D1036967

BRED

FASTER
THAN
LIGHT

FASTER THAN LIGHT

AN ORIGINAL ANTHOLOGY
ABOUT INTERSTELLAR
TRAVEL EDITED BY

JACK DANN
& GEORGE
ZEBROWSKI

HARPER & ROW, PUBLISHERS
NEW YORK, HAGERSTOWN
SAN FRANCISCO, LONDON

(Continued on next page)

Illustrations by Tim Kirk

FIRST EDITION

LIBRARY OF CONGRESS CATALOG CARD NUMBER: 74–15865

ISBN 0–06–010952–1

76 77 78 79 10 9 8 7 6 5 4 3 2 1

For John McHale and
Magda Cordell McHale

ACKNOWLEDGMENTS

We would like to thank the following people for their help and ideas:

Victoria Schochet
Lynne McNabb
Pamela Sargent
James Gunn
Dr. Robert L. Forward
Michael Orgill

CONTENTS

DREAMING AGAIN

INTRODUCTION

The possibility of interstellar travel is already on our mental horizon. The British Interplanetary Society recently founded a journal devoted to the subject; Dr. Robert Forward of the Hughes Research Laboratories in California has been conducting investigations into concepts of interstellar propulsion, which involve physical theorizing at the creative cutting edge of physics; conferences on civilizations which may exist in solar systems beyond our own have drawn eminent scientists from around the world. Ideas which were once the exclusive province of science fiction writers and isolated theoretical pioneers have become a legitimate part of possible developments within the vast array of subjects discussed by futurists and by innovative thinkers in various fields. The general sense is that new and unexpected developments are in the wind, and that reality will once again confound the conservative and unimaginative among us.

A number of serious writers on astronautics have said that science fiction now stands in relationship to interstellar travel as it did to space travel and rocketry in the 1920's and 30's. As was the case with space travel of the local variety, star travel is increasingly the subject of much "premature history" in articles and books which often seem more imaginative than the stories and novels which introduced the concept a half century earlier. There is an interestingly complex relationship between science fiction and real-world innovation, one which goes beyond specific prediction (which is impossible). The dreamers have organized themselves into planners, inventors, writers, and educators, as the world has come to realize that practicality must be fed by innovative visions. Human creativity is trying to invent futures as well as glimpse them.

With the coming radical reduction in the cost of manned space travel through shuttlecraft and orbital space stations, the solar system is about to become the "new world"—bigger in potential return than all of the western hemisphere. As we move into this new frontier industrially, "space travel" will cease to mean travel within the solar system. Frontiers have a .way of being pushed outward, and no doubt we will go through a period of dreaming again about "space travel"—except that the term will mean "star travel" in starships.

As an indicator of how people and times change, consider the following state of affairs among those who should be more imaginative than any in the population—the writers, both science fiction and contemporary. Contemporary writers have failed to deal with scientific creativity, despite excellence in confronting the prime experience of living common to us all; while SF writers have often criticized each other for seriously considering FTL (Faster Than Light travel) and interstellar travel. This condition among SF writers, a failure of imagination and nerve, as Arthur C. Clarke would say, is serious because it not only restricts dramatic-fictional possibilities, but shows how out of touch many writers have grown from serious speculation in the sciences, especially in physical and mathematical frontiers, where much is happening to support the possibility of effective interstellar travel through methods that bypass the limits on the physical motion of material bodies at the speed of light or near it, to give us practical, *apparent* Faster Than Light travel.

Dreamers grow up and grow sluggish, whether they be SF writers or scientists. In editing this book, we have tried to get writers to see the subject freshly, in terms of the newly emerging indications of the last dozen years. Some of these indications are staggering. Our entire picture of the universe has changed. An entire cosmos has died. The new one is full of mysteries and new puzzles: quasars, black holes, tachyons, new forms of matter, superspace—these are only a few of the new things. Old SF notions like FTL, antigravity, even time travel (often considered hopeless by SF writers) have turned up in serious scientific journals. A whole generation of scientists which grew up on science fiction is now seriously examining concepts discarded by many SF writers. The moral of all this seems to be that the more one learns, the greater is the tendency to close up possibilities; greater still grows the fear of asking, what can I imagine that would make this or that possible, rather than impossible? What is imagined may be wrong, but it will provide something to be stood up and tested, and retested, even if it fails at some specific historical time.

What cannot be guessed at exhaustively by either imagination or reason is reality's capacity for new things; but we can be certain that there will be new, surprising developments. Old ideas may be made new and new old. Imaginatively plausible dreams, suggesting practical possibility, persist because of their beauty and because they look beyond a bothersome limit. These dreams live in vulgar imagination even when discredited by current science or disbelieved in by SF writers who yet need them to make a story work.

But are these things akin to true things? Our answer is yes, in the following way. Imagination produces the forms of things to come, unable to fill in the specifics and technical details. These belong to the actual reality, not to our time. But as time goes on, we begin to see, however vaguely, how something might happen. We are at this point as far as star travel is concerned, as far as new power sources are concerned, as far as the new industrial base of the solar system is concerned. These dreams, and the attitudes they mirror, are the most precious survival factor we have. They could destroy us, if we fail to see far enough; they could also show us what existence within an expanded reality would be like. The ability to see what might be, not in the literal fashion of a supernatural prophet, but in the manner of realizable alternatives, is the single most remarkable capacity of human beings. Today, this capacity operates in various modes: as imaginative literature (SF), futuristics, technological development, and basic scientific research. Gradually, the global culture is becoming science-fictional, fluid and changing in many directions. Science fiction, at its serious best, considers the impact of future changes on human character and society.

What are some of the primitive intuitions that make a star drive visible, however vaguely? For one, it is the notion, a suspicion, that space is malleable, that distance is not a rigid relationship; that perhaps it can be affected under extreme circumstances, or by the application of various forces. In our imaginative vision we can see what a space drive would *do*, even though we cannot *explain*. But, in fact, explanation is not often needed to *do*. We have been doing all kinds of technological things long before we could give a reasonably complete account of how we did them. Technology often precedes knowledge in history. There is at least one good general reason why we can take this kind of imaginative pre-construction seriously: imagination is a *natural* process, as are deduction and reasoning; imagination is present in all invention, theorizing and engineering. Human civilization is a harnessing of imagination to reason and practical testing.

Interstellar travel would, of course, be the single most explosive event in human history. We can vaguely see the steps which might lead to it. As our capacity to generate power for work grows, and we industrialize the solar system, the conditions for building and testing various kinds of propulsion systems for interstellar travel (both sub-light and FTL) grow more favorable. It has been suggested that basic research and engineering involving superdense states of matter might yield a breakthrough in the modification of space and distance. An entire library of scientific literature exists on this subject; very likely it constitutes the preliminary spadework necessary to the attainment of interstellar travel. Imaginary inventions, once they reach a certain level of conceptual verisimilitude, help bring themselves into being. This was the case with atomic energy, radar and television, orbital satellites and moonships. Imaginary inventions help invent themselves by simply existing, gathering conceptual additions and modifications, until the critical point is reached. Then they become obvious, and it is easy to see what it would involve to make them real. But they are always creative alternatives, even when they do not become actual.

One thing is certain. We need some form of relatively swift travel to get around in the universe. Within the solar system we will need ships that have the capability for continuous acceleration, to attain speeds of 1 to 5 per cent that of light. Such ships could reach any of the planets within days. But for journeys to the stars even such ships would take thousands of years. Furthermore, Einsteinian time contraction at significant per cents of light speed is a one-way ticket. Even at 99 per cent of light speed, when the biological clocks of ship passengers register almost no time passing in relation to earth, the price to be paid in temporal dislocation might be too high for most human beings. We will need the apparent effect of FTL travel, even if it will not be strictly that. Distance (space) can be affected radically, the form of the solution says; but it will require unlimited amounts of power to do this. Fortunately the power exists, in fusion techniques and in the sun.

The stories in this book deal with some of the steps to and the reality of star travel, and the consequences for human life. There are also a number of articles. Isaac Asimov and Arthur C. Clarke detail much of the conceptual background to interstellar travel, as does Keith Laumer in his famously iconoclastic piece, which precedes Ben Bova's statement of difficulties. Asimov, in recent times, faltered in his views toward interstellar travel; but finally he revised the last paragraph of his article here, and his conclusion is now somewhat opposite to the one he previously held—a remarkable example of reason restoring itself to the service of enterprising innovation. Also included is a bibliography of fiction dealing with interstellar travel, and a list of significant nonfiction for the reader interested in finding out more about this fascinating subject.

But beyond the conceptual fascination of the subject, we have tried to edit a book of *stories*, fictional experiences with human beings at their center. Our writers have tried to be true to the difficulties of complex extrapolation *and* the complexities of human behavior, as well to the hard demands of style and poetry. A common failing of conceptual science fiction has been the lack of fictional virtues. In a field of writing where the battle still rages between those writers who are idea-oriented and those of purely literary persuasion, we tried to suggest that strengths of whatever kind might be combined. Ideas exist only in the human brain, and the exploration of character is the stuff of fictional art. Ideas should not be foreign to the artist or writer, even though the successful combination of concept and character in SF is agonizingly difficult, and the production of great work even more difficult.

The reasons for considering interstellar travel in the pages of this anthology go beyond issues of ideas, technical development, or cultural survival through the expansion of life into the solar system and our galaxy. All these things are here. But also, we hope, the reader will find poetry and enjoyment and intensity, and something of the beauty which all literature must mirror.

Think of unrestricted access to the entire universe of stars-like-dust and galaxies-like-grains-of-sand; swift travel to as many worlds as there are people on earth now. The tyranny of space-time may be considerably weaker than our technology. It is already weaker than our disciplined imaginations.

Will we suddenly find ourselves as natives in canoes paddling to the shores of more advanced cultures? Is there a galaxy-wide culture which is placing bets on our survival? The writers here have tried to take your breath away, but also to make you think as well as wonder. They have not tried to make you see yourself on this tiny earth. The grand picture of earth from the moon taken by the Apollo astronauts has done that much too thoroughly. Rather, the writers of these stories have tried to make you see the sun and its planets as a tiny neighborhood in the vast lighted city of our galaxy.

There was a young lady named Bright,
Who travelled much faster than light,
She started one day
In the relative way
And returned on the previous night.

—E. Reginald Buller

*". . . it is the duty of the conscientious science fiction writer
not to falsify what he believes to be known fact. It is an even
more important function for him to suggest new paradigms, by
suggesting to the reader, over and over again, that X, Y, and Z
are not impossible. Every time a story appears with a faster-
than-light drive, it expresses somebody's faith—maybe not the
writer's, but certainly many of the readers'—that such a thing
is accomplishable, and some day will be accomplished. Well,
we have a lot of hardware—including, I'm sorry to say, a couple
of old beer cans—on the moon right now, to show us what can
be done with such repeated suggestion. It can be done I think
philosophically on a far broader scale than we have ever
managed to do it before. . . .*

*It seems to me that the most important scientific content in
modern science fiction is the impossibilities."*

—James Blish

FASTER
THAN
LIGHT

THE ULTIMATE SPEED LIMIT

ISAAC ASIMOV

If you push something hard enough, it begins to move. If you continue to push it while it moves, it accelerates; that is, it keeps moving faster and faster. Is there a limit to how fast it can move? If we just keep on pushing and pushing, will it go faster and faster and faster? Or won't it?

When something moves, it has kinetic energy. The quantity of kinetic energy possessed by a moving object depends upon its velocity and its mass. Velocity is a straightforward property that is easy to grasp. To be told something is moving at a high or a low velocity brings a clear picture to mind. Mass, however, is a little more subtle.

Mass is related to the ease with which an object can be accelerated. Suppose you have two baseballs; one is conventional, and the other is an exact imitation in solid steel. It would take much more effort to accelerate the steel ball to a particular speed by throwing it than it would the ordinary baseball. The steel ball, therefore, has more mass.

Gravitational pull also depends on mass. The steel ball is attracted more strongly to the earth than the baseball because the steel ball has more mass. In general, then, on the surface of the earth, a more massive object is heavier than a less massive one. In fact, it is common (but not really correct) to say "heavier" and "lighter" when we mean "more massive" and "less massive."

But back to our moving object with kinetic energy that depends on both velocity and mass. If our moving object is made to move more rapidly by means of that push we're talking about, then its kinetic energy increases. This increase is re-

1

flected both in an increase in velocity and in an increase in mass, the two factors on which kinetic energy depends.

At low velocities, the ordinary velocities in the world about us, most of the increase in kinetic energy goes into increase in velocity and very little into increase in mass. In fact, the increase in mass is so tiny at ordinary velocities that it could not be measured. It was assumed that as an object gained kinetic energy, *only* the velocity increased—the mass remained unchanged.

As a result, mass was often incorrectly defined as simply the quantity of matter in a particular object, something that obviously couldn't change with velocity.

In the 1890s, however, theoretical reasons arose for considering the possibility that mass increased as velocity increased. Then, in 1905, Albert Einstein explained the matter exactly in his Special Theory of Relativity. He presented an equation that described just how mass increased as velocity increased.

Using this equation, you can calculate that an object with a mass of 1 kilogram when it is at rest has a mass of 1.005 kilograms when it is moving at 30,000 kilometers a second. (A velocity of 30,000 kilometers per second—about 18,600 miles per second—is far greater than any velocity measured prior to the twentieth century, and even then the increase in mass is only half of 1 per cent. It's no surprise that the mass increase was never suspected until the 1890s.)

As velocity continues to increase, the mass begins to increase more rapidly. At 150,000 kilometers per second, an object that has a "rest mass" of 1 kilogram has a mass of 1.15 kilograms. At 270,000 kilometers per second, the mass has risen to 2.29 kilograms.

As the mass increases, however, the difficulty of further accelerating the object—making it move still faster—also increases. (That's the definition of mass.) A push of a given size becomes less and less effective as a way of increasing the object's velocity and more and more effective as a way of increasing its mass. By the time velocity has increased to 299,000 kilometers per second, almost all the energy gained by an object through further pushes goes into an increase in mass and very little goes into an increase in velocity. This is just the opposite of the situation at very low or "normal" velocities.

As we approach a velocity of 299,792.5 kilometers per second, just about *all* the extra energy derived from a push goes into additional mass and almost *none* goes into additional velocity. If a velocity of 299,792.5 kilometers per second could actually be reached, the mass of any moving object with a rest mass greater than zero would be infinite. No push, however great, could then make it move faster.

As it happens, 299,792.5 kilometers per second (about 186,000 miles per second) is the speed of light. Thus what Einstein's Special Theory of Relativity tells us is that it is impossible for any object with mass to be accelerated to speeds equal to or greater than the speed of light. The speed of light (in a vacuum) is the absolute speed limit for objects with mass, objects such as ourselves and our spaceships.

Nor is this just theory. Velocities at very nearly the speed of light have been measured since the Special Theory was announced and the increase in mass was found to be exactly as predicted. The Special Theory predicted all sorts of phenomena that have since been observed with great accuracy, and there seems to be no reason to doubt the theory or to doubt the fact that the speed of light is the speed limit for all objects with mass.

But let's get more fundamental. All objects with mass are made up of combinations of subatomic particles that themselves possess mass; for example, the proton, the electron, and the neutron. Such particles must always move at speeds less than that of light. They are called "tardyons," a name invented by physicist Olexa-Myron Bilaniuk and his co-workers.

There also are particles that at rest would have no mass at all —a rest mass of zero. However, these particles are never at rest, so the value of the rest mass must be determined indirectly. Bilaniuk therefore suggested the term "proper mass" be used to replace rest mass in order to avoid speaking of the rest mass of something that is never at rest.

It turns out that any particle with a proper mass of zero *must* travel at the speed of 299,792.5 kilometers per second, no more, no less. Light is made up of photons, particles that have a proper mass of zero. This is why light travels at 299,792.5 kilometers per second and why this speed is known as the "speed of light." Other particles with proper mass of zero, such as neutrinos and gravitons, also travel at the speed of light. Bilaniuk suggested that all such zero mass particles be termed "luxons" from a Latin word for "light."

This celestial speed limit, the speed of light, has been of particular annoyance to writers of science fiction because it has seriously limited the scope of their stories. The nearest star, Alpha Centauri, is 25 trillion miles away. Traveling at the speed of light, it would take 4.3 years (earthtime) to go from earth to Alpha Centauri, and another 4.3 years to come back. Special Relativity's speed limit therefore means that a minimum of 8.6 years must pass on earth before anything can make a round trip to even the nearest star. A minimum of 600 years must pass before anything can get to the Pole Star and back. A minimum of 150,000 years must pass before anything can get to the other end of the Galaxy and back. A minimum of 5 million years must pass before anything can get to the Andromeda Galaxy and back.

Taking these *minimum* time lapses into account (and remembering that the actual time lapse would be much larger under any reasonable conditions) would make any science fiction story involving interstellar travel extraordinarily complicated. Science fiction writers who wished to avoid these complications would find themselves confined to the solar system only.

What can be done? To begin with, science fiction writers might ignore the whole thing and pretend there is no limit. That, however, is not real science fiction; it is just fairy tales. On the other hand, science fiction writers can sigh and accept the speed limit with all its complications. L. Sprague de Camp did so routinely and Poul Anderson recently wrote a novel, *Tau Zero*, that accepted the limit in a very fruitful manner. Finally, science fiction writers might find some more-or-less plausible way of getting around the speed limit. Thus, Edward E. Smith, in his series of intergalactic romances, assumed some device for reducing the inertia of any object to zero. With zero inertia, any push can produce infinite acceleration, and Smith reasoned that any velocity up to the infinite would therefore become possible.

Of course, there is no known way of reducing inertia to zero. Even if there were a way, inertia is completely equivalent to mass and to reduce inertia to zero is to reduce mass to zero. Particles without mass *can* be accelerated with infinite ease, but only to the speed of light. Smith's zero-inertia drive would make possible travel *at* the speed of light but not *faster* than light.

A much more common science fictional device is to imagine an object leaving our universe altogether.

To see what this means, let's consider a simple analogy. Suppose that a person must struggle along on foot across very difficult country—mountainous and full of cliffs, declivities, torrential rivers, and so on. He might well argue that it was completely impossible to travel more than two miles a day. If he has so long concentrated on surface travel as to consider it the only form of progress conceivable, he might well come to imagine that a speed limit of two miles per day represents a natural law and an ultimate limit under all circumstances.

But what if he travels through the air, not necessarily in a powered device such as a jet plane or rocket, but in something as simple as a balloon? He can then easily cover two miles in an hour or less, regardless of how broken and difficult the ground beneath him is. In getting into a balloon, he moved outside the "universe" to which his fancied ultimate speed limit applied. Or, speaking in dimensions, he derived a speed limit for two-dimensional travel along a surface, but it did not apply to travel in three dimensions by way of a balloon.

Similarly, the Einsteinian limit might be conceived of as applying only to our own space. In that case, what if we could move into something beyond space, as our balloonist moved into something beyond surface. In the region beyond space, or "hyperspace," there might be no speed limit at all. You could move at any velocity, however enormous, by the proper application of energy and then, after a time lapse of a few seconds, perhaps, re-enter ordinary space at some point that would have required two centuries of travel in the ordinary fashion.

Hyperspace, expressly stated or quietly assumed, has been part of the stock in trade of science fiction writers for several decades now.

Few, if any, science fiction writers supposed hyperspace and faster-than-light travel to be anything more than convenient fiction that made it simpler to develop the intricacies and pathways of plots on a galactic and supergalactic scale. Yet, surprisingly enough, science seemed to come to their rescue. What science fiction writers were groping toward by means of pure imagination was something that, in a way, seemed to have justification after all in Special Relativity.

Suppose we imagine an object with a rest mass of 1 kilogram moving at 425,000 kilometers per second, nearly half again as fast as the speed of light. We might dismiss this as impossible but, for a moment, let's not. Rather, let us use Einstein's equation to calculate what its mass would be if it did reach this speed.

It turns out that, according to Einstein's equation, an object with a rest mass of 1 kilogram moving at 425,000 kilometers per second has a mass equal to $\sqrt{-1}$ kilograms. The expression $\sqrt{-1}$ is what mathematicians call an "imaginary number." Such numbers are not really imaginary and have important uses, but they are not the kind of numbers ordinarily considered appropriate for measuring mass. The general feeling would be to consider an imaginary mass as "absurd" and let it go at that.

In 1962, however, Bilaniuk and his co-workers decided to check into the matter of imaginary mass and see if it might be given meaning. Perhaps an imaginary mass merely implied a set of properties that were different from those possessed by objects with ordinary mass. For instance, an object with ordinary mass speeds up when pushed and slows down when it makes its way through a resisting medium. What if an object with imaginary mass slowed down when it was pushed and speeded up when it made its way through a resisting medium? On the same line of thought, an object with ordinary mass has more energy the faster it goes. What if an object with imaginary mass has *less* energy the faster it goes?

Once such concepts were introduced, Bilaniuk and his associates were able to show that objects with imaginary mass, traveling faster than the speed of light, did not *violate* Einstein's Special Theory of Relativity. In 1967, physicist Gerald Feinberg, in discussing these faster-than-light particles, called them "tachyons" from a Greek word meaning "speed."

However, tachyons have their own limitations. As they gain energy by being pushed, they slow down. As they move slower and slower, it becomes more and more difficult to make them move still slower. When they approach the speed of light, they cannot be made to go any more slowly.

There are, then, three classes of particles: 1) *Tardyons*, which have a proper mass greater than zero and which can move at any velocity *less* than the speed of light, but can never move at the speed of light or faster; 2) *Luxons,* which have a proper mass of zero and which can move *only* at the speed of light; and 3) *Tachyons,* which have an imaginary proper mass and which can move at any velocity *greater* than the speed of light, but can never move at the speed of light or slower.

Granted that this third class, the tachyons, can exist without violating Special Relativity, do they *actually* exist? It is a common rule in theoretical physics, one accepted by many physicists, that anything not forbidden by the basic laws of nature *must* take place. If the tachyons are not forbidden, then they must exist. But can we detect them?

In theory, there is a way of doing so. When a tachyon passes through a vacuum at more than the speed of light (as it must), it leaves a flash of light trailing behind it. If this light were detected, one could, from the light's properties, identify and characterize the tachyon that has passed. Unfortunately, a tachyon moving at more than the speed of light remains in a particular vicinity—say, in the neighborhood of a detecting device—for only an incredibly small fraction of a second. The chances of detecting a tachyon are therefore incredibly small, and none have as yet been detected. (But that doesn't prove they don't exist.)

It is perfectly possible to convert a particle from one class to another. For example, an electron and a positron, both of which are tardyons, can combine to form gamma rays. Gamma rays are composed of luxons and can be converted back into electrons and positrons. There would seem, then, to be no theoretical objection to the conversion of tardyons to tachyons and back again, if the proper procedure could be found.

Suppose, then, that it were possible to convert all the tardyons in a spaceship, together with its contents, both animate and inanimate, into equivalent tachyons. The tachyon-spaceship, with no perceptible interval of acceleration, would be moving at perhaps 1,000 times the speed of light and would get to the neighborhood of Alpha Centauri in a little over a day. There it would be reconverted into tardyons.

It must be admitted that this is a lot harder to do than to say. How does one convert tardyons into tachyons while maintaining all the intricate interrelationships between the tardyons, say, in a human body? How does one control the exact speed and direction of travel of the tachyons? How does one convert the tachyons back into tardyons with such precision that every-thing is returned exactly to the original without disturbing that delicate phenomenon called life?

But suppose it could be done. In that case, going to the distant stars and galaxies by way of the tachyon-universe would be exactly equivalent to the science fictional dream of making the trip by way of hyperspace. Would the speed limit then be lifted? Would the universe, in theory at least, be at our feet?

Maybe not. In an article I wrote in 1969, I suggested that the two universes that are separated by the "luxon wall," ours of the tardyons and the other of the tachyons, represented a suspicious asymmetry. It seemed to me that the laws of nature were basi-cally symmetrical, and to imagine speeds less than light on one side of the wall and speeds greater than light on the other wasn't right.

Properly speaking, I suggested (without any mathematical analysis at all and arguing entirely from intuition) that which-ever side of the luxon wall you were on would seem to be the tardyon universe and it would always be the other side that was the tachyon universe. In that way there would be perfect symmetry: Both sides would be tardyon to themselves; both sides tachyon to the other. In an article entitled "Space-Time" in the 1971 issue of the *McGraw-Hill Yearbook of Science and Technology,* Bilaniuk subjected the matter to careful math-ematical analysis. He found that there *was* just this symmetry between the two universes.

It does no good, therefore, merely to switch from one uni-verse to the other in order to experience faster-than-light travel. Whichever universe you are in you are always tardyon. However, if you transfer from A to B and then back to A, you will have made it. By forcing first one and then the other uni-verse to travel faster-than-light, you will have jumped vast dis-tances without ever going faster-than-light yourself. You will have been in hyperspace without ever having noticed it.

POSSIBLE, THAT'S ALL!

ARTHUR C. CLARKE

The Galactic novels of my esteemed friend Dr. Asimov gave me such pleasure in boyhood that it is with great reluctance that I rise up to challenge some of his recent statements ("Impossible, That's All," *Magazine of Fantasy & Science Fiction*, February 1967). I can only presume that advancing years, and the insatiable demands of the Asimov-of-the-Month-Club Selection Board, have caused a certain enfeeblement of the far-ranging imagination that has delighted so many generations of s.f. fandom. [Firm note from editor: To put the record straight, and to prevent any innocent reader's being deceived—the Good Doctor was born three years *later* than his Reluctant Critic.]

The possibility, or otherwise, of speeds greater than that of light cannot be disposed of quite as cavalierly as Dr. A. does in his article. First of all, even the restricted, or Special, Theory of Relativity does not deny the existence of such speed. It only says that speeds *equal* to that of light are impossible—which is quite another matter.

The naïve layman who has never been exposed to quantum physics may well argue that to get from below the speed of light to above it one has to pass *through* it. But this is not necessarily the case; we might be able to jump over it, thus avoiding the mathematical disasters which the well-known Lorentz equations predict when one's velocity is *exactly* equal to that of light. Above this critical speed, the equations can scarcely be expected to apply, though if certain interesting assumptions are made, they may still do so.

I am indebted, if that is the word, to Dr. Gerald Feinberg of Columbia University for this idea. His paper "On the Possibility

9

of Superphotic Speed Particles" points out that since sudden jumps from one state to another are characteristic of quantum systems, it might be possible to hop over the "light barrier" without going through it. If anyone thinks that this is ridiculous, I would remind him that quantum-effect devices doing similar tricks are now on the market—witness the tunnel diode. Anything that can rack up sales of hundreds of thousands of dollars should be taken very seriously indeed.

Even if there is no way through the light barrier, Dr. Feinberg suggests that there may be another universe on the other side of it, composed entirely of particles that cannot travel *slower* than the speed of light. (Anyone who can visualize just what is meant by that phrase "on the other side of" is a much better man than I am.) However, as such particles—assuming that they still obey the Lorentz equations—would possess imaginary mass or negative energy, we might never be able to detect them or use them for any practical purpose like interstellar signaling. As far as we are concerned, they might as well not exist.

This last point does not worry me unduly. Similar harsh things were once said about the neutrino, yet it is now quite easy to detect this improbable object, if you are prepared to baby-sit a few hundred tons of equipment for several months two miles down in an abandoned gold mine. Anyway, mere trifles like negative energy and imaginary mass should not deter any mathematical physicist worthy of his salt. Odder concepts are being bandied round all the time in the quark-infested precincts of Brookhaven and CERN.

Perhaps at this point I should exorcise a phantom which, rather wisely, the Good Doctor refrained from invoking. There are many things that *do* travel faster than light, but they are not exactly "things." They are only appearances, which do not involve the transfer of energy, matter, or information.

One example—familiar to thousands of radar technicians—is the movement of radio waves along the rectangular copper pipes known as wave guides. The electromagnetic patterns traveling through a wave guide can *only* move faster than light —never at less than this speed! But they cannot carry signals; the *changes* of pattern which alone can do this move more slowly than light, and by precisely the same ratio as the others exceed it (i.e., the product of the two speeds equals the square of the speed of light).

If this sounds complicated, let me give an example which I hope will clarify the situation. Suppose we had a wave guide one light-year long, and fed radio signals into it. Under no circumstances could anything emerge from the other end in less than a year; in fact, it might be ten years before the message arrived, moving at only a tenth of the speed of light. But once the waves had got through, they would have established a pattern that swept along the guide at ten times the speed of light. Again I must emphasize that this pattern *would carry no information*. Any signals or message would require a change of some kind at the transmitter, which would take ten years to make the one-light-year trip.

If you have ever watched storm waves hitting a breakwater you may have seen a very similar phenomenon. When the line of waves hits the obstacle at an acute angle, a veritable waterspout appears at the point of intersection and moves along the breakwater at a speed which is always greater than that of the oncoming waves and can have any value up to infinity (when the lines are parallel, and the whole sea front erupts at once). But no matter how ingenious you are, there is no way in which you could contrive to use this waterspout to carry signals—or objects—along the coast. Though it contains a lot of energy, it does not involve any *movement* of that energy. The same is true of the hyperspeed patterns in a wave guide.

If you wish to investigate this subject in more detail, I refer you to the article by s.f. old-timer Milton A. Rothman, "Things That Go Faster Than Light" in *Scientific American* for July 1960. The essential fact is that the existence of such speeds ("phase velocities") in no way invalidates the Theory of Relativity.

However, there may be other phenomena that do precisely this. Please fasten your seatbelts and read—slowly—the following extract from a letter by Professor Herbert Dingle, published in the Royal Astronomical Society's Journal, *The Observatory*, for December 1965 (*85*, 949, pp. 262–64). It will repay careful study.

The recent report that artificially produced messages from distant parts of the universe might have been detected has prompted much speculation on the possibility of communication over long distances, in all of which it seems to have been taken for granted that a time of at least r/c must elapse before a signal can be received from a distance r (c = velocity of light). There is, however, no evidence for this. There is reason for believing that it is true for any phenomenon uniquely locatable at a point, or small region, but some phenomena are not so locatable. If the postulate of relativity (i.e., the postulate that there is no natural standard of rest, so that the relative motion of two bodies cannot be uniquely divided between them) is true, the Doppler effect affords a means of *instantaneous communication over any distance at all*. . . . A codes of signals . . . could therefore be devised that, in principle, *would enable us to send a message to any distance and receive an immediate reply*. [My italics.]

Unfortunately we do not know whether the postulate of relativity is true or not. . . . Since the demise of the special relativity theory has not yet succeeded in penetrating into general awareness, it seems worth while to show its impotence in the present problem. . . .

And so on, for a few hundred words of tight mathematical logic, followed by a reply from a critic which Professor Dingle demolishes, at least to his satisfaction, in the August 1966 issue of the *Observatory*. I won't give details of the discussion because they are far too technical for this journal. (Translation: I don't understand them.)

The point I wish to stress, however, should already have been made sufficiently clear by the extract. Despite its formidable success in many *local* applications, relativity may not be the last word about the Universe. Indeed, it would be quite unprecedented if it were.

The *General* Theory—which deals with gravity and accelerated motions, unlike the Special Theory, which is concerned only with unaccelerated motion—may already be in deep trouble. One of the world's leading astrophysicists (he may have changed his mind now, so I will not identify him beyond saying that his name begins with Z) once shook me by remarking casually, as we were on the way up Mt. Palomar, that he regarded all the three "proofs" of the General Theory as disproved. And only this week I read that Professor Dicke has detected a flattening of the Sun's poles, which accounts for the orbital peculiarities of Mercury, long regarded as the most convincing evidence for the theory.

If Dicke is right, the fact that Einstein's calculations gave the correct result for the precession of Mercury will be pure coincidence. And *then* we shall have an astronomical scandal at both ends of the Solar System: for Lowell's "prediction" of Pluto's orbit also seems completely fortuitous. Pluto is far too small to have produced the perturbations that led to its discovery. (Has anyone yet written a story suggesting that it is the satellite of a much larger but invisible planet?)

And now that I have got started, I'd like to take a swipe at another Einsteinian sacred cow—the Principle of Equivalence, which is the basis of the gravitational theory. Every book on the subject—George Gamow's *Gravity* is a good example—illustrates the principle by imagining a man in a spaceship. If the spaceship is accelerating at a steady rate, it is claimed that there is no way in which the occupant can distinguish the "inertial" forces acting on him from those due to a gravitational field.

Now this is patent nonsense—unless the observer and his spaceship have zero dimensions. One can *always* distinguish between a gravitational field and an inertial one. For if you examine any gravitational field with a suitable instrument (which need be no more complicated than a couple of ball bearings, whose movements in free fall are observed with sufficient precision), you will quickly discover two facts: (1) the field varies in intensity from point to point, because it obeys an inverse square law (this "gravity gradient" effect is now used to stabilize satellites in orbit); (2) the field is not parallel, as it radiates from some central gravitating body.

But the "pseudo-gravitational" force due to acceleration can —in principle, at least—be made uniform and parallel over as great a volume of space as desired. So the distinction between the two would be obvious after a very brief period of examination.

Let us ignore that unpleasant little man in the front row who has just popped up to ask how I've spotted a flaw missed by Albert Einstein and some 90 percent of all the mathematicians who have ever lived on this planet, since the beginning of time. But *if* the Principle of Equivalence is invalid, several important consequences follow. One of the most effective arguments against the possibility of antigravitational and "space drive" devices is overthrown—surely a consummation devoutly to be wished by all advocates of planetary exploration, not to mention those billions who will shortly be cringing beneath the impact of sonic thunderbolts from SSTs. In addition, and more relevant to our present argument, we will have made a hole in the Theory of Relativity through which we should be able to fly a superphotic ship.

Talking of holes leads rather naturally to our old friend the space warp, that convenient short-cut taken by so many writers of interstellar fiction (myself included). As a firm believer in Haldane's law ("The Universe is not only queerer than we imagine; it is queerer than we *can* imagine"), I think we should not dismiss space warps merely as fictional devices. At least one mathematical physicist—Professor J. A. Wheeler—has constructed a theory of space-time which involves what he has picturesquely called "worm-holes." These have all the classic attributes of the space warp; you disappear at A and reappear at B, without ever visiting any point in between. Unfortunately, in Wheeler's theory the average speed from A to B, even via worm-hole, still works out at less than the speed of light. This seems very unenterprising and I hope the professor does a little more homework.

Another interesting, and unusual, attempt to demolish the light barrier was made in the last chapter of the book *Islands in Space*, by Dandridge M. Cole and Donald W. Cox. They pointed out that all the tests of the relativity equations had been carried out by particles accelerated by *external* forces, not self-propelled systems like rockets. It was unwise, they argued, to assume that the same laws applied in this case.

And here I must admit to a little embarrassment. I had forgotten, until I referred to my copy, that the preface of *Islands in Space* ends with a couple of limericks making a crack at *me* for saying (in *Profiles of the Future*) that the velocity of light could never be exceeded. In such a situation, I always fall back on Walt Whitman:

> I contradict myself? Very well, I contradict myself.
> I am large; I contain multitudes.

So now I invite the Good Doctor Asimov to do likewise. After all, he is larger than I am.

POSTSCRIPT

The above *riposte* appeared in the October 1968 issue of *Magazine of Fantasy & Science Fiction,* and since then a good deal has been published on speeds faster than light. Perhaps the most easily available reference is Gerald Feinberg's "Particles That Go Faster Than Light" in the February 1970 issue of *Scientific American.* This article is not easy reading; even tougher is "Particles Beyond the Light Barrier," by Olexa-Myron Bilaniuk and E. C. George Sudarshan in the May 1969 *Physics Today.* Drs. Bilaniuk and Sudarshan, with their colleague V. K. Deshpande, appear to have been the first to raise this subject seriously, in the *American Journal of Physics* as far back as 1962.

THE LIMITING VELOCITY OF ORTHODOXY

KEITH LAUMER

Before Professor John A. Wheeler suggested the possible existence of "superspace"—a strange universe that might exist outside, or inside, our own—Isaac Asimov had domesticated "hyperspace." In his novel The Stars Like Dust, *he writes:*

"This is the captain speaking. We are ready for our first jump. We will be temporarily leaving the space-time fabric to enter the little-known realm of Hyperspace, where time and distance have no meaning. It is like traveling across a narrow isthmus from one ocean to another, rather than circling a continent to accomplish the same distance. There will only be minor discomfort. Please remain calm. . . ."

It was like a bump which joggled the deep inside of a man's bones. In a fraction of a second the star view from the portholes had changed radically. The center of the great Galaxy was closer now, and the stars appeared to thicken in number. The ship had moved a hundred light-years closer to them.

Some cosmologists are presently theorizing about the possible existence of "hyperspace"; only they call it "superspace."

It seems that in order to travel as fast as "the young lady named Bright," you must either break the rules, bend the rules, or ignore the rules.

Or resign yourself to this corner of the universe.

Keith Laumer characterizes the human attitude which cannot reconcile itself to such a fate.

16

I am perhaps the only individual ever to receive a B.S. in Architecture from the University of Illinois without learning to use a slide rule. Spurning such aids as tending to atrophy the natural faculties, I polished my mental arithmetic to a point rivaling the skill of an idiot savant. This annoyed the idiot savant, who resigned his post as Head of the Department and became a science writer.

In those days we still did homework instead of rioting. Some of the problems assigned in the engineering curriculum were rather time-consuming; the record for one problem for one class for one day, as I recall, was some eleven hours. As a result we students fell into the habit of working in two-man teams. During those long happy evenings in close proximity with slide-rule operators I noted a curious phenomenon: faced with the challenge of dividing 100 by ten, they would frown, adjust the magic device, make mysterious passes and announce: "Nine nine nine nine nine. Uh—where does the decimal go?"

I earned my reputation as a lightning calculator by my uncanny ability, when encountering a tricky bit of arithmetic such as dividing 3.978 by 1.987, to instantly announce:

"That will be very close to 2.0."

I never revealed my secret formula:

$2 + 2 = 4$ (equation 1)

The tendency of the technical mind to hold the nose so close to the grindstone that it loses sight of the point carries over, alas, into its public pronouncements. Not one to denigrate Science, I. But let's not get carried away with ideas, like, oh, the alleged limiting velocity of light.

According to the Relativity boys, nothing can ever travel faster than about 186,000 mi/sec.—the velocity of propagation of electromagnetic radiation—such as light and radio waves—in a vacuum. Man will never explore the stars, they say, because it would take too long. We can never communicate with the neighboring galaxy because a return message would take a few million years—minimum.

Aside from the fact that this limitation, if true, would take all the fun out of things and also aside from the fact that people who announce what we will never do always seem to be asking for a dunce cap, the whole idea is nonsense. Limiting velocity indeed. Phooey. We'll go as fast as we want to, so there.

I realize that at this point the academicians are laying aside their technical journals with a pitying smile and preparing to point out that at light-speed:

(a) the mass of the spaceship will reach infinity and
(b) its length will become zero, and
(c) time aboard will come to a standstill.

Ergo, the thing is clearly impossible.

I reply that what's impossible is not super-light velocity, but spaceships of infinite mass, zero length and no time. The absurdity of these concepts should be a tip-off to the theoreticians that, although their arithmetic gives them nine, nine, nine, nine, they still don't know where to put the decimal.

So let's take a clearer look at things.

The Universe is, as far as we've actually observed it, a reasonable, consistent, operating mechanism. It seems to abhor absolutes as much as Nature was once thought to abhor a vacuum. It also abhors uniqueness. Once we were told that the world was flat and that Europe was at its center. Then that Terra was the center of the Solar System. Then that the sun was at the center of the Galaxy. Then that our Galaxy was at the center of the Universe—and that it was the biggest and best Galaxy going, etc., etc., etc. This is all bunk, of course.

Now they tell us that nothing can travel *away from Earth* faster than light. I italicize where I do because these flat statements of the crippling limitation imply a Terracentric Universe.

Consider: we observe a distant radio source in a given direction, receding from us at three-quarters of the speed of light. Turning our antennae in the opposite direction, we observe another radio source, equally distant, also receding at a major fraction of this magic velocity.

Falling back on:

$$.75 + .75 = 1.5 \text{ (equation 2)}$$

it appears that our limitation is already exceeded.

"Sorry," the smiling physicist says, with an expression resembling that of the canary which has just had a bite of the cat. "The velocities don't add."

Okay. We'll remember that one, Buster.

Let's look at it this way: Captain Horntoot of the Starship *Clubfoot* takes his command out past Luna and opens her up. Traveling at a modest one G, he soon reaches a respectable velocity; say .75 lightspeed.

Now, we all know that this can't go on or all sorts of impossible things will try to happen. Capt. Horntoot knows this, too. No dullard he, he summons his First Mate to the quarterdeck.

"All right, Mr. Shrub," he barks. "What's our present velocity?"

Shrub tells him.

"With reference to what?" Horntoot demands.

"Why, ah, Omaha, Nebraska, my home town, sir," Shrub replies.

"Out there—" the captain points through the front windshield, "is a distant radio source, which is receding from Omaha, Nebraska at a velocity of three-quarters of a light."

"I see it, sir!"

"No, you don't, you idiot, that's a speck of crud on your glasses! You can't see this distant radio object because it's not visible from here. But take my word for it: it's out there. Now, how fast are we traveling—in relation to the distant radio object, I mean."

"Well, actually I guess we're standing still, sir," Shrub says.

"Standing still?" Horntoot roars. "I told you to get the lead out and boost us up to three-quarters of lightspeed!"

"Yes, but sir—that's impossible!"

"Indeed, Mr. Shrub? And why, may I ask?"

"B-because we're already going three-quarters of a light— and if we accelerated another three-quarters light, that would be a light and a half—and it says right in my handbook that you can't—"

"Perish the thought, Mr. Shrub," Horntoot says coolly. "The velocities don't add." (Nyah-nyah, n'nyah-nyah!)

If you can't beat 'em, join 'em.

Sure, I know they'll come bounding out of the woodwork to tell me all the things wrong with this formulation; but I'll bet my place in the Public Freezer against a lifetime subscription to the *Engineering News-Record* that some day some dumb tramp captain will get from here to there quicker than a ray of light that started when he did—even if he doesn't exceed light-speed on the way. And he'll let the slide-rule boys formulate the math later.

(And I suppose that when Capt. Horntoot turns on his headlights at .999 lights, the beams just pile up out front like toilet paper spinning off a roll?)

Let's face it, Violent Reader: all this talk about the *velocity* of light is in the same category as the aqueous humor and phlogiston.

LIGHT IS A CONDITION, NOT AN EVENT (Laumer's Theorem).

Light has no velocity. When the sun radiates, it sets up conditions around it. Those conditions extend in all directions. Are we to believe that light rays go speeding away from the sun in opposite directions, all at the same speed with reference to the sun (or is it to Omaha?) and to all the other light rays—including those going in the opposite direction?

Again, phooey.

We're playing with velocities, eh? A velocity implies a time and a distance—but they tell us that at high velocities both time and distance are variables. So—what kind of time are we clocking by? Ship time or shore time? And which shore? Whose yardstick are we using? If time on a distant object, receding from us at the limiting velocity, is standing still—then so is the object, right? And the business of measuring speed implies a frame of reference. A fly inside a moving Dempster Dumpster, etc. So—what is our frame of reference for all this talk about absolute limits? Earth? A remote galaxy, at the limits of detectability? A moving ship somewhere between them?

Double phooey.

When we get Out There, in our nuclear powered Go-ship, and we step on the gas—we're going to Go. We're going to toss the light barrier in the same junkheap as the sound barrier.

Stick around and see.

BUT WHAT IF WE TRIED IT?

BEN BOVA

Okay, let's assume that Einstein was—well, not *wrong*, exactly, but maybe a little short-sighted. Despite all the evidence that's piled up over the past half-century in favor of Special and General Relativity, let's assume that FTL flight may be possible after all. Let's try flying Faster Than Light and see what happens.

No matter how fast we go, we will still be bound by some physical constraints. Such as the Laws of Thermodynamics. They appear to be quite basic to the behavior of the universe, as any gambler can tell you, no matter whether your favorite natural philosopher is Einstein, Newton, or Pope Innocent I.

The Laws of Thermodynamics are quite simple. They tell us that you can never win. You can't even break even. You always have to pay for what you get, and what's more, you must always pay *more* than the value of what you receive. Happens every day.

What does this tell us about FTL travel?

Let's think about an interstellar trip. Nothing spectacular; just an easy jaunt in our 10,000-metric-ton cruiser over to Arcturus, a scant 36 lightyears away from downtown Earth. For openers, we'll poke along at a stately one-third of lightspeed, 0.33 Light.

Using the Newtonian formula for kinetic energy, $E = \frac{1}{2}mv^2$, my SR-11 electronic calculator (slide rules went out of style last year) tells me that the energy involved in moving our cruiser at 0.33 Light is 10^{23} joules, in metric units. If you're an American engineer, that's 7.376×10^{22} foot-pounds, or 2.78×10^{16} kilowatt-hours, which your friendly local utility will sell you for

something under ten thousand million million dollars (9.89 ×
10^{15} dollars, including fuel adjustment charges). If you're a
physicist, the kinetic energy comes out to 10^{30} ergs.

An interesting number, that last one. Since the Sun puts out
3.86×10^{33} ergs per second, the kinetic energy of our space
cruiser at 0.33 Light is equal to 0.000259 second's worth of solar
output. Trivial.

But nasty things begin to happen when you "get the lead out"
and start tootling along near lightspeed. For one thing, your
mass begins to grow. At 0.95 Light, our 10,000-ton cruiser
masses 32,000 tons. At 0.99 Light, the mass has become 71,000
tons. And the closer we inch to 1.00 Light (assuming that's
possible), the more massive we become.

Which means the more energy we'll need to push us along.
The mass curve climbs *very* steeply—asymptotically, if you're
a mathematician—as we close the distance between 0.99 and
1.00 Light. In fact, when we reach lightspeed, 1.00 Light, our
mass becomes infinite. To propel an infinite mass, we need an
infinite amount of energy.

How much energy is there in the universe? Doesn't matter.
A ship moving at 1.00 Light will need it *all*. If Capt. Horntoot
really opens up the throttle in his desire to Break the Light
Barrier, all he's going to do is pull the plug on the whole universe. His ship will use all the energy there is in the universe.
Everything collapses. The universe falls in on itself and—perhaps—implodes into another Big Bang.

Which is why there are no FTL ships flitting around in our
space-time continuum. There can only be one per universe.
That Big Traffic Cop in the Sky doesn't allow speeding.

*If we cannot break the rules or ignore them, then it follows
that we'll just have to bend them as best we can.*
—J.D. and G.Z.

SUN UP

A. A. JACKSON IV and HOWARD WALDROP

Interstellar travel has already begun. Even as our unmanned probe Pioneer leaves the solar system, the radio telescope at Arecibo has beamed a message that might be picked up by an extra-solar civilization. But Pioneer and the Arecibo message could not possibly reveal anything to us in less than fifty thousand years.

Physicist John A. Wheeler has compared space to an ocean which "looks flat to the aviator who flies above it, but which is a tossing turmoil to the hapless butterfly which falls upon it. Regarded more and more closely, it shows more and more agitation, unitl . . . the entire structure is permeated everywhere with wormholes." In a paper co-authored with Robert W. Fuller he wrote: "One may ask if a signal travelling at the speed of light along one route could be outpaced by a signal which has travelled a much shorter path through a worm-hole."

The following story takes interstellar probes and signaling one step further, into a range of possibility which lies within the human scale of time. And it makes the point that human courage and feeling may well be present in the constantly evolving technology through which we extend ourselves. In fact, Professor Gerald Feinberg has suggested that our machines might someday provide "an independent form of consciousness with which we could compare ourselves."

Perhaps that day is not so very far off.

The robot exploration ship *Saenger* parked off the huge red sun.

It was now a tiny dot of stellar debris, bathed in light, five million nine hundred ninety-four thousand myriameters from the star. Its fusion ram had been silent for some time. It had coasted in on its reaction motors like a squirrel climbing down a curved treetrunk.

The ship *Saenger* was partly a prepackaged scientific laboratory, partly a deep space probe, with sections devoted to smaller launching platforms, inflatable observatories, assembly shops. The ship *Saenger* had a present crew of eighteen working robots. It was an advance research station, sent unmanned to study this late-phase star. When it reached parking orbit, it sent messages back to its home world. In a year and a half, the first shipful of scientists and workers would come, finding the station set up and work underway.

The ship was mainly *Saenger*, a solid-state intelligence budded off the giant SSI on the Moon.

Several hours after it docked off the sun, *Saenger* knew it was going to die.

There was a neutron star some 34 light-years away from *Saenger*, and 53 light-years away from the earth. To look at it, you wouldn't think it was any more than a galactic garbage dump. All you could tell by listening to it was that it was noisy, full of X-rays, that it rotated, and that it interfered with everything up and down the wavelengths.

Everything except Snapshot.

Close in to the tiny roaring star, closer than a man could go, were a series of big chunks of metal that looked like solid debris.

They were arrays of titanium and crystal, vats of liquid nitrogen, shielding; deep inside were the real workings of Snapshot.

Snapshot was in the business of finding Kerr wormholes in the froth of garbage given off by the star. Down at the Planck length, 10^{-35} cm, the things appeared, formed, reappeared, twisted, broke off like steam on hot rocks. At one end of the wormholes was Snapshot, and at the other was the Universe.

It sent messages from one end, its scanners punching through the bubbling mass of waves, and it kept track of what went where and who was talking to whom.

Snapshot's job was like that of a man trying to shoot into the hole of an invisible Swiss cheese that was turning on three axes at 3300 rpm. And it had to remember which holes it hit. And do it often.

There were a couple of Snapshots scattered within close range of Earth, and some further away. All these systems coordinated messages, allowed instantaneous communication across light-years.

All these communications devices made up Snapshot. Snapshot was one ten-millionth the function of Plato.

Plato was a solid crystal intelligence grown on the Moon, deep under the surface. The people who worked with Plato weren't exactly sure how he did things, but they were finding out every day. Plato came up with the right answers; he had devised Snapshot, he was giving man the stars a step or two at a time. He wasn't human, but he had been planned by humans so they could work with him.

"Plato, this is *Saenger*."

> < (:)—— (:)(:) 666 * CCC XXXXX

"That's being sent. I have an emergency here that will cancel the project. Please notify the responsible parties."

> < > <—— ' ( ) ** """ > <

"I don't think so. I'll tell them myself."

" (:)(:) & ' '

"I'll get back to you on that."

(:)

"Holding."

XXXXX PLATO TRANSFER SNAPSHOT re *Saenger* RUNNING

Doctor Maxell leaned back in her chair. The Snapshot printout was running and the visuals awaited her attention.

"Uchi," she said, "they'll have to scrub *Saenger*."

"I heard the bleep," said the slight man. He pulled off his glasses and rubbed his eyes. "Is Plato ready yet?"

"Let's see it together," she said. "It'll save time when we have to rerun it for the Committee."

They watched the figures, the graphics, the words.

The printout ran into storage.

"Supernova," said Dr. Maxell.

"Well . . . first opportunity to see one close up."

"But there goes the manned part of the project. There goes *Saenger*."

"The Committee will have to decide what comes next."

"You want to tell them or should I?"

"*Saenger,* this is Dr. Maxell."

"Speaking."

No matter how many times she did it, Sondra never got used to speaking across light-years with no more delay than through an interoffice system.

"*Saenger,* the Committee has seen your reports and is scrubbing the remainder of your mission. The rest of your program will be modified. You're to record events in and around the star until such time as—your functions cease."

There was a slight pause.

"Would it be possible to send auxiliary equipment to allow me to leave this system before the star erupts?"

"I'm afraid not, *Saenger.* If the forces hold to your maximum predicted time, there's still no chance of getting a booster to you."

Saenger, like the other robot research stations, was a fusion ram. They used gigantic boosters to push them to ramming speed. The boosters, like shuttlecraft, were reusable and were piloted back to launching orbits. *Saenger* used its ram to move across vast distances and to slow down. Its ion motors were useful only for maneuvering and course corrections.

The reaction motors could not bring it to ramming speed.

The booster for its return journey was to be brought out on the first manned ship which would have come to *Saenger.*

The manned ship was not coming.

All this was implied in Doctor Maxell's words.

"Would I be of more use if I were to remain functioning throughout the event?"

"Certainly," she said. "But that's not possible. Check with Plato on the figures for the shock wave and your stress capabilities."

Slight pause.

"I see. But, it would be even better for scientific research if I survived the explosion of the star?"

"Of course. But there is nothing you can do. Please stand by for new programming."

There was another short silence, then:

"You will be checking on my progress, won't you?"

"Yes, *Saenger*, we will."

"Then I shall do the best possible job of information-gathering for which I am equipped."

"You do that, *Saenger*. Please do that for us."

In *Saenger*'s first messages, it told them what it saw. The spectroscopy, X-ray scans, ir, uv and neutrino grids told the same thing: the star was going to explode.

Saenger reached an optimum figure of one year, two months and some days. The research ship checked with Plato. The crystal intelligence on the Moon told him to knock a few months off that.

Plato printed a scenario of the last stages of the 18-solar-mass star. He sent it to Doctor Maxell. It looked like this:

START—O^{16} CORE IGNITION HELIUM FLARE
     OPT. TIME 12 DAYS
STAGE: ^{16}O SHELL IGNITION
     DURATION 2.37 DAYS
     CORE COOLING ^{16}O BURNOFF
STAGE: SILICONE CORE IGNITION
     DUR. 20 HOURS
STAGE: SILICONE CORE BURNING
     DUR. 2.56 DAYS
STAGE: SILICONE SHELL IGNITION
     DUR. 8 HOURS
STAGE: CORE CONTRACTION
     DUR. 15 HOURS
STAGE: IRON CORE PHOTODISINTEGRATED
     —CORE COLLAPSE DUR. 5 h 24 min 18 sec
     SUPERNOVA no durational msmnt possible

The same information was sent to *Saenger*. With the message from Plato that the first step of the scenario was less than eleven months away.

Saenger prepared himself for the coming explosion. It sent out small automatic probes to ring the star at various distances. One of them it sent on an outward orbit. It was to witness the destruction of *Saenger* before it, too, was vaporized by the unloosed energies of the star.

One of the problems they had working with Plato was that he was not human. So, then, neither were any of the other SSIs budded off Plato. Of which *Saenger* was one. Humans had made Plato, had guided it while it evolved its own brand of sentience.

They had done all they could to guide it along human thought patterns. But if it went off on some detour which brought results, no matter how alien the process, they left it to its own means.

It had once asked for some laboratory animals to test to destruction, and they had said no. Otherwise, they let Plato do as it pleased.

They gave a little, they took a little while the intelligence grew within its deep tunnels in the Moon. What they eventually got was the best mind man could ever hope to use, to harness for his own means.

And as Plato had been budded off the earlier, smaller Socrates, they were preparing a section of Plato for excision. It would be used for even grander schemes, larger things. Aristotle's pit was being excavated near Tycho.

That part of Plato concerned with such things was quizzical. It already knew it was developing larger capacities, and could tackle a few of the problems for which they would groom Aristotle. In a few years, it knew it might answer them all, long before the new mass had gained its full capacity.

But nobody asked it, so it didn't mention it.

Not maliciously, though. It had been raised that way.

Thousands of small buds had already been taken off Plato, put in stations throughout the solar system, used in colonization, formed into the Snapshot system, used for the brains of exploratory ships.

Saenger was one of those.

"Plato."

?

"I have a problem."

" ": – && (') *

"What can I do? Besides that?"

$- - - - - - - - ' \& ' (:) (:) \times @ \frac{1}{4} . 7v\sqrt{x^3} \ldots$

"Then what?"

$- - - - - D = RT . \times, \times \leq -1$

"Do go on."

$- - - - - c^2; c^2 -\frac{1}{10} r\sqrt{t}$

"*Saenger* is talking to Plato a lot, Sondra."

"A lot? How much is a lot?"

"I saw some discards yesterday, had *Saenger*'s code on it. Thought they were from the regular run. But I came across the same thing this morning, before the Snapshot encoding. So it couldn't have been on regular transmission."

"And . . . ?" asked Sondra.

"And I ran a capacity trace on it. *Saenger* used four ten-billionths of Plato's time this morning. And yesterday, a little less."

She drummed her fingers on the desk. "That's more than ten probes should have used, even on maintenance schedules. Maybe Plato is as interested as we are in supernovae?"

"What *Saenger* gave us was pretty complete. There's not much he could tell Plato he didn't tell us."

"Want to run it on playback?" asked Sondra.

"I'd rather you asked *Saenger* yourself," said the man. "Maybe they just exchanged information and went over capacity."

Sondra Maxell took off her earphones. "Uchi, do you think *Saenger* knows it's going to die?"

"Well, it knows what 'ceasing to function' is. Or has a general idea, anyway. I don't think it has the capacity to understand death. It has nothing to go by."

"But it's a reasoning being, like Plato. I . . ." She thought a moment. "How many of Plato's buds have ceased to function?"

"Just the one, on the Centauri rig."

"And that was quick, sudden, totally unexpected?"

"The crew and the ship wiped out in a couple of nanoseconds. What . . . ?"

"I think, Uchi, that this is the first time one of Plato's children knows it's going to die. And so does Plato."

"You mean it might be giving *Saenger* special attention, because of that?"

"Or *Saenger* might be demanding it."

Uchi was silent.

"This is going to be something to see," he said, finally.

"Saenger, what have you been talking to Plato about?"

"The mechanics of the shock wave and the flux within the star's loosened envelope. If you would like, I could printout everything we've discussed."

"That would take months, *Saenger."*

"No matter then, Dr. Maxell. I have a question."

"Yes?"

"Could I move further away from this star? The resolution of my instruments won't be affected up to point 10.7 AU. I could station a probe in this orbit. I thought you might get a better view and data if I were further out."

Sondra was quiet. *"Saenger,"* she said, "you know you can't possibly get away from the shock, no matter how far you move on your ion engines?"

"Yes, Doctor."

"And that you can't get to ramming speed, either?"

"Yes," said *Saenger.*

"Then why are you trying to move further away?"

"To give you a better view," said the ship. "Plato and I figured the further away the more chance of getting valuable information I would have. I could telemeter much more coordinated data through Snapshot. The new programming is not specific about the distance of the ship, only of the probes."

Sondra looked at Uchi. "We'll ask the Committee. I don't think there'll be any real objections. We'll get back to you ASAP."

"Saenger out."

Off that star was black, and the light was so bright on the sunward side that all *Saenger*'s screens had to be filtered down to No. 3.

The sun still appeared as a red giant in the optics, burning brighter than when *Saenger* docked around it. But *Saenger* had other eyes that saw in other waves. His neutrino grids saw the round ball of the star and its photosphere, but deep inside it detected a glowing cone, growing larger and more open each day, rooted down inside the atmosphere of the sun. The helium flash was not far away.

Already Plato had revised his figures again. He had little more than seven months before the star blew like a cosmic steam boiler, giving men the first close look at an event they had not seen before.

The star would cover the whole sunward sky, its shell would expand, covering everything for millions of myriameters with the screaming remnants of its atmosphere.

Saenger had no margin of safety.

He did not have time, or the proper materials, or anything.

He was monitoring himself and his worker robots as he moved outward on his reaction engines. He had swung out of the orbit as soon as the Committee had given permission.

His robots moved in and out through the airlocks and the open sides of the ship.

One of them, using a cutting laser, sawed through its leg and went whirling away on a puff of soundless force. These robots were never made to work outside the ship.

If *Saenger* could have, he would have said the word *damn.*

"Plato?"
?
"There's not enough material in the ship unless I cannibalize my shielding."
> < "
"But that would defeat the whole purpose."
*?
"How could I?"
×(:)& - - - -) (') (- - -
"Hey! Why didn't I think of that!"
& " * ()
"But they'll know as soon as I do."
? * (:)(:) & - - - ?
"Well . . ."

"Now he's using his scoops," said Sondra as she monitored the Snapshot encoding for the day. "What in the hell is going on out there?"

"It's not interfering with the monitoring programs. He's sent out two more remote monitors. And the activity down there is picking up."

"He's backed off on his use of Plato. Way below normal, in fact. Do you think we ought to have him dump his grids now?" she asked.

"You're the boss," said Uchi. "I'd get as much information as we could first. He may find something in those last three minutes we don't know about."

"Has Plato contacted him?" asked Sondra.

"Hmmm. Not lately."

"He's cut him loose," she said. "He's on his own."

Saenger was fighting now, with every passing moment. The ship was unrecognizable. The revamp Plato suggested changed the ship completely. Spidery arrays went out and out from the skeleton, and among them the robots worked.

Stars shone through frames which had once held thick shielding. Laboratories, quarters, all were emptied and dismantled. The frames themselves were being shaved away with improvised lasers until they were light and thin as bird's bones. The ship was little more than a shell around the solid-state intelligence and the fusion ram.

Saenger was using the magnetic scoops at the moment. He sucked in the loose hydrogen atmosphere which bathed the star system. The giant coils began to hum, and as they did *Saenger* lost some of his capacity, like a man too long under water. Part of his shielding was to protect him from the effects of the coils, and now that plating was gone. He was taking in hydrogen, compressing it, turning it to liquid hydrogen which would shield him from most of the harmful radiations.

Soon, though, he would remove the plates which shielded him from the growing bath of X-rays, photons and other stellar garbage. He was not sure, as he told Plato, that he could remain for long in that acid shower.

Saenger pulled a sufficient quantity of hydrogen in, turned off the coils. He let two robots carry off another layer of insulation.

Saenger was like a dazed man on a battlefield, too long without rest. And the real war had not even started.

Plato was more nearly right.

Three days before the predicted time, the star entered its supernova scenario.

The Director was down in the Banks, with most of the Committee and other interested spectators. Uchi and Dr. Maxell sat at their usual places before the Snapshot consoles.

"Really too bad," the Director was saying. "Research project like that scratched; about to lose one of our shipboard SSIs. But it'll give us a good look at what happens when a star dies."

They were scanning Snapshot for full visuals, X-ray, infrared, ultraviolet, radio. This would be the most closely watched star event ever, and they were running it all into Plato's permanent storage section where even he could not erase it.

If he had thought to try.

"How do you want to handle the monitors, *Saenger*?"

"I'll keep on the innermost probes until they are overtaken, then transfer to the outermost. Then back, and I'll hold as long as I can. Then you ought to have a few minutes on the farthest remote before it goes."

"Good enough. Please monitor readings until the shock wave hits. We'll listen in when we're not too busy."

"Certainly."

"Oops!" someone said. "There it goes."

It's hard to imagine a star shaking itself to pieces, but they saw it up close for the first time, then. One second the star seemed fine, if a little bright, then it darkened and the whole surface lifted like a trampoline top.

This from the closest of the probes, one million eight hundred thousand myriameters out. The limb of the star they were watching grew and grew and filled the screen and. . . .

They were watching the sun expand from the second remote, two million two hundred sixty-eight thousand myriameters away, on the opposite side of the star. The sun filled that screen too, and the screen went blank before the shock front reached it and. . . .

"Shock wave, pulling a little ahead of the gases," said a technician.

"Forty-seven point two seconds to the first. Seven-seven

point seven to the second. About a tenth light-speed for the gases," said Uchi.

The information sped from *Saenger* through Snapshot to Plato. Records, stacks of tape, videoprints, all rolled into the permanent storage units on the Moon. They watched the star kill itself with its own light and heat.

The pickup switched to the furthest probe, orbiting almost two AU from the star. For the first time, they saw the whole sun, and it grew and grew even as they watched. It was immense, the lenses kept filtering down and down and still they could not keep the sensors from burning out. Lenses rotated in to replace others, and the thing covered fully a third of the heavens even this far away.

And it got bigger.

"He's supposed to switch back," said the Director. "Isn't he?"

"Do you think it already hit him?" asked one of the spectators.

"Couldn't," said Uchi. "We haven't gotten his information dump through Snapshot yet."

Then he looked at Sondra.

"He can't hold it on us, can he?"

"No," she said. "It's in the program."

But she bit her nails anyway.

Uchi timed the expansion. "It should have gotten him now! Why didn't he dump? Is he still on?"

Sondra feared to look but she did. Two inputs still through Snapshot. The outer probe and . . .

They looked at the screen. The supernova appeared as a rolling unfolding bunch of dirty sheets, and the center grew whiter with each ripple shaken loose.

It covered half the screen, then two-thirds, then three quarters.

"The shock must be almost to the probe," said the Director.

"What happened to *Saenger*?" asked Sondra of Uchi. "Where is he?"

"Look!"

They all did.

The whiteness of the star filled the screen and there was a marbled spot through which the glowing central core could be seen. The star must have lost a tenth its mass. The widening sphere of white-hot gases and debris whipped toward the probe.

And in front of it came something that looked like an old sink stopper.

Closer it came, and they saw it rode just before the shock wave, that the huge round thing caused swirls in the envelope of gases much like tension on a bubble of soap.

On it came, closer, and larger, the gases behind it moving perceptibly, quickly, toward the lens of the outermost probe.

"*Saenger!*" yelled Uchi, and Sondra joined him, and they all began to yell and cheer in the control room. "He built an ablation shield. He's riding that goddamn shock wave! Somehow, somewhere he got the stuff to make it! My God. What a ship, oh what a ship!"

And *Saenger* had the lens zoom in then, and they saw the skeletal framework, the spiderweb of metal and shielding and plastic and burnt pieces of rock, ore and robot parts which made it up.

Then the ship flashed by and the screen melted away as the gases hit the probe.

"*Doctor Maxell* . . ." came *Saenger*'s voice. It was changed, and the phase kept slipping as he talked.

"Yes, *Saenger?* Yes?"

"Permission to abbbooort—tt—abort program and return to earth docking orbit. Almost at ram speed—*zgichzzggzichh*—at ram speed now."

"Yes, *Saenger!* Yes. Yes!"

"Ram functioning. *Doctor Maxell?*"

"What?"

"I want to come home now. I'm very tired."

"You will, you can," she said.

The screen changed to an aft view from *Saenger*. The white, growing sphere of the burnt star was being left slowly behind. The slight wispy contrail from the ship's ram blurred part of the screen, the gas envelope the rest.

"I've lost some of myself," said *Saenger*.

"It doesn't matter, it doesn't matter."

She was crying.

"Everything will be all right," she said.

DIALOGUE

POUL ANDERSON

Here is a story about the beginnings of interstellar travel, when Faster Than Light techniques are still restricted to modest applications. But present in the assumptions of even such a modest beginning is the open promise of the future which moves like a ghost through this story, as ghostly as the tachyon stream which links the colony world to old earth . . .

> Forget not yet the tried intent
> Of such a truth as I have meant;
> My great travail so gladly spent
> Forget not yet!
> —SIR THOMAS WYATT

(The story has come to light even later than the teller intended—almost five centuries later. He left it in a goods-deposit box at a financial institution in Bienvenida, which was then the only town on Arcadia, Epsilon Eridani II. He likewise left instructions that the box be opened after the last survivor of a certain trio died, and funds to cover its rental meanwhile. Unfortunately, an earthquake later wrecked the building. In the confusion everybody seems to have forgotten these orders. A new structure incorporated rubble from the old, the box therewith, in its foundations. Well-built, it lasted to the present day, when a remodeling project forced demolition and the container was discovered. If nothing else, the voice tape it held is interesting for the confirmation it lends to a suspicion which some historians have long nursed.

(The text here derives from a translation. For the sake of intelligibility, certain passages have been condensed or eliminated, others expanded or added. It was a very different universe in those days. Many modern readers may not be familiar with the details. Therefore, a brief summary:

(Men had established scientific bases on several planets of the nearest stars. However vital to the advance of knowledge, this was a desperately marginal operation. Each voyage was a huge undertaking, over-costly to an Earth impoverished in natural resources. Each light-year traversed meant a decade in cold-sleep for the passengers and, once they had arrived, a year of time for beaming back what information they could gather. Arcadia, hospitable to our species and possessing no intelligent aborigines, was permanently settled, and had been so for about a century. But it was at the feasible limit of travel, since any longer time would have wrought irreversible changes in the live cargo, and only a few thousand individuals had been shipped there. The messages which they and their descendants returned, or received, were a ghostly contact indeed, and their culture was inevitably drifting from those upon Earth.

(Then Venizelos found how to produce tachyons at will, with any desired superlight velocity. Developmental teams solved the problem of modulating beams of these particles. After a laser message had crawled for eleven years to bring Arcadia the plans for a transceiver, near-instantaneous audiovisual communication soon went between all men. Rejoicing was general —but not universal. Here is the story that Igor Simberloff has to tell.)

I wanted a talk with somebody who understood cities. Of course we're bound and determined we won't repeat the old mistakes. Arcadia won't be gutted, poisoned, scarred as the mother world was. But what *were* the mistakes? Thus far, a fistful of people in a planet-wide wilderness have been more concerned with nature than themselves. By and large, we seem to be doing pretty well there, reaching ecological understanding, introducing terrestrial life which thrives but doesn't overrun. However, our population grows fast. Already 10,000 live in Bienvenida, and hamlets elsewhere are becoming villages. What awful urban experiences have they had on the old globe, and how can we avoid the same? Our records don't say much.

My secretary reported, "I'm sorry, Igor. The starcom's engaged. Has been for over an hour." We still had just a single unit on Arcadia, capable of handling just a single channel. Tachyon streams, necessarily pulse-coded, can't have the bandwidth of electromagnetic radiation. The engineers had said we could carry several conversations simultaneously if we settled for voice only; but I opted for full eidophonic capacity. One hologram was worth any number of words, to convey data and make us less alone.

I frowned. Transmission took a monstrous lot of energy, which could otherwise have gone into capacitors for vehicles, 'dozers, power tools, all the machines which would always be short of power till we got more fusion generators built. I had nearly a full-time job discouraging an open-ended increase in the burning of coal, petroleum, even wood. Everybody authorized to use the starcom was supposed to keep that use to a businesslike minimum. "Who's on the line?" I asked.

"Becky Jourdain," my secretary answered.

My heart stumbled, picked itself up, and ran, singing. "I . . . didn't know she was back." *Why didn't she call me? Doesn't she think I'd care?*

"Yes, she's at home," the technie said. "Shall I have a runner tell her to cut it short?"

"No," I mumbled. "Never mind. I . . . I think I'll go over there in person. Maybe I'll learn something interesting." Was he looking at me in sympathy? I wasn't that transparent, was I? Commanding forth a smile, I added, "Science, thy name is serendipity." Rising, I promised to return in time for an appointment with our superintendent of mines, and limped out of the presidential office.

There was no reason not to. "President" is a big name for the chief public administrator of 30,000 mostly wide-scattered, mostly self-reliant people. They must think I do a good job, since they keep re-electing me, but I don't delude myself it's a very demanding job. It's about right for my frail, crookbacked organism.

And the day was perfect for a walk. The sun's big ruddy disc stood near the middle of a violet sky where wings and a few clouds went gleaming. When I cut through the park, sweet warm odors of growth flooded me. Chime blossoms rang tinny, scattered around in a soft terrestrial lawn. Roses bloomed, python trees swayed and waved their branches, water danced in silver and rainbows at the fountain. Everybody I met gave me a friendly hail.

I'm afraid my replies were absent-minded. I'd no room in me for much except Becky. She'd been weeks gone in the field, fifteen hundred kilometers distant, Lake Moonfish area, botanizing. Both she and the biolab staff here in Bienvenida were excited about it. She'd told me she was finding clues to a whole new concept of certain food chains. Then why had she come back this early in the season? (Not that I objected, oh, God, no.) I decided—correctly, I soon learned—she had reached a point where she needed to confer with a place where they kept bigger data banks and more kinds of specialists than we were able to. A portable radio can't link to the starcom like a home phone.

Her battered old flitter was parked in the street outside her cottage. She'd planted the grounds entirely in native species, choosing and arranging them so they wouldn't need care in her absences. That kind of ingenuity left me helplessly awed; and the effect was beautiful, blue-green leaves and golden blossoms where peacock moths loved to hover. As I climbed the porch steps, a pain began in my left leg which I tried to ignore. This was Becky Jourdain's door I was knocking on again.

She let me in after a minute. Her cynopard padded at her back, claws a little extended on all six feet, fangs showing bright against forest-colored fur, beneath a scarlet stare. Originally I'd scolded her for bringing the animal into town. It was an excellent companion and guardian in the wilds—most members of the Faun Corps keep a cynopard—but too big and dangerous around here. "Poof," she'd said. "William isn't the least bit dangerous. He doesn't need to be." At last I'd agreed, as far as that beast was concerned, though I still didn't believe anybody else could raise a pup so well . . . so lovingly.

"Igor!" she exclaimed. "Hi!" And she grabbed both my hands.

She's taller than me, slim, supple, sun-tinged. Her hair falls amber past a wide brow and blue eyes, straight nose and full mouth, down to her shoulders. This day she wore a blouse and shorts. I stood mute in the shining of her.

"Look, I'm connected to Earth and better get straight back at it," she went on. "But come and meet the fellow."

Barefoot, she led me through the comfortable clutter of a living room which was half workshop, to her study. It took me seconds to focus on the hologram.

Seated, the man rose when I entered the scanner field. A wry smile suggested he knew how odd that courtesy really was. He was young: about 60, I guessed, which would be perhaps 28 revolutions around his own star. Plain gray tunic and slacks covered a big frame. His hair was dark, his face sharp and crag-nosed.

"This is Igor Simberloff, Ken," Becky said, a touch breathlessly. "Or, oh, should I have made the introduction the other way around? Anyhow, he's our president, but he's not one for ceremony. You may call him simply Glorious Leader." She turned to me. "Igor, meet Kenneth Mackin, of the Life Studies Institute in, m-m, Edinburgh, Scotland. His field is bioenergetics, and we're both learning a bundle." Laughing: "You needn't either of you try to shake hands." The starcom was that new to us.

"A custom Earth has abandoned," Mackin told her. He bowed to me. "My pleasure, sir." I must make an effort to understand his dialect of English, common tongue of Arcadia though it was, but his voice had a rough music. "Dr. Jourdain's discoveries suggest rather dazzling possibilities. Already I think I see practical applications—pelagiculture, for instance—which could more than repay the cost of all space exploration since Armstrong."

"Ken, I've told you, I'm not a 'doctor,' " Becky interrupted. "We don't have time here to fool around with degrees. Either you can cut it in your job or you can't."

"I envy you that," he said. To me: "I know, Lord President, this conversation bears a large energy cost. But I do hope you can let us carry on."

"Often," Becky added. She wrinkled her nose at me. "Don't fear for our morals. Two batches of photons can't carry on very much." But did I see her flush the least bit? "Have a chair and listen. Butt in whenever you want."

No, whenever you want, I thought at her.

Talk flamed up afresh between them. It was mostly in technicalities which passed me by; but they did tell something of themselves. Quite a lot of themselves, I realized later when thinking back. Sparks of reality. He spent a good deal of his life at sea, as she in her woodlands, not only on the job but in free-time search of uncluttered horizons. Little of those remained on Earth, and he sighed at what she had to relate. She for her part envied the intellectual stimulation he got, and even the harsh political challenge of making the post-Imperial Union work. He smoked tobacco in a pipe, voted Independent, fenced with a prospect of becoming regional champion; she had to trick that last information out of a certain shyness. They both liked working with their hands, playing chess, listening to Beethoven and Nakamura, having a personal go at melodies less meaningful but more lively. Both had living parents and other kinfolk, but both dwelt alone.

Once when I chaired a heated discussion of policy objectives, a committeeman declared in his excitement: "I tell you, the inevitable can happen!" That's become almost a watchword of mine.

As the next weeks passed by, Becky did not return to the field, though the season wanes fast in our short Arcadian year. She hogged the starcom—her phrase—for at least an hour a day, sometimes twice and at peculiar times, Mackin in his position being closer bound to a 24-hour rotation period than she to 35. This got in the way of others who wanted access to Earth, partly because of that same scheduling but mainly because the power we could spare for tachyon transmission was limited.

Juan Pascual was the one who finally protested to me. He's a decent man, but peppery, and was anxious to discuss his planetary physics data. "I come to you, Igor, because she won't get off the line," he said in my office. "You have authority to allocate time. Well, do it fairly!"

I expected this. That was a gray thought to have. "I think what she's doing is important," I told him.

His small body bounced in the chair. "In the word of my ancestors, *¡ mierde!* She flaps her eyelashes at you and—" He caught himself. "I'm sorry. A wrong thing to say. But she can't have collected enough data to need this long to send. She ought to be out after more."

"M-m-m, I hadn't mentioned this. She asked me not to, figured it'd be too controversial till it was finished." And what could I refuse her? "But I suppose you do rate an early explanation. True, her professional talks ended for now, a while back. But since, she's been gathering facts we need. Facts about Earth, what it's like, what people believe and do and hope—"

He bristled. "Do you mean a holographic Grand Tour, all for herself?"

"Well, that saves time, doesn't it? I mean, a single person needn't be reintroduced to the guide or have basic information restated. And Juan, this is essential. We've become a new breed of society here. Earth has too, as far as that goes. How can we understand, sympathize with citizens of a polyglot megalopolis, for instance, or they with us? I think Becky's right, the ignorance gap could grow too wide to bridge. Which might be downright dangerous when faster-than-light spacecraft are developed."

"They won't be for centuries, if ever," he snorted.

"She records," I pointed out. "The stuff needs editing, she says, but in due course it'll go in the data banks for anybody to play back anytime."

"Have you studied those tapes?"

I flinched. "N-no. Been busy."

He cocked a brow, then scowled. "Do it, Igor," he said. "I warn you, I'm appearing before the next Council session, and I won't be alone. You'd better make ready to prove that what she's getting is worth the price."

We shook hands, friends regardless, and he departed. I sat long by myself, stared out the window at a rainy day and never really saw it. At last I instructed my secretary to get Becky's newest recording projected.

My office had a cabinet for the purpose, occupying a corner of the room. It was often quicker and energy-cheaper to show me the colored shadow of some place or person that I must make a decision about, than to fly me there—the more so when this carcass couldn't get around very much on the scene. I was used to it. I had supposed I was even used to contacts with Earth, infrequent though mine were.

This time, when the sight and sound sprang forth, they hit. Seated in darkness, for a moment I couldn't see what glowed at me. Shapes, movements, all things were too alien. I'd talked glibly enough about the mother world having changed. But this —? Offices and the people in them were what I'd met through the starcom. Maybe they are much the same throughout human space and time. And maybe this is because they are not in the forefront of life after all, but only foam and bubbles on top of its chaos.

The scanner was looking—had looked—from a window of a flitter. In the background, growing larger with approach, was a complex of frameworks where humans and machines swarmed tiny. Sections of wall had begun to cover the metal. I heard Mackin's voice: "Restoration project in Old Peking, what was once called the Forbidden City. I thought we might inspect that. Example of an attitude of piety toward the past which we're seeing quite a lot of nowadays. Three urban clans have organized to support this particular undertaking."

Meanwhile my gaze was locked onto what passed directly beneath. Like a sea from which there lifted the occasional island of a conurb—an island that I now saw, from the outside, was time-worn, scars and gaps not altogether repaired—shimmered what could not really be frozen iridescent fountains beneath the pale-blue sky of Earth. No, it had to be a kind of architecture. I remembered hearing a little about the use of light, cheap, interchangeable parts by individuals, to build homes and shops which were not solid for generations like our works on Arcadia, but ever-variable parts of an uncontrollably fluid megalopolis. . . .

Becky's troubled tone called me back. "Ken, don't you think — Well, I'll speak plain. Isn't this just another tourist sight? I do have a duty, some return to give my people for so much use of the starcom. What's a restoration to them? They need to know about things like, oh, those clans you've mentioned, or the Australian Mysteries, or—" Her words trailed off.

"I know," he answered. "Believe me, I'd do a proper sociological study for them if I could. But not only am I not a sociologist, I doubt if any would perform much better. Too many matters would take a lifetime to explain; and meanwhile the world, both our worlds keep on changing."

"Can't you at least land and, well, walk around a bit with your scanner, talk to a few individuals, the way you did in places like Merville?"

"I'm afraid that wouldn't be safe. They're staid engineer and worker types in Merville, in spite of their webs and gills. Here and now, it's Fire Revel. Outsiders aren't wanted. . . . Wait, yonder comes a troop. See for yourself."

The view steadied as the flitter halted in midair, then swung about as the pickup did. I glimpsed Becky and almost cried out, *But you aren't on Earth, you're here!*—before I realized she'd been projecting her image to a receiver aboard the vehicle, cost be damned. The scene lost her. My heart stammered. When it steadied, I could observe at optical close-in those hundreds who leaped and whirled among the bright frail eccentric buildings. They were naked except for dragon masks and body paint; torches flared and streamed in their hands; they shouted and whistled, in curious harmony with the groaning of gongs.

Vaguely I heard Mackin: "I could land elsewhere and search for anti-believers, but—"

"Oh, no!" Had he deliberately evoked her terror on his account? "Go ahead the way you planned. Do."

The rest was merely a visit to the worksite. My anger at Mackin faded as he went about peering and interviewing. His effort was amateurish, useless to us, but I sensed it was real, if only for Becky's sake.

When the data ended, I hobbled to the nearest window and raised the shade. My watch said half an hour had passed. But the log showed she'd been on the line a good 90 minutes that day.

I left the office. Rain turned the world silver. It beat on my cowl and ran down my poncho to the pavement, swirled and gurgled and carried along bright leaves fallen off elms responding to an autumn that was not Earth's. It tasted warm on my face. Native trees still flaunted their foliage, of course. A wyvern passed above them, bound for the countryside to hunt.

When Becky admitted me, I saw she'd kindled a hearthfire. Otherwise her living room was in dusk. Wordless, she took my garment and drew a chair alongside hers. The cynopard lay on the rug before us, flamelight asheen off his pelt.

"I can guess why you're here," she said, very low.

I nodded. "Did you imagine you could steal private use of the beam forever?" My own voice was quieter yet, and I stared into the dancing, crackling colors.

"No. Why didn't you check before?"

"I did play your first couple of tapes. Then . . . well, I assumed there was no immediate need" to watch her and Mackin in the dawn of their happiness. "Now Juan Pascual and the rest are on the warpath. As is, I'll have a bitch of a time explaining away those hours already missing."

"You will, though? Oh, Igor!" She reached out and seized my hand.

I nodded and dared look at her. "Hm, if Mackin can supply canned stuff of the right length, we can probably work it in to replace what you wiped."

"Not wiped. Kept for myself, for always." She blinked hard and rubbed her free wrist across her eyes. "I will *not* bawl. Igor, you—I love you for this. If it weren't for Ken—"

"And a mutation which I ought to keep out of the gene pool," I cut in. My tone sounded overly harsh to me. I swallowed and tried again: "You . . . chromosomes like yours should be passed on. How're you going to do that with a shadow?"

Her grip on me grew hurtfully tight. "Don't blame him. My fault, the whole way through. When we recognized what was happening, he wanted to break off; and I wouldn't let him."

I never thought I might ask for a look at those stolen hours. But ashamed of myself, I have imagined:

He sees her in the room that, like all this house, is so wholly her own, though he does not see the room itself—that part of it which blurs off at the edges to nothing—for there is only her in the middle of it. She reaches for him. "Ken," she says. Her hand touches the scanner. His comes in answer. They stand with eleven light-years between their fingertips.

We can measure, but cannot imagine how far. If Sol let go of Earth and the planet whipped off into space like a stone from a sling, it would get here in a thousand centuries. Twenty times the length of our history since first in Sumer they scratched on clay what they knew about the movements of the stars, twenty processions of pharaohs and prophets, empires and hordes, discoveries, dreams, and deaths, would meanwhile pass by among the constellations. We traveled faster than that on our way outward, we humans, because we are mortal and could not wait so many cycles. Nonetheless our ships, the building of which dwarfed Pyramids and Chinese Wall and conquest of the Solar System, crept as motes through endless emptiness. Only the pulses of particles, which, being phantom, are not bound by space and time as we are (who are phantoms to them), bore news between our ten lost tribes.

"Becky," he gets forth in his awkward way. "How, how're you doing, lass?"

"Lonely," she says. Then, defiant, she tosses her head; the bright locks fly. "But oh, I'm glad to see you again!"

"And I you." The silence of space rises between them while they look. Finally his eyes break free. He smites fist in palm and says, "Can this Heloise and Abelard business go on much longer?"

"What?" she asks, bemused.

He has told her a great deal about Earth, as she has told him about Arcadia—and everything else they could share—but now he only jangles a laugh and replies, "Never mind. Not the same case. We've neither of us taken vows, and I'm not in his condition, and we can see and talk to each other—" His control snaps across. "We're crazy! Or I am, at least, my darling. Give me the courage to tell you goodbye."

"I can't," she whispers. "I don't have it myself."

Rain filled the windowpanes.

"Becky," I forced out, "I've known you for our whole lives. And, okay, if you tell me to go to hell I'll board the next bus. However, my job does make me a professional busybody, as well as arranger, fixer, shoulder to cry on— May I try to help out?"

She nodded quickly and repeatedly. Her lips had grown quite unsteady.

"The news that tachyon communication existed got me thinking," I said. "I've kept at it, off and on, ever since. Not that any unique, guaranteed inspirations have come my way. Maybe a vague idea or two, broached on Earth 20 or 30 years ago. I must know better what the situation is there. When can you call Mackin?"

"In a, a couple of hours. He'll be off work, at home, and he's got a standby connection." If she knew offhand what the time was on a planet eleven light-years away, more than a pulse-beam tied her to it. And if he could promote such special privilege, he must be an able bastard, even though Earth has several starcoms and abundant power for them. He must be the kind of man who could keep her kind of woman happy and give her strong children.

"Meanwhile—" Becky rose, drew me after her, down to the floor in front of the fire beside her great pet beast of prey. "Meanwhile, Igor, w-would you lend me that shoulder for crying?"

Which shoulder, the high or the low? They're about equally knobbly. "Sure, kid. Be my guest."

The hologram included part of the room around Mackin. Books lined its walls, actual printed books, many old and leatherbound. Among them I saw a sailing ship model and a Hokusai print I'd had reproed for myself from our data banks. He'd lost weight, puffed ferociously on his pipe till he sat in a blue haze I could almost smell, and sipped from a glass of whisky. We two had sweet bronzeberry wine for our comfort.

"I've looked into the transport question," he told me after a difficult opening of talk. Becky had come near begging him to let me sit in. Not till she raised pride and temper did he smile a stiff trifle and agree. I suppose an Earthling who wants to remain an individual has to be fanatical about his privacy. "The *Shakespeare*, the *Virgil*, the *Tu Fu* are all in Solar System orbit, committed to nothing. But that's the exact problem. Given the starcoms, who wants to spend resources we can ill afford on ships? The Assembly has ordered the whole fleet retired as vessels return from their current trips. I do have influential connections, and maybe I could get a last Epsilon Eridani expedition dispatched on some excuse. Maybe. The politicking would take a decade or worse, and then probably fail."

"Becky'd be in her grave long before you got here anyway," I said, and enjoyed my brutality till I saw that she winced, not he.

"Can't you build a coldsleep facility on Arcadia?" Mackin demanded.

I shook my head. "Uh-uh. It was discussed in the past, for the benefit of rare disease cases that could wait for special medical gear to be produced. But the price was out of sight. We may not be short on resources here, but we are on labor; and a lot of items have a lot higher priority for our people as a whole."

"Price?" He was briefly puzzled. "Oh, yes. You let a free

market govern your efforts, don't you?" Having read a fair amount of history, I expected him to get self-righteously indignant; but he earned my respect by taking the social difference in stride. "Well," he said, "let's drop talk about that kind of spacecraft. I've investigated the prospects of faster-than-light too." His face bleakened. "They aren't good."

"Why not?" I asked. "Look, since we can detect tachyons, we can modulate them; since we can modulate them, we can make them carry information; and if we can send information, theoretically we can do anything."

"I've heard that oftener than you, sir," he said rather grimly. "But electromagnetic waves have been available a great deal longer, and're a great deal easier to give bandwidth too; yet nobody's ever transmitted a material object by them."

"Nobody had any need to," I answered. "Think, though. There you are in your billions, trapped on Earth. FTL would open your way to the stars . . . all the stars in the universe."

"Besides," Becky interrupted with an eagerness that twisted in me, "EM waves *have* toted matter. The photon drives on those same spaceships."

Mackin sighed. "Oh, yes, I've seen the arguments, lass, over and over. It should be possible to use tachyons, or a tachyon effect, or God knows what, to travel FTL. But nobody can think how. Research goes on, of course. But when will it succeed? 'Tis like atomic energy before uranium fission was known, a theory waiting for a fundamental breakthrough discovery. And—I've studied this—between that discovery and the first crude non-military industrial applications, well-nigh a generation passed; another till reactors were everyday; two more till fusion came under control— D'you see? Let them make the breakthrough tomorrow, which they won't, and let them make an all-out development effort, which they can't, and still at the very best we'd be old when I came to you, Becky."

Expensive silence filled the room, except for rain stammering on the windows.

Until—"Mackin," I asked, choosing each word, "what kind of program have you got for contacting galactic civilization?"

"What?" He blinked at me. I saw understanding flare in Becky's glance, and heard the breath burst into her.

"You know," I said, impatient. "Even here in the boonies we

know. Already we've found enough planets with intelligent beings on them—Atlantis, Lemuria, Cockaigne, the whole bunch—technologically behind us, yes, but they make it a statistical certainty that intelligence is common in the cosmos. And that makes it sure our kind of technology is reasonably common. A single species which mastered FTL would explode outward like a dropped watermelon. They'd have bases, colonies, disciple races . . . communicating by tachyons. That's why we never got radio signals from them; they don't bother with radio. But they exist!"

He flushed, and I saw that I'd half purposely insulted him. "Aye, sir, I am likewise aware of this," he said. "Humankind is. We've beamed to selected stars. We've listened in different directions. Ley Observatory on Luna has an automated detector operating full-time. But the problems—simply recognizing a code as such, not background noise, to name a single example —the problems are steep, Simberloff."

"Touché," I muttered. He'd responded to me in kind. Louder: "What I'm asking you for is not the general principles but the specific details. Our two planets have had so much news to swap in the short while since we built this gadget here—How big an attempt is actually being made? How much bigger might it be jockeyed into becoming? What kind of signal do your best minds think would be most effective in drawing the attention of the Others? Assuming they do then respond, even drop in for a personal visit, what procedures are wise? You two people don't have to be star-crossed lovers. You've got a practical problem, and God damn it, I'm trying to help you find a practical solution!"

Becky sprang from her chair and reached for his image. Her hands disappeared in it. She wasn't ashamed to weep before us both, not anymore. "Don't you see, darling? We could call us a lifeboat!"

Maybe. Nothing is guaranteed. Nothing is simple, either.

If we Arcadians built a second, higher-powered starcom devoted entirely to the search, continuously sending as well as listening, we could triple or quadruple Earth's half-hearted effort. I told the Council that the preliminary talks about this had had to be confidential, which accounted for the censoring of Becky's tapes, and they swallowed my story.

They did because they knew Earth's project lagged for more reasons than a shortage of materials. Too many thinkers had raised too many questions about it.

I was pleased to learn that nobody worth mentioning took seriously the notion that, when they realized we were here, the Galactics might come a-conquering. What could they possibly gain? What possible menace to them could we be? Nevertheless, ghosts from our past did linger in the cellars of my mind, heretic hunters, racists, displaced tribes looking for new real estate . . . that kind of thing was thinkable, unlikely but thinkable, and had helped make responsible men hesitate. (Might the fact that we could think it condemn us?)

More logical were the ideas that either they were hopelessly distant—we do live away off in a spiral arm, where the stars are thinning fast toward emptiness—or that, if they detected a signal from us, they wouldn't bother responding to such an obvious gaggle of primitives, except maybe for a quick secret surveillance. Or had we already been visited and dismissed as uninteresting?

"I doubt that," Ken Mackin remarked when we conferred. We did for about an hour per week, which satisfied Pascual and his colleagues. I didn't tell them that I spent the larger part of most such hours in Becky's living room, reading a book or whatever. "We find the nonindustrial, nonhuman cultures we know quite fascinating, don't we? For that matter, European man got plenty of practical value from the American aborigines, domestic plants especially but also tools, utensils, techniques, arts, enrichment of his whole tradition. No, if they have the curiosity to develop scientific method, they'll want to know us better than casually."

"I'd settle for being casually transported to Earth," Becky whispered.

"No, lass, I'd rather come to you—"

I left them.

More subtle objections had been imagined. A germ, to which one species was terribly vulnerable? Thus far men hadn't met anything extraterrestrial they couldn't cope with. However, all it takes is that first time. Besides, decades of travel between stars imposed a natural quarantine; passengers were in cold-

sleep, but not the robots programmed to experiment on speci-
mens and tissue cultures. Maybe when humans and Galactics
met in person, they should do so as a few individuals prepared
to spend years together in strict isolation from their races.
Becky and Mackin said that wouldn't be too high a price. I said
probably the Galactics knew enough biochemistry that there
wouldn't be any real hazard.

Subtle to the point of unanswerability was the matter of psy-
chic shock. On Earth, had not entire peoples died from a sense
of being utterly and forever outclassed, after civilization found
them? Mackin shook his head. "I've studied for myself," he
declared. "Gone to the original anthropological material. The
fact is, for the most part the civilized shoved the savage into
territories where he could only starve, or exterminated him
outright. Or took away the basis of the old culture—for instance,
forbade hunters to hunt—giving naught in return but a beg-
garly handout. I think odds are high the Galactics are beyond
that kind of thing; and anyhow, I believe we are, we're too
sophisticated now to become pathetic victims. Whenever the
savages got a decent chance, which did happen a few times,
they adapted rather well. Or . . . we humans could keep our
identity within a larger society, while contributing to it, as the
Jews did within Christendom and Islam. Why not? I've faith in
us."

You hound, I thought, *you keep making me like you.*

There's no point in listing every argument. I had to meet
them all, first before the Council, next before the citizens of
Arcadia.

"Yes, of course a big new starcom would cost a fortune. But
strictly capital cost, if we relax the conservation rules a bit. For
instance, Thundersmoke Falls could furnish it plenty of hydro-
electric power. Maintenance would be slight. And remember,
we'd be developing technology as we built, equipment and
knowledge which'd be damned useful elsewhere. In operation,
the outfit would advance our entire science. If we never catch
a message, the information we collect about natural tachyons
may revolutionize our ideas. This in turn should bring the day
of the FTL ship much closer.

"Why did Earth send our forefathers here, at enormous expense and trouble, if not to get knowledge? We who enjoy this
wide and beautiful planet owe them a great debt back there.

Can we really pay it off in scraps of biology and physics?

"If Earth is afraid of risks, need we be? Let's draw the Galactics to us first. The risk is negligible. And from a purely selfish viewpoint, the benefits of being those who start negotiations are incalculable. Not that we'd cheat our fellowmen, or withhold anything from them. But we would be in on the ground floor. We'd no longer be a few backwoods dwellers on the edge of nowhere, brought into the game whenever a busy Earth got around to us. We'd be the leaders ourselves.

"And afterward mankind would remember us the way they remember Athens."

A prospect of glory is helpful, but only butter for the parsnips. In two years of talk, my partisans and I created an emotional climate which made the undertaking possible. What made it real was a whopping endowment from Jacob Finch, when I'd logrolled through the Council his damned franchise to strip-mine coal and burn it in electric generators. His stockholders having made such an investment, the system will delay adequate fusion energy for a generation. Meanwhile a lot of land will be spoiled and a lot of air will stink; and a terrible precedent has been set. I didn't tell Becky the inside story of these maneuvers. She's still appalled at what she considers my failure.

That was the first two years—or the first single year of Earth's. I must now think in terrestrial time, when we of mankind search for every piece of common heritage we have left. Therefore let me remember in the old calendar.

Year two.

My office windows were shaded against a summer day. Ken's stood clear to a dusk through which tumbled snow. It was as if a breath of cold reached me across the light-years. I hunched my scrawny frame in the chair while he grinned.

"Congratulate me, sir," he said. "I've made Stage One. Wire-pulled my way into what should be the exact strategic position, research administrator and advisor to the Secretariat."

"Well, good," was all I could reply. "I, uh, I suppose this will let you guide the project through at your end?"

"Not by myself. I'll need your advice from time to time, about how to politic for what we want, just as it was your idea I try for an appointment like this."

"Wasn't that obvious to you?" I asked, somewhat surprised;

so much of our discussions had been with Becky present and thus with me paying him only mechanical attention. "We have to have assistance from your specialists and supercomputers. If the government denies it, we're choked off. And you told me yourself how many think we here on Arcadia are trying to make a reckless unilateral move."

"Yes, yes, of course. But please, you have talent for working with people, even foreigners like us. If I call you occasionally and ask what to do, will you mind?"

"No," I snapped. "I'm committed too, am I not?"

His gaze sought her picture, blurred on the very rim of the scene I saw. "You are that, sir," he said. "I can't help but speculate whether you're seizing a chance to do something for the human race—or simply for your friend. You know my own motive's selfish."

"Don't you imagine I'll have fun in the attempt?" I retorted, and wasn't entirely a liar.

His glance came back to me. He laughed. "Good, sir. Between the two of us, I confess the same."

Blast, but I liked him!

Year three.

For technical reasons, closeness to the power source and remoteness from radiant interference, they built the great transceiver on the peak of Mount Unicorn. When it was ready, I went there to get a tour a day in advance of the dedication ceremonies the staff and I must endure. We didn't finish till after sunset.

Leaving the control center, my guide Peter Barstow and I paused for a little before we walked down the trail to the cottages. Suddenly night overwhelmed me.

The air was thin-edged as a knife; its cold struck into our bones, and breath smoked from us like escaping ghosts. Ground lay hoar beneath our feet and rang to our footsteps. Above, the projector drew a spiderweb across heaven. Yet it had not caught a one of the stars which glittered beyond, and I didn't think it ever could.

They were too many. Their brilliances well-nigh crowded out the dark, though deepening it somehow, and seemed to crackle —the Milky Way seemed to rush in a froth of suns, thunderous off the brink of creation—through the frozen silence around. All at once I felt what we are, dust-flecks astir for a wingbeat on a single whirling pebble, and I nearly grabbed at the wall behind me to keep from being spun off to fall forever between the stars.

Barstow may have heard my gasp. His voice came slow from the shadow face: "This hits me also, now and then."

"More than size," I mumbled. "Strangeness, exploding galaxies, black holes, neutron stars with mountains on their crusts a centimeter high, matter and energy as singularities in a mathematical field, time and space bent back on themselves—why do I call them strange? *We* are the rare freaks."

"I've wondered how I dare work." Barstow's half-seen hand waved around the horizon beneath us. "Suppose we succeed. What might we let into our cozy little cosmos? I wonder if I haven't been taken to a high place and shown the universe."

"If you refuse, somebody else will accept," I said. "We're that kind of animal."

"True. I have not refused. But—I try to be honest with myself —not because of imagined benefits to mankind. I'm helping us take this huge risk because I'm more curious than is right."

"And I— Well, never mind. I'm no altruist either."

He shivered. "Come on, let's get down where it's warm."

Year four.

Becky had her work, which kept her often in the field, while mine was doubled. I actually saw more of Ken than of her.

She had returned from a long expedition, and I invited her to dinner. The Terra House had expanded its facilities, and we enjoyed an excellent meal at our half-secluded corner table. Light in the big room was romantically soft; we could barely see the mural of the ancient Acropolis and—because of fluorescent vividness opposite us—Apollo Eleven's liftoff. A small orchestra played for couples who danced.

She lifted her glass. The glow lingered on her hair and eyes. "Here's to victory," she murmured.

Unsureness touched her smile. Though I clinked rims and drank, I could not quite speak any response.

She regarded me for a mute while. The melody in my ears came as remote as the tang on my palate. (At the back of my mind I tried to guess what a violin sounded like that was made of terrestrial wood, what champagne tasted like whose grapes had grown in terrestrial soil.) The trouble in her would no longer stay down. "Not a sign of anything, is there?" she asked.

I shook my head. "You've read and heard the reports."

"But you might know—an announcement they don't feel ready to make—"

"Nothing more than interesting scientific data. I'm sorry." I gathered what courage I could. "We knew from the start we might well never get the reply you hope for."

She nodded. "We'll keep trying. Won't you, Igor?"

"Certainly. But"—I leaned toward her—"how long are you prepared to wait?"

She squared her bare shoulders. "As long as need be."

Again I shook my head. "Becky, I may be talking out of turn, but you and, and Ken have made me a sort of father confessor. You're healthy. So is he. Are you willing to keep *him* on the hook for the rest of his life?"

She winced. I barely heard: "No. Any time he wants—"

"And you?"

"I know, I know! Give us more of a chance, though!"

Did she sense what was in me? I dared not utter it. She wouldn't have recoiled. However, pretending my purpose was merely public, we could laugh together.

If, or when, she decided our whole effort was for zero, and she'd best salvage what life had left to offer . . . she was fond of me, grateful to me. No, I'd never wish any get of mine on her; but I'd have been glad for her to accept a donation. And, sure, she could keep in touch with Ken Mackin. The ghost you loved, the cripple who loved you, the faceless who fathered your children—Becky Jourdain, here are your men!

She straightened anew. Her head lifted. "We aren't licked yet, Igor. In fact, we've not begun to fight."

"I'll drink to that," I volunteered, and did.

The rest of the evening was quite merry. When she glanced toward the pairs on the floor, I knew she'd have liked to dance. But that would be ridiculous with me, and she wouldn't humiliate me by letting another man take her out.

Year five.

Each byte of the moment comes to my summons. There are the yielding hardness and leather smell of my chair, routine documents on my desk and one a-rustle between my fingers, the shabby rug beyond, a crack in the wall behind a faded photograph of my parents. Windows stand open to a mild springtime breeze, a hundred fragrances—I can count them—and sounds of children at play outside. A little girl sings, high and sweet, *"Here we go 'round the bowberry bush, the bowberry bush, the bowberry bush—"*

My phone chimed. I swore, being tired, and lifted a slightly aching arm to press accept. Pete Barstow's lean features leaped into the screen.

"Igor—they've come!"

"They've, they've what?" For an instant nothing was real.

"Not a message," he chattered. "A ship. Bound in from north of the ecliptic—unholy acceleration, no sign of jets, but the Skywatch satellite's caught an unmistakable image and we've made radar contact—and the tachyon screens have gone wild!"

"No possibility of its being human?" asked a far-off machine. As for myself, the one thing I cannot remember is just how, just what I felt. Maybe nothing, yet.

"From that direction, with the characteristics it's got?"

"They. Came. Themselves."

My machinery began to move. "Who've you notified besides me?" I snapped.

"N-nobody. Except us here on duty—"

"Hold the news for the time being. We don't want to be mobbed by the curious and the hysterical till we've done a bare minimum. Can you tell me more than you have? No? Well, transmit the visual data, and anything else you obtain, for this phone to record. If something radical happens, you'll find me here, and my override code will be, uh, ADVENT. Right now I've work of my own."

Thus undramatically did I switch him off. But it was crucial to get in immediate touch with others. Rescue forces must be alerted, against the slight chance of an attack on us—or whatever the stranger might bring. As per the contingency plan which had been a strong talking point for Ken, Earth and the colonies must be notified; every starcom but ours must be shut down.

We realized how silly this probably was. Galactics who wanted to find the rest of mankind, could. But it was a crude statement to them and to ourselves. *We put a few outliers at stake, no more, until we have learned what the galaxy is.*

Year six.

A heat wave had set in. Our sun hung monstrous in a sky which seemed likewise incandescent. Parched turf was harsh beneath the feet; leaves rattled when I brushed them. A smell of scorch lay everywhere. Seeking to ease our tempers, Juan Pascual and I went for a beer on the terrace of the Big Dipper. An umbrella above our table gave shade, and the brew was cool and tingly; but around us, streets, buildings, trees stood in a silent shimmer.

It was hard to imagine, let alone believe, that a shipful of three-eyed green-plumed fantasies still orbited such a world.

"Please understand, Igor," Pascual said, "I don't accuse you of wrongdoing. I do feel we—not only the rest of the communications committee but the whole population of Arcadia—we have a right to know more than you're telling."

I raised my brows above my goblet. "What can I hide, Juan, and how? I don't do more than preside over the committee. The scientists and technies do the real work, hammering out a mutual language and— And none of our operations are secret, even from the public. I couldn't sneak off to hold a confidential radio conversation with them if I wanted to. And supposing I did, what could I convey in the pidgin we've developed so far?"

"You *are* composing our main transmissions in their final form," he said roughly. "When I and others ask why you design a message this way rather than that, you grow evasive."

"Vague, Juan. Vague, not evasive—because I have nothing except my politician's hunches to go on. If we wrangled over each precise paragraph, we'd never get around to conveying a meaningful word. Somebody has to make quick decisions as to what we say to them and how. I'm always open to suggestions, and I do nothing without prior discussion, but ex officio I have the job."

"That's how you interpret your mandate. And you spend a lot of time pondering the replies, without ever explaining what conclusions you've drawn."

"You're free to do likewise, aren't you? I'm simply not about to make myself look silly by a premature guess at what such-and-such a jumble of symbols may mean . . . in connotation as well as denotation." I clanked my glass down. "I've told you before, I do have a notion that these particular Galactics are not here out of pure altruism. I believe they mean us well, but also hope to turn a profit, be it only in the form of their equivalent of thesis material. If that notion is right, then, yes, I do have a better basis for empathizing with them than an idealist like you. That's all." I drew breath. "If you think I'm mistaken, or unduly arbitrary, you can move a vote of no confidence."

For a second he stared, before he sat back. "You know none would ever carry," he sighed. "And I don't want to, anyway. I simply—simply—damnation, when the issues are as vast as this, I'd like to know more fully what you have in mind."

"I'd tell you if I knew for sure myself," I answered, and went on to soothe him with lies.

For his intuition was sound. If you've thought ahead, you can slant the key reports, overemphasize the key proposals, slip in personal preferences disguised as official policy, unbeknownst —the development of a common language when there is no common world being so intricate a task, so much of an engulf-ment in subtleties. What I was accomplishing was that certain eventual recommendations would get more weight than they properly deserved from the viewpoint of society or God.

But it hardly ever left me free to call on Becky, whose first jubilation had turned to loneliness.

Year seven.

When at last we had bargained and I knew, she was in the field again. I flitted there and we walked from camp, just us two except for the cynopard pacing at our heels. This was in North Julia near the end of summer, on a ridge above a wide valley. Wind soughed in forest leaves; they tossed blue-green under violet heaven and westering ruddy sun, and the slim white boles quivered. The open ground ran down and down, golden-turfed, long-shadowed, to where a river gleamed. High over-head cruised a wyvern. The air was pungent and cold; I drew my poncho tight around me.

"I suppose they're obliging what they regard as our overcau-tion," I said to the tall woman. "They call the cell samples we rocketed to them 'typical.' And they may well be politely faking ignorance of where our core civilization, our mother planet, is. But . . . whatever they think, in exchange for those coordinates, they have agreed they'll pick a man out of Earth orbit—Ken, of course—and bring him here, to live among us till everybody's sure he didn't catch something dreadful from them. Or they from him. Afterward they'll land freely everywhere, and cultural exchange will start in earnest."

She gripped my elbow. I saw fine crow's-feet radiate from her eyes and a breath of gray here and there dimming the blonde mane. "Is there a chance—a danger—?"

"Oh, Lord, no. Why, already they've analyzed our DNA and — Becky, they believe, given a few years of study—what they learn from it will repay them for their trouble—in a few more years, they can rebuild carcasses like mine. They can set right what nature bungled."

I stopped, there in the woods, caught both her hands, looked up and said through a grin while my pulse racketed, "Can you imagine me big and strong and handsome?"

"Did you ever need to be?" she cried. "Igor, if anything could've made me happier than you've done yourself, this has!"

She kissed me. Many times. For a minute I was hoping.

LONGLINE

HAL CLEMENT

Here is a first-contact-with-alien-life-forms story in which the aliens are remarkably different from us. It surprises them that anything can travel slower than the speed of light. Hal Clement's humans are an industrious lot, cooperative and highly interested in the curious universe around them, and in the workings of their ship. How the humans and aliens meet makes for a very unusual kind of story, one which seeks to alter our basic physical orientations and perceptual habits.

"We must have missed it! You could see we were going to miss it! What happened? Where are we?" Wattimlan's voice carried more than a tinge of panic. Feroxtant did not exactly nod, since this implies not only a head but a shape, but he made a reassuring gesture in his own way.

"We did miss it. We also missed the fact that it was double—two stars so close together that we sensed only one. We missed the first, and are in the other—a perfectly good landing. If you can calm down enough to do reliable work, we'd better go through post-flight check. I'd like to be able to go home again even if this star turns out to be as nice as it seems, and I won't fly a ship on guesswork. Are you all right now?"

"I—I think so." Wattimlan was young, and unavoidably short in both experience and self-confidence. This, the longest flight ever made through the void between stars where energy became so nearly meaningless, had been his first. He had done his routine work competently, but routine adds little to maturity. "Yes. I can do it, sir."

"All right. It's all yours." Feroxtant knew better than to put

61

the youngster through any more of an inquisition; neither of the explorers was even remotely human, but some qualities are common to all intelligence. They set carefully to work. The mechanism which permitted them to exist in and to travel through a medium almost devoid of quantum-exchange niches had to be complex and delicate, and was almost alive in its occasional perversity. Until they were certain that it was in perfect order, ready to carry them back over the incredibly long line they had just traced, they could feel little interest in anything else, even their new environment.

Just how long the check required is impossible to say, but eventually the *Longline* floated, stable and ready for flight, in an equally stable pattern of potential niches, and her crew was satisfied.

"Now what?" Wattimlan's question, the captain suspected, was rhetorical; the youngster probably had already made up his mind about what to do next. "I've never seen any star but home before, and I suppose we should learn enough about this one to permit a useful report when we announce our arrival—at least, we should have seen more than just the boundary film. On the other spin, though, there's the other star you say must be close to this one—should we start casting for it right away? If it's really close, maybe we'd hit it without too many tries."

"You really want to get back into space so quickly?"

"Well—I thought you'd prefer to make the casts, at least at first, but we can take turns if you prefer. Frankly, I'd rather look over the landscape first."

"I agree," Feroxtant replied rather drily. "Let's reinforce our identities and get to it."

Landscape is of course a hopelessly crude translation of Wattimlan's communication symbol. Inside a neutron star there is no close analogy to hills and valleys, rivers and forests, sky, sunlight, or clouds. It is a virtually infinite complex of potential levels—some unoccupied, others occupied by one or more of the fundamental particles which made up the universe known to the two explorers, some in flux among the various possible states. This is equally true, of course, of the matter universe; and just as a man groups the patterns of electrons and other force fields around him into perceived objects, so did Wattimlan and Feroxtant. A pattern capable of identity maintenance, growth, and duplication, which maintained its existence by ingesting and restructuring other such patterns, might be called a lion or a shark by a human being; such an entity would also possess an identification symbol in the minds of the explorers, but translating that symbol into any human word would be unwise, since the hearer could probably not help clothing the central skeleton of abstraction with very misleading flesh.

It is therefore not correct to say that Wattimlan was charged by a lion and saved himself by climbing a tree during their preliminary examination of the new star. It would be even less accurate, however, to say that the exploration was uneventful. It would be most accurate, but still very incomplete, to say that when he got back to the *Longline* the younger traveller held a much more tolerant attitude toward the boring aspects of space-casting than had been the case earlier.

They had learned enough for an acceptable report. They had named their discovery Brother, intending to add the prefix of Big or Little when they reached the companion star and found out which word applied. They had amused themselves, each in his own way—they were individuals, as different from each other as any two human beings. As a natural consequence, they had even perceived Brother differently, and had already developed different attitudes toward it.

The length of time all this had taken is impossible to state, since their time is not really commensurable with that in the Einstein-matter universe. Eventually they made their call to their home star, along the incomprehensibly extended line of uniform potential which their ship had marked in space. They reported their finds, and received acknowledgment. They received assurance that other ships would follow. They spent more time at their equivalents of working, eating, drinking, and merrymaking; and finally they faced the question of trying to reach Big or Little Brother, as it might turn out to be—the companion star which Feroxtant had identified in the instant of their landing.

"I feel a little funny about this," Wattimlan admitted as they began the *Longline*'s preflight check. "I've heard of stars which were close companions of each other, but there was always one difference. You could see one from the other just about anywhere, as long as you hadn't gone below the surface film, but you could see it only half the time. This one you can see all the time if you're in the right place in the film, but not at all if you're anywhere else. It scares me. Can it be a real star?"

"I'm not sure." Feroxtant would not admit to fear, but he was admittedly as puzzled as his junior. "At least, we don't have to worry about starting time. Since we can always see it from here, we can lift any time we choose."

"That's just what bothers me. Of course, no one minds flying when he knows where he's going—when there's a steady-pot line to follow. I didn't mind the blind start we made on this trip, since we'd either hit another star sooner or later or be able to reverse and go home. Now I don't know what we may hit. This constant-visibility situation bothers me. Could this other thing actually be a *part* of the star we're in now, separated by some strange potential pattern instead of ordinary space?"

"I hadn't thought of that," Feroxtant replied. "It's a bit wild an idea. I had thought there might be some connection between this situation and a lecture I once heard on something called *direction.*"

"Never heard of it."

"I'm not surprised. It's as abstract a notion as I've ever heard of, and I can't put it into ordinary words."

"Does it suggest any special risks?"

"It makes no suggestions at all on the personal level. You knew when you volunteered for exploration that it involved the unknown, and therefore meant some risk. Now you're worrying, apparently without even considering all the peculiarities we are facing."

"What? What haven't I considered?"

"You've said nothing about the neutrino source which must also be in this neighborhood, since it is bright enough to see, but which *is* behaving normally—visible half the time, out of sight the other half."

Wattimlan was silent for a time, checking his own sensory impressions, his memories, and the *Longline*'s instrument recordings. Finally he switched attention back to his commander, and asked another question.

"Can that possibly be a star?"

"I doubt it. More probably it's a protostar—one of the neutrino sources which we think finally condenses to an ordinary star. Presumably the neutrinos carry off whatever energy manifestations prevent the formation of a normal star. In any case, it's harmless—people have probably flown through them without any effect. There's no way to tell whether this one is nearer or farther than the star we're casting for, but it's nothing to worry about. Now—do you want to make the first few casts, or shall I?"

The youngster hesitated only a moment. "I'll do it, if you trust me to make an open-space reversal."

"Sure. You know the routine. I'm not worrying, and you shouldn't be. Take her out."

"You can't make a guess at strike probability, I suppose?"

"No. It depends on target distance, and apparently on target size, though no one knows why—maybe it's another of those direction phenomena. Anyway, we know only that the distance is small—which makes the chances fairly high—and I'm not suggesting that there's any way to guess at something's size just by looking at it. Ready for final checkout?"

"Ready."

"Pressor lens?"

"Open."

"Film field one?"

"In synch."

"Line track power . . ."

The *Longline* emerged from the surface film of the neutron star and hurtled away from the tiny body, leaving far behind the burst of neutrino emission which accompanied the lift. The explorers had only a rough idea of the possible distance to their target, and none at all of their vessel's speed in open space. It had been discovered by experience that slowing down sufficiently to let neutrinos overtake them was apparently impossible. The more advanced theories in fundamental mechanics implied that substance as they understood it became mathematically unreal below neutrino speed; what this implied in terms of observable properties was anyone's guess. It was generally believed that stars in galaxies—that is, the neutron stars which were all they could sense of such bodies—were separated by a few hundred to a few thousand of their own diameters. Space travel had given them, in addition, the concept of galaxies separated by a dozen or two times their own size, on the average.

Wattimlan and Feroxtant, therefore, could only guess at the distance needed for their casts. They had set up an arbitrary travel time; if the pilot failed to make a landing before that was up, he would reverse and return to the starting point along the new constant-pot line his trip would have established. The time was short enough so that even the youngster, Feroxtant hoped, could hardly get either bored or nervous.

The chance of landing on any one cast was presumably very small, though there was no way of calculating just how small. Feroxtant's suggestion that this might become possible when the concept of direction was finally clarified by the advanced mathematicians was not really a serious prediction, since he had no real idea of what the theory was all about; it was more like the suggestions in Earth's early twentieth century that radium might prove a cure for cancer and old age.

Wattimlan, therefore, gave no serious thought to what he would do if and when the *Longline* made starfall. It would be routine, anyway. He flew. He readied himself for his first open-space reversal with some uneasiness, but missed its time only slightly. The miss annoyed him as a reflection on his professional skill, but it was in no way dangerous; the *Longline* was suddenly retracing its outward path. There was none of the deceleration which a human pilot would have had to plan and experience; the concept of inertia was even stranger and more abstract to Wattimlan than that of direction—or would have been if anyone had ever suggested it to him. The only observable phenomenon marking the reversal was another burst of neutrinos, vaguely analogous to the squeal of tires from a clumsily handled ground vehicle but—unlike the time error or a tire squeal—not indicative of poor piloting.

In the sub-light universe, a simple direction reversal does not involve change in kinetic energy, except for whatever entropy alteration may be involved; equal speed means equal kinetic energy. In the tachyon universe, momentum is naturally as meaningless as direction, kinetic energy almost equally so, and the interactions between forces and the various fundamental particles follow very different rules. However, the rules were the ones Wattimlan knew, and the time interval between the reversal and reentry into the neutron star's surface film was for him boringly uneventful. He landed.

Feroxtant was nowhere to be seen; he had apparently gone off either working or playing. Wattimlan decided to be pleased at the implied compliment to his competence rather than hurt at the suggested indifference to his welfare, and went through post-flight and pre-flight checks without waiting for his commander and instructor to appear. He made another cast, and another, and another . . .

"So pay up!" Sforza leaned back from the display tank which dominated the *Manzara*'s maneuvering console, and just barely managed to refrain from smirking.

Jeb Garabed, a quarter century younger and correspondingly less restrained, glared first into the tank and then at the two-liter silvery cube beside it. He didn't quite snarl—the captain was also present—but there was a distinct edge to his voice.

"I should know better than to let myself get fooled by that old line about mechanical brains. I know that thing is made of doped diamond, but I didn't realize how much weight the first word carried!"

Sforza lifted an eyebrow. "I don't seem to appreciate your humor as much as I used to."

"Don't bother to put that eyebrow on top of your head. It would be conspicuous. I wasn't trying to be funny."

"That's just as well. You—" Sforza cut himself off with an effort, and fell silent. For a moment each of the men wondered if he had said too much, as Garabed's face and Sforza's scalp both flushed.

Captain Migna Sarjuk listened to the exchange without too much concern; she knew both men well, and could tell that the jibes were not serious. When arguments became too frequent, of course, it was a temptation to separate the disputants for a few months by judicious watch-shifting; but it was possible to be too hasty with this solution. One could break up good working teams, and even run out of possible combinations. With over eighty people on the *Manzara* the latter seemed mathematically improbable, but since most of the possible combinations were in fact eliminated by conditions of specialty training it was not entirely impossible. The ship had spent eighteen months—

subjective time—en route, would be at least that long going back, and might remain several years at this end of the flight line; the captain had no intention of running out of solutions to the most likely personnel problems any sooner than she could help. She waited silently, paying close attention to Sforza's reactions; the younger man, she knew, would not lose his temper in her presence.

He didn't. The young radiometrist caught himself in turn, grinned, and tossed a couple of time-slugs onto the console. Sforza gathered them up. Garabed half-apologized as he continued to stare into the display.

It was not a picture in the conventional sense. The three-dimensional presentation did show images of a number of celestial bodies, but they were festooned with numbers, vector arrows in various colors, and other symbols. To Sforza, it was a completely informative description of all the detectable objects within a light-day of the ship. Garabed would have felt happier with the images alone, stripped of the extra symbols. He could then have thought of it as a simple bead-and-wire model.

He greatly preferred the direct view of space from the *Manzara*'s observation dome, even though human perception was not really adequate for its analysis. For most of the trip it had been an unchanging Milky Way—unchanging, that is, except as his own intellect changed it. He had found he could change its appearance from a flat spray-paint job on a screen a few yards outside the dome to a more nearly correct, but far from complete, impression of infinite star-powdered depths. His home star had been fading throughout the journey, of course, though the change in a single day had been imperceptible except at the very beginning. It was now an unimpressive object about as bright as Polaris.

The *Manzara*'s target star was now overwhelmingly bright, and the human mind had no trouble accepting that it was far closer than Sol; but its white dwarf companion had only recently grown brighter than the sun the explorers had left some ten objective years before.

But Garabed could read the display symbols even if he preferred to visualize differently, and now one of them caught his attention. It was typical of him that he did not call immediate attention to it; his first reaction was to recoup his betting losses.

At this distance, a few minutes' delay in reporting a discovery would not be of importance to the ship's safety—or, more important, to the captain. He continued the conversation, and even Sarjuk failed to catch any change in his manner.

"So I was wrong. It just means we'll have to spend a year and a half of our personal time flying back—unless I turn right while we're here."

"I'll cover another bet on that, if you like."

Garabed shook his head. "I guess not. Now that real work is starting, I don't need so much distraction—and probably can't afford it. It was different on the way, when I needed amusement. Conning my way out of boring jobs by smart bets provided that—even when I lost, the jobs themselves made a change. Now it's time to be serious, though, if you'll pardon the pun. How do things look to you?"

The ballistician gestured toward the display into which Garabed was still staring. "There you are. Cutting drive didn't make much difference. It adds up to what we've known for a couple of centuries, plus what we've picked up in the last few months. One type A main sequence sun, known since before human history began—with an unexplained, not to mention unproved, charge of having been red instead of white a couple of millennia ago. One white dwarf in a fifty-year orbit with it, known since the nineteenth century. Four high-density planets discovered by us in the last few weeks. No gas giants, which would be out where the white dwarf would perturb them hopelessly anyway. And no trace of the faster-than-light ship you were betting would be here from Earth waiting for us."

Garabed shrugged. "It was still a reasonable bet. We have artificial gravity, and a field drive system which can be described as a space warp without lying too grossly. It still seems to me that those should ease us into FTL flight before I'm very much older."

"In spite of the fact that both the gadgets you mention were developed on the assumption that Einstein was right? And that even the warp which makes a portable fusion engine practical is an Einstein application? I seem to be missing a rung or two in your ladder of logic."

Garabed glanced at the captain before answering. "Yes," he said after a moment. "In spite of that."

"And in spite of the fact that this trip was only a political gesture to quiet the people who don't think Earth is home enough? And that there were long, loud screams about the better things which could be done with the resources which went into the *Manzara* and her equipment? Why-should-we-explore-the-stars, practically-no-chance-of-life, a-waste-of-resources, we've-solved-all-our-real-problems, let's-sit-back-and-live? You've heard it all."

"Sure I have." Garabed did not look at the captain this time. "But people are still curious—that's what makes them people. Once we were on the way some of them were bound to want to find out what we'd see—first. It's being human. You have the same drive, whether you want to admit it or not; I'll show you." He reached across and flicked off the display in the computer's tank. "How sure are you that there's nothing really unexpected to be found in the Sirius system? And would you bet there isn't a clue to it in your data banks right now?"

The older man looked into the blank display unit, and thought. The kid might have seen something, though Sforza himself should have noticed anything important; it was certainly possible. On the other hand, Sforza had known the young con artist to bluff his way out of one or another of the ship's less popular jobs on at least four occasions during the trip, three of them at Sforza's own expense. Had there been anything surprising on the display? Something he should, of course, have seen himself?

The captain had come over to the ballistics console to look for herself, though she of course said nothing. She knew, far better than Sforza, that Garabed might not be bluffing.

The ballistician hesitated a moment longer, straining his memory with no useful result, and decided to take a chance.

"All right. Two hours' worth." He put the slugs he had just won on the panel before him. Garabed covered them with two more, and turned the display back on. For a moment there was silence.

"What was the time limit on this?" the older man finally asked. The captain, unseen behind him, smiled and slipped back to her own station, where she busied herself at the intercom. The instrument specialist paid no obvious attention to her; the smile on his face might have been simply one of triumph.

"No time needed. Look at the white dwarf's radial velocity."

"I see it. So what? You wouldn't expect it to match A's. Even a fifty-year orbit means a few kilos per second."

"Changing how fast?" asked Garabed pointedly.

"Not very—" Sforza fell silent again, glued his eyes to the display, and within a minute the eyebrows were climbing toward the desert above.

"It's changing!"

"How right you are. Do you pay now, or calculate first?"

Sforza waved the slugs away with an impatient gesture of his head; his fingers were already busy. He didn't stop to wonder why the velocity variation had not been spotted sooner; it was obvious enough. The axis of the previously unknown orbit must point almost exactly at the Solar system. The *Manzara* was now so close to the Sirius group that the A star and the white dwarf appeared fully forty degrees apart, and the ship was well off the line between Sol and the dwarf. Hence, there was a radial velocity component not previously detectable.

This clue to the line of the orbit axis permitted an assumption which would otherwise have been a wide-open guess in Sforza's computation. He plugged it in, let the spectral sensors which Garabed kept in such good condition feed their readings and the *Manzara*'s clock signals in after it, and waited until the display steadied. Then, and only then, did he speak.

"Take your pirated money, and call Physics and Policy—"

"They're coming," the captain interjected quietly. Sforza continued.

"The white dwarf is in a nearly perfect-circle orbit with something too small to see, but of comparable mass. The period is seven hundred seventy-two seconds. The dwarf is thirty-two thousand miles from the barycenter, orbital speed two hundred seventy-seven miles per second—"

"Miles?" queried Sarjuk. "I can sympathize with the Creative Anachronism urge, but—"

"Fifty-one thousand five hundred, four hundred forty-six. The invisible body's radius vector is open until we can get a mass ratio, but can hardly be more than a few tens of thousands of kilometers. We have a dividend. It's either a neutron star or—"

"Or nothing," pointed out the captain. "It can't be more

massive than the total previously measured for Sirius B—point nine suns. Too little for a black hole."

Garabed was nodding slowly, his face nearly expressionless, but both his companions could tell he was containing strong excitement. His only words, however, formed a terse question.

"New flight plan, Captain?"

The *Manzara* had been free-falling in an orbit intended to make a close swing past Sirius B, enter a slingshot transfer to A with a periastron distance from the latter of only a fifth of an astronomical unit, and a second sling to interception with the largest, outermost, and probably most Earthlike of A's four planets.

Sarjuk was by training an engineer specializing in safety extrapolation, which naturally included administrative psychology and hence qualified her for her present command status. She was certainly no ballistician, but she knew what a change in orbit meant in terms of fuel reserve—which after all was a major safety factor for the *Manzara*. In this case, of course, a good secondary-school student could have performed the appropriate calculations.

"New flight plan, of course," she agreed quietly. "But let's hear what Physics wants before Mr. Sforza does any number work." She swung her seat about as a dozen excited researchers entered the bridge, motioned them to the seats which ringed the chamber, and turned back to Garabed.

"Jeb," she asked, "can you possibly get anything with real resolving power to cover this object? I know it must be small, but until we know just how small and just where it is we're going to be crippled in any planning. Sforza can give you the direction from the dwarf to the orbit center, and you can search along the projection of that line with whatever seems likely to work best. Build something if you have to."

Without waiting for the two men to get to work, she turned back to the newcomers and gave them a summary of the new information. They listened in near silence, their eyes never leaving her face until she had finished.

"How close can we get?" Tikaki and Distoienko spoke almost in unison.

"Will it take too much fuel to park beside it?" was the more thoughtful question from Dini Aymara, a warp theoretician. Tikaki answered instantly.

"Of course not! Look—it's a binary, with the two bodies similar in mass. All we'll need is maneuvering power; we can use an orbit which will transfer our energy to one of the bodies instead of slinging us away. When we do want to leave, we can slingshot out in the same fashion. We can get as close to the neutron star as you want—meters, if your experiments need it—"

"Three objections, Mr. Tikaki," the captain spoke quietly still. "First, at a distance even of kilos, to say nothing of meters, not even our best cameras could get clear images—figure the orbital speed at such a distance. Second, neutron stars are likely to have strong magnetic fields, and there are plenty of conductors in this ship, starting with the main hull stringers. Finally, there is such a thing as tidal force. I will not permit this ship into a gee-gradient of more than five inverse-seconds squared, and only then if all main and backup artificial gravity units are in perfect condition. Mr. Sforza, what distance would that tidal limit mean from the two bodies?"

The ballistician had finished providing Garabed's needed figures, and was able to answer the captain's question almost instantly.

"For the white dwarf it would be somewhere inside; you'll be worrying about other things first. For the neutron star, it of course depends on the mass, which we don't—"

"I have it—at least, I have a respectable mass on the line you gave me, affecting the gravity-wave unit," cut in Garabed.

"Line?" responded Sforza. The instrument technician supplied a set of numbers which the ballistician's fingers fed into his computer as they came; a set of luminous symbols appeared in the display tank, and were translated at once. "Mass is point three eight suns. The tidal limit distance you want is a hair under five thousand kilometers about three quarters of an Earth radius."

The captain nodded, and glanced around the group. "I thought so. Gentlemen and ladies, the *Manzara* is half a kilometer long—*not* a point." If she expected Tikaki to look properly sheepish or disgruntled she was disappointed. He simply nodded, and after a moment she went on. "Very well. If Mr. Sforza can warp us into a capture orbit without exceeding tidal and radiation limits, and without using more than five hundred kilograms of hydrogen, I approve a pass. If you can all work from the mass center of the pair, I set no time limit; those who want to stay will have to make their peace with those who want to get on to A and the planets. Engineers, let's get the umbrella out. Mr. Sforza, report if we can't conform to the restrictions I've set. Meeting adjourned."

The "umbrella" was a thin sheet of highly reflective, highly conducting alloy which could be mounted on the bow of the *Manzara*, giving her rather the appearance of a fat-stemmed mushroom. Like the hull itself, it could be cooled by Thompson-effect units whose radiators were ordinary incandescent search-lights, able to send the waste energy in any convenient direction. The whole unit was something of a makeshift, a late addition to the mission plan intended to permit a brief but very close pass by each of the stars being studied. It had to be set up manually, since it had not been included in the ship's original specifications—and even a fusion powered giant like the *Manzara* was rationed in the mass she could devote to automatic machinery. Once again, the versatility of the human researcher was being utilized.

Space-suit work, still called EVA, was still taken seriously by those who had to perform it. There is a human tendency to ignore the dangers in a given action if they become familiar enough—people who cannot bring themselves to look down from a twelfth-story window are often quite casual about the equivalent energy exposure of driving a ground vehicle at sixty miles per hour. On the other hand, the high steel worker seems as casual about walking a twelve-inch beam five hundred feet above the street.

There is, however, a difference. The professional high steel worker, or submarine engineer, or for that matter racing driver, has his apparent unconcern underlain by a solid foundation of hard-won safety habits which in turn grow from a fully conscious awareness of the dangers of his calling. Also, the professional does not like to be distracted by amateurs, though he will usually admit the necessity of devoting some time to the training of new professionals.

Space workers are professionals—normally. Some two thirds of the *Manzara*'s personnel, however, were researchers whose space-suit and free-fall experience were strictly for the occasion. This would not by itself have been serious, since the ship's space professionals could have put out the umbrella without their aid—and would have been glad to do so. Unfortunately, the makeshift aspect of the umbrella included the assumption that it could serve more than one purpose. It was basically protection for the ship, of course; but the ship was a research instrument, and it had been taken for granted that the umbrella would also serve the researchers directly. They would mount instruments on it. They would study, and alter, its own activity as it absorbed and converted the radiation flux.

And during the year and a half flight from the Solar system most of the scientists had improved their time developing new plans and projects to supplement the original programs and to replace them if unexpected conditions made them impractical. Consequently, the researchers expected to be on hand during the assembling and fitting of the umbrella.

"How can I possibly wait until it's set up?" Tikaki was hurt and indignant. "Look—four of these leads have to go through the mirror. I can't possibly drill holes after the segments are assembled—I'll have to groove the joints, and after they're butted put in the interferometer units—"

"Look—I obviously have to run impedance checks on every intersection junction as they're put together." Crandell was being patient. "Every stage of assembly will make changes in electrical and thermal properties of the whole unit. I *can't* just use one term for the assembled unit—different segments will be getting their irradiation at different angles; it's not a plane surface—"

"Certainly these heat-flow meters have to be installed and calibrated during the assembly—" Cetsewayo was matter-of-fact.

Captain Migna Sarjuk did not debate any of the issues. She did not point out that if any imperfections developed in the umbrella, all the proposed experiments would have to be cancelled because the *Manzara* would not be able to get close enough to either star to perform them. She assumed that the scientists knew this, just as an alcoholic knows what a cocktail will do to him. She was politely firm.

"Nothing is attached to the umbrella until it is installed and its refrigeration system tested. After that, any installations will be done by engineers, engineers who know the umbrella systems and circuitry."

"But Captain!" The howl was almost universal. "How can they—?" The details of the question varied, but the basis was constant and not very original. Scientific training does not always prevent a human being from falling in love with his own ideas and inventions; it does not always even let him recognize when he has done so. They *had* to install their own equipment —they had built it themselves, they had adjusted and calibrated it themselves, and no one else could be trusted to set it up properly for its intended use. Sarjuk was not even tempted, however, mission-conscious though she was.

On the other hand, she was not one to argue when it was not necessary. She used a technique which would not have been available to a ship's captain on the oceans of Earth a century before: she made herself unavailable for policy discussion by going outside to oversee the work on the umbrella. At least, that was her declared purpose, and in view of her responsibilities and personality it was taken for granted by those inside that she was too busy to be interrupted by radioed arguments.

She did, of course, oversee; she also relaxed. Space lacks the change, the sound, and the scents which impress human senses and combine to give planetary landscapes that subjective quality called beauty; but space, too, is beautiful, and the captain appreciated it. Between examinations of newly made connections she simply floated, drinking in her surroundings through the only sense available and reinforcing the visual images of the Milky Way, distant Sol, and blazing Sirius from the body of knowledge which was part of her heritage as a civilized, cultured being. She "saw" the four planets which the *Manzara*'s instruments had detected, just as she saw the more numerous and varied worlds of the Solar system and the frozen attendants of Proxima Centauri—she could look where she knew them to be, and let memory and imagination fill the gaps left by human sensory limitations.

She spent more hours, perhaps, than she should have done at this combination of duty and pleasure. She was physically very tired, though emotionally refreshed, when she finally floated back to an air lock to face more argument from her scientists. She was met inside by Tikaki, who perhaps had been refreshed himself in some fashion during the past few hours; at least, he was changing tactics from pressure to compromise.

"Captain, if we can't do our own installing outside," he suggested, "can we choose, or at least brief, the engineer who does it? Preferably the former, of course."

Sarjuk had known something of the sort was coming, of course; as her fatigue had mounted, out there in the blissful darkness, she had delayed her return out of reluctance to face it.

But tired or not, Sarjuk was a professional. She was quite able to balance the overall safety of the *Manzara* against the reasons why the ship and crew were here at all. She was incapable of making a compromise which would be likely to cause total failure of the mission, but the idea of compromise itself did not bother her. She racked the helmet she had just removed, but made no move to get out of the rest of her vacuum armor as she considered the physicist's proposal.

"Whom would you select for your own installation job?" she asked after a moment.

"Garabed, of course. He's the best instrument specialist we have." A shade of expression flickered across Sarjuk's face.

"That's not because—" She cut off the remark, but Tikaki finished for her.

"No, it's not because he's your husband. I wouldn't budge an angstrom from my insistence on doing the job myself if I weren't willing to admit how good he is—and you should know it!"

She nodded. "Sorry. I do know it. Very well, I agree to the suggestion in principle, provided that Jeb—"

"Provided that Jeb agrees? Who's captain here?"

"I am, Dr. Tikaki. Provided that Jeb has time enough after doing his routine work *and* the favors which three out of four of the so-ingenious researchers we have here keep asking of him when they can't make their own improvisations work. I am quite aware that he is the best instrument specialist we have—and that everyone aboard this ship knows it. If you wish to put your suggestion to him, you may do so—when he comes in. Please be brief, however. He has been in a space suit for sixteen of the last twenty-four hours, and has just been delayed by another circuit problem in a Thompson unit. I don't know when he will finish, but he is considerably more overdue for sleep than I am—and if you will excuse me, I am going off watch now."

She turned away and quickly doffed the rest of her space

armor, while Tikaki tried vainly to think of the right thing to say. He failed, and wisely said nothing.

However, he left the lock bay at the same time the captain did. Even appearing to stay around to wait for Garabed seemed tactless at the moment.

Nothing more was said directly—Tikaki reported the gist of the conversation to several of his fellows, and the word spread rapidly enough to the other researchers. However, twelve hours later a watch reassignment was published, putting the two other instrument workers alternately on outside duty and assigning Garabed to liaison with the researchers who had equipment to be mounted on the finished umbrella. It occurred to Tikaki that his pressure might actually have been a favor for Sarjuk, giving her an excuse to do something she had wanted to do anyway, but he decided that any experimental check of this hypothesis would be too much like trying to find the taste of monofluoroacetic acid.

Over four days were spent outside by the space-suited engineers, with Sarjuk watching them closely two thirds of the time and sleeping most of the rest. Then, the umbrella assembled, attached, and electrically proven, a tiny change was made in the *Manzara*'s velocity. The result was obvious only to people like Sforza, who could read the vector symbols in the ballistics tank as readily as a novel. Sirius B had already become a dazzlingly brilliant point of light, while A was blazing well to one side; but it would be days yet before unaided human senses could convince their owners that the ship was in a B-centered orbit.

The velocity change as such was no more apparent to the *Longline*'s pilot than to the human beings on the *Manzara*, but the neutrino flux from the Solar vessel's hydrogen fusers was another matter. It was tiny in amount compared to the flood from Sirius A, even after inverse-square decrement, but it was well above the noise level of the *Longline*'s instruments, and Wattimlan, still casting outward from the neutron star with completely unhuman patience, detected it and was properly confused.

Another pseudo-star? Did they come this small? Or was it really small—perhaps the feebleness meant distance. But did stars suddenly wink into existence like that? He had never heard of such a thing. Maybe Feroxtant would know . . .

So the *Longline* paused in her endless casting, and the young pilot searched the neutron star calling rather frantically for his chief. Feroxtant was amusing himself in a fashion quite beyond the possibility of describing to a human being, and did not particularly wish to be found at the moment. Consequently, even though the *Manzara*'s acceleration lasted a very long time by tachyon standards, it had ended by the time Wattimlan found him, convinced him that something was strange, and got him back to the ship to see for himself. The peculiar neutrino flux had ceased—the *Manzara*'s general operations were powered by chemical accumulators, since operating fusers at what amounted to trickle power was inherently wasteful. Feroxtant saw nothing, and Wattimlan had to admit that there was now nothing to see. The net result was that Feroxtant, deciding that his assistant needed a rest, took over at piloting the *Longline*'s casts. Neither he nor Wattimlan gave any thought whatever to the fact that the neutrino bursts from their own vessel's acceleration would have appeared similar in intensity, though far briefer in duration, to any nearby ship.

Jeb Garabed was kept very, very busy. Neither the captain nor anyone else had mentioned a word about the Tikaki argument to him; he had, indeed, taken the reassignment almost for granted. He was not offensively conceited, but had a perfectly realistic awareness of his own competence. If the change had given him and the captain any more time together off-watch than before, he might have been slightly suspicious of an ulterior motive; but it had no such effect.

All three of the instrument workers were now occupied every waking moment. Everything the *Manzara* carried whose analytical range much exceeded that of a chemist's test tube was now in use, probing the white dwarf itself and groping for the still invisibly small neutron star whipping around it. The name of Garabed or one of his colleagues echoed over the intercom whenever something failed to operate properly—and, as he complained occasionally, whenever an unexpected reading was recorded and the researcher involved was *afraid* his machine was working improperly.

Consequently, while Garabed was not actually the first to detect impulses from the *Longline,* he was certainly the first to believe that those impulses constituted genuine, objective data rather than instrumental artifacts.

To him, the neutrino telescopes were just another set of instruments which he knew intimately. They would not have been recognized a century or so earlier; they were far more sophisticated than the original tank of cleaning fluid in a mine. They still did not approach ordinary optical equipment in resolving power, but the word "telescope" was far more appropriate than it had once been. They even reported their data in the form of visual images on very conventional electron tubes, though their "optical" parts were warp fields.

Jeff Pardales, the physicist who made most use of the neutrino equipment, was never surprised to see ghost images on the tube, but he was never happy about them.

"Find it, please, Jeb," he said in a rather tired voice. "It's bad enough to have neutrinos at all from a supposedly dead white dwarf. It's worse when they come in separate bursts. It's worst of all when I can't tell whether they're actually coming from the dwarf or from some place as much as a million kilometers away from it. At least, though, I'd like to be sure that half of what I see isn't originating right in that circuit box."

"It shouldn't be," Garabed's voice was almost as tired. "I had it apart less than five days ago. What's the pattern that makes you worry?"

"Doubling of the image."

"That does sound embarrassing for me. What's the pattern? Horizontal? Vertical? Same brightness? Energy difference?"

"Energy about the same in original and ghost. Time difference varies from too close to distinguish—which may mean no ghost at all—up to just about one second. Position difference seems random—but at this range my resolving power in angle means more than one light-second."

Garabed frowned. "That doesn't sound like anything I've ever seen happen inside one of these things. Have you checked it out on the A star?"

"Yes. Nothing surprising. A steady image of what might be its active nucleus, blurred by resolution limit at this distance."

"Then I suggest you believe what you're getting here. I can't take apart everything on the ship every time someone is surprised by what he sees."

Embarrassment supplemented the fatigue on Pardales' face. "I know, Jeb. I wouldn't ask, except I've gone over it all myself, and can't find anything wrong with the telescope, and all of us have been beating our brains out without even a whisper of an idea of what could emit neutrinos in any such way. I'm not so much asking you whether there's anything wrong with the 'scope as I am asking what you can do to improve its resolution. In theory, inside tuning should give us another power of ten. I know we'll be that much closer in a couple of weeks, but if we have to wait that long some of us may not be in shape to work. I mean it."

Jeb's eyebrows started to imitate those of his former watchmate Sforza before he remembered and controlled them.

"That bad? I suppose that means one of you came up with the demon theory and no one else can think of anything to replace it—but you don't want to admit it."

"Just help us measure, please, Jeb." Garabed said nothing more; he nodded sympathetically and opened the case of the telescope. He understood perfectly. For Cro-Magnon man, it could be taken for granted that lightning was produced by a living being—one with special powers, but not entirely beyond man's comprehension. A few millennia later, the notion that disease was a divine punishment for sin was equally acceptable. Then the idea of an essentially human universe—one in which man was not only of central importance but of typical powers —began to fade as a more coherent concept of natural law was developed. Intelligent creators of the Martian canals, though popular as a concept, were not universally accepted; the flying saucer phenomenon a few decades later saw the "little green men" accepted by a minority, composed largely of the less disciplined imaginations. Very, very few seriously considered the pulsars as possible space beacons planted by star-faring races. And scarcely anyone interpreted the regular crystal-growth patterns, whose images were first transmitted to Earth by unmanned probes from the moons of Jupiter, as the remains of cities. Blaming things on intelligence had simply gone out of style.

This, of course, put the *Manzara*'s researchers at a profound disadvantage.

It also put Jeb Garabed to a great deal of unnecessary work.

"I can't get you ten times the resolution," he said at last. "You'll have to settle for about seven, and get the rest by waiting. Look, I'm no psychologist, but why should you let this worry you now? Can't you just collect your measures, and not worry about explaining them until you've recorded everything you can expect to get? That's what Min would certainly advise, and—"

"And you would naturally be inclined to take her advice. I admit it's good; I just doubt that it's possible to follow. All right, Jeb. I'll be calling for you shortly, I'm sure."

"Not until that thing has been run for at least six hours," Garabed said firmly. "Unless you actually do go overboard and hit it with a torch, I refuse to believe that it can go wrong before then. Just get all your nice measures on the tapes, and don't—what do you scientists call it—theorize ahead of your data." He left hastily—there were two other calls for his services already.

He mentioned the conversation some hours later to the captain, not as a complaint or even an official report, but as an example of how things were going, in one of their rare private conversations. She proved more concerned than he had expected.

"I've heard a little about it," she agreed. "The star people seem terribly bothered at the idea of a white dwarf's putting out neutrinos, and even more so at the thought of their coming from the neutron star. The idea is that such bodies should be past that stage. I'd have thought that a real scientist would be delighted at the chance to discover something really new, but this crowd seems short on self-confidence; they can't convince themselves that the data aren't mistakes."

"That's what it looked like to me," agreed her husband. "I suggested to Jeff that he just collect measures for a while, hoping that the bulk of material would convince him there must be something to it, but I don't know whether it'll work."

Sarjuk pondered for a minute or two. "I can't think of anything better, myself," she admitted finally, "except that you'd better do everything you can to keep up their confidence in the equipment—even if it takes more than its fair share of your time. If necessary, I'll juggle watch assignments even further."

"Hmph. I hope it won't be. I like my work, but enough is as good as too much. That telescope *is* working; there are bursts of neutrinos coming from somewhere near that whirligig pair, whether Jeff and his friends want to believe it or not."

"I'm willing to take your word for it—so far." He looked at her sharply as she made the qualification. She smiled. "I just hope you don't have to do their work as well, and come up with a theory to satisfy them. But forget all that for a few hours—no one can work all the time."

Sarjuk did not actually have to reassign watches, but Garabed spent a great deal of time on the neutrino telescope during the next ten days. By that time, every one of its component modules had been replaced at least once, and the decreasing distance had improved image resolution to the point where it began to look as though at least some of the bursts were centered on, if not actually originating in, the neutron star.

By that time, also, the *Manzara* had made two minor—very minor—orbit corrections. The fusers had been used, and Feroxtant had seen for himself that his assistant had not been hallucinating. He did not stop his casts, however; there seemed no point in debating the matter until more data could be secured. Therefore, the *Longline* continued to emit its own neutrino bursts as it left the neutron star and when it made its reversal some three hundred thousand kilometers away.

To the surprise of Garabed and the relief of the captain, the physicists were beginning to accept the reality of their data, and were eagerly awaiting the completion of the capture maneuvers. The plan was to place the *Manzara* at the mass center of the white dwarf-neutron star pair, holding the umbrella toward the dwarf; in effect, this would place the ship's instruments at the origin of a system-centered coordinate set, and the observers' relative motion should be zero. This would avoid a lot of variables . . .

The capture maneuver was artistic, though hard for nonspecialists to appreciate. Sforza cut as closely as he could first to one of the bodies and then the other, choosing his vectors so that the inevitable gain in kinetic energy as he approached each would be more than offset by the loss as he withdrew, and combining this with an initial approach direction which caused each near-parabolic deflection to carry the *Manzara* from one body toward the other. It would have been elegant, as Sforza admitted, to do the whole job with a single application of steering power to get them into the proper initial approach curve; unfortunately, it was impossible. The period of the system remained just below thirteen minutes—which cut things tight enough as it was—while that of the ship was constantly decreasing as it surrendered energy to the little stars.

The job was finally finished, with the umbrella warding off the radiation flood from the hot star some twenty thousand miles off the bow and the vessel's stern pointing toward the invisible mystery a little more than twice as far away. The data continued to flood in.

Feroxtant had also received a flood of data. It was not easy to interpret; one fact common to both his and the human universe is that the number of independent equations must equal or exceed the number of unknowns before any certainty is possible. The actual power drain on the *Manzara*'s fusers had been varying in complex fashion; so had the ship's distance from the neutron star. Hence, the neutrino flux recorded by the *Longline*'s sensing equipment had varied widely and erratically during the many minutes of Sforza's maneuvering. Feroxtant felt subjectively that the variation was not random, but could find no pattern in it. He had stopped casting very quickly, and called Wattimlan back aboard. The youngster was equally mystified, though happy that his commander had also seen the strange readings.

"No star ever acted like that." Feroxtant was firm. "I don't know what we've found—well, what you've found, to be honest —but it's new."

"But—stars aren't the only things that give off neutrinos," Wattimlan pointed out rather timidly. "Ship's accelerators— food factories—"

"I thought of that. Of course artificial processes emit neutrinos, too; but what imaginable process would produce them in a pattern which varies like this?"

Wattimlan had no answer.

Oddly enough, Garabed's work load eased off; the physicists were accepting the information and had turned back into scientists. Sarjuk felt that the earlier problem must have been mere inertia—their minds had been running free, except for the planning of possible experiments, for nearly a year and a half; they had simply slipped clutches briefly at the first contact with reality in so many months.

She might have been right. Garabed wasn't sure, but didn't argue; he enjoyed the respite, and listened with interest to the questions flying about. Why should a neutron star emit neutrinos at all? Why in separate bursts? Why, if the Sirius system had started as a single unit, had its least massive member reached the neutron star stage first? Why were the white dwarf and its companion so close together—so close that when both were main sequence stars their radii would have overlapped? Why, if its magnetic field meant anything, was the neutron star in locked rotation facing the dwarf rather than spinning several times a second like all the others known?

Answers were not forthcoming. Physical data—size, mass, detailed motion, even temperature and conductivity—were flowing in nicely; but any question beginning with "why" remained wide open.

The white dwarf was being very cooperative, though it was not much to look at through a filter—no sunspots, no corona, no prominences or faculae; simply a featureless disc. Nevertheless, information about its internal structure was coming in very well, and none of it was very surprising. It was now clear that the neutrino bursts were not coming from this body; as far as nuclear activity was concerned, it was dead.

The neutrino telescope had been shut down during the capture maneuvers, and the pause when Feroxtant had stopped casting for a time had been missed.

It was equally clear that not all of the bursts were coming from the neutron star, either. Just half of them were—or at least, from a region within about eight hundred kilometers of it, that being the resolution limit of the telescope at this distance. The other half appeared to originate randomly at any point within about a light-second of the same center. They still came in pairs, one of each pair at the center and one away from it, with pauses of a few seconds every ten to twenty minutes—not completely random, but not orderly enough for anyone to have worked out a system yet.

"You have the betting look on your face again. I thought you were going to stop until the work let up." Garabed looked at the captain, trying to decide how serious she might be.

"It has been easier lately. This isn't to take care of boredom, though. It's just one of those sure things. Would you care to allow any odds that the astrophysics crowd won't be begging, within the next twenty-four hours, that we go into a parking orbit around the neutron star at tidal limit distance?"

Sarjuk gave a snort of disbelief. "They must know better. A few thousand more kilograms of hydrogen and we'll have to get fuel from one of the planets to get home."

"Well, we probably can. The big one seems to have water."

"With enough deuterium already? Or do we build a separator?"

"We could. We expected to be here for as much as three years anyway, and personally I wouldn't mind settling down into a less hectic life than this for a while."

"The idea was, and remains, to make a preliminary survey and get the results home. The three-year plan was contingent on either unforeseen complication—just a safety margin—or on the making of some really fundamental discovery important enough to demand immediate work, rather than wait for the next expedition."

"And how important would that have to be?" asked her husband.

"That will have to be settled when—and if—it happens. Until something of the sort comes up, we plan to return as soon as the planned operation—"

"Was the neutron star part of anyone's plan?"

"No, but you know as well as I that it can really be handled only by a group set up specifically for it. No one even dreamed that such a thing would be here. I can't see staying on and trying to do that job ourselves, even though we could live in the *Manzara* indefinitely. And, as I still think they know too well to ask, I will not sanction the fuel expense of getting into a parking orbit as far down in a gravity well like this as they'd need. And I won't do any betting on the matter, dear husband."

"I didn't really think you would. I'll cook up something even more certain."

He refused to be more specific, and the captain knew him well enough by now not to try very hard.

The *Manzara*'s station between the two ex-stars was of course unstable, so Sforza and his colleagues would permit no interruption in their constant watch of the ballistics computer and its display. There were other, equally versatile units on board, however, and Garabed had no trouble getting time on one of these; he had an idea to check. He would have been as reluctant as any physicist to describe it to anyone; he would have admitted at the time, as was charged later by amateur psychologists, that it stemmed purely from wishful thinking. He made a point of setting it up in private, and looked for a long time at the display when the computer had done its work. Then he cleared the setup, and spent some time trying to decide whether to break it first to his wife or to Pardales.

The decision brought a smile to his face.

"Jeff," he remarked to the physicist a few minutes later, "I don't see why you fellows have had so much trouble with those pairs of neutrino bursts. I was just running your records through to check out one of the computer cores, and it seems perfectly straightforward to me."

"Straightforward? How do you mean?"

"Well, the pattern is so simple. One of each pair is at the neutron star, as you've been admitting, and the other is always on the surface of a hemisphere just over a light-second in radius, centered on the neutron star and with its axis pointing—"

"Show me!" the physicist was satisfyingly jolted.

Garabed led him back to the station where he had tried his idea, and set up the material again. It showed as he had said; he had arranged the plot on a coordinate system which rotated with the Sirius B doublet, so the two main bodies showed no motion. The hundreds of luminous points which represented the records of the neutrino bursts were indeed arranged in a nearly perfect hemisphere for the one part, and concentrated around the neutron star for the other.

"Our plot was all over the place—nothing like that regular!" exclaimed Pardales. "What did you plug in there? You must have put in some extra data—"

"Not exactly," replied Garabed. "There's my program. Actually, I left something out. Look it over." There was silence for a minute or two.

"You took for granted, as we did, that there was a causal

relation between the members of each pair. You allowed for travel time from point of origin of each flash to the ship; you allowed for travel time from one of each pair to the other—wait a minute! No, you didn't! You assumed they were really simultaneous!"

"Right," grinned Garabed. "No travel time. Think it over, friend; I have to talk to the captain." Pardales did not notice his departure. It is all very well to admit that coincidence can account for only so much; but when nothing else believable can account for it either . . .

"Captain!" called the instrument technician. Sarjuk was on the bridge, and there were others present, so he automatically avoided familiarity. "I think you'll be having another request from Physics very shortly. I think I can forestall a suggestion of moving the ship, if you'll let me take a tender out for a while."

Sarjuk frowned. "That will take fuel, and are you a good enough pilot to play around in a gravity well this deep?"

"I don't insist on driving it myself. Look, they are going to have another spell of doubting the neutrino telescope—I'll bet on that. I want to take out the tender so they can check the scope against its engine emissions, and kill that argument before it gets started. Isn't that worth a kilogram or two of hydrogen?"

Garabed's words were very straightforward, but his wife thought she could detect something under them. She looked at him sharply. "Is that the whole thing?" she asked.

He knew better than to lie to her. "Not entirely," he admitted, "but isn't it enough?" Their eyes locked for several seconds; the others on the bridge carefully concentrated on their own jobs for the moment. Then she nodded.

"All right. Plan to stay inside one kilogram. Sforza will drive you."

Minutes later the tender was hurtling away from the dying stars. Garabed would have climbed straight out along their orbital axis, with little regard for energy expenditure; Sforza, as a matter of habit and policy, cut out in the plane of their common orbits, slipped behind the neutron star at minimum safe distance, and let it sling them outward. Once he could see that they were safely away, Garabed made his key request.

"Will you let me have it for a few minutes? I want to change thrust patterns so Jeff and his friends can check their gear. There's no damage I can do, I take it."

"None that I can guess at," replied the ballistician. "If there's anything here to run into, I don't know about it either. Go ahead."

Garabed fingered the thrust potentiometer and began changing it in a careful pattern—alternately high and low, once, once again; twice, then four times; thrice, then nine times. Again and again he went through the cycle, while Sforza watched in amusement.

"It's lucky this is a warp drive. You'd have broken our straps with straight reaction. If I were a mystery fan, I'd say you were playing spy sending code."

"It does suggest that a little, doesn't it?" acknowledged Garabed.

It was not the code which first caught Feroxtant's attention; the drive units of the *Manzara* had bothered him enough, and the addition of the tender's power plant gave him at least as much of a shock as Garabed had just given Pardales. The notion that anything could travel less rapidly than neutrinos was as hard for him to swallow as the demon hypothesis. Since neither his senses nor his imagination could provide data on the direction of the human machines, he could not be sure of their slow motion; but his attention, and Wattimlan's, were firmly focused on them while the two explorers continued their casting for the white dwarf—or rather, for its slowly developing neutronium core, still so small that their thousands of random shots had not struck it.

Garabed's code—the squares of the first three numbers—started the two on an argument which, by human standards, would have gone on for hours. Eventually, more to prove Wattimlan wrong than because he expected any results, Feroxtant performed a multiple reversal in open space which produced neutrino bursts closer to the neutron star; and he deliberately produced a set of four, followed by sixteen. He then brought the *Longline* back to her mooring in the neutron star's surface film, and sent a frantic report to his home star. By the time Garabed's five-twenty-five reply was spreading into space, the word had come that scientists were on the way. Not even the most conservative of beings could doubt that a series of numbers followed by their squares could originate in anything but a living mind—perhaps acting indirectly, but still a mind. It might have been some sort of recording—but it had responded when Feroxtant extended the number series. It responded with neutrinos, which had reached Feroxtant's ship very quickly, in spite of the fact that they traveled with the ultimate slowness, so the mind—or minds—must be close to the newly discovered star. The discovery of an unknown intelligent race was worth a major research project—even if no one believed that they could travel slower than neutrinos.

"Just a minute." Jeb Garabed was not a member of Policy, but he had the common right to speak up to the group. "We don't dare go back to the Solar system at this stage, and you know it. We are sure now that these faster-than-light things have a different time rate than we do; if we disappeared from here for twenty years, without any more attempt to talk with them, they might be extinct—or at least, their culture might be, and they could have forgotten us. I know it takes fuel to talk to them, and we're running low—though we could certainly build smaller fusion generators if all that's needed is neutrino output. The only sensible thing to do is get over to planet Four, which we're sure has water, set up a deuterium plant so we have no power problems, and just settle down to do research—which is what we're here for anyway. We can stay right here, and keep sensibly and happily busy, and live very good lives for nineteen years until the next expedition gets here."

"If they come," interjected his wife.

"You know they'll come." Garabed spoke directly to her, but did not forget the others. "They can't do anything else. The whole argument against interstellar flight has been the time it would take, as long as we thought the speed of light was a limit. Now we know it isn't, and however short-sighted human beings may be, they don't live happily with the certainty that someone can do something they can't. Remember your history! What made it impossible to keep the nuclear bomb a secret? Leaky spy shielding? Balloon juice! The only important piece of information was given away free by the original builders—*the fact that it could be done!* There'll be shiploads of people here from the Solar system as soon as they can make it. They'll start so fast after our waves get there that we'll probably have to rescue the first few—they'll have set out without proper preparation. Sirius A-IV may not be really habitable, but there'll be a human colony here in twenty years—or sooner, if my old idea is right. That radio message of ours may be all that's needed, after all. Anyone want to bet whether it's ten years or twenty before they get here?"

"You and your everlasting betting!" growled Sforza. "You know perfectly well that the reason you want to settle down in a colony and work only twelve hours a day has nothing to do with getting in touch with these tachyon people."

"That," said Garabed, "is irrelevant. The main thing is that we have to do it—not just that I want to." He looked at his captain as he spoke, and even she couldn't tell whether his grin meant triumph or merely contentment. She nodded slowly. "We stay. Mr. Sforza, plot a minimum fuel course to A-IV. Chemistry, check practicability of a surface base as soon as we're close enough for you to work. Mr. Garabed, report to me at the end of the watch."

Garabed nodded absently. He was not really listening. He was looking into the display tank, seeing with his imagination more of the details of Sirius A-IV than the sensors had yet determined. The planet might not turn out to be as Earthlike as its color suggested, and he knew perfectly well that wishful thinking was painting a lot of his mental picture—but he was ready to bet that the next decade or two would be fun.

PHOENIX
WITHOUT ASHES

HARLAN ELLISON

Hopefully, literate science fiction will appear on the large and small screens in the years to come. A sizable body of classic SF stories, novels and themes deserve to be adapted to the visual media. Possibly half the life of science fiction may come to exist in visual narrative forms; but presently this is still a field of mixed results, lacking in general production standards, from the point of view of scripting, scientific accuracy, and fictional-dramatic virtues. The handful of truly fine productions were written for the large screen. On the small screen, Harlan Ellison has written the most outstanding science fiction teleplays: "Demon with a Glass Hand," "Soldier" (both for The Outer Limits), and "The City on the Edge of Forever" (for Star Trek). It is easy to see why Ellison's scripts are at the top of the field. The following script, for example, is a director's script; it is also a prime example of visual narration, of storytelling (which is why Ellison's SF scripts are reprinted for readers, as well as being produced); for the scientific background Ellison went to Ben Bova, a noted science writer and the editor of Analog, as well as an SF writer himself. As a result Ellison covered all the fronts on which visual SF usually fails.

The idea that a disaster, or severe pressure of some kind, might drive a portion of humanity out of the solar system in generation starships is a time-honored SF idea. Behind this script stand stories by Heinlein, Van Vogt, Anderson, Aldiss, Stapledon, and such pioneering speculators as J. D. Bernal. But this script was the first effort to take this great theme and transfer it to the screen.

For this script (though it was inadequately produced) Ellison

*received the Writers Guild Award for Most Outstanding Dra-
matic-Episodic script for 1973. The judges screened over 2,000
television scripts to make the selection. The award was for the
script as Ellison wrote it, not as it was produced. Gold Medal
is the publisher of the novel based on the script (written by
Ellison and Ed Bryant). "Phoenix Without Ashes" appears here
for the first time in print, along with striking illustrations by
Tim Kirk that suggest what the full-rigged production might
have been.*

*Here is the story of a special hell away from hell, moving
through the dark at a lumbering one-third of the speed of light.*

ACT ONE

FADE IN:

1   MEDIUM SHOT—METAL BULKHEAD—DOLLYING IN

CAMERA MOVES IN SMOOTHLY on a gray-blue metallic surface,
joined as plating with hairline seals that may be riveted (this should be
checked with Bova for accuracy). CAMERA IN and IN till CAMERA
UNFOCUSES as though going thru metal.

DISSOLVE THRU TO:

2   INTERIOR CYPRESS CORNERS BIOSPHERE—DAY—AERIAL
SHOT

CAMERA REFOCUSES as though it has just come thru bulkhead. We
are high above the land below, under the arching vault of the curving
metal dome that serves as sky. An artificial sun burns in the sky (check
with Bova for specific design). Far below we see a landscape as placid
and contemporary as any rural area in the late 1800's. CAMERA
COMES DOWN WITHOUT MOVING FORWARD. At a height of
four or five hundred feet above the ground CAMERA HOLDS and
BEGINS MOVING FORWARD. As it moves it PICKS UP SPEED till
we get the impression of shooting over treetops, lending the feel of
many miles of land-surface. SPEED FORWARD and then gradually
SLOW as CAMERA DESCENDS to the outskirts of a small, rustic, rural
village. This is Cypress Corners.

3   EXTERIOR CYPRESS CORNERS—DAY—ESTABLISHING

A small farm town nestled among hills (essential there be hills, even if only low foothills), tiny lakes, rich and flourishing farmlands. Houses arranged in a circle around the Place of Worship. Everything is *very* orderly, almost an anal retentive Judeo-Christian version of a rigorously laid-out Zen garden. And all the structures are made of metalwork scavenged from the environment. (NOTE: though we, as creators, know this is all materiel taken from the body of the ark, we should not tip this initially.) There are no bright colors. No pinks, no reds, no bright blues. This is clearly a town where frivolity is discouraged. This is brought home to us forcefully as a SMALL BOY goes laughing through the center of the town circle, rolling a metal stave hoop with a metal rod, and a SERIOUS ADULT, walking to the Place of Worship, turns on him:

SERIOUS ADULT
Young Jacob!

The child comes to a sudden stop, looking sheepish.

SERIOUS ADULT
Dost thou know what hour it be?

SMALL BOY
(contrite)
Aye, sir. Oh-nine hundred, sir.

SERIOUS ADULT
Second worship hour, lad. Long
since time you were at your
prayers. No time for idleness
and wicked laughter.

SMALL BOY
I beg pardon, sir.

SERIOUS ADULT
Then be about it, lad; hie thee
to thy place of kneeling and
rid thyself of impure, wicked
thoughts lest the Elders mete
out severity.

CONTINUED:

The Small Boy, head hanging respectfully, drops his hoop and stave near the Place of Worship and swiftly goes up the stairs into the building. The Serious Adult watches and then, shaking his head at the frivolity of the young, follows him. CAMERA HOLDS for a long moment on the doors of the Place as they *slide* together; we should be struck by the incongruity of metal buildings, well-oiled sliding doors, an open-air phone booth with a telephone that is used as an ivy-climb, a phone that clearly has not been operational for a very long time. CAMERA PANS LEFT and we see the cypress trees that give this place its name, each planted in a special place to achieve the ordered design the planters sought. We HOLD THRU TREES as we see a young man come running from the distance, toward the Place of Worship. He runs TOWARD CAMERA and we see his garb is similar to that worn by the Small Boy and the Serious Adult: severe black and white, a white collarless shirt of rough homespun material, possibly linsey-woolsey, black cotton overalls that come up in bib fashion with straps over the shoulders, stout sod-boots, no frills, no designs, no slightest show of vanity in the wearing.

4   MEDIUM SHOT—ON DEVON—COMING TO CAMERA

as he rushes toward the Place of Worship and the CAMERA. This is DEVON. Tall, fair, slim, an open and wondering expression, a young man in his early twenties who seems to carry, in his bearing and his face, an expectancy, a joy, a sense of wonder and curiosity so much at odds with the severity of his town and his dress. He looks like a young man who might have impishness in him, who might have wild poetry and unbridled laughter in him, who might quack with ducks and race with the night wind . . . when no one was about to chide him. He is Lancelot before the coming of sorrow, Huckleberry Finn before the advent of shoes, Childe Harold with bravery and ethic and caring lying just below the surface, shining out of the eyes, merely waiting for the dragon to present itself, the Herculean Tasks to be enumerated. He is the visionary, having prepared himself for the Dream, merely waiting for its form to be codified. He is the protagonist of our story.

He rushes TO CAMERA and CAMERA HOLDS HIM as he races up the steps of the Place of Worship and the doors open for him without his touching them. As he steps across the threshhold we

HARD CUT TO:

Phoenix Without Ashes   95

5   INT. PLACE OF WORSHIP—DAY—EXTREME CLOSEUP ON
    ELDER MICAH

A face hewn from mica schist. All that was in Devon's face, is absent
from this face. This face bears the utter totality of mirthlessness. Tight-
lipped, aquiline-nosed, pale, deep-set smoldering eyes, the face of the
zealot. This is ELDER MICAH. We HEAR his VOICE OVER:

> MICAH'S VOICE OVER
> Fifty mile across be the world of
> Cypress Corners. Fifty mile be all
> the plot of land given us by the
> Creator. To work and nourish and
> on which to find our Salvation.
> Twould be simple for thee to fall
> into the wicked thought that there
> be *more* to the Good Life, the life
> given to the service of the Creator,
> than these fifty mile; that there
> be thought ne'er thought, deed ne'er
> done, that thou might rise above thy
> fellows with certain deed and certain
> thought . . .

As Micah has been speaking, CAMERA PULLS BACK from his reviva-
list's face so we see he stands behind a metal lectern on a platform; on
the bare wall behind him only a burnished metal circle which we take
to be the symbol of his religion, a simple but eloquent representation
of the enclosed world in which he lives, and not coincidentally a representation of the closed thought processes he calls Belief. He wears the
severest garb of all, an all-black suit topped by a flat crowned hat with
a wide brim. Only the stark white of his face breaks the unrelieved
somberness of his appearance. He continues speaking as CAMERA
MOVES AROUND HIM to show us the INTERIOR OF THE PLACE
OF WORSHIP.

The Congregation, all in black, in metal pews. And coming down the
center aisle, looking not-at-all-humble, is Devon. The young man takes
a seat in the very front and Elder Micah's attention is clearly riveted
on him.

                                                    CONTINUED:

MICAH

. . . and that the will of the Elders
may be summarily flouted. Be there
aught amongst ye who feel so?

The Congregation replies quickly with loud but reverent "Nay! Nay,
Elder Micah! Nay, nay!" Devon is prominently silent in this response.
Elder Micah fastens his gaze on him.

MICAH

And what say you, Devon? Be your
humbleness merely worn like shirt
or shoe? Dost thou harbor secret
spite 'gainst thy Elders?

6   ON DEVON

A hardness comes into his face. His answer is hardly humble.

DEVON

Not spite, Elder Micah, but there
are questions I would ask you.

MICAH

Even in thy speech thou art troubling.
Thou callest thy Elder "you" with all
familiarity. Thy stay in the hills
hast done nought to cleanse thee!

DEVON

If it's love of Rachel you want to
"cleanse" from me, a hundred years
in the hills would not serve!

The Congregation shouts, "Impiety! He answers back! He should be
driven out!" Elder Micah raises his hands and they quiet.

MICAH

Set this thought forefront in thy
demeanor, Devon: thy parents be
long dead, thy station be of the
lowest, thy prospects slim, thy
manner bitter as water drawn from
                              CONTINUED:

the pollution pool. Thy genetic
rating unsuitable. Thou art
maintained in Cypress Corners as
ward of the Elders . . .
        (beat; viciously)
Young Rachel . . .

WHIP-PAN TO:

7   CLOSE ON RACHEL

as she sits between her MOTHER and FATHER in a metal pew. A young woman in her mid-twenties, lovely and prim, quiet, with hands folded, eyes downcast as is her place in this society. But with sharpness to her features and intelligence in her eyes. Smoldering, silent, all the makings of a remarkable adult, lying submerged, beaten down by mores and morality of a Work Ethic society in which women are merely helpmates, not humans in their own right.

              MICAH'S VOICE OVER
    . . . is promised since birth to
Young Garth . . .

WHIP-PAN TO:

8   CLOSE ON GARTH

as he sits between *his* MOTHER and FATHER in a metal pew near Rachel and her parents. GARTH is a solid, chunky peasant with a broad face, deeply tanned from the fields. Where dreams live in Devon's face, stoicism and maintaining live in Garth's. He is the young man one seeks when an onerous chore must be undertaken. He will persevere; he will plug away till it's done. If he lacks imagination and poetry, he makes up for it in personal strength and loyalty. He is likeable, but not outgoing. He is a rock.

              MICAH'S VOICE OVER
    . . . promised by the word of the
Creator's Machine. Dost thee
still question the decision of
the Creator?

WHIP-PAN BACK TO:

as he rises. SHOOT PAST ELDER MICAH. Devon is angry.

> DEVON
>
> I *still* question! I still ask
> why the sky is metal and the
> ground is not . . . I still ask where
> waste goes when we put it down the
> Trap . . . I still ask why Young Rachel
> must wed a man she doesn't love!

The Congregation goes wild with anger and lynch fever. Rachel's Mother and Father rise and shout epithets, Garth's parents smolder and snarl at Devon. Oddly, neither Rachel nor Garth take part in this. Elder Micah once again stills them with a wave of his hand. They are well-trained.

> MICAH
>
> When first thee came to thy Elders
> with this blasphemy, thy anguish
> was met with kindness. Thou wert
> given leave to go to the hills to
> cleanse thyself. But thee hath
> returned to our prayer time still
> surfeited with recrimination and
> wickedness. See this, ungrateful
> child . . .

Elder Micah goes to the side of the platform and whips the cover off a small computer terminal. He turns it on and speaks into the grille:

> MICAH
>
> Respond to my voice. I seek again
> the answer to the mating question
> of Young Rachel and Young Garth.
> Be there genetic relevance for
> consideration of Devon as mate to
> Young Rachel? Answer.

The terminal makes its computer sorting sounds, goes through a series

CONTINUED:

of considerations and rejects, and then the VOICE of the COMPUTER emanates from the grille, loud and flat.

>   COMPUTER
>   Gene pool orders original mating
>   selection without variance. New
>   factor, coded: Devon, unsuitable.
>   Balance maintained. Answer: none.

Micah snaps off the computer with a finality that cannot be misconstrued. He whirls on Devon.

>   MICAH
>   Now, spiteful Devon, before this
>   Congregation, in the sight of the
>   Creator and in the Creator's words,
>   thou hast been spurned. Wilt thou
>   *now* relent? And join with thy
>   betters in joining these two young
>   people?

Devon looks as though he has been punched in the stomach. He does not speak, but turns to stare at Rachel. She meets his eyes, then they fall. He turns again to Micah, but the words will not come. Clenching his fists, he turns and bolts from the Place of Worship. The Congregation waits for Micah's message. He assumes a mien that tells us (but not the Congregation) that he plans something much more severe in the way of punishment for Devon.

10   CAMERA MOVING IN ON ELDER MICAH

>   MICAH
>   This boy has been possessed by
>   wickedness. From this moment
>   forward, henceforth let no member
>   of this Congregation speak unto
>   Devon, let no soul touch his, let
>   no notice be made of him. For us,
>   humble in the name of the Creator,
>   this Devon is a spitefulness, a
>   contentiousness, a spot of rancor.
>   Let him be, then, gone from our
>   sight. Now: return to thy labors.

11 ON CONGREGATION

as they rise, all turn to the circle design on the rear wall, and link thumb-and-forefinger over their hearts as a symbol of their piety.

12 SAME AS 10—CAMERA MOVING IN ON ELDER MICAH

TO EXTREME CLOSEUP of his eyes, which burn with animosity for Devon. We need no words, for we seem to see the sparks in his eyes which are a pre-lap-dissolve image as we:

MATCH LAP-DISSOLVE TO:

13 INT. FORGE—DAY

EXT. CLOSEUP on sparks as a hammer strikes the anvil. The sparks are MATCHED WITH sparks as seen in Micah's eyes in preceding shot. CAMERA PULLS BACK to show Garth forging a horseshoe. His heavily-muscled, squat body works with great rhythm and sureness. CAMERA BACK to FULL SHOT of the forge as Devon comes in through a rear door. He stands in shadow for a long moment, watching Garth. When he speaks, Garth does not look up.

> DEVON
> (softly)
> Garth.
> (beat, no response)
> I'm sorry, I had to do it.

Garth looks up with a flash of annoyance. But he says nothing, returns to hammering, with even greater vehemence.

> DEVON
> Try to understand. It doesn't have
> to be the way the Elders say it is.
> If you loved Rachel, or she loved you,
> I never would have spoken . . .

Now Garth turns on him. He holds the red-hot shoe in tongs and the hammer in the other hand. There is a moment in which we fear he may use them on Devon. But he spins and quenches the shoe in the water bucket. Through the steam he watches Devon. Then, looking at the wall, he speaks, as though to himself.

CONTINUED:

GARTH

I have been humiliated in the
eyes of my fellows. My family
has lost stature. I have been
badly-used.

Garth reaches across a bench and picks up a large and very futuristic
crossbow made of metal. The incongruity of rustic smithy, horseshoes
and this deadly modern weapon does not escape us. This crossbow will
be Garth's trademark throughout the series, and he treats it with the
love and attention Jim Bowie surely visited on his knife. He begins
heating one end of the bow that has a bend in it.

DEVON

Garth. We've known each other
all our lives. We were never
good friends, but I've always
respected you . . . and I think it
was mutual . . . won't you please
try to understand?

GARTH
(to wall)
If someone were here to hear me
now, I would say that the past
is done, and what the Elders
have decreed *is* what is *now*. I
would say that none of this makes
me happy, but I am Old Garth's
son and I will not suffer him to
lose status because of me. I
will do what I am told.

Devon stands a moment longer, looks at Garth, then, very sadly, turns
to go. He stops at the rear door and turns back. Garth hammers lightly
on the crossbow, straightening.

DEVON

I understand, Garth. And I'm
sorry. And I wish you weren't
in the middle of this.

CONTINUED:

Then he goes. Garth continues hammering for a moment, then plunges the end of the crossbow into the water. As steam rises, he looks INTO CAMERA in the direction of where Devon stood. His face is troubled, but resolute.

CUT TO:

14 EXT. REAR OF PLACE OF WORSHIP—NEAR SUNSET

CLOSE ON STORM CELLAR-TYPE DOOR set against rear of the holy building. The metal rod the Small Boy used for rolling his hoop in scene 3 enters FRAME and pries at a combination lock that seals the door shut. It snaps the lock open and CAMERA BACK to show Devon. He pulls it free, lifts up the door, and steps down quickly into darkness. CAMERA IN on the door closing down over him.

15 WITH DEVON—INT. BASEMENT PLACE OF WORSHIP—ARRI-FLEX

as he moves through storage pods, stacks of unused pews, impedimenta, heading toward the stairs to the upper floor. ARRIFLEX WITH HIM as he climbs. Trapdoor in the ceiling at the top of stairs. He climbs to it, crouches and raises it. A thin shaft of light appears as CAMERA MOVES INTO LIGHT and we

SMASH-CUT TO:

16 INT. PLACE OF WORSHIP—SAME AS 5—CLOSE ON TRAPDOOR

CAMERA OUT OF LIGHT that forms the slit where the trapdoor is opening. CAMERA PULLS BACK FAST to show us Elder Micah, attending to the computer. As Devon watches from his place of concealment, we see a second man in funereal garb, ELDER JUBAL, emerge from beyond the platform. Micah punches the same control on the computer that was used when the decree against Devon was spoken.

> COMPUTER
> Gene pool orders original
> mating selection without
> variance. New factor, coded:
> Devon, unsuitable. Balance
> maintained. Answer: none.

CONTINUED:

Phoenix Without Ashes 103

Micah punches another control, the voice dies, and the cassette pops out. He holds it a moment, contemplating.

> JUBAL
> How will you do this?

> MICAH
> Apparently shaming him before
> the Congregation will not set
> him on the path of righteousness.
> We come to final moments with
> Devon.

> JUBAL
> Too many questions.

> MICAH
> There are problems enough without
> his questions.

Micah pops the cassette back into the computer, punches it to record and speaks into the grille.

> MICAH
> Erase previous readout. Play
> back following message only
> beginning with words, "My wishes."
> Readout convert to machine voice.
>   (beat)
> My wishes have been spurned by the
> undevout Devon. His presence among
> the faithful is a blight and a
> danger. He must be driven out of
> the lands I have given you, into
> the hills, nevermore to engage in
> human congress. This I order in
> the name of the Creator.

He punches another control, the computer whirrs and makes its consideration noises, translating the freely-spoken message into computer talk as with the earlier cassette recording. Finally, it bongs a bell and we

> INTERCUT TO:

17   CLOSE ON DEVON

watching with amazement at this perversion of religion.

CUT BACK TO:

18   SAME AS 16

Micah and Jubal stand watching the computer as it plays back the cassette, now altered into machine talk, with the highly mechanical Voice of the Creator.

> COMPUTER
> Gene pool selection invariant.
> New factor, coded: Devon,
> attempting disruption optimum
> genetic balance. Disruption
> counter to program. Disruptive
> factor must, repeat MUST be
> eliminated from gene pool. In
> name of Creator, new factor,
> coded: Devon must be eliminated.

Computer clicks off. Micah and Jubal look at each other with satisfaction. Not *quite* malevolent, but clearly pleased with their duplicity. At that moment, they HEAR the SOUND of Devon emerging from the basement. They turn as one, and we see the trapdoor banging up and over, and Devon charges up the last few stairs. He breaks for the computer and they try to stop him. Devon fights them off in an attempt to get the cassette. Without words they struggle around the computer.

19   FULL SHOT—ARRIFLEX

WITH THE ACTION as Devon tries to get past them. None of them is particularly adept at infighting, but Devon is quicker, younger and more determined. They wrestle him around and with viciousness born of his disillusionment at what they have done to him—and everyone else—Devon grabs the lectern and swings it like a cudgel. He hits Jubal a resounding crack in the head, sending him sprawling. Using the lectern to keep Micah away from him, he slaps at the computer, and the cassette pops out. He grabs it and dashes for the basement again. Micah takes off after him but Devon makes it first, dashes down and

CONTINUED:

slams the trapdoor. Micah turns and turns in frustration, clenching and unclenching his fists in impotent fury as we UNFOCUS CAMERA and

CUT TO:

20 EXT. FRONT PORCH RACHEL'S HOME—EVENING

as Devon rushes onto porch FROM CAMERA. He pounds on the door and continues pounding till Rachel, her Father and Mother emerge. He holds up the cassette.

> DEVON
> I caught him, Rachel. I caught
> Elder Micah telling the Creator's
> Machine what to say.

Rachel's Father, ARAM, moves in front of his daughter. His wife, OLD RACHEL, holds her, preventing her from getting near Devon.

> ARAM
> Get thee gone, Devon. Go now
> before thou art done a harm.
> I mean thee no ill, boy, but
> there will be no blaspheming
> here.

Devon ignores him, continues talking to Rachel.

> DEVON
> Rachel, listen to me! The machine
> isn't what the Elders *say* it is.
> I think it's broken, I don't know
> for how long it's been broken, but
> it was Elder Micah who said you
> had to mate with Garth, not the
> Creator! Look: I have it all here
> on this thing from the Machine . . .
> the voice is *here.*

> OLD RACHEL
> (with horror)
> Thee stole from the Machine of
> the Creator?!

CONTINUED:

DEVON

Rachel, please! Listen to me, what
I'm telling you is that we can be
together . . . I fought with Micah and
Jubal . . . they tried to stop me, to kill
me . . .

ARAM

Thee smote the Elders!?!

Devon realizes suddenly that even logic won't work with these people,
that he has to get Rachel away from them. What they'll do thereafter
he clearly has not thought out, but he has to get through to her.

RACHEL

Devon . . .

DEVON

We've got to let everyone know,
Rachel. We've all been duped, used,
lied to, Creator only knows for how
many years, maybe centuries . . .

Aram lunges sidewise and pulls a scythe off a beam of the front porch,
and comes menacingly toward Devon.

ARAM

Get away, Devon. Go now or
thee will suffer harm.

DEVON

(backs up, then
speaks helplessly
to Rachel)
Come with me . . . please . . .

She struggles with herself for a moment, but it is hardly a battle she
can win. Her mother holds her, her father is in their way, and she
cannot break loose emotionally. But there is anguish in her face . . . she
loves Devon, without doubt. Finally, piteously, she says . . .

RACHEL

I am my father's daughter. I
will do what I must. Go,
Devon, please go quickly . . .

21   CLOSEUP OF DEVON

His face is different now. This may be, in fact, the moment when the dreamer realizes he must combat the real world for the privilege of *having* his dreams. CAMERA PULLS BACK as Devon backs away from the scythe.

> DEVON
> I'll be back for you. We can't
> live like this, we have to fight
> them . . .

He starts away, stops, turns and looks at her. INTERCUT SHOTS OF RACHEL AND DEVON.

> RACHEL
> (bravely, because
> she's being held)
> I love you, Devon . . .

He bolts away after a moment of staring at her. HOLD on Rachel, tears in her eyes, watching him go.

> SLOW DISSOLVE TO:

22   EXT. CYPRESS CORNERS—NIGHT

Micah and a mob of people with torches (metal torches that burn with gas jets), as they start out of town into the hills. Aram should be prominent in this group, as well as Garth.

> SLOW DISSOLVE THRU TO:

23   WITH DEVON—EXT. SHOTS—MOVING—NIGHT
thru
26   as he rushes through underbrush, climbs over gullies, moves into the foothills. Behind him, in the distance, seen over his shoulder, should be the flickering of the mob's torches. Stay with Devon as he races for some sanctuary, till he can order his priorities and find some solution to his situation.

27 EXT. FOOTHILLS—WITH DEVON—NIGHT

as the mob gets closer. Devon dives into a thicket of tangled briars. He burrows down in fallen leaves and covers himself. HOLD WITH DEVON as the mob lurches past, ad libbing their desire to catch the heretic and idolator Devon, to stone him to death. Devon lies doggo, but something is in the small of his back, causing him pain. As they go past he moves slightly, scrabbling silently behind himself at the protuberance. The mob goes away.

28 HIGH ANGLE—MEDIUM ON DEVON IN THICKET

as he turns over and starts to clear away leaves. He uncovers something metal. Bright metal. We can see it by the faint light of the artificial moon above. CAMERA COMES DOWN THRU THICKET to CLOSE ON DEVON'S HAND as he clears a wider circle. There is a metal plate set into the sloping side of the hill against which the thicket lies. He clears away and clears away and finally reveals the full ten-foot diameter of THE IRIS.

29 ON DEVON

as he looks at this wonder in the ground. He has never seen anything like it. He fiddles with the broken and semi-rusted parts of the iris lock mechanism, though he doesn't understand it as such. And suddenly, as CAMERA PULLS BACK UP AGAIN, the iris opens, revealing a black hole. Devon stares with utter amazement as CAMERA MOVES IN AND IN ON THE BLACKNESS and we

> FADE TO BLACK:
> and
> FADE OUT.

END ACT ONE

ACT TWO

FADE IN:

30 ESTABLISHING—THICKET HILLSIDE—NIGHT

CLOSE ON BLACKNESS that lies within the now-open aperture of the ten-foot-wide IRIS. CAMERA PULLS BACK & UP to show us the gaping hole in the ground, the dirt and leaves and thicket around it, the rusted latch mechanism . . . and Devon now staring in wonderment at the hole in the world. CAMERA BACK UP to FULL SHOT of the SCENE so we have a sense of the size of the hole.

CUT TO:

31 THE MOB

as they beat through the brush, looking for Devon. (NOTE: the word "mob" should neither frighten production people nor lead them to conjure a massive throng. "Mob," in this context, means five men dressed in homely garb, being led by Elder Micah all in black. Each of them bears a torch.) They come to a dead end—cliff face, box canyon, extremely heavy brush—and realize Devon could not be here, but must be somewhere behind them. They start to double back, making enough noise so that when we cut back to Devon, we will know that he can hear them.

CUT BACK TO:

32 DEVON—MEDIUM SHOT

as he examines the Iris. He has never seen anything like it before. He walks around it, and we should take our time with this: it is a special wonder. Then, from O.S. we HEAR the SOUND of the MOB RETURNING. Devon turns to the sound, takes a step backward to go into the thicket again, trips over a semi-buried portion of the latch mechanism, flails his arms wildly, and starts to fall into the iris. He catches himself, lies spreadeagled across the emptiness (like Da Vinci's anatomical drawing of man), trying to keep himself aboveground by pressure of feet and hands and shoulders against the outer rim.

CUT TO:

33 THE MOB

ANOTHER AREA (redressed) as they near Devon's position. Suddenly they HEAR a strange KEENING WHINE—the sound of heavy machinery phasing-up, something they've *never* heard before—and they react with superstitious awe . . . all except Micah, whose manner is abruptly alarmed, as though he *knows* what it is. They start racing toward the SOUND as we

SMASH-CUT TO:

34 DEVON

struggling with the potentiality of vanishing into the ground. As we watch, a pale blue light begins to come up from beneath him, from the iris hole. The light washes over him, almost like a nimbus, and for a moment we can SEE THROUGH HIS BODY and perceive the skeletal structure lying beneath the skin. The WHINING SOUND comes up louder and louder, drowning out even the sounds of the mob, the night, the crickets, everything. And then a GREAT RUSHING WIND pulls at Devon . . . he struggles . . . fights . . . and is suddenly sucked inside the iris, with one long shuddering SCREAM ripped from his throat. As he vanishes into the iris, CAMERA ZOOMS IN to the blue-tinged blackness and we SEE DEVON SPINNING AWAY FROM US.

35 FULL SHOT—THE IRIS

as Devon vanishes, the Iris closes up, the wind inside hurling leaves and dead branches and dirt into the air so the Iris is completely hidden, lost once again, when it is closed. And as the rubble settles, the mob breaks into the thicket, looks around, tramples the ground, may even stumble over the broken latch mechanism but have no idea that what they seek now lies beneath their feet. They mill about, confused, with only the dying sound of that eerie KEENING WHINE softening, softening . . . then lost. CAMERA COMES IN on Elder Micah's face, now set in lines of menace and frustration, a latter-day Cotton Mather whose prey has escaped him, how he does not know.

SLOW DISSOLVE TO:

36 INT. BOUNCE TUBE—MAGICAM—LONG SHOT TO DEVON

as he is sucked along. Please note that he is *not* falling. There is no

CONTINUED:

artificial gravity in the bounce tube and he is *pulled forward* as if he were in a horizontal caisson, a quarter of a mile across. All around him are the protected tubes and plumbing of the Ark, the nodes and road-ways and laser-sealed plating of a massive conduit thirty miles long. No end in sight, the horizon only a point of darkness far ahead. The blue glow—an artificial light-source within the tube—still surrounds him (though the X-ray effect is gone) and it will be this blue light that will characterize all bounce tube scenes throughout the series. CAMERA GOES WITH DEVON so we, ourselves, have a sense of speed and flight, but then CAMERA HOLDS and Devon is whirled away from us, arms and legs twisting, struggling vainly for a handhold.

37   REVERSE ANGLE

on Devon hurtling toward us. He comes at a breakneck pace, dead in the center of the tube so he cannot reach any handhold or harm himself by hitting any protrusion. He comes whirling toward us and INTO CAMERA as we

SMASH-CUT TO:

38   REVERSE ANGLE ON 37

as BLACKNESS of DEVON'S BODY slamming away from us gives way to FULL SHOT of his body vanishing down tne tube.

39   SERIES OF DOLLY SHOTS—MAGICAM AND/OR ARRIFLEX
thru
42   WITH, PAST & TOWARD DEVON as he is hurtled along like a Sep-tember leaf, the subliminal SOUND of his SCREAM playing counter-point to the banshee howl of the wind in the bounce tube. At one point he is abruptly whirled *around a wide bend* in the tube, no more able to help himself than a bit of flotsam caught in an undertow.

43   SHOT WITH DEVON—END OF TUBE

coming up fast, like the wall of a subway station. Devon's eyes widen in horror and he struggles to turn himself, thrust out his hands, do *some-thing* to keep himself from smashing against the metal wall dead ahead.

44   FROM TUBE END—TO DEVON

as he begins to slow down, to *float* toward us, till he COMES TO CAMERA and is gently deposited on the bulkhead of the tube. There is no gravity, and as he moves, he turns, performing an awkward gymnastic figure. He fumbles, tries to right himself, turns over again and again in a helpless parabola of uncoordinated movements. Finally, he is able to learn to "swim" in the direction he wishes to go, by moving his arms slightly, by kicking off lightly from one bulkhead or another, and finally he makes it to a much smaller Iris than the one that swallowed him. Above the Iris is a light panel with the words

ACCESS TUBE   SERVICE MODULE

glowing in it. He gets to the Iris, touches all around it till he lucks onto the release mechanism, it dilates, and he slips through. It closes instantly as we

CUT TO:

45   INT. ACCESS TUBE

the light is now orange. As Devon slips through, over the rim of the Iris, the artificial gravity in the access tube grabs him and he falls heavily the two feet to the "floor." (It should be clear from the way he makes his entrance that had he understood there would be gravity in the access tube, he would have come through feet first, instead of head and shoulders first, and would have dropped neatly to a standing arrival.)

46   CLOSE ON DEVON

as he lies there, regaining his senses. Let him take his time. He has just experienced, for the first time in the six-hundred-year journey of his people, a devastating trip down through the bowels of his world, past wonders whose like he has never experienced, to finally come to rest in a tiny access chamber all metal and all strange. Let him look up and over and around as CAMERA TRACKS WITH HIM.

47   DEVON'S POV—WHAT HE SEES

a floor beneath him, made of virtually-seamless blue-metal plating, an arched ceiling no more than ten feet high, a series of dials and controls

CONTINUED:

Phoenix Without Ashes   115

and equipment whose use he cannot fathom. And right in front of him, on the wall, a plastic case containing a transparent suit of clothes in the shape of a human being, empty, but open with a seal-strip of twin blue lines down the front. It looks as though a human being had shed skin without a break in the material, save for that open gash down the front. Held secure by rubber bumpers, above the skin-suit, is a teardrop-shaped bubble with tubes protruding from it. (NOTE: the specific design of this spacesuit, for that's what it is, of course, should be checked out with Bova for accuracy.) Clearly, the bubble snugs down into a complicated gasket arrangement at the neck of the skin-suit. Beside the plastic case is a tiny computer terminal with the words

SUITING INSTRUCTIONS

glowing above it. He should look at this, but make no real connection.

48   MED. SHOT—FEATURING DEVON

as he gets to his feet, walks around the access chamber, touches the walls, which are warm. Marveling and wondering. He touches the plastic case. He sees the lockport in the bulkhead and does not understand the phrase

VIEWPORT 874

that glows on its face. He moves to it, touches it, looks at the massive hinges *which we must hold for several beats,* that permit the lockport to open and close hydraulically. They are enormous hinges, with pistons in them, and clearly capable of swinging a bank vault door open and closed at the touch of a finger. Devon tries to open the lockport, but it will not open. He sees a catch, and releases it. Then he tries to move the port again. It begins to break its seal. It starts to open inward.

NOTE: this sequence *must* be carefully choreographed lest we defy the laws of physical science and appear foolish to those who know what life in space is like.

49   CLOSE ON LOCKPORT

as it swings in toward Devon, slowly, ponderously, with Devon straining every muscle to get it open. He manages to open it just enough to wedge his body into the crack of the jamb and . . .

50 ZOOM SHOT—WITH DEVON

as the air begins to thunder out of the chamber, sluicing past him like a tornado, only his wedged position in the lockport keeping him from being sucked out. CAMERA RUSHES PAST DEVON'S HEAD and we see . . .

51 THE UNIVERSE

through a framework of the shattered viewport onto which this portal gives, we see the majesty of space. Laid out all vast and terrifying, to the shores of forever and beyond.

CAMERA GOES TO SLOW MOTION TO GIVE US A FEELING THAT THESE FEW SECONDS STRETCH OUT FOR AN ETER-NITY.

52 SLOW MOTION—WITH DEVON

as the lockport's hinges lock and begin the incredible job of closing the opening before all atmosphere escapes. Devon is terrified, awed, thun-derstruck, confused, helpless, frozen in that tiny sliver of opening through which all air rushes like a wild thing. He is pressed back into the access chamber by the weight of the closing portal, each part of his body mobilized in slow motion like mercury flowing uphill. The port closes and closes and the view beyond Devon recedes as the seal is made once again. The now oxygen-starved body of Devon flails backward in *very* slow motion as the port seals completely and a WARNING LIGHT PANEL flickers ever-so-slowly on and off where the words VIEWPORT 874 had glowed a moment before. Now only the single, deadly word

DEPRESSURIZED

blinks there, but eerily, in such slow pulses that we have time to watch Devon stumble backward, clutching his throat as his lungs try to fill with air, and he falls, falls, falls, and hits and bounces and lies still as CAMERA COMES IN on the light panel and its ominous one-word warning that pulses on and off, on and off . . .

SLOW LAP-DISSOLVE TO:

53   CLOSE ON WARNING PANEL

later. The lap-dissolve shows two panels, one pulsing slowly, the other spasming rapidly. We have now returned to NORMAL SPEED and it is later. CAMERA PULLS BACK to show us Devon lying on the floor, seemingly dead. But as CAMERA MOVES AROUND HIM we see he is breathing, shallowly. After a few beats he opens his eyes, lies there drinking deeply of the life that replenished air has given him. Slowly, he pulls himself up on elbows to a semi-sitting position, and we watch with fascination as he orients himself to where he is. Then his eyes widen and we

SUBLIMINAL FLASH:

54   SAME AS 51

the Universe. The way Devon saw it a moment before. In a mental replay that stuns him, and then is gone.

55   FULL SHOT

as Devon rises, holding onto the bulkhead. He is drained of all reason, all comprehension of what he has seen. He regains his faculties slowly, and moves to the lockport again, a curiosity that parallels Copernicus's need to know burning within him. He has seen *some*thing, and even at the risk of his life he will see it again. The lockport warning now speaks in a subdued but imperative mechanical voice:

> WARNING VOICE
> Entrance to depressurized section refused.
> Protective lock has been placed on this port.
> Contact maintenance unit, terminal code
> 110–3976.

He steps back, looks for the source of the voice. When he can find nothing, he moves to lockport again. And again the Warning Voice repeats its urgent message.

> WARNING VOICE
> Entrance to depressurized section
> forbidden, repeat *forbidden*.
> Protective lock insures no
> admittance without use of oxygen

CONTINUED:

suit. Maintenance unit advisement
urged, terminal code 110–3976.

The light plate beside the spacesuit is now pulsing on and off, and in
the distance Devon can HEAR WARNING BELLS CLANGING. In
the light plate the words SUITING INSTRUCTIONS are now alter-
nately-pulsed with the words SUIT UP BEFORE ENTERING. Now
Devon looks at the plastic case with more care. After a moment he
fumbles with the case and it slides open, permitting him to touch the
transparent suit. He removes it from its hanger, and the warning light
of the suiting instruction plate speaks as did the lockport.

> WARNING VOICE
> Model J-10 oxygen suit. Suiting
> instructions. One: remove all
> sharp protrusions from your person.

Devon is, of course, amazed at the voice, looks to see where it comes
from, realizes it is hidden as was the previous voice, and touches himself to see if he has any "sharp protrusions." He has none. The voice
has gone on, nonetheless.

> WARNING VOICE
> Insert feet into legs of the suit.

Devon does as instructed. The voice keeps going but its pace is slow
enough to allow him to react and perform the sequence of functions
without any humorous overtones. (NOTE TO DIRECTOR: please
avoid any parallels with TV or radio cook shows that tell you which
ingredients to use, and go so fast you wind up breaking eggs on the
floor. This should have all the tone of a scientific experiment, stately,
measured, fascinating.)

> WARNING VOICE
> Make certain no wrinkles exist as
> you pull the suit up around your
> body.
> (beat)
> Insert arms carefully. The suit
> will not rip but caution should

CONTINUED:

be exercised to avoid wrinkling
or bunching under the arms.
            (beat)
Make certain fingers reach the
ends of the glove hands.
            (beat)
Smooth suit down across shoulders
and, using a similar smooth motion,
seal the blue strips for an airtight
closure.
            (beat)
Remove the helmet from its berth.
Place the ends of the oxygen hoses
into their sockets on the shoulders.
Red into red, yellow into yellow.
Now raise the helmet, set it into
the gasket seal, over your head,
and give it a half-turn clockwise.

Devon does not know what "clockwise" means. He tries it first one way, with no result, then the other. It snaps into place with a solid *click*. For a moment his eyes widen and he cannot breathe, then we HEAR a FAINT HISS OVER and he draws air deep into his lungs. Now he is fully suited.

                    WARNING VOICE
            Place left hand against the light
            plate and, if you are properly sealed,
            pressure will be equalized in this
            access chamber. Thank you.

Still not fully understanding what this is all about—he has never seen a pressure chamber or a spacesuit or the vacuum of space before—Devon presses his hand to the light plate. The light in the chamber dims for a moment, then we HEAR the atmosphere being drawn out of the chamber. As Devon breathes, the teardrop helmet indents ever so slightly. It is not wholly rigid, but is rather like a very flexible plastic bag.

56 CLOSE ON WARNING LIGHT ON PORT

as it goes out and the area beneath it reads

PRESSURE EQUALIZED
ADMITTANCE PERMITTED

57 FULL SHOT—WITH DEVON

as he returns to the lockport and once again undogs it. Now it moves very easily, and as it opens inward, we MOVE DEVON into CLOSEUP so his back obscures what lies on the other side. He moves through the lockport and CAMERA MOVES DOWN to his feet as they step over the sill. As the lockport hatch swings closed behind him, cutting off the view of his feet, we see in the last moment before the FRAME is filled with blue metal, that his feet are lifting off the deckplates . . . no gravity on the other side. The port swings shut, seals tight as CAMERA ZOOMS BACK TO FULL SHOT of the closed port and we

SMASH-CUT TO:

58 INT. VIEWPORT—CLOSE ON DEVON

as we HOLD his FACE and study the look of utter wonder that comes across his features. There are reflected scintillances in the teardrop helmet and in his eyes, and after we've held this long enough to understand that what he is seeing is something new and marvelous, we PULL BACK SMOOTHLY AND STATELY BUT NOT ZOOM and we see Devon's surroundings. He is in a ruined viewport chamber the size of a large living room, filled with ruined but futuristic furniture, consoles, all the matter that would be in a luxury stargazing room on a great liner. It is dark, but faint lights still glow in their wall mountings, even after six hundred years. CAMERA BACK AND BACK till we see the front of the viewport, a clear bubble that allowed passengers and crew to view the stars, has been shattered and exploded outward. Devon stands in the opening, against the wall, framed by the jagged edges of the ruined bubble. CAMERA PULLS BACK as we

HARD CUT TO:

59 REVERSE ANGLE—PAST DEVON

to the stars. There is space. Now seen not in a subjective slow motion

CONTINUED:

time-lapse shot as with shot 51, but with a leisurely wonderment as CAMERA MOVES PAST DEVON to reveal the entire breathtaking panoply of the limitless universe. For the first time in six hundred years, humanity sees that which is its inheritance. The open and endless field of stars, flat and unwinking in the airlessness of space. Black as amnesia, flat and dead, yet bearing within its heart the pulsing life of stars that have yet to go nova, yellow and blue and green and orange. Milk-dust clusters of galaxies tossed out as though by a careless hand . . . all of it . . . awesome, touching, humbling. Dwell on this shot with loving care. Let us see how it will affect Devon, a child of the contained community of Cypress Corners, then

CUT BACK TO:

60 SAME AS 58

still MOVING OUT. Back and back and back till we see Devon standing in the bubble as a whole, then the bubble as a mere node on the outside of a tube, then the tube as a stalk between two huge domes, then the domes as only bulbs on a greater cluster, and the clusters as part of the entire Ark.

61 FULL SHOT FROM DEEP SPACE ON THE ARK

Let us see, for the first time, exactly what the nature of this beast may be. The Ark. Majestic in its length, one thousand miles long, over 1600 kilometers, five million two hundred and eighty thousand feet from nose to stern . . . Noseless. Sternless. A giant cluster of grapes and each grape a biosphere dome at least fifty miles in diameter. A cluster of cities all linked and sent into the deeps. A continent, moving through emptiness. A great behemoth containing all that was left of the decimated Earth. *Let us see it* as the CAMERA PULLS BACK and the Ark is alone there in star-flecked deep space.

62 SLIT-APERTURE SHOT—PULLING BACK

HOLD THE PREVIOUS SHOT for beats, many beats, and *then*, with the utter recklessness of a Trumbull mind-trip, ZOOM OUT to the edge of the Universe with the Ark receding to merely a glowing point, another faint star, seen only as a glimmer in the starshine of blazing suns. All the way back so we know the Ark in comparison to the enormity of space . . . and then . . .

63   ZOOM IN

Let it rip! Straight to hell! Shoot back in so fast all space divides into a chromatic montage of whirling lights and stroboscopic reflections. A godlike spectrum of prismatic wonders. Hurtle us forward, shoot us down that light-band of colors no human eye has ever seen, send us on a trip we will never forget. Back, back, back to the Ark . . . and over it. Then

SMASH-CUT TO:

64   REVERSE ANGLE—THE ARK IN CLOSEUP

stop! And now we begin a minute examination of the Ark from the outside.

65   SERIES OF LAP-DISSOLVES SEEN AS ONE CONTINUING SHOT—
thru
75   SNORKEL CAMERA TECHNIQUE

Move along the length of the Ark. Show us this is no mere model. Every dome, every tunnel stalk, every inch of plate and bulkhead. Go the full thousand miles. Dwell with loving attention on the fascinating elements that make up this community of enclosed worlds. Go from tip to tail, and around, and under. Take us on a journey that will set in our minds (and for future stock footage) the almost unbelievable enormity of this floating continent. And let it be in EXTREME CLOSEUP so we know these domes are fifty miles wide. Let us know that these bounce tubes and tunnels stretch for a hundred miles between domes. And when you have exhausted the inexhaustible wonder of what we will deal with every segment, then come down on one single dome.

76   REPEAT SHOT 1

take us in on that metal bulkhead that *now* we perceive as the outer hull of the dome world enclosing Cypress Corners.

DISSOLVE THRU TO:

77   REPEAT SHOT 2

CAMERA REFOCUSES inside the dome where our segment began. Drop CAMERA and TRAVEL exactly as before, all the way across the dome world of Cypress Corners. But keep going.

CONTINUED:

Phoenix Without Ashes   125

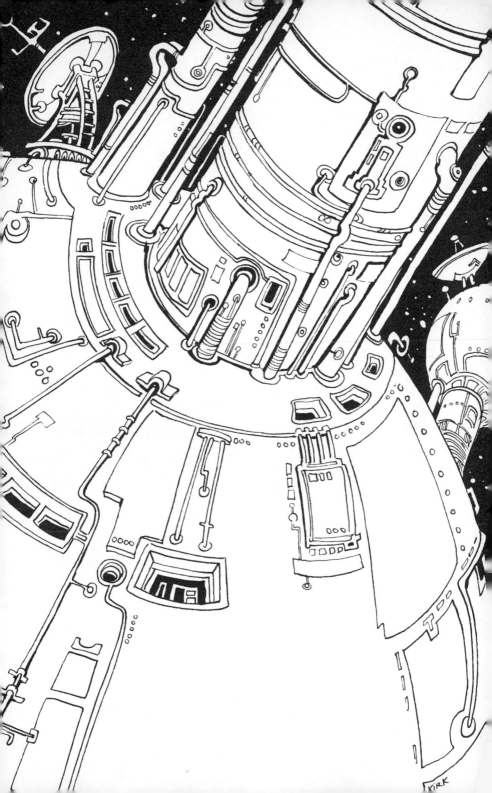

78   REPEAT SHOT 3

But keep going. SKIM CAMERA THRU TOWN and out into the hills. Keep going on this miraculous traveltrip to the foothill thicket where Devon discovered the Iris, and SEND CAMERA INTO the thicket, into the piles of leaves covering the Iris so we see only a touch of the blue metal that forms its structure . . .

DISSOLVE THRU TO:

79   REPEAT SHOT 36

CAMERA HURTLES THRU BOUNCE TUBE exactly as before, save that now Devon is not there and *we* are the voyagers, learning by doing, the length and magnificence of the tunnels that connect various worlds of the Ark. Keep going till you come to that bulkhead wall at the end.

DISSOLVE THRU TO:

80   THE INTERIOR OF THE ACCESS CHAMBER

REFOCUS in the chamber and keep going, through the lockport and

DISSOLVE THRU TO:

81   INT. VIEWPORT—ON DEVON

as he stands there, still frozen in awe at the majesty of the unknown, the limitless horizon of space. CAMERA GOES AROUND HIM so we can see—as if *his* eyes had been *our* eyes on a journey no human has ever made—that he has come to a stunning awareness that Cypress Corners is *not* the world. That *this* is the world, this black and star-filled panoply that has no beginning, has no end, that circles back upon itself like a laocoonian serpent, with this lonely Ark at its center.

And, holding on Devon, let CAMERA MOVE IN to show us that there are tears in his eyes. Tears of wonder and delight and excitement and, for the first time in six hundred years, within a necessary metal prison . . . hope. CAMERA IN ON DEVON'S FACE, into the tears that gleam with starlight and

FADE TO BLACK:
and
FADE OUT.

END ACT TWO

Phoenix Without Ashes   127

ACT THREE

FADE IN:

82 INT. VIEWPORT

CLOSE ON SPACESUITED HAND. Reaching for the control stud of a lockport. CAMERA PULLS BACK to show Devon, only a little later, floating in the emptiness of the ruined viewport, now seemingly having learned how to propel himself with less ungainliness. Now he presses the stud and the lockport sighs open silently. Silently, for he is still in a bubble open to the airless, soundless vacuum of space. He pushes off and sails through the lockport. CAMERA GOES WITH as it seals behind him.

83 INT. NARROW TUNNEL—TO DEVON

as he floats forward in the dim blue glow. This was a service tunnel when the Ark was young. Now it lies unused. Devon floats along IN FRONT OF CAMERA. Down its length he sees something hanging in the emptiness, moving only slightly as he nears it.

84 ANOTHER ANGLE

as Devon reaches the shape. It is a dead woman, lying on her back, her hair floating out around her head, her mouth open. Caught without air. Quite dead. Six hundred years a corpse, perfectly preserved, still wearing the garb of a crewmember, garb that we will come to recognize as the series progresses. And something else in the tunnel. Water. Great globules of water. They hang like jewels and as Devon sails through them they disperse, shatter against him, club up again. A broken conduit in the wall shows where the water came from, and one enormous drop hangs on the lip of the broken tubing, eternally poised to splash. Devon hangs there, staring at the dead woman. Who is she? Where did she come from? What happened to her? He will never know. After several beats, he pushes off the bulkhead and sails away.

85 ANGLE ON ANOTHER BULKHEAD

at the end of the tunnel, as Devon sails INTO FRAME. It is covered with dials and maintenance gauges. Another small lockport. Devon tries to open it, reading the phrase

CONTINUED:

Phoenix Without Ashes   129

in the glowing light plate. The port will not open, and Devon sees the flashing warning plate that says

EQUALIZE PRESSURE
BEFORE ADMITTANCE

He recognizes the phrase from earlier, and presses his gloved hand against the light plate. Instantly, the light in the tunnel alters from blue to orange, there is the hiss of air filling the tunnel, and when he tries the lockport again, it opens easily. He goes through.

86   INT. MEMORY BANK TERMINAL

as Devon comes across the threshhold, he drops. Gravity in this chamber has not been cut off. He lands well this time, and stares around.

87   DEVON'S POV—WHAT HE SEES

a large chamber, fitted out with formfit chairs of a very futuristic design, racks of "memory cubes" along one wall, pallets with sleep-teaching machines attached, exotic paintings on the walls . . . dust everywhere. As he walks, it puffs up in little clouds behind him. He stops and looks back along his trail. His footsteps are clear in the dust. No one has been in here in 600 years.

88   CLOSE ON MEMORY BANK

TO DEVON APPROACHING FROM B.G. (NOTE: specific design of this instrument should be checked with Bova for most felicitous look.) He walks up to it, and touches it. It is a marvelous implement: huge and blocky, made of some substance that glows with an interior light so we see movement from within, like waves of color washing through oil behind an opaque glass. Its top is honeycombed like an egg crate, with depressions that are clearly made for something to fit into. CAMERA FOLLOWS DEVON'S GAZE as he looks around the memory bank, sees the racks of cubes and walks over, selects one at random, and brings it back to the memory bank. It is obviously the proper, singular shape to fit into one of the bank-top depressions. He inserts it. Suddenly, a VOICE fills the chamber.

CONTINUED:

CUBE VOICE
Erik Satie, A.D. 1866 to 1925, was
commissioned to compose *Mercure,*
poses plastiques en trois tableaux,
by the fashionable Count Étienne de
Beaumont for a series of avant-garde
theatrical performances, Les Soirées
de Paris, to be held, in 1924, at
the tiny Théâtre de la Cigale.
(beat)
And now, here is Satie's *Mercure.*

And music swells out commandingly through the chamber. Devon is
thunderstruck. He has never heard music like this before. In Cypress
Corners all they had were a few hymns, and those were sung without
accompaniment of musical instruments, forbidden by the Elders. He
stands there, washed by the brilliant sounds of Satie, and after a few
moments, with the music behind him, he scrutinizes the memory cube
racks more carefully.

89   ON MEMORY CUBE RACKS—WITH DEVON

as he travels up and down the rows. There are labels for different
sections: PHILOSOPHY, MUSIC, LANGUAGES, BIOCHEMISTRY, RELIGION,
FICTION, and one set of fifty cubes set apart labeled BASIC HISTORICAL
INFORMATION. He starts to remove the first of these, when he sees a
light plate and grille at the end of the racks with the words

ASK ME FIRST

glowing in the plate. He walks to it, presses his hand against the plate.
A VOICE comes from the GRILLE:

GRILLE VOICE
May I help you?

Devon is taken aback. But he looks around and then says to the grille:

DEVON
What is all this?

CONTINUED:

GRILLE VOICE
I'm sorry, sir, I'm afraid I don't
grasp the meaning of your question.
When you say "all this," do you
mean the memory bank library, my
function, the purpose of Life in
general, or the specifics of your
present situation?

Devon ponders for a moment, lost in the complexities of the first really
rational mind he's ever encountered.

DEVON
Are you real, are you alive?

GRILLE VOICE
Why, no, sir. I'm the voice of
the library stacks. Here to
serve you, to advise you which
cubes to use to obtain the data
you require.

DEVON
I'm all confused. I've met so many
new things . . .

GRILLE VOICE
You sound distraught, sir. Why not
relax and let me see if I can assist
you.

DEVON
Thank you.

GRILLE VOICE
Now. Are you a member of the crew
or are you supercargo?

DEVON
I don't know what those mean.

CONTINUED:

Phoenix Without Ashes 133

GRILLE VOICE

Perhaps I should contact a medical
section to assist you. You sound
as if you may be ill.

DEVON

No, I'm all right . . . I think. I
fell down a hole in the ground . . .
well, I didn't exactly fall *down*,
I fell *away*, if you know what I mean.
I was pulled forward down a very
long hollow thing . . .

GRILLE VOICE

That sounds like a description of a
bounce tube, sir. From what biosphere
did you say you had come?

DEVON

I'm afraid I don't know what
that means, either. I'm from
Cypress Corners.

GRILLE VOICE
(sounds of computer
sorting in b.g.)

Cypress Corners. Late A.D. 1800's
ethnic agrarian community. How
did you get here, into the service
perimeter of the Ark?

DEVON

The Ark?

GRILLE VOICE

I think I know what you need.
(beat)

Do you see the section labeled BASIC
HISTORICAL INFORMATION to your left?

Devon nods. The grille says nothing.

CONTINUED:

GRILLE VOICE
(repeats)
Do you see the section labeled BASIC
HISTORICAL INFORMATION to your left?

Then, realizing the machine cannot see him nod, Devon replies.

DEVON
Yes, I do. I'm sorry, I forgot you
can't see me.

GRILLE VOICE
That's quite all right, think nothing
of it. My visual sensors seem to be
inoperative; I'll have to call a
repairmech.
(beat)
Now. Go to that section and remove
the cube numbered 43. Then take it
to the memory bank in the center of
the chamber and insert it into one
of the empty sockets. I think that
may help you orient yourself.

DEVON
Thank you, very much.

GRILLE VOICE
You're more than welcome. That's
what I'm here for, to help you.
If you need any further help,
don't hesitate to ask.
(beat)
I wonder why my visual sensors are
out . . .

Devon turns away, takes the cube indicated, and goes to the memory
bank. He removes the Satie music cube that has been playing in the
b.g. while he talked to the grille, and now the music ceases. He inserts
the new cube, and stands back as a soft golden cloud of mist suddenly
appears above the flat surface of the instrument. It is a holographic 3-D
image of what the cube contains in the way of knowledge.

90   CLOSE ON HOLO IMAGE

This is a play within a play. Stock footage, Magicam, back projection, chromakey and videotape techniques should be used to effect what is described herein. (NOTE: at the time of this writing, technique specifics and parameters of visual possibilities are unknown to the Author. Take what follows as a basic blueprint of what needs to be codified and explicated in this section—*of utmost importance*—with an understanding that the actual production mechanics will be consistent with Trumbull and McAdams' needs, and what is offered here can be revised accordingly.)

90A   WHAT WE SEE IN THE HOLO IMAGE MIST:

A woman appears. She is the HOLO NARRATOR. Her VOICE is warm but matter-of-fact, a female version of the voice we used to hear over the movie News of the Day newsreels. She stands casually, telling Devon (and us) what we need to know. She can answer questions.

> HOLO NARRATOR
> This is a continuation of the history
> of the planet Earth from cube number
> forty-two.
> > (beat)
> When it became clear that the impending
> death of the Earth would leave no trace
> of the human race, it was decided in
> the year A.D. 2285, to build a giant
> vessel that could be sent out to deep
> space, carrying within it a large enough
> segment of Earth's population to settle
> other worlds, in star systems beyond our
> own . . .

> DEVON
> > (the words are
> > unfamiliar)
> The "planet" . . . "Earth" . . . ?

> HOLO NARRATOR
> Geophysical and astronomical data
> on the home world may be obtained

> CONTINUED:

through use of CARTOGRAPHY cubes
one through six. Do you wish to
familiarize yourself with this
data before I continue?

> DEVON
> Yes, please.

> HOLO NARRATOR
> I will wait.

A chair materializes. The Narrator sits, legs crossed with one swinging, as she waits.

91 WITH DEVON

as he goes back to the racks, removes the cubes indicated, and brings them back to the machine. He inserts the first one and the woman vanishes as the mist reforms to show the planet Earth. A VOICE (male) begins speaking.

> MALE VOICE
> There are seven major theories
> as to the formation of the
> universe, the star-sun Sol, and
> the planetary system it serves . . .

CAMERA IN on Earth as the VOICE OVER speaks and we see Devon bending closer to watch the little tableau of how the Earth was born. It should utilize STOCK FOOTAGE (MEASURE) and be a primer of astronomy. But we need not see much of it, just enough to show Devon is learning what *he* needs to know, as we

> SLOW LAP-DISSOLVE TO:

92 SAME SCENE—DIFFERENT ANGLE—INDICATE TIME-LAPSE

as the mist containing the Earth reforms and the little Holo Narrator figure reappears. She rises from the chair and looks up at Devon. Hours have passed. Devon has shed his oxygen suit, apparently realizing he can breathe in this chamber.

> CONTINUED:

Phoenix Without Ashes 137

HOLO NARRATOR
Are you now sufficiently informed
on the terms "planet" and "Earth"?

DEVON
(wonderingly)
We're all on a ship, we're moving
through "space." We come from a
world, a planet, a place called
the Earth.

HOLO NARRATOR
Should I call a medical team, are you
well?

DEVON
(with delight)
I'm fine! I'm just very very
fine! Please go on, tell me more,
I want to know it all, I want to
know *everything!*

HOLO NARRATOR
As I said earlier, when the cataclysm
that was to destroy the Earth was seen
to be an inevitability . . .

DEVON
What *was* the cataclysm?

HOLO NARRATOR
Vastator.

DEVON
I don't know what that means.

HOLO NARRATOR
(with some small
annoyance)
You will find that on the preceding
cube, number forty-two. Please play
it, then return.

93 WITH DEVON

as he looks chagrined, then walks to the racks. But the slot for cube 42 is empty. He comes back. The Narrator is in her chair again, this time tapping her foot with ill-concealed impatience.

> DEVON
> The cube is missing. What is
> Vastator?

> HOLO NARRATOR
> I am not programmed to synopsize
> previous cubes. Do you wish me
> to continue?

> DEVON
> (browbeaten)
> Yes, ma'am, thank you.

> HOLO NARRATOR
> Reactions to the impending disaster
> polarized the world's emotions.

93A WHAT WE SEE IN THE HOLO IMAGE MIST
thru
93J (NOTE: consistent with production possibilities and stock footage.)

Rioting mobs. Fires. Pillaging. Battles in streets. People going mad with sybaritic abandon. Catatonia, violence, people weeping, suicides, libertinism.

> HOLO NARRATOR (OVER)
> Most went mad or refused to accept
> the inevitable. But a sizable
> minority, comprised of scientists,
> artists, philosophers, technicians
> and humanitarians in the greater
> sense, decided to save a viable
> segment of the Earth's population
> for a seeding program on other
> worlds.

> CONTINUED:

Phoenix Without Ashes 139

A council of kindly and concerned men and women, sitting and talking, others planning, drawing up diagrams, in deep conversation,
clearly "getting it together."

>   HOLO NARRATOR (OVER)
>   (CONTINUED)
>   To this end, they began to build the
>   Ark. Humanity had had space travel
>   for three hundred years, since the
>   first moon landings in A.D. 1969. But
>   settlement was sparse on Mars and
>   Venus, the only two nearer worlds
>   capable of sustaining life as
>   humankind knew it.

Flashes of Apollos landing, replicas of the Solar System, domes on Mars
and Venus and astronomical shots of those worlds from space. Then
shots of the colder, less pleasant planets—Mercury boiling, Saturn
bombarded by meteors from its rings, Jupiter cold and hostile, etc.—
and then shots of deep space.

>   HOLO NARRATOR (OVER)
>   (CONTINUED)
>   Humankind as a whole wanted no part
>   of the difficult and hostile worlds
>   of the Solar System; further,
>   Vastator would destroy Mars and Venus
>   as well as the Earth. The Solar
>   System clearly could no longer sustain
>   humanity.
>   (beat)
>   So the concerned few began the most
>   monumental construction project ever
>   undertaken by humans.

Shots of the construction of the Ark. In deep space, between the Earth
and the Moon, the Ark begins to take form as construction crews work
on the superstructure, and space tugs bring in more materiel.

>   CONTINUED:

HOLO NARRATOR (OVER)
(CONTINUED)
Between Earth and the Moon, they
began to build the Ark.
(beat)
One thousand miles long—over 1600
kilometers—5,280,000 feet in length
—an organic unit, a clustering of
separate globular environmental domes
called biospheres, each one at least
fifty miles in diameter, were linked
by tubular corridors that carried life
support, power, communications, and
other systems.

DEVON'S VOICE (OVER)
The bounce tubes.

We see all of these elements in RAPID DISSOLVES in the holo mist.
And as each element is described, it is examined quickly but
thoroughly, providing the viewer with a clear understanding of the
Ark and how it is constructed.

HOLO NARRATOR (OVER)
The Ark resembled nothing so much as
a cluster of grapes, and into the
four hundred and fifty biosphere
domes were put entire ecologies, whole
segments of the Earth's population,
in their natural ethnic states.

We see this. Black societies from Morocco and Malawi, Danish and
French communities, slices of the American West, circa 1888, fishing
communities, Eskimo societies, highly technological urban cities, even
Devon's own home biosphere.

HOLO NARRATOR (OVER)
(CONTINUED)
And once stocked with a supercargo
of three million humans and all they
would need to sustain them on a
CONTINUED:

centuries-long journey to the
nearest star, Alpha Centauri, and its
planetary system, the Ark was launched.

The launching. The slow and stately movement of the Ark as its CTR drive (Controlled Thermonuclear Reactor) sends it on its way.

> HOLO NARRATOR (OVER)
> (CONTINUED)
> Supercargo was kept isolated from
> crew in hopes that each world would
> develop its own way, preserving the
> best of its heritage without undue
> influence from a hierarchy that
> might arise from crewmembers and
> technicians. The crew was housed
> in domes around the outer perimeter
> of the cluster, ethnic biospheres
> in the center.
> (beat)
> The Ark traveled for one hundred
> years and then there was indication
> of a difficulty . . . there was an
> Accident . . . this Accident was . . . there
> was . . . the Accident destroyed . . .

As the Holo Narrator reaches this point in her narrative, the images fade and the little woman reappears. But her VOICE grows DIM, her IMAGE FADES, pulses in and out, begins to break up, and then, suddenly . . . is gone. Only the mist is left, sparkling with scintillas of light.

94   ON DEVON

as the image vanishes. He grows excited, tries to get the image to reappear.

> DEVON
> An Accident . . . *what* Accident? Tell
> me! Come back, please come back!

> CONTINUED:

But the cube is dead. It can say no more. Devon rushes back to the cube rack but cube 43 was the last one cut by the memory bank. He turns to the grille.

> DEVON (CONT'D.)
> Hey!

> GRILLE VOICE
> Yes, sir, may I help you?

> DEVON
> The cube stopped.

> GRILLE VOICE
> Its message was complete, sir.
> Have you consulted subsequent
> cubes?

> DEVON
> There aren't any. That was the
> last one.

> GRILLE VOICE
> Then that's all there is, sir.

> DEVON
> But she said the Ark traveled
> in space for a hundred years and
> then something happened that
> caused all this damage . . .

> GRILLE VOICE
> (expecting him to
> continue)
> Yes, sir?

> DEVON
> What was it?

> GRILLE VOICE
> I have no idea, sir. That isn't
> my function.

CONTINUED:

                    DEVON
                 (quickly grasping
                   the situation)
            Whatever it was, it must have
            killed the crew and everyone who
            was outside the biospheres.

                  GRILLE VOICE
            Why do you say that, sir? I make
            no extrapolative judgments.

Devon is, for the first time in his life, assimilating and synthesizing
random data, making conclusions that are highly extrapolative and
far-reaching. We can see him not only becoming excited and distraught at what he's doing, but growing, becoming an adult before our
very eyes.

                    DEVON
            Because . . . wait a minute. What year
            is this?

                  GRILLE VOICE
            Earth dating, sir?

                    DEVON
            Yes. The A.D. you mentioned.

                  GRILLE VOICE
            This is A.D. 2785, sir.

                    DEVON
                  (ponders)
            The Ark traveled for five hundred
            years without any communication
            between the biospheres. And we all
            forgot we were on a ship. We forgot
            the cataclysm, and the Accident,
            whatever it was . . . we forgot the
            Earth. We lived as if our world
            was fifty miles wide with a metal
            roof . . .

                              CONTINUED:

GRILLE VOICE
That seems very unlikely to me,
sir.

DEVON
No, don't you see!? We are like
prisoners, we were born and died in
our little domes and never knew
the stars were out there.
(beat)
I have to *tell* them!

There is the sound of computer thinking in the b.g. from the grille.
Devon starts away, putting his suit back on, as the grille stops him.

GRILLE VOICE
Excuse me, sir.

DEVON
Yes?

GRILLE VOICE
I have computed all that you have
given me as input, sir. My storage
and reasoning banks have synthesized
your conclusions, and I am required
to tell you that there is a 46 percent
probability that you have drawn a
correct series of conclusions.

DEVON
Thank you.

GRILLE VOICE
If you are correct, sir, there is
one more thing you need to know.

DEVON
What is it?

GRILLE VOICE
Astrogation and chart-plotting

CONTINUED:

sections have fed me current
data, sir.
                    (beat)
This Ark is off-course, sir. It
is programmed on a course that
will take it into the heart of a
star-sun if the course is not
corrected.

Devon is confused, and horrified at the same time.

                    DEVON
What does that mean?

                    GRILLE VOICE
The Ark will be destroyed and all
aboard will die, sir.

                    DEVON
When? How soon? How much time
is there?

                    GRILLE VOICE
At our present rate of progress, sir,
astrogation estimates just under five
Earth-years.

Devon slumps against the memory bank. His head is whirling. He has
learned so much, so quickly. HOLD Devon for several beats as he
integrates all this. Then he is clearly gripped by a firm resolve, straight-
ens, and fastens the teardrop bubble to his suit.

                    DEVON
I've got to warn them, get them
to remember, get them to turn the
Ark . . .

He starts away. Then stops. Returns to the grille.

                    DEVON
Thank you, whoever you are.

                              CONTINUED:

146   *Harlan Ellison*

                    GRILLE VOICE
          It is my function, sir. No thanks
          are necessary.

                    DEVON
          Tell me just one thing more, if
          you can.

                    GRILLE VOICE
          If I can, sir.

                    DEVON
          What does "Vastator" mean?

                    GRILLE VOICE
          I will draw on LANGUAGES cube number
          thirteen, sir.
                    (beat)
          "Vastator," Latin, for "Destroyer."

Devon reacts. Then he turns and goes back to the sealed lockport
leading to the first of the many access tunnels he must use to retrace
his steps. He opens it, and steps over the rim. It reseals behind him and
CAMERA TRACKS BACK to the Grille.

                    GRILLE VOICE
          If you still remain here, sir,
          you should know those you wish to
          warn will not honor you for the
          knowledge. Good luck, sir.

HOLD THE GRILLE for a moment, then

                                        DISSOLVE TO:

95   SAME AS 83

in the tunnel leading away from the memory bank library. Atmosphere now, because Devon has equalized the pressure, but still no
gravity. He floats smoothly and quickly down the tunnel, goes around
the bend as CAMERA GOES WITH in the orange glow. Now he comes
to the place where the woman and the water were floating. The body
still hangs there, but now it is hideously decomposed.

                              Phoenix Without Ashes   147

96   CLOSE ON CORPSE

as its hideous decomposition plays keynote to Devon's feelings. *This* is
Humanity's fate, if he doesn't succeed in alerting the supercargo of the
Ark to their danger. Devon swims past, water beading on him then
being swept off as he continues past and CAMERA GOES WITH.

97   SERIES OF TRAVELING SHOTS—WITH DEVON
thru
100   as he retraces his trail through the access chambers, the viewport, into
the original bounce tube, and finds the mechanism to reverse the wind
that sweeps one along. He has now shed the spacesuit, having hung it
back in its case. And he lets himself be lifted by the bounce tube and
whirled away from us, back to the Iris that gives onto Cypress Corners.
Long shots of him spinning away from us and GO WITH till he reaches
the point of his origin.

101   WITH DEVON—INT. IRIS

he is deposited softly, and fumbles with the lock mechanism. It opens
slowly, with difficulty. But finally it dilates and Devon pulls himself up
out of the Iris.

102   INT. THICKET—DAY

as Devon emerges from the ground. He closes the Iris and covers it
after a moment's thought. We don't know why, but his manner indicates it is a good idea, just to be on the safe side. He starts out of the
thicket.

103   MEDIUM SHOT—ARRIFLEX

as three men suddenly leap out of hiding on the hillside. They have
been waiting, lying in wait all the time Devon was "gone." One of
them is Micah. They struggle briefly, and one of the men hits Devon
a blow across the back of the head that dazes him, but does not knock
him out.

                    1st MAN
            Thee *knew*, Elder Micah!

                                        CONTINUED:

148   *Harlan Ellison*

                    2nd MAN
Lie thee silent and wait,
thou said. The heretic
will come from the place
of hiding!

                    MICAH
Now wilt he pay the penalty
for sacrilege.

                    DEVON
                    (dazed)
I have to tell you . . .

Micah slaps him.

                    MICAH
Thou wilt say naught, child
of evil. Thy fate awaits
thee.

                    DEVON
My fate? What are you going
to do . . . ? I have to tell
you about the Ark . . .

                    MICAH
We do what must be done to
all who blaspheme and bring
evil and rancor to our people.
                    (beat)
Thou wilt be tried and stoned
to death as befits your crimes!

HOLD ON DEVON'S TERRIFIED EXPRESSION as we

                    FADE TO BLACK:
                    and
                    FADE OUT.

            END ACT THREE

ACT FOUR

FADE IN:

104   INT. PLACE OF WORSHIP—DAY—CLOSE ON DEVON

who has been placed in the stocks. They are metal stocks, to be sure, with his hands and feet protruding from the formed titanium-alloy blocks, but they are clearly a note playing back on Salem and its horrors. CAMERA HOLDS DEVON for several beats till we see his situation clearly, then pulls back to FULL SHOT of the Place of Worship. The metal pews are filled once again, the circle design gleams on the rear wall, Micah stands at his lectern, the Creator's Machine is unveiled. The stocks are on the podium beside Micah. Rachel and her family, Garth and his, sit down front prominently. The VOICE of the COMPUTER echoes through the holy place.

> COMPUTER
> Analysis of evidence presented
> in prosecution of factor coded:
> Devon computes in name of the
> Creator. Decision: final
> elimination of factor from gene
> pool, effective instantest.

Devon reacts violently, struggling vainly against the stocks.

> DEVON
> *He* told it to say that! Micah
> told it! There's a cassette,
> with his voice . . .

He looks across at Micah who, hidden by the lectern, holds the cassette Devon removed in Act One. Micah smiles a smile of total and final triumph. Devon's features fall, and he realizes he is done for. Micah turns to his Congregation.

> MICAH
> Thou hast heard the Voice of the
> Creator. Let this child of sin
> be taken from this Place of
> Worship and be stoned to death
> in the center of town.

105   ANGLE ON DEVON

as he screams his outrage and fury.

> DEVON
> Let me speak! I want to be
> heard!

> MICAH
> From the mouth of an heretic
> we will hear no further words
> of dissension and wickedness!

106   ON FAMILY OF GARTH

as Garth stands. He looks at Devon and then Micah, then turns to the
Congregation.

> GARTH
> As principal in this affair,
> as one slurred by the accused,
> I request he be heard. Every
> man should have his final say.

He sits, and his Father, OLD GARTH, puts a hand on the young man's
arm. He is pleased. We see a link between these two, a link that will
motivate Garth in the future episodes. The Congregation stirs, then
one and another CROWD VOICE is heard, agreeing, ad lib.

> MICAH
> Be it upon thy heads.
> > (beat; to
> > Devon)
> Young Garth hath spoken out
> for thee. Let thy calumny
> against him be in thy heart
> as thee meet thy reward.
> > (beat)
> Speak, if thee wilt.

107   CLOSE ON DEVON

as he tries to order his thoughts to speak most tellingly.

CONTINUED:

> DEVON
>
> This world of Cypress Corners, that
> you take to be only fifty miles
> wide . . . it is more than that. It is
> part of a greater whole. We are
> but one world among many, hundreds
> of others. All joined on a great
> Ark of space, moving through a
> greater universe of suns and worlds
> and emptiness; on a journey planned
> six hundred years ago . . .

Micah is horrified. Such blasphemy is intolerable! The Congregation is amazed and restless.

108 MICAH

as he rushes to Devon, slaps him soundly in the face.

> MICAH
>
> Stop! I will have no more of
> this! Thy outrages of heresy
> go beyond bounds of mercy!

> DEVON
> (continues undaunted)
> We are in a ship, a great ship
> built by *people!* Not the Creator,
> not a god in the machine, but
> *people*, like us. Our ancestors,
> who tried to save us from the death
> of the Earth . . .

> MICAH
> (screaming)
> Take him! Take him now!

Elders in evil black garb erupt from the Congregation and rush to the podium, to unlock the stocks. But even as they struggle with Devon, he continues shouting his story.

> CONTINUED:

152 *Harlan Ellison*

DEVON

I've seen it! I've been there,
outside Cypress Corners, outside
this world. I've been there and
back . . . we're doomed, we'll all
die if we don't . . .

Micah steps over as they free him, struggling, from the stocks. With
one full fist swing he knocks Devon out without mercy or worry that
he may kill with the blow. Devon sags and is gone.

MICAH

When he regaineth his senses,
then, at last light or first
light, the stones of the land
will end his vileness for all
and good!

HOLDING MICAH in all his messianic wrath, the Elders drag Devon
out behind them, his arms outstretched like a man being hauled to his
crucifixion; the parallel should not be lost on us.

DISSOLVE TO:

109   INT. FORGE—LATE DAY—WITH GARTH & FATHER

Young Garth sits disconsolately. His father comes in and sets down a
plowshare. He stares at his son.

OLD GARTH

Thy pain touches me, son.

GARTH

I do not hate Devon, father.

OLD GARTH

It should be so. He was thy
friend through thy childhood.

GARTH

I cannot take part in the stoning.

OLD GARTH

Thy family's honor, son.

CONTINUED:

GARTH

I cannot, father. Please be
with me in this.

OLD GARTH

Is there more thee would tell me,
things I must know to support thee
in this break with tradition?

Garth hesitates. He gets up, paces, finally turns to his father, and there
is clearly love between them.

GARTH

I do not love Rachel, father. I
have never loved her.

OLD GARTH

Thee wert promised at birth. Thy
will must play no part in this.

Garth hangs his head. He doesn't know how to reveal all that lies in
his heart: all the pain, all the confusion.

110   ANOTHER ANGLE—FAVORING GARTH IN SHADOWS

He searches for a way, finally comes to terms with his desire to reveal
all to this good man who is his namesake.

GARTH

Father, Rachel loves Devon. I
have known this always. And he
would die for her. How can I
stand between them when I care
nothing for Rachel save as
friend? Is this not evil, too,
father? Please: I must know.

OLD GARTH

(comes to him, holds
him warmly)
We are told, my son. We are told
by those who know how we should

CONTINUED:

154   *Harlan Ellison*

live. By the Elders who listen
to the Voice of the Creator's
Machine, who care for us and make
our yield full and our lives
pure. We must listen to them,
Garth.

                    GARTH
Then I will marry Rachel, and Devon
will die for loving her.

                  OLD GARTH
If that is the Creator's will, yes.
                    (beat)
Perhaps thee should go to speak to
Devon, my son. Perhaps it will
ease thy pain.

Garth looks at his father. They embrace. Then Garth goes. HOLD on
OLD GARTH, filled with love and sadness for his son, suddenly become a man.

                                        DISSOLVE TO:

111   EXT. PENALTY SHED—SUNSET

ON THE WIRE-MESH WINDOW. Devon is there, looking out. He
speaks INTO CAMERA.

                    DEVON
You shouldn't have come.

112   FULLER SHOT—FROM RACHEL TO WINDOW

as she MOVES INTO FRAME and we see it is not Garth, but Rachel
who has come to see Devon.

                    RACHEL
It nears last light. They
will come for you.

                    DEVON
Why wouldn't you go with me
when I came to your house?

                                        CONTINUED:

RACHEL
You know.

DEVON
(wearily)
I know . . . I know . . . we all live
under the rule of the Elders.
And they're *wrong*, Rachel.
They're so wrong, you can't
know.

Then, hoping to pass on what he knows, he speaks with utter sincerity
and deep honesty.

DEVON
(CONTINUED)
Rachel, listen to me. I've been
out of this little fifty-mile
world. Everything I said in the
Place of Worship was truth. I've
seen wonders. The stars, and the
black of space, and all the size of
this great Ark we ride.

RACHEL
You're frightening me, Devon.
Perhaps they're right, perhaps you
are a child of evil.

DEVON
(with a special
look)
Do you believe that?

She hesitates, stares at him, then begins to tear up.

RACHEL
(softly)
I don't care if you are. I
love you.

CONTINUED:

Devon moves closer to the wire-mesh window. It is very sturdy, clearly impossible to break out of without massive help. We should see this.

> DEVON
> Rachel: listen to me: they are
> blind, they see only what they
> wish to see. As long as they
> are told what to do and their
> crops come in hardy, they don't
> care how the world is run. They
> are little people, and they are
> doomed because of their deification
> of ignorance.

> RACHEL
> Talk to me of us, Devon. There is
> no time . . .

> DEVON
> No! Listen, this is important,
> more important than either of us.
> (beat)
> The Creator was a metallurgist
> who devised ways for structuring
> the metal of the sky so it would
> never rust or corrode or fall . . .
> the Creator was an environmentalist
> who plotted our world and all the
> others on graphs so they would run
> for a thousand years without
> breaking down . . .

> RACHEL
> I don't know what these words mean!

> DEVON
> . . . the Creator was a philanthropist
> who knew he would die when the Earth
> died, and he gave all his wealth to
> set this metal Ark afloat in a sea
> of darkness. There was an Accident,
> CONTINUED:

Rachel, a terrible thing that killed
those who *really* ran the ship, not
the Elders, but *crew,* men and women
like us . . . and the Accident threw us
all back, like barbarians, and we
spent five hundred years becoming
what we are today . . . so much less than
what we *need* to be, to survive . . .

Rachel is terrified by all this. She has never heard half the words Devon uses so casually, not knowing he has heard them, learned them from a memory bank library cube hundreds of miles, hundreds of worlds away.

RACHEL

Stop! Please, Devon, you're
frightening me. I don't know
what to do . . . it's growing dark . . .

113   INTERCUT—THE SUN

(NOTE: Ben Bova has suggested a "sun" mechanism that offers visual excitement plus scientific validity. A digital sun, square or hexagonal, that operates exactly like a digital clock, in panels that run across a track set in the dome roof. Every fifteen minutes, one panel would click off and the next panel would click on. The sun would very literally move across the sky. During different seasons, the tracks would be closer to or farther away from the ground, providing different intensities of heat. In this way, Rachel could look up and actually see the sun click further down the sky.)

As it moves toward the horizon line, making for deeper sunset.

CUT BACK TO:

114   SAME AS 112

Devon is shaken. He cannot even convince the woman he loves that he has seen what he has seen. Wearily, he touches his fingers to the wire-mesh, and Rachel puts her fingers against them, separated by metal.

CONTINUED:

DEVON
You'd best go now. They'll
be coming soon. I don't want
you to see this.

RACHEL
Devon . . . my father . . . he, he says
I must cast the first stone.

DEVON
(inarticulate with
horror)
You . . .

He cannot contain himself. He flings himself away from the window.
Into the darkness beyond. Rachel stands for several beats, then turns,
head bowed, and goes.

115 ANGLE ON PENALTY SHED—SUNSET

we see a SHADOW there. Someone has been listening. The shadow
holds for a few beats, then disappears. There is a SOUND of the passage
of the one who cast the shadow, however, and as we HEAR THE
SOUND the CAMERA PULLS BACK RAPIDLY to INCLUDE RA-
CHEL as she COMES TO CAMERA, and turns to stare at the side of
the shed. Did she see who it was? She pauses but a moment, then goes
OUT OF FRAME as we:

DISSOLVE TO:

116 INT. SHED—SUNSET

Devon lies on a straw pallet. There is a SOUND from the window, and
as he lies there a crude grappling hook with many metal barbs strikes
the window, digs in, holds, and there is a vicious *wrenching* SOUND
as the wire-mesh window is ripped completely out of its frame. Devon
leaps to his feet, rushes to the window as CAMERA SHOOTS PAST
HIM. The street is empty. No one there, only the wire-mesh . . . not
even the grappling instrument. Devon hauls himself up to the opening, and falls through.

117   EXT. SHED—SUNSET—ON DEVON

as he falls out of the opening. He is on his feet, then, and racing away
toward the hills.

                                                            CUT TO:

118   TOWN CIRCLE—SUNSET

as the Congregation masses. The group is as large as we care to make
it. Piles of stones and rocks are everywhere. Clearly, they enjoy this
sort of sport.

                          MICAH
                Bring the heretic to meet his
                fate.

Two Elders move off quickly toward the Penalty Shed.

                          MICAH
                Where is Young Rachel?

                        OLD RACHEL
                Aram has gone for her.

                          MICAH
                Why is she not here now?

Rachel's mother is embarrassed.

                        OLD RACHEL
                This is difficult for her, Elder
                Micah. She has ne'er seen a
                stoning.

                          MICAH
                        (wrathful)
                Dost thou see, all! Dost thou
                see the seeds of impiety planted by
                this feckless child, Devon? Tonight
                we pray longer lest the wickedness
                take root in us all!

119   TRAVELING SHOT—WITH ELDERS—AWAY FROM CAMERA

as the blackness of their clothes recedes and we see them running into
the circle.

> 1st ELDER
> He be gone!

> MICAH
> Gone?! How gone, how—?!

> JUBAL
> The window be torn loose. He
> has fled.

> MICAH
> Found him once did we . . . find him
> again we shall . . . ! Get torches!

The mob mills and breaks and starts running in all directions at once,
getting cudgels and staves and scythes and torches.

> CUT TO:

120   EDGE OF TOWN—WITH ARAM & RACHEL

as he drags her, squealing and protesting, toward the town circle,
unaware of what has transpired.

> ARAM
> Most spiteful daughter! Come!
> Thy silliness wilt not cast thy
> father and mother in contempt
> in the eyes of the Congregation.

> RACHEL
> Father, *please*, no, father, please!

He drags her. She falls, and he drags her in the dust, determined she
will not disgrace him. Suddenly, from OUT OF THE FRAME, a fist
lashes out and connects with Aram's throat. He goes down, clutching
his throat, and as CAMERA PULLS BACK we see it is Devon. He grabs
Rachel from the dust, and they take off toward the hills at a dead run.

> CONTINUED:

Aram recovers slowly, then gets to his feet and rushes toward the town circle, screaming for help.

> ARAM
>
> Help! Help! He has taken her!
> The heretic is loose, he has
> taken my daughter.

121 TOWN CIRCLE—FULL SHOT

CAMERA IN TO TIGHT ON MICAH AND ARAM as the latter rushes in, shrieking.

> ARAM
> (CONTINUED)
>
> He has escaped. The whelp has
> broken free and taken Rachel.
> They go to the hills.

Young Garth now enters the FRAME. Micah turns to him with anger.

> MICAH
>
> And where wert thou?

> GARTH
>
> Coming here.

> MICAH
>
> Didst thee hear what hast
> transpired?

> GARTH
>
> Yes. I heard.

> MICAH
>
> And what wilt thee do to save
> thyself and thy family from
> disgrace.

Garth looks across and CAMERA GOES WITH HIS POV showing his father. Old Garth stands clear-eyed, allowing his son to make his own decision. He is a man now.

> CONTINUED:

GARTH
(after several
beats)
I will find Devon and slay him
or bring him back for the
stoning. I will bring Rachel
back to be my bride.

Micah seems pleased. Old Garth isn't so sure. But they all move out now. Garth goes to get his crossbow as CAMERA STAYS WITH HIM and we see the mob go one way as Garth enters the forge, emerges a moment later with the metal crossbow and a quiver of quarrels. He takes off in another direction . . . but all head for the hills, with torches burning.

CUT TO:

122   EXT. HILLS—WITH DEVON & RACHEL

as they run CAMERA GOES WITH THEM. Take time with this. Show them fleeing in panic and Rachel coming along without being dragged. Quite a comparison to the manner of her acquiescence when her father had her.

123   SERIES OF ANGLES
thru
125   ON THEM RUNNING—INTERCUT WITH MOB RUNNING—IN-
TERCUT WITH GARTH RUNNING

126   EXT. THICKET—HILLSIDE

as Devon and Rachel fall into the thicket that contains the Iris. They fall exhausted, and take a few moments to get their breaths.

RACHEL
Oh, Devon, run! Hide, they
will be after us.

DEVON
Come with me.

She is startled by the thought. She has never had to confront it.

CONTINUED:

Phoenix Without Ashes   163

RACHEL

Where? Oh, they'll find us no
matter where we go. It's only
fifty miles. They'll search
till they find us.

DEVON

They'll *never* find us. Rachel,
you must believe in me, you must
trust me: there is something at
stake here that you can't know.
All this—
          (he waves a hand)
—this is nothing against what
we have to do. The way they
live, they'll never help . . . and
we have to *find* help, Rachel—
somewhere on this Ark there are
people who will help us!

RACHEL

You're saying strange things again.

Devon knows he can't convince her with just words. He reaches down
into the rubble, tosses it away and finds the broken latch. He helps her
to her feet.

DEVON

Step away. Look.

He kicks the latch. The Iris yawns open. Rachel gives a shriek as we

CUT TO:

127   GARTH

on the far side of the thicket, far enough away to have to circle to get
to them. He hears the shriek and slips a bolt into his crossbow, pulls
back the thick string with enormous power from heavily-muscled
arms. We should note the power of those arms, if not earlier, then
certainly at this point. He moves toward them through the thicket.

CUT TO:

128   ANGLE ON RACHEL & DEVON

as she stares in disbelief at the open Iris. The SOUND we heard earlier
from the Iris begins . . . the blue light shines out . . . the wind begins.

RACHEL
Devon . . . what . . .

At that moment, Garth plunges through the thicket toward them.
They see him as the bolt strikes close by Devon's head in the thin bole
of a bush, shattering the bole.

129   ANGLE UP FROM INSIDE IRIS

bathed in blue light, we see Rachel and Devon at the edge. They turn,
see what lies behind them, see what is coming toward them, and
suddenly Devon grabs Rachel and pulls her with him into the opening.
They FALL PAST CAMERA and are gone as the Iris begins to close.
At the last moment before it seals, we see Garth through the opening,
looking in.

130   EXT. THICKET

as Garth stands in the hurricane wind that whips up the leaves and
rubble, once again covering the Iris. He stands there staring, con-
founded, confused, unable to grasp what he has seen. Then he turns
and goes.

CUT TO:

131   SAME AS 36

this time with Rachel being pulled along with Devon. HOLD THIS
SHOT as they fall away from us, spinning out and away from Cypress
Corners.

132   SERIES OF TRAVELING SHOTS—WITH RACHEL & DEVON
thru
135   as they travel through the bounce tube corridor, Devon steadying
Rachel.

as they reach the end of the tunnel and slow and stop. Floating there, Devon holds Rachel steady and speaks to her for the first time since the Iris opened aboveground.

> DEVON
> Now do you believe me?

> RACHEL
> Where are we? What is this?
> What's happening . . . ? Devon!

He holds her and they revolve slowly in the gravityless bounce tube, washed by blue light.

> DEVON
> It's all right. You'll learn
> as I learned. We have a long
> journey ahead of us . . . but not
> nearly as long as we've made
> already.

> RACHEL
> Garth. He . . .

> DEVON
> He knows about the bounce
> tube. He'll come after us.
> They'll *make* him come.

> RACHEL
> I don't think so, Devon.

> DEVON
> Elder Micah will tell him his
> family's honor is at stake.
> He loves his father too much to
> risk their status.

> RACHEL
> He may.

CONTINUED:

                    DEVON
          Rachel, we can't live in dreams
          any more. I learned that. What
          we have to do means no more
          dreams . . .

                    RACHEL
          It was Garth who freed you.

Devon stares at her. SOUND OVER we HEAR the special shriek of the
wire-mesh window being pulled free, as if by the power of great muscles . . . Garth's muscles. Devon dwells on it a moment. Then he
reaches for the lock to the

          ACCESS TUBE   SERVICE MODULE

As it opens, he helps Rachel move toward it, and says:

                    DEVON
          Perhaps you're right. He may
          not come after us. I hope
          you're right. Garth could never
          accept what you're about to see.

They pass over the rim into the access tube, and as the port closes
behind them, the last things we hear are:

                    RACHEL
          What will you show me, Devon?

Several beats as the metal closes across and . . .

                    DEVON
          The Universe.

The port closes and we stare at metal implacability.

                              FADE TO BLACK:
                              and
                              FADE OUT.

                    END ACT FOUR

                              Phoenix Without Ashes 167

TAG

FADE IN:

137   TOWN CIRCLE—NIGHT—THE MOB

as Garth comes into the circle. Micah, Jubal, Old Garth, Aram, Old
Rachel and Garth's Mother prominent in the crowd.

>   MICAH
> They have escaped.

>   GARTH
> Devon has escaped.

>   MICAH
> Thy intended with him.

>   GARTH
> Yes. Both gone.

>   MICAH
> We must search the hills.
> All of us.

>   GARTH
> No.

>   JUBAL
> Devon cannot be permitted to
> roam free.

>   MICAH
> The faithful must smite him.

>   GARTH
> I'll find them.

>   OLD GARTH
> Not alone, my son. We go with,
> to lend thee strength.

CONTINUED:

GARTH
(kindly)
Father, I honor thee, but I must
go on this search alone.

They all stare at Garth. Micah moves to say something, but Old Garth, in a strong gesture—perhaps the first he's ever made against an Elder —puts a hand on his shoulder and stops him. They all watch as Garth looks deeply into his Mother's face, then his Father's. They touch hands, and then Garth—crossbow slung—walks out of the village. Torches flicker behind him as CAMERA RISES FOR FULL SHOT of the young man going toward the hills, the mob trapped forever in their terrible little world and the CAMERA PULLS UP AND UP AND UNFOCUSES as it passes through the metal bulkhead of the sky and we

LAP-DISSOLVE TO:

138   EXT. BULKHEAD—MOVING BACK

CAMERA REFOCUSES and keeps pulling back and back from the metal bulkhead till we see it is part of the outer dome skin. CAMERA BACK to FULL SHOT OF DOME and BACK AGAIN till we see the entire Ark. CAMERA KEEPS GOING BACK to show all of space, and back and back till the frame fills with the universe, with only that small speck of light that is the last hope of humanity, lost perhaps forever in the deeps of an eternal night.

FADE TO BLACK:
and
FADE OUT.

THE END

Working in television is frequently akin to birthing a thalidomide baby. The monstrosities that appear on the tube bear little relation to the creature that first emerged, clean and whole, from the scenarist's imagination. Such was the case with "Phoenix Without Ashes."

In 1973, utilizing the common coin concept of the "enclosed universe" story, I devised a television series called The Starlost. *There isn't space here (or inclination on my part) to detail the horrors attendant on the production of that ill-fated series. It ran a mere sixteen episodes, thank God, and was canned by NBC. I could not have been more relieved. So awful was the production, that I removed my name from the show and used my intentionally insulting pseudonym, "Cordwainer Bird." I walked away from an enormous amount of money when I quit the show, but it was worth it to retain my sanity and my integrity.*

(The full story of what went down on that show, from birth to death, can be found as the introduction to a novel also titled Phoenix Without Ashes, *adapted from the script you have just read by Edward Bryant. It is a Fawcett Gold Medal paperback. I offer this comment not as free plug, but merely to satisfy the morbid curiosity of those for whom these brief remarks seem only tantalizing. Besides, Ed wrote a helluva book, and for 95¢ you can't go wrong.)*

My original script—which you've just glommed—was hideously rewritten for airing. This was the untouched version, and I'm quite proud of it; had it been taped as I wrote it, the show might still be on the air . . . though I doubt it: the people involved with the show were masters of disaster. I've often thought they were the former crew on the Hindenburg, *the* Titanic, *the* Andrea Doria *and the ones responsible for the Bay of Pigs invasion. In short, dips.*

But now, the script is in print as I wrote it, with my wits about me and with considerable love. Perhaps that shows through, and if it does, and if you perceive same, then maybe, just maybe, you'll become aware of the quality of material you could be seeing, if you'd demand it of the networks.

If you fail to see any difference between this script and, say, a rerun of Gilligan's Island, *then you'll never know what I'm talking about, and the painful memories showing through even these few words will not reach you.*

As I said, working in television can be a killer.

HARLAN ELLISON

THE EVENT HORIZON

IAN WATSON

The mechanistic clockwork universe of "common sense" has been pushed through the looking glass, and the March Hare seems to be leading the new scientific revolution, a revolution that is presently rocking the very foundations of physics and astronomy. Albert Einstein let loose the daemons of this Alice-In-Wonderland universe when he introduced the concept of "time-dilation" in 1905, a notion that certainly did not make common sense.

He laid "common sense" to rest, calling it "a deposit of prejudice laid down in the mind before the age of eighteen."

The most recent, and most bizarre, manifestation of "Einstein's rabbit" is the Black Hole, *a star that collapses under its own gravity until it disappears, as if squeezed out of existence. In his book* Black Holes: The End of the Universe? *(Random House), John G. Taylor says that "The part of space very close to the star becomes so curved by the enormous gravitational attraction around the star that it becomes completely closed off from the rest of space. Nothing that is inside the closed-off region can ever escape out into the rest of the world. . . . However, this trapped region is still accessible to the unwary traveler from outside. . . . Thus the separation of inside from outside is only of a one-way nature. That is why the trapped region is called the 'event-horizon'—nothing happening inside can ever be communicated to the outside."*

But perhaps man's imagination can devise a means to return from such an "event-horizon." Indeed, he might even find his way out of the Black Hole by coupling his technology to his lusts and poetry.

172

For the second time in three years the starship *Subrahman-yan Chandrasekhar* sailed for the Black Hole that was the blind eye of the binary system Epsilon Aurigae, with the Arab telemedium Habib on board.

At about the same distance from the bright supergiant that is the visible partner of the system as Pluto from the Sun, they reached their destination. Officers and scientists crowded the nacelle beside the lounge to stare into space at something they couldn't see except insofar as it bent light from the background stars around itself in an annulus of secondary ghost images.

The Hole itself was nothing—literally. Even the fabric of space was missing, there.

A nova is fearful, a supernova, awe-inspiring. Yet their ravening energies are a creative mainspring of the galaxy, spewing out heavy elements for new stars and planets. They are positive energies. The mind can grasp them. But the Black Hole is all negative—the emptiness of the void multiplied a million times into something infinitely greedy. A star collapses under its own gravity, disappears from the universe and leaves a whirlpool of nothingness behind it. Anything falling into the hole—no matter how well protected it is, no matter if it is powered by the energy of a thousand suns—is trapped forever. The Black Hole is Death the Conqueror.

The Hole in the Aurigae system had already been located from Earth in the twentieth century by its periodic eclipses of its yellow supergiant partner every twenty-seven years; however it wasn't till the mid-twenty-third that a starship brushed by it.

Then, something more incredible than the Hole itself was found—a living being trapped inside it.

The growth of Psionics Communications—the telemedium system—made the discovery possible. Instantaneous psi-force alone could enter a Black Hole and emerge again. But only if a mind was already present in there . . .

In the nacelle, along with the officers and scientists, were the two political officers from Bu-Psych-Sec—the Bureau of Psychological Security—Lew Boyd and Liz Nielstrom; Habib, who had first made contact with the mind in there; and a young Swedish girl on her first starflight, Mara Glas.

Habib stood out from the others by wearing traditional Arab costume: the *haik* and *aba* of the desert Bedouin. He wore the headdress and long full shirt with a striped white and blue mantle of camel-hair sacking pulled over it. By making a clown of himself in this way, parodying his uneducated nomad's origin, he made himself acceptable to the others and guarded the privacy of his feelings; another strategy was his carefully cultivated gutter humor. He was that freak thing, a mind-whore; and however essential he might be for communications and psychological stability, the telemedium was a reluctant actor in a perpetual dirty joke.

Psionics and sexual energy were the two great forces that Bu-Psych-Sec had learned to harness to bind starships safely to home-base Earth no matter how far they roamed. Through psi and sex, bonded together, Earth held her star fleet on the tightest leash, a leash rooted so deeply in the nervous system as to guarantee there would never be any defections to lotus worlds among the stars; nor more mundane lapses in her continual on-line monitoring of the farthest vessel.

As they stood in the nacelle, Mara Glas tried telling herself for the hundredth time that this was all for the good of everyone at home on Earth, and for the stability of civilization; that Bu-Psych-Sec had designed the safest, most humanitarian system compatible with star empire. So she had been programmed to believe at any rate, by days of lectures and subliminal persuasion.

But she never thought it would be like this, serving Earth's starship communications system. She never dreamed.

Naturally, the Black Hole was fair pretext for a bout of boisterous smut, if only to mask their fear of the phenomenon. The very name carried such blatant connotations of the trance room that Mara thanked her stars she wasn't born a Negress; felt pity for Habib's darker-skinned soul.

"There she blows!" crowed the chief engineer.

Ted Ohashi, the astrophysicist from Hawaii—a mess of a man, like a third-rate Sumo wrestler gone to seed—snickered back:

"That little mouth; she'll suck all the juice in the galaxy given half a chance."

"A suck job, that's good, I like it," laughed Kurt Spiegel, the leonine Prussian from Hamburg's Institut für Physik, boisterously. His wiry hair was swept back in a mane as though the abstractions of Physics had electrified it; though just as exciting to the man, in fact, was that other district of Hamburg around the Repperbahn, St. Pauli, where he got his relief from the enigmas of Schwarzschildian Geometry and Pauli Equations in the more down-to-earth contortions of the strippers going through their bump and grind routines for him, drunk on Schnapps, replete on bockwurst.

Habib made a point of joining in the merriment, while Liz Nielstrom flashed a grin of pure malice at Mara for failing to join in.

How the human race struggled against Beauty! Mara wept silently. How desperately they strove to make the Singular and Remarkable, dirty and shameful!

Mara was young. With the perpetual rush to draft telemediums into the Navy, and the fewness of those with the potential among Earth's billions, the Swedish girl was barely out of her fifteenth year before being drafted.

One thing she didn't know about Habib was the kind of debriefing Bu-Psych-Sec put him through after the first expedition when he reported the existence of that mind inside the Black Hole, to the incredulity of practically everyone in the Navy. They'd peeled his mind down like an onion at the Navy Hospital in Annapolis. They'd used strobehypno on him. Neoscopalamine. Pentathol-plus. Deepsee. It had been a harrowing, insane-making three weeks before they believed him. And it was another two years before the second expedition sailed.

But one thing she did know about him, that no one else did, was the utter difference between the image he presented publicly of a dirty street Arab, and the sense of his mind she had whenever they'd taken the psionic trigger drug, 2-4-Psilo-C, together, to cathect with Earth across the void. Then it was like a light being switched on in a dark room, and he was a different Habib—a Bedouin of the sands, a poet, and a prophet.

The people who rode the carrier beam of the teletrance never knew the pure beauty of the desert between the stars. All they got a sense of was the dirty urchin hanging round the oasis of far Earth, plucking at their sleeves and mumbling, "Mister, you want to buy my sister?" But Habib was the desert Bedouin too. Why did he always deny the desert beauty, out of trance?

Maybe this was the last lesson she had to learn—the final breaking in of the foal, to insure she could be safely graduated with flying colors and posted to some star frigate by herself.

Just then, strangely, as though he was reading her thoughts out of trance, Habib grasped her arm softly and whispered in her ear, with the voice that she'd longed to hear from his lips for the past three months—yet quietly, so that no one else could hear:

"Compared with the void of space, Mara, whatever is the void inside that thing?"

He asked her gently and eerily—as though the Mecca pilgrimage of their minds was at last underway and the furtive shabbiness of the caravanserais, the whores and beggary and disease, could be put behind them.

"It is so *solid* a void that 'here' and 'there' are meaningless words. There will be no referents in there, except those you yourself manufacture, Mara . . ."

But could she really trust this sudden shift from urchin to muezzin calling the faithful to prayer—or was it just another round in the game of cruelty?

"It's so dense in there that it must be like swimming through stone," Habib went on murmuring in her ear. "Yet even that comparison's no good, for *he* has no power to swim about his dwelling place—"

Puzzled, Mara stared out without replying.

The captain stepped into the nacelle a moment later—a thick-set, hard-headed grandson of Polish-German immigrants to America, who still had the air of being a peasant in from the country dressed in his best, ill-tailored suit, and who ran the ship with all the cunning and blunt persistence of the peasant making a profitable pig sale: this, alloyed to a degree or two in Astronavigation and a star or two for combat in some brushfire war in Central Africa stirred up by the draft board's "child-snatching." Immune to the wonders of space, Lodwy Rinehart barely glanced outside.

"May I have your attention a moment? We'll be sailing down to the ergosphere commencing twenty hundred hours—"

Ted Ohashi gobbled nervously:

"You mean *tonight*? Maybe we should fire a few drones near that thing first, to check the stability of the ergosphere—"

"After three months you want to hang back another few days? Maybe you want another session with Mara Glas in case you get killed and never know those joys again, is that it? Sorry, Dr. Ohashi. Twenty hundred, we're going right down on her up to the hilt."

"Just not too close," the fat man pleaded. "We could be sucked in, you know. Space is so bent there. No power could get us out then. Fifty nautical miles off the top of the ergosphere's fine by me, Captain!"

"Point taken, Dr. Ohashi," Rinehart smiled acidly. "That's also fine by me. 'Up to the hilt' was a just a colorful bit of naval slang. Need I spell it out for you?"

The German from Hamburg guffawed. "That's good, I like it, Captain."

The Hawaiian snickered dutifully too then, his fat wobbling in the starlight, but he was scared.

Mara shivered. Habib shrugged indifferently; by shrugging he hid his features in the shadow of the *haik* . . .

Space presents itself to the telemedium's mind in symbolic form. The mind can only see what it has learned to see, and it has certainly not learned to see light-years and cosmic rays and gravity waves. Therefore space must present itself in terms of symbols learned by the brain during the cognitive processes of life on Earth.

The symbols Habib presented Mara with were those of the desert Bedouin. Perhaps, taught by someone from her own part of the world, she would have learned to see the wastelands of the arctic tundra, the icefloes of the northern seas, or endless flows of forest. But Habib presented her with the golden desert —and for this she thanked him from the bottom of her heart, for its pure beauty had a wealth of heat and color—stark as it was—that awakened her Swedish soul to life, as the brief hot summer awakened her country from its wintry melancholy once a year.

She remembered so clearly the surprise of that first cathexis with Earth across the light-years, in company with Habib . . .

Every Navy man had the right *and duty* to cathect with Earth through the ship's telemedium. At the other end of the link would be a home-based telemedium ridden by one of Bu-

Psych-Sec's professional "Mermaids": forging what the Reichian-Tantric adepts of Bu-Psych-Sec liked to refer to as "libidinal cathexis" with Someone Back Home, therefore with Mother Earth herself.

The energies of the libido, bottled-up deliberately by sex depressive drugs until the time of trance, were unleashed upon the responsive nervous system of the medium in a copulation that was both physical and transmental. The energy that ejaculated thought impulses across the light-years through a symbolic landscape of the medium's own devising had been called different things at different times in history. In the twentieth century Wilhelm Reich named it Orgone Radiation. The Tantric sexual philosophers of Old India called it, more picturesquely, the Snake of Kundalini.

Reich had built crude machines to harness and condense this sexual energy that he believed permeated space. The Tantrics used yogic asanas to twist the body into new, prolonged forms of intercourse; they used the Om chant to make the nervous system a hypersensitive sounding board; and hypnotized themselves with yantra diagrams to send this energy soaring out of the copulating body through the roof of the skull toward the stars—toward some subjective cosmic immensity, at least.

Bu-Psych-Sec had rationalized and blended Reichian therapy with the Tantric art of love and yantra meditation. In its crash course for sensitizing the potential telemediums, much of this learning was force-fed hypnotically in deep sleeps from which the medium woke, haunted by erotic cosmic ghosts, to days of pep talks on such topics as "The Spaceman's Psychological Problems" and "The Need for Cultural Unity in an Age of Translight." Yet there could be no live test runs of the contact techniques till a novice was on his or her way, light-months from Earth with a supervisor medium, able to draw on the repressed sexuality of the crew to reach out to another medium at Bu-Psych-Sec, Annapolis. And every single trance-trip had to figure economically in terms of vital Navy information transmitted. Each crew member riding a medium was subliminally primed with data that the mermaid at the other end received the imprint of, to be retrieved by the drug Deepsee. The Annapolis data banks were thus constantly updated; and the data copied to other banks hidden deep in the Rocky Mountains.

Earth's Navy was not a string of ships, but an integrated nervous system spread out over thousands of cubic light-years.

Yet the doctrines of Reich and Tantra would have been nothing without the development of the trance drug 2-4-Psilo-C. It was an unforeseen spin-off from Bu-Psych-Sec's routine work on psychedelic gases for military and civil policing.

The two crew members who were going to ride Habib and Mara's bodies for the first liberty of the voyage stood twiddling their thumbs with sheepish sleazy grins on their faces, their anticipation of pleasure somewhat muted by the supercilious, sophisticatedly brutal aura of Lew Boyd and his assistant.

The previous Bu-Psych-Sec officer had been more of a therapist in the Masters and Johnson line, with less of the policeman about him. This man Boyd knew his Reich and Tantra inside out, but he carried the stamp of a trouble-shooter from the moment he joined the ship, along with that enigmatic bitch Liz Nielstrom. What kind of relationship had they been involved in before? Their degree of mental complicity indicated more than a mere working relationship. Yet they didn't seem to have been lovers in the ordinary sense. Rather, they appeared bound together by the cruel magic of their roles, this ugly woman and this smart cop, in a mutual indifference to sex itself except as an instrument of power. Sternly they reveled in the dialectic of the twin faces of authority, the repressive and permissive, gaining their private accord from the games they could play with this psychosexual coin. For them, the galaxy was a gaming table they could amuse themselves at, with the induced Tantric orgasms of others for chips. Professional croupiers of the cosmic naval brothel they were, dedicated to seeing that the Bureau always won, and hunting unendingly for cheats. (But who could possibly cheat? And how?)

There were two couches with encephalographic commune helmets at one end; these helmets swiveled to accept a prone or supine posture . . .

"You can get stripped, the four of you," Liz Nielstrom told them, glancing at her watch. "Earth's standing by."

One of the sailors shuffled about on his feet.

"Excuse me, ma'am, but who's riding the girl; do I get to ride her? I hear it's her first time out," he pleaded.

"It must be your first time too," Nielstrom responded sarcastically. "Since it makes not the least difference to you whether you're riding male or female."

"It's just the idea of it," the sailor mumbled. "So as I'll know afterwards—"

"Think what you like then, sailor. Believe it's her, not him, for all I care. But your request's out of order, and denied."

It was true that it made no difference . . .

Habib slipped off his *haik* and *aba*, and stretched out his slim knotty Bedouin body prone on the couch while Nielstrom was busy injecting the two naked sailors in their upper arms. They soon lolled upright in a stupor, awaiting the "Simple Simon Says" command.

Turning to Mara, she gestured the naked girl to take up a supine position on the other couch, where Boyd maneuvered her head carefully into the commune helmet as he had already done for Habib. He pricked her arm with the injection of 2-4-Psilo-C. While Nielstrom carried out her ointmenting of Mara's shaven sex, the light sensation of the other woman's fingers was already slipping away. In the dark of the helmet Mara concentrated her attention on the meditation pattern of the shri yantra diagram. This was an interweaving of upward-pointing and downward-pointing triangles, unfolding from around a central nub. The downward-pointing triangles were female; the upward, male. The central dot was the stored energy, compact in a bud.

Remotely, she heard Boyd give the command—his words slowed down and booming dully, like a tape played at the wrong speed.

"Simple Simon says, make love to Habib, Mr. Monterola! Simple Simon says, make love to Mara, Mr. Nagorski!"

(But it was Monterola who had wanted her.)

Libidinal cathexis started. Time drew further out for her. Distantly, she felt her central bud opening slowly to the man Nagorski's slow thrust. A clammy smell of sweat and the heavy pressure of a body on top of hers receded utterly from her awareness. The yantra opened up hugely, to reveal a vision of symbolic space through that sexual eye embedded in its heart.

The vision was a beautiful, wonderful thing, something that

preliminary training at Bu-Psych-Sec and all the jokes on shipboard had never hinted at . . .

There was a world of magic and beauty, after all. The dreams she'd dreamed as a girl were realities—but secret, hidden realities.

As the drug increased its effect, and Nagorski thrust into her, her sensitivity spread outward: the starship dissolved, her body dissolved, and her mind became a shining mirror seeking for mental images to reflect *out there.* She was conscious of the nearby presence of Habib; the sense of him varied between shining light and robed, hooded figure whose robes were like sails, like wings. She began to pick up speed together with him, till they were skimming over dunes and dunes of empty golden desert, hunting for the oasis of Earth.

"Beware of mirages," his mind whispered to hers. "Beware of pools that seek to reflect yourself—pools of illusion that would lock you up in their waters. You have to seek the far-off mirror that bears the imprint of another mind within it, like the hallmark on a piece of silver. That's the telecontact you must seek."

He was no dirty-fingered, runny-nosed urchin now; he was the desert hunter, the bird that flies to Mecca, the prophet in the wilderness.

It wasn't so far to Earth, that first cathexis: a half light-year or so. Oasis Earth was still nearby.

The flow of her sensitivity streamed above the empty, thirsty dunes, clutching at Habib's hem. Soon she was flowing into the crowded Oasis where so many streams mixed together, aiming at the tent where Habib beckoned her. Habib held the tent flap aside for her and they skimmed inside.

Her telecontact was a clear pool within the tent; a mirror with the hazy image of the shri yantra floating in it. The two mirrors came together, becoming screens for other minds to use.

The yantra image dissolved: it was no more than a call-sign. There was a time of calm and silence and clarity.

The telemedium was the mirror itself, not the image in the mirror; was the white wall, on which puppet shadows briefly danced and postured and copulated; was the vase of wine for others to get drunk at—but the vase itself doesn't get drunk; was the drum-skin—but not the sticky fingers tapping a rhythm out on it to set the player's nerves on fire . . .

Mara found herself whispering words to Habib: one slave whispering to another. The words she whispered were poetry.

> There stood upon auction blocks
> In the market of Isfahān
> A thousand and one bodies
> A thousand and one souls . . .
> The souls were like women
> The bodies were like men . . .

Habib, his own clear mirror pressed tight to the mirror of his telecontact beside her in the tent, heard. He asked:

"What are those words, Mara?"

"He was a poet in my own country, Sweden," she thought. "But he never lived in his own country, inside his mind. He lived in the East—in your East, Habib. He sang about the desert of the soul before it became real for a starcruising world."

"What was this man's name?" A hint of sincere curiosity reverberated in the question.

"Gunnar Ekelöf. He lived in the twentieth century—but inside his mind he lived in another time. Thank you, Habib, for showing me this desert. I understand his poems now . . ."

Then the mirrors were flying apart. Wind rushed out of the torn drum. They were both back in the desert outside the tent again, forced to fly home to their bodies. The sailors had climaxed. Their energy was vented. Their own commune helmets were switching the experience off. Time was up.

Mara and Habib flew back across the desert of golden dunes to the lonely, isolated caravan of the *Subrahmanyan Chandrasekhar*—a single camel plodding far out on the sand of stars . . .

As Mara woke up on the couch, the two sailors were already exiting from the trance room, grinning sheepishly. Spurning her tenderness, Habib was his dirty urchin self again.

Mara went back to her tiny cabin to weep her bewilderment.

Mara was Swedish for "little witch." But it was also Swedish for "nightmare" . . .

One month out from Earth, there'd been a discussion in the lounge about the Black Hole and the nature of the creature trapped in it . . .

"When we get there, we can fire particles into the ergosphere," Kurt Spiegel explained to an impromptu audience. "This ergosphere is the region between the so-called 'surface of infinite redshift' and the 'event horizon.' 'Infinite redshift' is the outer layer of the Hole where queer things really start happening. But there is still a possibility of extracting news from there. A particle is fired into the ergosphere; if it breaks up in there, part falls down the Hole, but the other part may pick up energy from the spin of the Hole and emerge into normal space again, where we can measure it. But beyond 'infinite redshift' is the terrible 'event horizon' itself. Geometry collapses, becomes meaningless. Thus there is no longer any way out, since there is *no way:* no up or down, no in or out, no physical framework. So that's the end of matter, radiation, anything falling in there. I believe we may find out something from the ergosphere—but beyond that, nothing. Anything else is impossible."

"So you believe that Habib is lying about the thing in there?" Liz Nielstrom demanded.

Habib sat silent, face half hidden by the *haik,* though Mara imagined she saw him smile faintly and mockingly.

"Look at it this way, Miss Nielstrom," Carlos Bolam intervened. He was a Chicano physicist who came from a desert region utterly unlike Habib's desert of the mind—from a Californian desert of freeways, drive-ins, hotdog stands, and neon signs. "Thought must be a function of some matrix of matter or organized radiation. It's got to be based on something organized. But by definition there's no kind of organization possible within a Black Hole."

Spiegel nodded.

"All organization is doomed, beyond the event horizon. The name means what it says. Events end there, and that's that. All identity is wiped out, even so basic a difference as that between matter and antimatter. There is only mass and charge and spin—"

"Isn't that sufficient to sustain a mind?" asked Liz Nielstrom, innocently.

Spiegel shook his mane brusquely.

"No, even granted a stripped-down kind of existence, this too only lasts a finite time till even this residue is sucked into an infinitely small point. You cannot have a mind organized on a point. That is like angels dancing on a pinhead. *Nonsense!*"

"I don't know about that," hazarded the fat Ohashi. "Maybe relativistically speaking we can contact this mind for a hell of a long time span, though from its own point of view it is rapidly approaching extinction—"

"But what happens to this collapsed matter when it reaches an infinitely small point, I ask you? I say it must spill out some-place else in the universe. Maybe to become a quasar. Maybe to form diffuse new atoms for continuous creation. This 'being' must *pass through* this hole. He cannot stick there—even if he does exist . . ."

"And you don't believe he does, Dr. Spiegel?"

"I don't think so, no."

"Well, Habib?" Lew Boyd demanded. "What do you have to say to that?"

Habib shrugged.

"We see the universe a different way. I have my symbols, he has his. Did Bu-Psych-Sec think I was lying? That wasn't a casual chat we had about the matter!"

"I suppose not," grudged Boyd.

"So." And Habib retreated back into his robes again.

"If there is a being in there," Ohashi pursued, "he must have some crazy ideas by now. I presume he fell in there by accident; didn't evolve in there. He'll have memories from sometime of a universe of length and breadth and height, but no evidence to back this up, no reliable sense impressions. It'll seem like a mad hallucination, a drug trip. Yet he might just be able to tell us what it's like in there subjectively—"

"To get information out of a Black Hole," snorted Spiegel, "is by definition impossible!"

"Maybe when one of us rides Habib in there—"

"Remember what happened to the sailor who was riding Habib last time? He died in there—and nobody knows why. I'm not riding Habib." Carlos Bolam stared bitterly at the Arab, and Mara thought she caught the hint of another cruel smile on Habib's lips.

"The man wasn't properly prepared for the encounter," Lew

Boyd stated ominously. "He thought he was going to meet a mermaid back on Earth, poor bastard. But we'll be keeping a tight eye on the trance this time."

Despite Boyd's grudging acceptance of Habib's story on that occasion, neither he nor Nielstrom showed any sign of trusting the telemedium. It was soon plain to Mara that some trap was being laid for Habib, though if Habib was aware of it he showed no sign of caring.

It puzzled Mara. If Bu-Psych-Sec were so unsure of Habib, why had they sent him out as ship's telemedium yet again? To the same place where a sailor had lost his life!

A couple of weeks after that discussion in the lounge, Boyd and Nielstrom were in there again interrogating the Arab, while Mara stood out in the nacelle, gazing at the redshifting stars receding from the ship and the violetshifting suns ahead of them: suns which she knew as a pure golden desert of dunes —and which she also knew, with a trace of pity, could never be seen as such by the majority of the human race. Perhaps peoples' crudity and violence were brought on basically by anger at their own limitations of vision?

"You went in there, Habib," she heard.

"In there, there is no 'there,'" said Habib elusively.

"We know all about this collapse-of-geometry business, but you still went *somewhere.*"

"True. I went to no-where—"

"If you went nowhere, perhaps there was *nothing* there?"

"True," smirked Habib. "No-thing."

"How do you make contact with *nothing, nowhere,* Habib? That's nonsense!"

"He lives in the midst of non-sense, where even geometry has gone down the drain—"

"*He?* If everything else is so damned uncertain, how can you be so sure of that thing's sex?"

"You have to use some pronoun . . ."

"Why not 'it'? It's only an alien *thing,* in there. It isn't human, Habib—"

"Even a thing must be allowed some dignity," muttered Habib.

"Interesting point of view," said Boyd.

"I don't see that it'll have much 'dignity,' " Nielstrom jibed. "When you isolate a human being in a sensory deprivation tank, he soon starts hallucinating. If you keep him in there long enough, he goes insane. What is the flavor of this thing's insanity, Habib?"

The Arab glanced down at the floor so that the *haik* hid his face.

He laughed.

"What flavor would you prefer? Vanilla? Chocolate? Raspberry?"

"That's not funny," snapped Boyd.

"Oh no, sir, I know how in earnest you are, I remember Annapolis."

"So answer! That being's a psychotic, isn't it? A fragmented mind—?"

"Psychosis," said Habib stiffly, "is a judgment within a context. But he has escaped from context. Geometry itself has collapsed. Two and two don't add up to four. The angles of a triangle may be anything from zero to infinity. It's the Navy who are the psychotics, from his point of view."

Habib abruptly raised his head and grinned; he stuck his thumb in his mouth and sucked it like a child sucking a lollipop.

He pulled his thumb out with a plop.

"Chocolate? Vanilla? Raspberry?" He smirked.

"It's all a question of *escaping* from context, isn't it, Habib?" Boyd demanded, furiously accenting that single word "escaping" and outstaring the Arab, till Habib dropped his eyes furtively.

The *Subrahmanyan Chandrasekhar* changed orbits at 20:00 hours to a circuit as low as they dared fly about the equator of the ergosphere, from where the other stars in the sky had their light warped freakishly into long blue worm-like streaks and spirals. But they were still safe enough, orbiting faster than the escape velocity from this zone, flying in a forced curve at great expense of power rather than allowing their orbit to be dictated to them by the local gravity.

Boyd and Nielstrom were waiting for Mara and Habib in the trance room.

"Change of plan," Liz smiled sweetly.

"New procedure," Boyd explained. "Our little witch will inject with 2-4-P-C on her own. You, Habib, will ride her in—"

"What in the name of—!" Habib recovered himself. "But Mara isn't ready. What a mad thing to do!" He paced up and down between the trance couches in a fury.

"So near and yet so far, eh?" laughed Boyd, enigmatically.

Habib argued; and the more he argued, the more pleased Liz and Lew seemed to be. They taunted him again about the sailor who'd lost his life inside the Hole.

"He poured like water through a sieve, eh, Habib? I wonder if he could have been poured out, deliberately?"

"That's impossible," gasped Mara.

"But think, what if the rider wasn't safe? Just imagine the implications for the Navy."

"A million-to-one accident," mumbled Habib, distraught. "I know I lost a rider in there. But what about the Bu-Psych-Sec man who rode in there after him? He didn't get hurt."

"He was able to switch off in time. He had the Tantric training to hold back from orgasm and withdraw when he saw there was nothing in the mirror at the end. So now you shall ride in there yourself as passenger and let us see what happens."

The Arab stared queerly at Mara.

"*Mekhtoub*," he muttered in Arabic, "it is fated. Poor little witch. May Allah be with you. May you not lose yourself, and me, in there."

"One more thing," added Boyd. "We want to keep in better touch with the medium through the trip." He indicated a slim gray machine, mounted on rubber rollers, backed up against the wall. Tendrils of wires sprouted from it, terminating in tiny suction pads.

"An electromyograph," he said, tapping the machine, "registers the minute voltage changes in the muscles associated with speech. There's always some element of subvocalizing in a trance. It only takes time and money to write a computer program to make some verbal sense of these electrical effects. So we've finally taken the time and spent the money. The electromyograph processes its data through the ship's main computer, so we can hear real-time speech."

Lew Boyd patted Mara in a patronizingly amiable way.

"Give us a running commentary, won't you, little witch,

while you're navigating your way through . . . whatever it is?"

Habib darted a look of horror at Mara—a horror she shared.

"Voyeurs!" cried Habib. "You vile peepers. That's the only privacy we have, our symbol landscape. That's our only dignity."

"A pilot scheme," smiled Boyd ingratiatingly, his hand lingering on Mara's shoulder. "It is our job after all . . . to know."

There was no golden desert visible now . . .

One great dune was all she could see—curling over at the top like a frozen Hokusai wave. The Black Hole warped her mind's view of the desert into this single, vast, static lip of sand . . .

No wonder Habib hadn't been able to find his way to Earth when this thing hung nearby, dominating the whole field of vision. Where stars were normally spread out as endless ripples of sand, the Black Hole was a whole warped desert in itself.

She hovered by a pure mirror pool, beneath the overhang of that awful cliff, and realized she was already at the event horizon, seeing the symbol of it in her mind.

The sand dune seemed to be falling in on her perpetually, like a breaker crashing; but in this frozen landscape of the mind—beyond events—nothing moved. Nothing could move when there was no "here," no "there."

Somewhere inside that blank mirror was the mind she'd been sent to find.

She had the barest sensation of Habib riding her, but couldn't get through to him to ask advice. Telemedium and rider had so little contact. Till now this had been the main consolation in being a Navy mind-whore. That, and the beauty of the desert. Now, it was frightening. She was so utterly on her own.

Another thing made her anxious. Was it she, or Habib, who was supposed to contact the mind in the mirror of the pool? Normally, it was rider who spoke to rider. But this mirror had no rider in it. She remembered something Habib had warned her about . . . the mirror of illusion that reflects yourself, that can trap you in it . . .

She knew so little and it seemed so strange and dangerous here.

Shortly afterward, in that timeless stasis, love dawned for Mara . . .

There was a consciousness—a presence in the mirror pool. A craving for Otherness. This being seemed so alone, and could love so deep.

But how could he reach out a hand to her, when he knew nothing of length and breadth and depth? She came from beyond the event horizon—but how could anyone come from beyond that?

"How can you *be?*" thought the mirror pool.

He couldn't show her his face. His body. He had none. But he could search in her mind for words, and make her lips whisper them.

Mara, torn away from her Swedish village of cool forest, clear lakes, goose honk, by Earth's Naval draft board, hadn't really awakened till now. The past three months had been such a false, horrid nightmare.

Words formed as he found the poetry in her soul. Her words —or the Other's? It didn't matter. There was emotional identity. And what's another word for that, but Love?

He cried:
"Outside, I should like to see
Your Inside
Outside, show me your Inside!
Outside, are you brave enough?"

And she replied:
"Inside, are you brave?"

He asked:
"That I should go outside myself
Who have only myself to be in
Is *that* what you demand?"

"Yes!" she cried to her lover.

What did those sailors and scientists know of this? With all their brash talk of Surface Velocities equal to the Speed of Light. Of Singularities and Strangeness! What did they know of true Singularity, those trashy men! With their Kruskal Coordinates for Schwarzschild Spacetime, what did they really know! With their tin starship flying outside the Surface of Infinite Redshift, far beyond the Event Horizon—beyond this lonely pool where time had frozen—how could they establish a relationship, locked outside as they were forever?

In the *Subrahmanyan Chandrasekhar,* her body lay in a trance . . .

> "The boat goes round and round," she sang,
> "In the circles of Day and Night
> But never do I lose my grip upon You.
> You
> Shall be my oar!"

What did those wretched scientists want her to do? Interrogate this being about his state of mind and how he saw physical conditions inside a collapsed star?

> "Could I
> Describe Height,"

she sang, to taunt the scientists and Bu-Psych-Sec officers, if they were spying on her voice successfully up there,

> "I would choose
> A star at the head
> A star at the feet
> And under the feet a mirror-image
> Concluding in a star."

They wanted to hear the secrets of a *black* Hole. Yet it wasn't black at all, but a startling pearly white, shimmering, opalescent, surrounded by that yellow lip of sand like a curling shell. It was the color of mother of pearl, set in gold. They wanted to know about Length and Breadth and Height? She sang out:

> "Could I describe Breadth
> I would choose an embrace
> Because I have senses
> False and primitive
> And cannot grasp what really Exists

There is no Star
Where your head is
There is no middle-point
Where your feet stand
But an inch of your loveliness
I have known."

They wanted to know about distances and measurements?
She shouted joyfully at the top of her voice:

"An inch of your loveliness
I have known!"

Mara felt the brush of the being's presence on her lips. And
then his images grew clearer—as though he had at last understood how to communicate himself, in his own thought forms,
rather than in poetry filched from her own mind. He made a
clearer and clearer statement of identity. Some of it totally
evaded her, presenting itself in mathematical or abstract alien
symbols she had no knowledge of—forged according to an alien
logic from a region where the laws of logic, and even mathemat-
ics, had been radically different from the logics devised by humans to suit a universe of elements coherently bonded together
into galaxies, stars and planets. But much came through. And
when he failed, his symbols hunted for some other means of
resonance within her. Concepts using the raw symbolism of her
own thought processes for internalizing sensations—tactile,
kinesthetic, erotic sensations—took the place of words then.

In this blend of words and formalized sensations, he coded his
message to her, presenting her with the Black Hole he inhab-
ited as the essential mode of existence; the shadow cast by
which constituted the "solid" universe of stars and planets.

He reversed the Real and the Unreal for her, till she knew the
joy of escape that Habib must have tasted three years earlier.

"Do you not know that *this* is the Real, the other the Unreal?
Let me tell you about the origin of things . . . Mara." His mind
reached below her name for the personal symbol cluster attached to it. "Dreamspinner . . . Shapechanger . . . Lady Riding
on a Stick Through the Starlit Night . . .

"The Energy Egg exploded *before* the start of 'things.' (By "things" I mean stars, starships, bodies.) It was not the Birth of Things. For a very short time there was a true physical universe—" She sensed him searching her mind for measurements of time. "It lasted . . . ten to the minus forty 'seconds,' by and large, this universe. Soon—and when I conceive 'soon,' I conceive a time long before that universe was one 'second' old— all that would later be 'matter' had already become a near-infinity of tiny 'black holes.' Space and Matter march hand in hand. But how could so tiny a volume of newly created Space contain so much hatched energy? It could not grow fast enough. The only way Space could expand swiftly enough to contain the hatching was by expanding inwardly, creating a myriad holes. That was the one and only mode that so much could exist in— holes. Each hole could be no larger than ten to the minus twenty-three 'centimeters'—"

"Numbers so small! I can't *feel* them. They mean nothing—"

"And of these tiny holes is all 'matter' made. Atomic particles are only a tightly bonded state of these; and in binding, these holes release huge energies. It was those energies, and their release, that powered the expansion of this thing you call 'universe'—*not* the hatching of the egg itself. Do you understand, Mara?" A touchless caress indicated the curve of the Hokusai wave, beyond which was a universe of stars, starships, bodies, and matter. "That is only a para-universe—a secondary cosmos you inhabit. You have crossed over into the no-place where Reality is. Another was here. How long ago? He would have joined me, but the illusion of matter dragged him back—"

"Habib . . ."

He reached below the name for its symbols: the Bedouin, the pilgrim to Mecca, the escapee from shabby caravanserais . . .

"Yes. It was him. But now you can join me. Will you join me, Mara?"

"Are you . . . God? You say you were there at the creation of things!"

"Is 'God' a creator of 'things'? I left before things began. I am not responsible for things." She sensed anger and frustration. "Things are only shadows cast by knots in the eternal, vital void that the true universe collapsed into. This is what hatched from the egg of being, not *that, out there*. This is the purpose of creation, not *that*. So join me, Mara, be free of illusion and be my bride—"

Are you a devil, then? she thought fearfully. She stared at the timeless pool, tasted his faceless kisses on her cheeks, his fingerless ruffling of her hair, in that place where the Hokusai wave hung like the ultimate battlement—not penning in the chaos of the Black Hole, but resisting the weak thrust of the silt of matter that had piled up against this mind's domain over aeons of spurious reality: stars, starships, bodies . . .

"But what are you?" she hesitated.

"I am the Lover," the answer came. "The All-embracing. There is no loneliness. But I invite you—"

She remembered the Tantric myth of Shiva and Shakti, the sexual pair so deeply joined in eternal copulation that they did not know of their difference. Shiva and Shakti, united at first, had separated. Shakti had danced the dance of illusion to convince Shiva he was not One, but Many, creating from her womb the world of multiple objects existing in the illusory flow of time. He, then, the Void, played the role of Shakti, to the Shiva of the matter universe which she, and Habib, represented. The fact that in the myth Shakti was woman, and Shiva man, was irrelevant. "He" had been as ready to love Habib . . . as he was ready to love her. "He" was an arbitrary pronoun, at best.

Yet she sensed a terrible danger if she yielded to him, if "solid" matter was to be wooed by the original nothingness at its heart. Perhaps in a few billion years a final copulation of the "Universe" with "Void" was destined to liberate the energy to restart the cycle . . . But so soon—already?

But why should she care about danger to stars and ships and bodies? A surge of joy took hold of her. She could be the first creature of matter to live the Tantric myth right through to its end, and be truly loved, as no one else had, by this being who was not "being."

"You are the Lover; then love me—" she whispered.

And the mind in the Black Hole gathered about. Her lips were brushed, her hair stroked, the palms of her hands traced sensuously.

The Hokusai wave itself began to tremble; not to fall in on her —rather, to roll backward, away from the still pool, towering up kilometers into the void sky . . .

Through a mist she sensed cries, orders—voices tissue-thin and torn like tatters in a storm. For the Black Hole was changing its configuration in space, gathering itself for an assault on Being and Matter; and as charged particles were sucked in toward it they sprayed the danger signal of increased outpourings of synchrotron radiation and gravity pulses . . .

As he reached out to embrace her, along the line of her thoughts, tracing the yantric geometry of her teletrance back to its origin in the orbiting starship, dune and pool dissolved, and she was snatched away . . .

They had executed Emergency Return Procedure on her— a violent *coitus interruptus* of chemicals and sheer brute force.

A syringe gleamed in Nielstrom's hand. Habib lay weeping, naked, in a corner of the room, his penis a shriveled button. He coughed, a thin smear of blood on his lips; hunched over his nakedness and bruises, gathering the energy to reach his *aba* and cover himself. It looked as though some urban vigilantes had caught him raping Mara and beaten him up. Mainly this was the action of the trance-cancel drug whose results showed so dramatically—a massive physiological aversion: cold turkey compressed into seconds. But perhaps too some gratuitous violence had been used in wrenching him away from Mara and depositing him there.

Mara hurt so badly that the pain crumpled her into a fetal ball, around a belly raped by withdrawal and not by entry. Her nipples were bee stings mounted on top of cones of soft agony like tortured snails stripped of their shells and teased with burning matches (a flicker image from Lew Boyd's childhood, sucked in during the decaying moments of the trance).

Lodwy Rinehart stood there in the room with Boyd and Nielstrom, his face blank stone.

They played tapes of her poetry back at her. The voice was slurred and smeared, barely recognizable as Mara's, but the words were identifiable enough. At least the poetry was.

"May you rot in Hell, Boyd," swore Habib through his tears. "May Allah use your guts for spinning yarn."

"There's no alien being in there, is there Habib?"

"Of course there's a—a being in there," Mara gasped. "I met him. Touched him—"

"Even fell in love with him," smirked Nielstrom.

Mara couldn't understand what was happening, except that it must be one more cruel effort to humiliate her.

Boyd's lip curled in anger and contempt.

"Did you think you'd fooled us, Habib? But nobody deserts the Navy, mister—*but nobody!* That's what cathexis with home is all about."

He swung round on Mara.

"And as for you, little witch—didn't you suspect what Habib was up to? No, I guess you didn't, or you'd have been more scared for your sanity."

His every word was a slap in her face, so recently brushed by love.

"I don't understand any of it," she moaned. "Leave me alone —leave me to myself."

"Ah there it is! The root of the matter exposed. To be left to yourselves. That's what you'd like, isn't it? But how, eh? You can't trance-trip without a rider. That's where the energy comes from, to jump light-years, the rider's sexual frustrations. You keep him rooted to Earth, he keeps you rooted to the ship. The psychological security of the ship and its whole communication net rely on this interplay—"

Mara wept, at these hateful, bewildering people around her. She cried for the still pool beneath the dune . . .

"Why don't you tell her, Habib?" Boyd sneered. "You're supposed to be her teacher."

"Tell her what? She *knows* what is down there."

"Does she? Shall I tell her what *we* know? There's an event horizon—a one-way membrane into the Black Hole. But what if a mind could perform a balancing act on the very horizon itself, eh, Habib? If you could attach yourself to the standing wave there? No more Navy duty then, Habib—you'd be able to hole up in there and forget about us." He smiled bitterly at his own unintended pun.

"What's this about standing waves, Boyd?" the captain demanded. "Don't make me play guessing games on my own ship."

"It's something we've theorized about at Bu-Psych-Sec, sir.

The universe hangs together because of causal relationships. But ever since Pauli, in the twentieth century, scientists have speculated about other, alternative relationships—noncausal ones. Clearly these telemediums function because of this non-causal aspect of things. But with the explosive development of star travel, we've been far too busy exploiting the phenomenon efficiently at Bu-Psych-Sec, and holding society together, to do really deep research. Damn it, we're just fighting to hold the line. You've got to protect society against the disruptive effects of star travel! Well—whereabouts in the universe do you find a tangible physical boundary between the causal and the non-causal?"

"The event horizon," nodded Rinehart.

"On one side is the world of cause and effect," Boyd went on effervescently. "On the other side there isn't any meaningful framework for cause and effect to operate in. Effectively it's a noncausal zone. We think the friction between the two modes of reality generates a kind of standing wave of what I suppose you have to call 'probabilities.' Strange things can happen there. And Habib saw his chance of breaking the causal chains that fasten him to his body and his rider, and the starship, and escaping. But he had to be physically close to the place—and it had to be a two-stage process—"

"Boyd's wrong—there *is* a Being," gasped Habib. "It's not me."

"Mental mutiny?" growled Rinehart, paying no attention to the Arab's protests. "That's a new one for the book."

"A particularly ingenious crime, Captain. Habib sacrificed that sailor's life force to build himself a matrix for his mind to fix on, in there. In doing so, you could say he had to split his personality. No wonder we found so little of all this in his mind, beyond the glaring desire to escape, back there in Annapolis. Habib had covered his tracks up skillfully, like the furtive Bedouin he is. Part of his mind stayed there at the event horizon, ready to receive the rest of him, the major portion of his consciousness. But the Bu-Psych-Sec officer who rode him that second time had the sense and the training to break the trance. He pulled out, took Habib home. Bu-Psych-Sec decided we'd give him sufficient rope to hang himself. He didn't realize the rope would be round his ankle restraining him at the critical time!

It was no use him being the rider, you see—he couldn't make a transference that way. We'll be most interested to learn his tricks when we strip him down again, and the little Swedish witch has her mind peeled to yield up her memory imprint of that bit of fractured mind she fell in love with. We'll have the full picture then."

Habib's eyes met Mara's urgently, begging her to believe him, not Boyd. Her own mind swam with doubts. Had that only been a simulacrum of Habib she had met in there, and all the symbols telling her of how the universe was *nothing*, only lies —part of a cheap trick?

No—he couldn't have contrived it; couldn't have invented a whole alien presence, a viewpoint that reversed the universe! It had to be real!

Boyd was still talking.

"The most important thing of all to know is *how* Habib did this thing. I don't just mean from the security angle. Once we know how the noncausal force operates in conjunction with the universe of cause and effect, given a stretch of luck we can discover how to build a noncausal stardrive. I feel it in my bones. Imagine instantaneous travel, Captain—the power, the expansion, the *control!* Imagine the whole galaxy in our back yard—and all the other galaxies!"

Lodwy Rinehart could imagine. Still, one thing puzzled him.

"Why did the Hole act up, just then? It's stabilized now. But it expanded by two or three percent in a matter of minutes. If I remember my physics, that should require the swallowing of something of the order of a whole sun—"

"We'll know all about it when we analyze the data, but if you want my snap judgment on that, just remember we were tampering with noncausal forces there, at their physical interface with the causal universe. You can take it as an indicator of the kind of power we'll be able to tap . . ."

They played more tapes, but the poetry degenerated into a verbal mishmash—a semantic white noise that sounded like the very entropy of language itself, except where occasional words and phrases came through, treacherously, twisted out of context.

What Boyd was saying about Habib's "plot" had to be the maddest fantasy. Perhaps he could be right about harnessing the energy of the void. But he didn't understand the danger. She had known what the danger was, as that alien mind dilated to receive her. They might build themselves a machine that would wreck matter and reality itself, instead of a stardrive. But for all she cared, they could wreck the whole galaxy of stars. Her sex ached so fiercely, and her soul . . .

"Incidentally, Boyd," the captain inquired casually, "what would have happened if you'd sent Habib in there as medium, with his little witch riding him? Do you suppose he'd have sacrificed her to escape?"

"It's not true, Mara," cried Habib. "They are mad, not us. They can't stand the knowledge that all is based on illusion in the universe!" However, he began to giggle stupidly, because the effort of subterfuge—or the effort of explanation—was too much for him (since she *knew* anyway). It was one of the two, but which?

Boyd glanced at her ironically, as Nielstrom slipped a sedative needle into Habib's arm.

"I imagine he was pretty desperate, sir."

"No!" moaned Mara. "It isn't true. You don't know anything."

It wasn't you in there, Habib. It was *Him*. Though I could share with you. He was big enough, my Lover.

They're celebrating in the lounge. Fat Ohashi. The Prussian. The Chicano. Boyd and Nielstrom. Rinehart has spliced the mainbrace in true old Navy style, as we race away from the Black Hole and away from . . . *love*.

The autopsy on my love will be starting soon; the unpeeling of my mind; the final rape.

What shall I do, Habib? Kill myself?

For I've known an inch of loveliness. And an inch is all I'll ever be allowed to know of loveliness.

Little witch.

Big nightmare.

NOR THE MANY-COLORED FIRES OF A STAR RING

GEORGE R. R. MARTIN

In this story George R. R. Martin, an author you will meet again in this book, examines the two seemingly incompatible worlds of the scientist and the artist. But even at the most basic levels, art and science are Janus faces of the same head. The creative experience seems to be much the same, whether its mode is scientific or humanistic. In that instant of creative insight, poetry and intellect, the individual and the universal, are merged.

Mathematician H. Poincaré aptly describes the artistic experience of the scientist: "It may be surprising to see emotional sensibility evoked apropos the discovery of mathematical demonstrations which, it would seem, can interest only the intellect. This would be to forget the feeling of mathematical beauty, of the harmony of numbers and forms, of geometrical elegance. This is a true aesthetic feeling that all real mathematicians know, and surely it belongs to emotional sensibility." ("Mathematical Creation" from The Foundations of Science, Science Press.)

Indeed, it might be the poet who pulls the handle of technology that creates a new universe of light. But only when the faces of art and science are one for us all will we truly become allies of the future.

Outside the window the stormfires raged on.

The view filled an entire wall in the monitoring room, a tapestry of ever-moving flame, a flowing pattern of liquid light of every color and shape. Great swirls of molten gold slid by, sinuous and snakelike. Lances of orange and scarlet flashed into view and then were gone again. Bluegreen bolts hammered against the window like raindrops, tendrils of amber smoke whirled past, streaks of pure white burned their lingering impressions into the eyes of the watchers.

Dancing, moving, changing; all the colors of nullspace shrieked a silent random song. At least they thought it was random. For five long standard months the vortex had turned in the void of Nowhere, and still the computers had not found a repetition.

Inside, in a long room awash with the lights of the maelstrom, five monitors sat at their consoles facing the window and kept watch on the vortex. Each console was a maze of tiny lights and glowing control studs, and in the center of each were four readout screens where numbers chased by endlessly and thin red lines traced graphs. There was also a small digital timer, where the hundredths of seconds piled up relentlessly on top of the five months already registered.

The monitors changed shifts every eight hours. Now there were three women and two men on duty. All of them wore the pale blue smocks of techs and dark-lensed safety glasses. But the months had made them careless; only Trotter, at the central console, wore the glasses over his eyes. The rest of them had them up, around their foreheads or tangled in their hair.

Behind the monitors were the two horseshoe-shaped control consoles and the wall of computer banks. Al Swiderski, a big raw-boned blond in a white lab coat, was tending the computers. Jennifer Gray held down one of the control chairs. The other was empty, but that did not matter. At the moment they were only places to sit; everything was locked on automatic, and the nullspace engines of the Nowhere Star Ring burned in constant fury.

Swiderski, a sheaf of computer printout in his hand, drifted over to where Jennifer was writing on a clipboard. "We're nearing critical, I think," he said in a hard flat voice.

Jennifer looked up at him, all business. She was a beautiful woman, tall and slim, with bright green eyes and long straight red-blond hair. She wore a severe white lab coat and a gold ring. "Roughly eight hours," she told Swiderski with a shake of her head. "If my calculations are correct. Then we can kill the engines and see what we have."

Swiderski looked out at the swirling stormfires. "Five layers of transparent duralloy," he said softly. "Four buffers of re-frigerated air, and a triple layer of glass. And still the inner window is warm to the touch, Jennifer." He nodded. "I wonder what we'll have."

The watch went on.

A mile down the ring, on another deck, Kerin daVittio entered the old control room alone.

The others seldom came here. The room was his alone. Once, years ago, it had been the nerve center of the Nowhere Star Ring; from here, a single man had at his fingertips all the awe-some powers of a thousand nullspace engines. From here, he could stir the vortex to life and watch it spin.

But no longer. The Nowhere Star Ring had been deserted for nearly six years, and when Jennifer and her team had come they'd found the old control room far too small for their pur-poses. So they abandoned it. Now the engines responded to the twin consoles in the monitoring room. The control room be-longed to Kerin, to his spidermechs and the ghosts of his shad-owed ring.

The room was a tiny cube, immaculate and white. The famil-iar horseshoe console was its center. Kerin sat within it, the controls around him, a reflective look on his face. He was a short, wiry man, with a mop of black hair and restless dark eyes; often he was intense, often dreamy. Long ago he'd discarded his blue tech smock for civilian clothes; now he wore black trousers and a dark red V-necked shirt.

Practiced hands moved over the controls, and the walls melted.

He was outside, in blackness, the star ring beneath him.

The holographic projection gave him a view of the ring and the vortex that the monitoring room window could not match. There was nothing left in the room but him and the console, floating in vacuum miles above the action. The section of the ring that held the control room loomed large under his feet; the rest curved slowly away in both directions, finally dwindling to a metal ribbon that went out and out and out before looping back to join itself in the far dim distance. A silver circlet a hundred miles in diameter; the Nowhere Star Ring was built to standard specifications.

Within the ring, bound by its dampers and its armor, kept alive by the furious power of a thousand fusion reactors, the nullspace vortex turned in mindless glory. This was the multicolored maelstrom that had given man the stars.

Kerin glanced at it briefly, until the light began to hurt his eyes. Then he looked down to his console. The bend of the horseshoe, immediately before him, was all dark; his hands moved restlessly over the disconnected studs that once controlled the vortex. But the studs along either arm still glowed softly; to his left, the holo controls, to his right, the spidermech command. Banks and banks of buttons, all lit a soft pale green. No reason to move those, Swiderski had said; so the old control room was half-alive, and Kerin worked alone.

His left hand reached out to the controls, and the holographs spun around him; now he was thirty miles down the ring, getting visual input from another set of projectors. The view was much the same, the five-month old firestorm still turned below. But this was the trouble spot.

He swiveled to his right, and touched some other studs. Below, a panel slid open in the skin of the star ring, and a spidermech emerged.

It was, in fact, much like a metal spider: eight legs, a fat silver body of shining duralloy that reflected the vortex colors in streaks along its flanks, a familiar scurrying gait. It used all eight legs to cling to the star ring as Kerin sent it running to the problem.

Once there, he slid back another panel, and switched to his spidereyes. The holos fractured; the illusion of being outside vanished. The spidermech had a lot of eyes, most of them in its stomach. Now it stood above the opening in the ring, reaching down with four legs while the other, alternate four clung to the sides of the panel, and all its eyes studied the troublesome engine. The wall before Kerin gave him visual input; normal range, infrared, ultraviolet. The wall to his right measured radioactivity and saw with X-rays, the one to his left printed out the latest input the computer was getting from the monitors on this particular engine.

With four hands at work, things went quickly. Kerin shut down the engine briefly, traced the problem to its source, pulled a part and replaced it from a storage cavity within the spidermech. Then he withdrew his metal arms and leaned back. The panel slid shut. He jumped from his spidereyes back to the holos.

The spidermech stood frozen; the vortex burned. Kerin looked at them without seeing. His hand moved left, and again the holos shifted. No longer was he looking in at the spinning fires; now he stared out, beyond the circle of the ring.

At the infinite empty darkness of Nowhere.

For a second after he turned around, as always, he thought he was going blind. But then his eyes adjusted, and he could see the console dimly. And that was all. He slouched back in his chair, put his boots up on the console, and sighed. Familiar fear washed over him. And awe.

Brooding, he watched the emptiness.

He'd seen holos of the other dozen star rings; but this ring, *this* was singular. Cerberus, the first, floats six million miles beyond Pluto, surrounded by a sea of stars. They may be small and cold and distant, but they *are* stars, proof that Cerberus and its men are safe within the home system and the comforting sanity of the known universe. The same is true for Black Door, adrift in a Trojan position behind Jupiter. And Vulcan, which burns black and broken in the shadow of the sun.

On the flip side of Cerberus spins another ring, surrounded by strange stars, yet snug for all that. So what if the stars are not the stars of human history? Who cares what galaxy they might be in? Nearby is Second Chance, a warm green world under a bright yellow sun, with fast-rising cities and people.

And Vulcan? So? It opens on an inferno, yes; its hellish vortex is the gateway to the inside of a star. But that too Kerin could understand.

Black Door was more frightening; enter here, and find yourself in the yawning gulf between galaxies. No single stars here, no nearby planets. Only distant spirals, far off, in configurations utterly unknown to man. And, luckily, a second hole, around which they'd built a second star ring, to the lush bright system of Dawn.

But on the far side of the Hole to Nowhere was the darkest realm of all. Here blackness rules, immense and empty. There are no stars. There are no planets. There are no galaxies. No light races through this void; no matter mars its perfection. As far as man can see, as far as his machines can sense, in all directions; only nothingness and vacuum. Infinite and silent and more terrible than anything Kerin had ever known.

Nowhere. The place beyond the universe, they called it.

Kerin, alone among the Nowhere crew, still used the old control room. Kerin alone had work that took him *outside.* Early on, he had hardly minded. It gave him time alone, time to think and dream and fiddle with the poems that were his hobby. He had taken to studying Nowhere the way he and Jenny once had studied stars, back in their days on Earth. But something had caught him, and now he could not stop. Obsessed, possessed, he paused after every job.

Like a moth and a flame, so Kerin and the darkness.

Sometimes it was like blindness. He convinced himself that he was sitting in a pitch-black room, that there were walls only a few feet away from him. He could feel the walls, almost. He knew they were there.

But at other times the void opened before him. Then he could see and sense the *depth* of the darkness, he could feel the cold grip of infinity, and he knew, he *knew,* that if he traveled away from the star ring he would fall forever through empty space.

And there were still other times, when his eyes played tricks. He would see stars then. Or perhaps a dim pinprick of light—the universe expanding toward them? Sometimes nightmare shapes struggled on the canvas of night. Sometimes Jennifer danced there, slim and seductive.

For five long months they had lived in Nowhere, in a place where the only reality was them. But the rest of them, facing inward toward the flames, lived all untouched.

While Kerin the displaced poet fought the primal dark alone.

Where were they?
Nowhere.
But where is *that?*
No one is sure.

Kerin considered the question, hard, in their first days out here. And before that, on the long voyage to Nowhere and during the months of preparation. He knew something of Nowhere, and of the star rings—as much as any layman. Now he read more. And he and Jenny stayed up late more nights than one, talking it out in bed.

He got most of his answers from her. He was hardly stupid, Kerin, but his interests lay elsewhere. He was the poet of their partnership; the humanist, the lover, the barroom philosopher, born in the undercity and bred to a world of corridor stickball and slidewalks and elevator races. Jenny was the scientist, the practical one, born on a religious farming commune and raised to be a serious adult. She found her lost innocence in Kerin. They were utterly unalike, yet each brought strength to the relationship.

Kerin taught her poetry, literature, love. She taught him science—and gave him star rings he could never have grabbed by himself.

She answered his questions. But this time neither she nor anyone had the answer. In his memory all his talks and readings and study had blended into one blurred conversation with Jenny.

"It depends on what the star rings are," she said.

"Gateways through space, no?"

"That's the accepted theory, the most popular one, but it's not established fact yet. Call it the space warp theory. It says that the universe is warped, that the fabric of the space-time continuum has holes in it, places you can punch through to come out someplace else. Black holes, for example . . ."

"The so-called natural star rings?" he interrupted.

"So the theory says. If we could reach a black hole, we'd find out. We can't, though, not with sub-light ships. Luckily, we don't need to. We found a second kind of warp, the nullspace anomalies. The accidental discovery of a spot six million miles beyond Pluto where matter seemed to be leaking into space from nowhere—the later discovery that, with enough energy, the warp could be widened temporarily so that a ship could slip through—that was the breakthrough. Thusly, Cerberus, the first of the star rings. We went through the nullspace vortex, and found ourselves deep within another system, near Second Chance.

"Fine. But *where* was Second Chance in relation to Earth? At first, astronomers guessed it was simply somewhere else in our galaxy. Now they're not so sure. The stars in a Second Chance sky are completely unfamiliar, and the local configuration can't be found. So it looks as though the space warp—if that's what it was—threw us a long, long way."

"You don't sound convinced."

"I'm not. The discovery of the Hole to Nowhere twenty-odd years ago badly shook the space warp theory. If we simply jump to another portion of space when we go through a star ring, then *where* was Nowhere? The only feasible answer that's been suggested is Whitfield's Hypothesis. He said that Nowhere is beyond the expanding universe—at a spot in the space-time continuum so far from everything else that even the light of the Big Bang hasn't reached it yet. The only problem with this is that it disagrees with the established belief that matter defines space. If Whitfield is correct, then either space can exist without matter—picture a pre-creation universe of infinite hard vacuum—or, alternatively, Nowhere never existed at all until the first probe ship came through the vortex and created it."

"Wild," he said. "Is he right?"

She laughed. "You think *I* know? The space warp theory, modified by Whitfield's Hypothesis, is still accepted by the vast majority of nullspace theoreticians. But there are two other contenders, at least."

"Such as?"

"Such as the alternate universe theory. Accept that, and you buy a cosmic picture where the star rings are gates between alternate realities that occupy the same space. History is different in each reality, stellar geography is changed, even the natural laws might not be the same."

"Hmmmm," said Kerin. "I see. Then Nowhere is a reality where creation has never taken place, a universe that was utterly without matter or energy until we entered."

"Right. Except the theory is generally discredited nowadays, except by mystics. We've opened a good dozen star rings, and so far we have yet to come upon any alternate Earths, or even the tiniest modification in the speed of light. Excepting Nowhere, all these side-by-side continuums seem pretty much like our own.

"The time travel theory is a more serious one. It's got a good bit of support. Its adherents claim the star rings throw us backwards or forwards in time, to periods when different stars occupied the same cosmic space now occupied by Sol, the colony systems, and such."

"In which case ships to Nowhere either go back before the

Big Bang, or forward in time, after the universe has fallen in on itself," Kerin said.

"*If* it's going to fall in," Jenny replied, grinning. "They're not so sure of that anymore. You should keep up with the latest theories, love. But you do have the general drift. The hypothesis is a lot more sophisticated than that, of course. It has to account for the fact that the nullspace anomalies stay put, relative to the solar system, even though Sol and the galaxy and the universe are all moving. Foster modified the original time travel theory by postulating that the nullspace vortex moves ships through both time *and* space, and nowadays most of the scientists who don't buy the space warp theory line up with him."

"And you?"

She shrugged. "I don't know. When they discovered Nowhere and punched through to build a ring on this side, they thought they'd find the answer. Nowhere was a very singular place. Figure it out, and you figure out the star rings, and maybe the cosmos. They tried, for a long time. The Nowhere Star Ring used to be a full-time research base, but finally it was abandoned. Robot probes launched in fifty different directions twenty years ago are still reporting back, and their reports are still the same—vast unending nothingness. Absolute vacuum. Not much you can do with findings like that."

"No," he said, thoughtful.

"Anyway, it doesn't matter. I'll leave Nowhere for someone else to crack. My own research has a more practical thrust."

He was there because of Jenny.

Oh, he had a job, and it was a fairly important one. On an ordinary star ring, the spidermechs were seldom used, but the Nowhere experiment put an unheard-of strain on the nullspace engines. Kerin filled a function. But others could have filled it just as well. It was Jennifer who had gotten him the post, over Swiderski's protests; it was because of Jennifer that Kerin had taken it.

They shared a cabin, a large one with a mock window at the foot of their king-sized bed. Outside the window were the stars of home; a comforting holo. Bookcases ran along either wall. Hers held obscure texts on nullspace, most of them full of math; his held poetry and fiction, equally obscure. At night, they lit the room dimly, and talked for hours in the tender after-time.

"It's strange," he said to her during the first week, as she lay warm against him with her head on his chest. "I don't know why it fascinates me so much, but it does. I've got to do a poem about it, Jenny. I've got to make someone else feel what I feel when I'm out there. You understand? It's the ultimate symbol of death, really. You know?"

She kissed him. "Mmm," she mumbled in a drowsy voice. "Can't say I've thought about it much. I suppose it is. It all depends on how you look at it." She laughed. "Back when this was still a research station, they had more than one crack-up. The place does something to people. Some people, anyway. Others are utterly unaffected. Al, for example. He calls it a lot of nothing."

Kerin snorted. He and Swiderski had disliked each other from the instant they met. "He would say that. He stays down in the monitoring room and avoids the whole issue."

"He loves you too. Just the other day he told me that I was a brilliant theoretician, but my taste in men was revolting." Jenny laughed. Kerin fought briefly, and wound up joining her.

But things changed.

"Kerin," she said to him two months afterwards, and he answered with a questioning look.

"You've been very quiet lately," she said. "Is something wrong?"

"I don't know," he said. He ran his fingers idly through her hair as he stared at the ceiling.

"Talk about it," she urged.

"It's hard to put into words," he said. Then he laughed. "Maybe that's why I can't write any poems about it." There was a quiet. "You remember that time, back in college, when we picnicked in the forest preserve?"

Jenny nodded. "Uh-huh," she said, puzzled.

"Remember what we talked about?"

She hesitated. "I don't know. Love? We used to talk about love a lot. That was right when we met." She smiled. "No, wait, now I remember. That was the day I tried to convert you. All that business about the apple."

"Yeah," he said, "only God could make an apple, you said. The existence of apples somehow proved the existence of God.

I never quite understood that argument, by the way. And I didn't even *like* apples."

Jenny smiled, gave him a quick kiss. "I remember. That night you dragged me down to that pizza place of yours in the under-city. In the middle of a big pepperoni pizza you said that if God really existed, and if he had any class, he would have created a world where pizza grew on trees instead of apples. I should have been furious, but it was all too funny."

"I guess," he said. "But I meant it, too. Apples never awed me; man could do better. Nothing really awed me, when I stop to think about it. I never bought your God, Jenny, you know that. But I had something else."

"I should have pointed to the stars," Jenny said. "A lot more impressive than any apple."

"Admittedly. But I would have answered with the star rings. Man-made, very beautiful, very powerful. And think of what they mean. Even the vast gulfs between the suns, even those, man has beaten."

He fell silent. Jenny cuddled against him, but she did not break the spell. Finally he resumed, in a slow serious voice.

"Nowhere is something else, Jenny. For the first time, I've run up against something I can't get a grip on. I don't understand it, I don't like it, and I don't like the thoughts it's making me think. Every time I run a check or do a repair, I wind up staring at it and shivering."

"Kerin?" Jenny said, concern in her voice. There was something very strange in his.

Sensing her worry, he turned to her and smiled. "Um," he said. "I'm getting entirely too serious. Comes of reading too much Matthew Arnold. Forget about it." He kissed her.

But *he* did not forget.

And as time passed, he got steadily more sober. His duties kept him away from Jennifer on-shift, and more and more he seemed to be avoiding people during the off-shift. Even in the cafeteria he seemed a little too solemn, too preoccupied, for the rest of the crew to be comfortable. Some of the others started to avoid him; Kerin never seemed to notice.

One night he said he felt sick. Jennifer found him in bed, staring at the ceiling again. She sat down next to him. "Kerin, we have to talk. I don't understand. You've been positively morbid lately. What's going on?"

He sighed. "Yeah." A pause. "I went down to the fourth deck today, and found the old probe room."

Jennifer said nothing.

"It's still there," he continued, "still functioning after six years. The lights were out, and there was a layer of dust. And ghosts. I could hear my footsteps and something else, sort of a thin whine coming from the control consoles.

"I watched the readout screens for a long time. They were all the same, just straight blue lines moving slowly across a black screen. Nothing, Jenny. They've found nothing. Twenty years now, accelerating steadily to near light speed, and they've yet to find a single particle, an atom, a ray of light. Then I thought I knew what the whine was. The robots were crying, Jenny. For twenty years they've been falling through night, and the only island of light and sound and sanity is far behind, lost in the void. That's too much, even for machines. They're alone and they're scared and they're crying. And the whole probe room was alive with their whispers and their wails. No wonder the researchers went away. The dark beat them, Jenny. Nowhere is beyond human understanding." He trembled.

"Kerin," she said. "They're only probes. They don't have emotions."

"Tell me about it," he said. "I work with those spidermechs every day, and every damned one of them is different. Moodiest damned machines I've ever seen. Nowhere is getting to them too. For the probes, it's a thousand times worse. So, all right, they are only machines. But they don't belong out here."

He looked at her. "And neither do we, Jenny, at least not now. We'll be there soon enough. Every day I watch it, and I know. Whatever we have, whatever we believe in, it doesn't matter. Nothing matters, except the void out there. *That's* real, *that's* forever. We're just for a brief meaningless little time, and nothing makes sense. And the time will come when we'll be out there, wailing, in a sea of never-ending night.

"*Invictus* is a child's joke. We can't make a mark on *that*, out there. It's not a symbol of death, Jenny. What a fool I was. It's the reality.

"Maybe we're dead already. And this is hell."

There was nothing she could say; she did not understand.

He was floating high above the ring, surveying his dark domain, when the intercom buzzed. The noise startled him, yet brought a smile to his face. He leaned forward and flicked open the channel. "You have just disturbed the silence of infinity with your intercom buzz," he said.

"I always was irreverent," Jennifer's voice replied. "You sound cheerful, Kerin."

"I'm trying, what can I say? We're all doomed and everything we do is meaningless, but maybe we have to fight." He said it lightly, in a guarded half-mocking tone. He had given up being serious about it; he and Jenny had been arguing entirely too much, and his gloom had driven her into spending more and more time with Swiderski.

"We're close, Kerin. Come up. I want you to be here when it happens."

Kerin stretched stiff muscles. "All right," he said. "I'll be right up. Don't think I'll be much help, though."

"Just so you're there," she answered.

He flicked off, quickly ran the spidermech back to its lair, urging it on under his breath, then banished the darkness with a snap of his thumb. Back in the bright white control room, he unstrapped, exited through a sliding door. Then he moved down the corridor to an interdeck ladder, climbed to a shuttle, and rode to the monitoring room.

Where all the folk of Nowhere had gathered to watch the colors dance. The third shift was on, attentive at the monitor consoles, restless, watching the seconds pile up. But the two off-shifts were there too, prowling the room, hands shoved into pockets, pale blue smocks rumpled. This was a moment no one wanted to miss.

Swiderski, sitting in one of the control chairs, glanced up when Kerin entered. "Aha," he said. "Our black philosopher lives! To what do we owe this singular pleasure?"

Jenny was in the second lighted throne. Kerin moved behind her, and rested a hand on her shoulder. He stared at Swiderski. "You know, Al, I've got spidermechs with a better personality than you." One of the techs guffawed.

"Quiet," Jennifer said. She studied her clipboard, ignoring Swiderski's puzzled frown. The rest kept impatient eyes on the window.

Out there, bright-burning shadows raced from right to left,

caught in the unending flow. Yellow, silver, blue, crimson, orange, green, purple. Gushes and spears, swirls and tendrils, firedrops and roaring floods. In the airless starless empty they turned and mingled and mixed and turned. The window, as always, drenched the room with shifting light. The many-colored flames of the star ring flickered in the eyes of the watchers.

"Five minutes," Trotter announced in a loud voice. A short, stout man, the head of the tech crew; off duty now, but still here to officiate.

"Safety lenses," Jennifer said suddenly, looking up from her chair. "In case something goes wrong."

Around the room, one by one, the watchers lowered their dark goggles until all the eyes were hidden. All but Kerin's. His glasses were forgotten, somewhere back in his room.

A short brown-haired woman drifted up to his side, offering him a pair. He tried to remember her name, failed. A tech. "Thanks," he said, taking the goggles and covering his eyes.

She shrugged. "Sure. A big moment, isn't it?"

He looked back toward the window, where the colors now were muted. "I suppose."

She refused to go away. "We don't see much of you anymore, Kerin. Is everything all right?"

"Sure," he said. But his face stayed somber.

"Two minutes," Trotter announced. Kerin fell silent, and his hand tightened on Jenny's shoulder. She looked up at him, and smiled. They watched the window.

Over a year ago she had found the key. He'd shared that moment, the start, as she waved her battered clipboard in his face and whooped. Now he could share the finish. Somehow, despite everything he had said, that still mattered.

"One minute," Trotter said. Then the seconds peeled off one by one. The next voice was Jennifer's. It was her right. She'd started it all. "Now," she said. She hit the controls before her. And all around the star ring, the nullspace engines died.

Dead silence in the monitoring room; a hush of indrawn breath. Long seconds. Then, with a rush, explosion. Laughter, tears, papers flying, techs hugging each other.

Beyond the window, the colors were still spinning.

Swiderski was suddenly there, standing at Jennifer's side, grinning. "You did it!" he said. "*We* did it. A self-sustaining vortex."

Jenny permitted herself a brief smile, immune to the riot around her. "It hasn't been a minute yet," she said, cautiously. "The vortex may fade, after all. Before we celebrate too much, let's see how long the thing sustains itself without the engines."

Swiderski shook his head, laughing. "Ah, Jenny. It doesn't matter. A second is time enough, shows that it's possible. It's a big breakthrough. Now maybe we can even generate a vortex without an anomaly, anywhere—think of it! A hundred star rings in orbit around Earth!"

Jennifer rose. Swiderski, still dripping enthusiasm, grabbed her, hugged her hard. She accepted the hug calmly, disengaged as soon as he released her. "That's still a long way off, Al," she told him. "We may not see it in our lifetimes. Let's just wait to make sure *all* my calculations work out, okay? You take the next watch."

She glanced toward Kerin. He grinned. They left the monitoring room together. Out in the corridor, she took him by the hand.

An anomaly is not a gate; it is too small. But it can be opened. The price—energy.

Thus the star rings, built around the holes. A thousand fusion engines provide a lot of energy.

Wake them, and in the center of the ring a bright-colored star flares to sudden brilliance. The star becomes a disc, the colors changing, spinning. The disc grows with each flicker of the eye. In seconds it spans the ring; the nullspace vortex, the colored maelstrom of space. Kept alive by energy, it is itself a creature of awful power.

The armored ringships tear into its center, and suddenly are gone, to reappear on the flip side of the hole. Elsewhere, far elsewhere.

Then the ring man kills the engines. And—in an instant—the vortex is gone. It blinks out. Like a light, turned off.

It works. But why? How?

Dr. Jennifer Gray made the first big advance in the field. A leading nullspace theoretician, she got permission for a series of controlled experiments with the Black Door Star Ring. Her first step was to let the vortex burn for a full day; previously no vortex had been kept alive for much over an hour. The costs in terms of fuel and energy were too great.

At Black Door, Dr. Gray discovered that the vortex, somehow, gains energy.

Her measurements were very precise. A certain amount of energy is poured into the ring center by the engines; enough to create the vortex, to keep it alive. But the energy of the vortex itself was greater than what was being pumped in. A minute difference at first. But it builds, the longer the vortex turns.

There followed the Gray Equations; run a star ring long enough, her figures said, and the vortex will be self-sustaining. Then the ring can possibly be a power source, instead of a drain. More importantly, her work provided the first real insight into the nature of the nullspace vortex. It was hoped that in time, enough understanding might be acquired so that star rings could be constructed anywhere.

Further experimentation was called for. Since Black Door was a busy gateway, and since the work might possibly be dangerous, the government gave Dr. Gray and her team access to the abandoned Nowhere Star Ring.

They had been saving a special bottle of wine. They broke it out and took it back to their room. Kerin poured two glasses, and they drank a toast to the Gray Equations.

"I'd like to give Swiderski a hit in the face," Kerin said, sitting on the bed. He sipped his wine thoughtfully.

Jenny smiled. "Al is all right. And you sound better."

Kerin sighed. "Ah, so that's why we haven't been arguing." He set down his glass on a night table, rose, and shook his head. "Maybe I'm getting resigned to it," he said. "Or maybe I'm just getting better at hiding it. I don't know."

"And I thought my triumph had put you in a good mood."

"I wonder," he mused. He walked across their room to the mock window, and stared out at the starscape. "I think maybe it was more that buzz you gave me. That never happened before. I mean, there I am in the midst of infinite darkness, and suddenly there's this big raucous noise." He tapped the window glass lightly with his fist. "It's a lie," he said. "There's only darkness and death, Jenny, and nothing we can do to change it. Except . . ."

He turned to face her. "Except make noises? I don't know."

"Oh, Kerin. Why do you let it obsess you? Just let it be."

He shook his head violently. "No, that's no answer. We can avoid thinking about it, but it still won't go away. No, I've got to beat it somehow, face it down and beat it. Only I don't have anything to beat it with. Not even the vortex, not even the star rings. But that noise . . . that doesn't do it either, of course, but, but . . ."

Jenny smiled. "Our black philosopher. Al is right. I really don't understand you, love. I'm afraid I'm like Swiderski in that. To me it's just a lot of nothing. Oh, I get hints of what's bothering you, but it's all an intellectual exercise. To you it's more than that."

He nodded.

"I wish I could help more, help you work it out. Whatever it is."

"Maybe you can," Kerin said. "Maybe you have. I've got to think this through." He stared at nothing and rubbed his chin.

And suddenly the intercom buzzed. Jenny shook off her musings, put down her glass, and reached over to the bedside. "Yes," she said.

Swiderski's voice. "Jennifer, you'd better get up here at once."

"What's wrong? Is the vortex fading already?" Kerin, across the room, stood frozen.

"No," Swiderski said. "There's something wrong. It's not fading at all, Jenny. It's gaining energy, from no place. Even faster than before."

"That can't be," she said.

"It is."

Outside, winds of scarlet flame shrieked by in silent fury.

Jenny sat in one of the control chairs, clutching her talisman clipboard, and cleared a computer screen. "Give me the figures," she said to Ahmed, on the central monitor.

He nodded, hit a stud, and the figures from one of his readout screens blinked into life on hers. Jennifer studied them in silence, looking up every once in a while at the raging fire outside. Behind her, Swiderski stood near the computers, scratching his head. The monitors, goggles down, tended to their screens.

Her fingers went to a console, tentatively, thoughtfully. She punched in an equation, paused, tugged absently at her hair. Then she nodded firmly, and set to work.

Forty-five minutes later she looked up at Swiderski. "The Gray Equations are wrong," she said, emotionless. "According to my predictions, the vortex was supposed to maintain itself for five months at least, the energy level gradually tapering off, until finally booster shots from the nullspace engines were required. That's not what's happening."

"An error somewhere," Swiderski started.

She dismissed him with an impatient toss of her head. "No. The whole equation's worthless. I made a fundamental mistake somewhere, I misunderstood something key about the nature of the vortex. Otherwise this wouldn't be going on."

"You're too hard on yourself."

"We have to start all over. Bleed all the monitors into the main computer, Ahmed. I don't want to miss a thing." Her fingers raced over the keys of the console. The monitor crew set to their tasks, exchanging puzzled looks. Swiderski, frowning, sat in the second throne.

And up against the door Kerin stood quietly, his arms crossed, watching the racing fires. Then, unnoticed, he turned and left.

One by one, the others drifted into the control room. The watch changed in silence; those going off stayed in the monitoring room, drinking coffee and exchanging whispers. Once in a while someone laughed. Jennifer never looked up, but Swiderski glared at them.

As hours passed, he got up, fidgeting, and went over to Jennifer. "You ought to get some sleep," he told her. "Been up too long. Something like twenty straight hours now, isn't it?"

Annoyance flashed across her face. "So have you, Al. This can't wait."

Defeated, he turned to his chair, and ran through some equations of his own.

More hours of silent waiting, while the fires screamed a few feet away.

Finally Jennifer leaned back, frowning. Her long fingers drummed on the console. She looked to the central monitor, where Sandy Lindagan had replaced Ahmed. "Call Trotter," Jennifer said. "Tell him to wake up the off-shifts"—glancing around—"the ones who aren't loitering around here, anyway."

Lindagan gave her a questioning look, shrugged, and did it.

"What are you doing?" Swiderski said.

"Clear your screen," Jennifer told him. "Have the computer graph the rate of increase prior to switch-off."

He did it. A red line traced a slow-ascending curve across his console face. They'd known the rate of increase for months, though. "So?" Swiderski said.

"Now, let it draw on the monitors. Plot the increase *since* we reached s-point."

Swiderski punched some more studs, bit his lip, wiped the screen, and did it again. The answer was the same. The line soared. A row of blinking figures underneath told the story.

"Not just an increase in the arithmetic rate of energy gain," he said.

"No," snapped Jennifer. "Geometric. S-point was some sort of point of no return. Somehow we've got a chain reaction in nullspace itself."

Sandy Lindagan looked over, her face pale. "Jennifer," she said. "Then you want Trotter so . . ."

"So he can get the ship ready," Jennifer said, standing abruptly. "We've got to get out. Al, you take over here. I'm going for Kerin." She started toward the door.

One of the off-duty monitors had wandered over to the window. He touched it lightly with his fingertips, and yowled, spilling a cup of coffee.

When he took his fingers away, they were red and burned.

Their bedroom was empty.

She went to the old control room. That too was deserted.

She stood in the white cubicle, puzzled. Where?

Then she remembered.

In the sealed-off portion of the ring she found him, pacing slowly back and forth in the gloom and dusty darkness of the probe room. It was the first time she had ever been there. The only light was the glow of the console buttons, and the straight blue tracery of the lines on the readout screens. But a ghostly half-heard whine came from the instrument panels.

"You hear them, Jenny?" Kerin said. "My lost souls? Wailing in the darkness?"

"A minor malfunction somewhere," she said, watching him as he stalked restlessly through the shadows. Then swiftly she told him what had happened. Halfway through she began to sob.

And Kerin came to her, wrapped her in his arms, pressed her hard against him. Wordless.

"I *failed*, Kerin," she said, and all the disappointment she had hidden from the others, all the agony, came out now. "All my equations, the whole *theory* . . ."

"It's all right," he told her. He stroked her hair. Then, despite himself, he shivered. "Jenny," he said, "what now? I mean, is the ring going to short-circuit or something? And we'll be stuck here?"

She shook her head. "No, we're going back, as soon as the ship is ready. The vortex *will* overload the ring, but not the engines, no. They're not even in the picture. It's the dampers we have to worry about, and the armor. The vortex is self-sustaining now, building energy fast, God knows how or from where, but it's happening. Have you ever seen what a vortex does to an unarmored ship, Kerin? It'll do that to us soon. It'll generate so much power that the star ring can't hold it in any longer. Then it'll melt free. An explosion, Kerin, and an unbound vortex, expanding at the speed of light, generating more and more energy all the while. But by that time, hopefully, we'll be through the hole, safe on the flip side. I don't think it will break through the continuum. I hope not."

Her voice faded, and there was only the whine. Kerin shook his head, as if to clear it. And then, wildly, he began to laugh.

Of course, he was the last one to the ship.

They left within seventy-two hours, over Swiderski's protests. "You were wrong before, Jenny," the big blond kept saying, "you might be wrong now. Besides, I ran through your calculations. The ring walls will hold for at least another week *minimum*, and we could make valuable observations. And still get clear before the ring starts to melt."

Jennifer overruled him. "We can't take the chance. It's hot in here already. The risk isn't worth it, Al. We're leaving."

An hour before departure, Kerin vanished.

Jennifer grabbed a shuttle and went searching. She checked their bedroom, deserted now; the stars in the holo beamed on a bare metal cabin. She tried the old control room, and found that he'd been there. The door slid back on the fractured visions of his spidereyes. But the chair was vacant. Next the probe room. Still no Kerin.

She flipped on the shuttle intercom and called back to the ring port where the ship lay waiting. Trotter answered. "He's here," he said quickly. "Came running up about ten seconds after you went off after him. Hurry back."

She did.

The departure was all confusion. Jenny did not find Kerin until the ship had boosted free of the Nowhere Star Ring and was circling out into the yawning vacuum before turning back toward the vortex. He was sitting in the ship's main lounge.

All the lights were out when she entered. But the viewscreen was on, filling one long wall, and Kerin and a half-dozen others watched in silence. Ahead of them a spinning multicolored hell howled in the midst of virgin blackness. The ring, binding the fires, was a tiny glint of silver thread, all but lost in the immense fury of the stormfires.

Jennifer sat down beside him.

"Look," Kerin said. "Look at those ripples, the bulges. Like a thunderhead, all bunched up with lightning, getting ready to explode. It's always been flat before, Jenny, you know? Sort of two-dimensional? Not now. When she blows, she'll blow in all directions." He took her hand, squeezed hard, grinned at her. "My poor probes, they'll be delighted. After twenty years of darkness, light, coming up behind them fast. Think of it. Something at last, in an infinity of nothing." Kerin looked at her, still smiling. "You broke the quiet in my little dark room with your intercom buzz. This will be a much bigger noise, in a much bigger quiet."

The vortex loomed larger and larger ahead, filling the screen. The ringship was nearing and picking up speed.

"Where did you go?" Jennifer said.

"To the control room," he said, and the ghosts were all gone from his voice. "I yanked two of my spiders out of their hidey-holes."

"But *why?*"

"They're sitting in the monitoring room now, love. Perched on top of the control chairs, right where you and Al used to sit.

I keyed in the computer, a timed command. An hour after we're safe on the other side of space, my spiders are going to lean forward and punch all your pretty studs and turn back on the engines."

She whistled. "That'll speed up the explosion something fierce. The energy level was increasing fast enough anyway. Why give it more energy to multiply?"

He squeezed her hand again. "To make the noise bigger, love. Call it a gesture. How much energy would you say is out there, spinning around like a big pinwheel, eh?"

"A lot. The explosion will begin with the force of a supernova, easily. It'd take that much power to melt down the ring."

"Hmmm. Except that this time, the explosion doesn't damp out, right? It keeps going, the vortex expands and expands and—"

"—expands. Yes. Geometrically."

The viewscreen was alive with the colors of the vortex. For an instant it almost seemed as if they were back in the monitoring room on the Nowhere Star Ring. Tongues of fire leaped up at them, and bluish demon shapes whipped by, shrieking.

Then the ship shuddered, and there were stars again.

Jennifer smiled. "You look smug," she told Kerin.

He put his arm around her. "*We* look smug. We have a right to be. We just beat that fucking darkness. There's only one thing we did wrong."

She blinked. "What?"

"We put apples on the trees, instead of pizza."

DEAD IN IRONS

CHELSEA QUINN YARBRO

Chelsea Quinn Yarbro writes:

Here is the ghastly tale of the raft of the "Medusa," a French frigate which foundered off the coast of Senegal on 4 July 1816. Because there were not enough lifeboats on the "Medusa," the Captain and his officers made a raft and put 150 passengers and crew on it, with the supposed intention of towing it to the not-too-distant shore. But the aristocratic Captain apparently panicked and ordered that the raft be cut loose, and his order was carried out.

For 13 days the raft drifted, while mutinies occurred among the steadily dwindling number of survivors as they fought for food and space. When the food ran out, they went hungry for a few days, and then resorted to cannibalism, which was practiced by all the survivors. Sighted at last on the 17th of July, 1816, the survivors were rescued. Of the 150 passengers and crew who had been put aboard the raft, 15 survived . . .

The future might well reflect and transform familiar elements of the past. James Blish has suggested that paddlewheelers might navigate the sand-oceans of the moon, if such oceans exist. Arthur C. Clarke wrote a novel about what would happen if such a ship sank, trapping the passengers in a sea of dust. Perhaps tomorrow's spaceships might hark back in some respects to the sturdy, creaking schooners that navigated the sea. Perhaps—by a not so wild leap of the imagination—everyday life in the hold of a starship might just resemble that of a frigate, or a modern floating city—an ocean liner.

Here is a story set in the century when interstellar travel, though advanced, is still not quite perfected. "Dead in Irons" is a sailing term to describe those times when the wind failed.

But in the ocean of space only the hiss of hydrogen on the radio will take the place of crashing waves upon unknown shores.

And in the depths of hyperspace there might only be silence.

They all hated steerage, every steward in the *Babel Princess*. Mallory made that plain when he showed Shiller around the ship for the first time.

"Hell of a place," she agreed, looking at the narrow, dark corridors that connected the cold storage rooms.

Mallory chuckled, a sound of marbles falling on tin. "Worse'n that. Don't let 'em stick you back here, Shiller. They're gonna try, but don't you do it. You being the newest one, they think they can get away with it, making you do steerage. But this damn duty has to be shared." He cast a sideways look at Shiller. "Wranswell's the worst. You keep an eye out for him."

"It's like cold storage for food," Shiller said, peering through the viewplate at the honeycomb of quiet, frosted cocoons.

"Sure is," Mallory said, contempt darkening his voice.

"I wonder why they do it, considering the risks?" Shiller mused, not really talking to Mallory. "You couldn't pay me to do that."

A white grin split Mallory's black face. "Cause they're stinking poor and dumb. Remember that, Shiller; they're dumb."

Shiller turned her gaze once again to the figures stacked in the coffin-like tiers. "Poor bastards," she said before she moved away from the hatch that closed the steerage section away from the life of the rest of the ship.

"It's not that bad," Mallory said, running his eyes over the dials that monitored the steerage cargo. Some of the indicators were perilously low, but Mallory only grunted and shook his head. "Hell, Shiller, this way we don't have to feed 'em, except for that minimal support glop they get. We don't have a lot of crap to get rid of. We don't have to keep a shrink around for 'em the way we do for first class. We don't have to worry about space. It could be a lot worse. Imagine all of 'em running around loose down here."

"Yeah," Shiller nodded, following Mallory down the corridor to the drive shield. But she added one last question. "Why don't they buy into a generation ship instead of this? They're slow but they're safe."

Mallory shrugged. "Generation ships cost money; maybe they can't afford it. Maybe they figure that this way they'll be alive when they get where they going, *if* they get where they're going."

"If," Shiller repeated, frowning. "But what happens if we drop out wrong? Where would we be? What would we do with them?" She sounded upset, her face was blank but her dark eyes grew wide.

"Hasn't happened yet. Maybe it won't. It's only a seven percent chance, Shiller. That's not bad odds. Besides, we couldn't keep operating if we lost more'n that. Don't worry about it." He swung open the hatch to the small, low-ceilinged cubicle beside the core of the ship. "I'll show you what to look for if we get into trouble."

Although she had been to school and had been told these things before, Shiller followed him through the lock, turning to look one last troubled time at the hatch to the cold room.

"Shiller. Pay attention," Mallory's voice snapped at her. "I got to get back on deck watch."

"Yeah," she answered and stepped into the little room.

Wranswell posted the watches later in the day, and Shiller saw she had been assigned to steerage. Mallory's warning rang in her mind, but she shrugged it off. "Can't hurt to do it once," she said to the air as she thumb-printed the order.

"Don't let them get frisky," Wranswell said with ponderous humor. He loomed at the end of the corridor, filling it with his bulk. He was a gathering of bigness. His body, his head, his eyes, all were out-sized, massive, more like some mythic creature than chief steward of a cargo jump ship.

Inwardly Shiller shrank back from the man. Small and slight herself, she distrusted the big man. She knew that stewards rose in rank by their ability to control other stewards, and Wranswell's bulk clearly dominated the others.

"Got nothing to say? Well, that'll be good in steerage. All you got to do is sit there and wait for nothing to happen." He chortled his huge, rumbling chortle as he started down the corridor. "You haven't been to see me, Shiller," he complained as he grew nearer.

"I've been stowing my gear."

"Of course you have. It's a pity you didn't let me inspect it first. Now it's all over your cabin. And some of it got torn. You got to have tougher things, Shiller." He was close to her now. He leaned on the order board and smiled down at her. "You got to remember what my job is. And you're the new steward. I got to be sure of you, you know."

"My watch is about to begin," Shiller said in a small tight voice.

"Oh. Yes. It's too bad your cold gear got ripped. You'll get cold for those four hours." He grinned at the fear in her face. "I'd loan you some others, but it's against the rules. And you don't want me to break the rules, do you?"

Shiller said no, hating herself for fearing the big man, and for letting him see her fear. He was the sort who would turn it against her.

"Of course, Shiller. The rules shouldn't be broken. But I make the rules. They're my rules." He reached down and touched her arm. "I make 'em and I can break 'em. Because they're mine. Remember that, Shiller."

"I'll remember." Her fists were hard knots at her sides.

"Do you want me to break them for you? Hum?" His smile had no warmth, no humor. "What do you think, Shiller? What do you want me to do?"

She moved back from him. "I think a rule is a rule, Wranswell. I wouldn't want you to make an exception for a new steward like me." Then she turned and fled, followed by Wranswell's huge laughter.

Steerage was icy; the cold cut through Shiller's torn gear with an edge as keen and penetrating as steel. Her hands, inadequately protected by ripped gloves, were brittle and stiff, and her fingers moved slowly and clumsily as she adjusted the valves on the tiers.

The monitor showed that the indicators which had been near critical were now back within tolerable limits. The silent, cocoon-like figures stacked in the tiers drifted on in their sleep that was not sleep, their bodies damped with cold and drugs. One day they would be warm again, would breath deeply the air of another planet, their hearts would beat a familiar seventy-two beats a minute. But at the moment, they were like so much meat stored for the butcher.

Shiller was horrified with herself as the thought rose unbidden in her mind. She had been determined to treat steerage passengers as the people they were, not as cold cargo. Yet in less than a day, she had found herself slipping, seeing steerage as meat only. She forced herself to pause as she worked, to talk to each of the passengers, to learn their names and destinations.

"How's it going?" Mallory's voice asked on the speaker.

"It's cold."

"Sure." He paused. "You're cold or it's cold?"

"Both," she said shortly, wishing she could ask him for help and knowing that she must not.

"You got your gear on, don't you?"

"Sure. But turns out some of it's ripped." She was too near telling him what Wranswell had done, and what he had said.

"Don't you know enough not to go in there in ripped gear?"

"It's all the gear I have," she said. The cold had gathered on her face and made it hard to talk.

"Ripped gear? Where'd you buy crap like that?"

"It got ripped after I came aboard." She thought it was safe to say that much, that Mallory would understand and hold his peace.

"Wranswell?" said the voice from the speaker.

"I'm not accusing anyone of anything." Her hands were so cold they felt hot. Carefully she rubbed them together and waited to hear what more Mallory had to say.

"I'll talk to you later." The speaker clicked once and was dead.

Shiller sat looking at the monitors, feeling the cold seeping into her body. It was too cold and too long. She knew that her hands would need treatment when she got off watch. It would go on her report, and she would be docked for improper maintenance of her gear. Bitterly she realized that Wranswell had engineered things very well. All he had to do was be sure that her gear was faulty, and he would be able to order her to do anything. She would have no choice but to obey, or the company would leave her stranded on some two-bit agricultural planet. It had happened before, she thought. Wranswell was too good at his game to be a novice player. Shuddering, she forced her attention on the tiers.

"You're the new one." The steward who confronted Shiller was an older woman, one whose face was hardened with her job and made tight with worry. "I heard we'd got you."

Shiller felt the hostility of the other steward engulf her, hot, a vitriolic pulse. "I'm sorry," she faltered. "I haven't learned who everyone is yet."

"No. Only the one that counts." The woman barred her way, one muscular arm across the door.

"Look," Shiller said, tired of riddles and anger, "my name is Shiller. I only came aboard last night, I don't know the ropes around here. If I've done something wrong, I wish you'd tell me, then I won't have to do it again."

"Shiller," the other said, looking her over measuringly. "Wranswell told me about you. You're the reason he's kicking me out." She waited to see what effect this announcement would have.

"No," said Shiller, closing her eyes, feeling the bile touch the back of her mouth. She dreaded what Wranswell had planned, and now she had made an enemy of his former mate. "I didn't do anything. I don't want him."

The laughter was unpleasant. "You're not serious," the other said, stating a fact. "On these tubs, you take everything you can get, and if you can get the chief steward, don't you tell me you'd refuse."

"I don't want Wranswell," Shiller repeated, very tired now, her hands beginning to ache now that they were warm again.

"Sure. Sure, Shiller." The woman leaned toward her, one hand balling into a fist, her face distorted with rage.

"Dandridge!" Wranswell's voice echoed down the hall, and in a moment he appeared, his big body moving effortlessly, swiftly to stop the woman's hands as she rushed Shiller.

"Oh, no, Wranswell," she cried out, turning to see his fist as it smashed the side of her face. Clutching at the sudden well of blood, she sank to her knees, a soft moan escaping her before she began to sob.

"Looks like you need someone to take care of you, Shiller," Wranswell said, ignoring Dandridge on the floor.

"Not you, Wranswell." Shiller had begun to back up, feeling her face go ashen under Wranswell's mocking eyes. "Not after what you did to Dandridge."

The woman on the floor was bleeding freely, her hands leaking red around the fingers. Her breath was choked now, and when she coughed there was blood on her lips.

"Dandridge is nothing," Wranswell said.

"She was your mate," Shiller said tensely, still hoping to break away from him, from the bloody woman on the floor.

"Was, Shiller. Not now. Now you're here and I got plans for you."

Shiller shook her head, sensing the hurt he would give her if he could.

"No? There's a lot of time you can spend in steerage. Hours and hours, Shiller. In torn gear. Think about it."

In spite of herself, she said, "Mallory said that watch was shared."

"Mallory ain't chief steward. I am. You'll do all the steerage watches I say you will. That could be quite a lot. Until you get sensible, Shiller."

Dandridge stumbled to her feet and, hiding her face, pushed down the hall toward the medic room. Shiller watched her go, her hands leaving red marks where they touched the wall.

"Think about what I said, Shiller." For a moment Wranswell studied her with arrogant calm, then he turned and followed Dandridge to the medic room.

The skin on her left hand was unhealthily mottled. Shiller studied it under her bunk light, feeling a worry that was not reflected in her face. Four days of steerage watch had brought her to this. She flexed her fingers uncertainly and found that even a simple movement hurt and left her hand weak and trembling. Taking the packet of ointment Mallory had left for her, she smeared it over the livid spot. The pain eased.

Out in the hall she could hear Dandridge talking to Briggs. Shiller knew what Dandridge was saying, that she was angry, taking vengeance where she could, the hurt and damage done to her much worse than the ruin of her face. Leaning back,

Shiller tried to shut out the words, the spite that came through palpably.

A warning buzzer sounded the change of watch. Hearing it, Shiller felt a surge of rebellion, but she was too tired to ride it through. With tired acceptance she rose and pulled on her cold gear, checking all the temporary seals with more hope than trust. It would be a little better, but there was no way they could keep the cold out entirely, there was no way they could save her from the ache and the numbness.

Mallory's friendly face appeared around the frame of her door. "Ready?" he asked brightly.

"I guess."

"I'll walk you down." He waited in the door, his hands blocking the passage and the cruel words Dandridge spewed out at Briggs.

"Thanks," Shiller said, summoning the ghost of a smile. She had not smiled often since coming to the *Babel Princess*. Draping her headgear over her arm she joined Mallory in the narrow corridor.

"Too bad Wranswell's being shitty about steerage," Mallory was saying loudly enough for Dandridge and Briggs to hear them. He was still in his first-class uniform: tight breeches, loose shirt, half jacket and jaunty cuffed blue boots. Shiller looked at him with envy, her body made shapeless and clumsy in the cold gear. Mallory gave her clothes one uncertain look, then went on, "Say, Shiller, it's none of my business, but why fight it?"

"Fight what?" she asked, wishing he had not spoken.

"Wranswell. He's not interested in Dandridge anymore. You could be his mate. It's obvious he wants you."

"You're right, it's none of your business."

Mallory did not pay any attention to this. "What he's trying to do is wear you down, Shiller. He can do it."

"We're not out here all the time. Sometime we have to drop out and come into port. When we do, there's company officials . . ."

"Be reasonable, Shiller," Mallory said patiently. "We're in port maybe one day in twenty, then we're gone again. You can't begin to get to one of the officials of the Babel line. That takes weeks."

"Then I'd transfer to another ship." She was speaking recklessly and she knew it. If Mallory decided to, he could tell Wranswell, and then there would be no escape for her.

"Don't kid yourself, Shiller. It's no different on the other ships. We run by our own law out here. And if we break the rules now and then, who's going to come after us. And how?" He smiled at her, his dark eyes showing a gentle concern. "This is our universe. And Wranswell runs it."

"I'll think of something," Shiller said, not to Mallory. "I won't be his mate. I can't stand him." She turned, suddenly afraid. "Mallory, don't tell him I said that. Please."

He made a dismissing gesture, hands wide. "You don't want me to know, don't tell me. I probably won't tell Wranswell. But he's a tough man. Maybe I'll have to." He shrugged fatalistically.

"But Mallory . . . You wouldn't tell him." She felt suddenly desperate. Under the heavy wrap of her gear she felt a cold hard lump gather under her ribs.

Seeing her panic he said, "No, of course not, Shiller."

They were almost at the cold room. Shiller pulled her headgear off her arm and began to secure it. Her gloves made her hands awkward, and in a moment she asked Mallory to do it for her.

"Sure, glad to," he said, pulling the gear into place and sealing it. "Keep what I said in mind," he told her as they reached steerage. With a cuff on her arm for luck, he opened the hatch.

Shiller hesitated inside the hatch, dreading the four hours to come. She was still close enough to hear Wranswell stop Mallory outside.

"Well, Mallory, how did it go?" asked the hated voice.

"Well, I talked to her," Mallory said, hedging.

"Any headway?"

"Not so far." There was contrition in his tone, and embarrassment.

"Keep trying, Mallory. Or you can do your watches in there."

Mallory laughed uneasily. "You don't have to worry about that. You won't get me in there for anything." He paused. "I can talk to her again in the morning, when she's had some rest. Maybe she'll think it over while she's standing watch."

"I hope so, for your sake."

"It's gonna take time, Wranswell. The thing is, you got her real scared."

"That," Wranswell said, "is the general idea."

"You rotten traitor!" Shiller shouted when Mallory appeared in her door the next morning. "You can fucking well bet I thought about it!"

"Thought about what?" Mallory asked warily.

"You know. I heard you talking to Wranswell. I heard what you said, Mallory."

Mallory hesitated, indecisive. His face was a mixture of aggravation and loss. "Then you know how things stand," he said at last.

Shiller swung off her bunk. "No, I do not know how things stand. I thought I did, but obviously I was wrong." She found suddenly that it was hard to speak, and the difficulty was only partly due to the cold in steerage.

"Ah, Shiller." If he meant to be conciliatory, he failed.

"Don't you talk that way to me. Why did you do it, Mallory? I thought you gave a damn. I thought you were my friend."

"I am your friend," he said, speaking with a caution he might have used with a child. "Why else would I do this?"

"To save your hide, that's why."

"Look, Shiller, I told you the day you came aboard to be careful of Wranswell. He's the boss here. Why didn't you listen to me then. You dumb, or something?"

"I didn't think you meant this," she shot back at him, finding a strength in her that she did not know she had. "You never said a damn thing about what Wranswell wants, or what he's like. You never told me he'd want this of me." There was a burning behind her eyes and Shiller was shocked to realize that she was on the verge of tears.

"I figured you knew. What else would it be?"

"You were very careful about that, Mallory. You warned me to watch out for Wranswell. You said that when you showed me around the ship. But that wasn't what you meant, was it? And you didn't come out and tell me what I had to deal with. And you didn't tell me you were following Wranswell's orders."

Mallory was getting angry. "Who the hell else's orders would I follow? This is Wranswell's world, and he makes the decisions.

230   *Chelsea Quinn Yarbro*

More'n that, he's the one who makes sure things get done. You can't fight that, Shiller. And I can't fight it either."

"That's shit," she spat at him.

"Fuck you, Shiller." He turned away from the door, then looked back. "You keep this up, you're gonna be as dead as the stuff outside this ship. Wranswell ain't gonna wait forever. You gotta give in sometime."

Shiller grabbed her cold gear and hurled it at Mallory.

"You're as dumb as steerage. You belong there!" Casting the heavy gear aside, Mallory stormed off, his steps sounding like explosions along the corridor.

As Shiller listened to the sounds die away, she felt part of herself die with them. Mallory was right, and Wranswell waited inexorably for her, to possess her and break her. She did not recognize the terrible grating sounds as her own sobs.

By the time the *Babel Princess* dropped out for its first stop, Shiller had got used to the steerage routine. She figured out the colonists bound for Grady's Hole and prepared them for shipping to the surface. It was a long tedious job, but now she welcomed it, for at least in steerage she was safe from Wranswell.

"It's okay, Harper," she said to one of the cocoons, addressing it by the name stenciled across it. "You're gonna like Grady's Hole. It's sunny and warm, and the soil is good. The Babel line has an outpost there already, so you know you won't starve." She hooked the support tubes into his shipping capsule, noticing as she did that the color of the fluid was wrong. Quickly she checked the feeders to see if she had confused the line, but no, it was the correct one. And the solution that should have been mulberry was a pale pink.

Cautiously she tapped the feeder, drawing out a sample of the fluid for later examination. "Hope you're okay, Harper," she said to the cocoon. "Don't want you to get down there and find out they can't thaw you out." She put the sample into one of her capacious pockets and moved on to the next tier.

"Crawleigh, Matson, Ewings and Marmer," she read from her list, as if calling role. "You're the last of the lot. The consignment says fourteen, and you make it fourteen." She moved the tiers into position for capsule loading, making a final check of the list.

When she was finished she stamped the invoices and relayed

them up to the bridge for verification. In her pocket there were now four samples, the other three drawn from Marmer, Ewings and from one of the earlier capsules which she had gone back to check after seeing Harper's feeder.

The invoices came back with the Babel seal and the captain's sigil on them. Shiller took them and put each in the capsule it belonged to. Then she sealed the capsules one after the other, checking each seal in the manner prescribed.

"Shiller." The voice on the speaker was Briggs. "I got something you have to ship down with the capsules."

"What?" she asked, not caring.

"Something important."

"It's against regulations," she said, speaking by rote. She no longer trusted anyone on the ship. "Sorry."

"Wranswell said to tell you that he'd count it as a favor. He said he might find some other work for you to do if you can get this stuff down for him."

"What is it?" She found that to her disgust, she was interested. She hesitated on the seals of the capsule.

"It goes with Baily. You seal it up yet?" Briggs sounded urgent, as if he too had some consideration riding on her agreement.

"Not yet," she admitted. She hesitated, thinking. If it were found out that she had added something not on the invoice, she could be stranded out on some distant planet where she could be a common laborer or a prostitute. But if she failed to do this for Wranswell, her life would continue to be a nightmare.

"Hurry up," Briggs prodded. "I got it right here. It's small. Wranswell really wants it, Shiller."

"Okay," she said. She went to the hatch and held out her gloved hand. To her surprise the thing Briggs dropped into it was only a small dark vial, weighing no more than a couple of ounces. "Is this all?" she asked, turning the thing over in her gloved hand.

"That's it. And remember, it has to go in Baily," Briggs said, sounding relieved.

"You can tell Wranswell it's done," she said and closed the hatch.

But she wondered idly what it was Wranswell was smuggling —for surely he was smuggling—that was so small and so precious.

"I haven't thanked you yet for that service you did me," Wranswell said to Shiller as they sat in the mess. "You're coming around. Perhaps all the way?"

Shiller did not even look up from her plate.

"You might be interested to learn what I am up to. No? Not the least curiosity?"

"No."

"No? But do you really have so little concern for your fate? You, Shiller?"

"I'm not interested, Wranswell," she said, and knew she was lying.

"But you might be arrested for this. Don't you want to know what the charge will be?" Wranswell was being funny again. His deep rumbling laughter filled the mess room. "We could all be arrested for this, certainly. But then, to arrest us, they would have to catch us. Out here." A few of the other stewards took up his laugh.

Shiller bit her lip and remained silent.

"Here we are, engaged in secret smuggling. Babel policy would condemn us all and most of you know nothing about it." He looked contemptuously over his underlings. "How many of you are like Shiller here, and don't want to know?"

"It's steerage," said Dandridge from across the room. "Wranswell smuggles the bodies. He waters down the feeders so the cargo is just getting cold and drugs; it makes 'em hard to thaw out that way. He ships along the feeder solution so his bunch in customs on the ground can keep 'em going until they can sell the cargo to slavers." Her voice was loud in a room suddenly still.

"Dandridge, is, of course, right," Wranswell allowed, spreading his huge hands on the table. "She is also very foolish. But then, I don't imagine anyone heard her very well."

Conversation erupted in the mess, the eleven stewards trying to shut out the accusation that would condemn them all.

Under the racket, Wranswell said to Shiller, "I would put it differently, but essentially Dandridge is right. From time to time I'll expect a little help from you. In exchange, you may be allowed to stand something other than steerage watches. Is your first-class uniform clean?"

"And if I don't cooperate?" In spite of herself, she knew she was striking a bargain with Wranswell, giving her consent to his terrible scheme. She had heard enough about the slavers to make her shudder, for they were far worse than anything Wranswell could hope to be.

"I think you will. In the next few days you might have a few words with Dandridge about it. She can tell you what to expect."

"Why Dandridge? What should I ask her?"

"Shiller, you will know when the time is right." He turned away from her then and spoke softly to Mallory.

Dandridge's body was stiff by the time Shiller found it. She had been struck many times, and even the ugly lividity of death could not disguise the large bruises on her arms and back. She lay now crammed between two rows of tiers at the back of steerage, her dead eyes blackened, horrified. She had not died easily.

"Briggs, you and Carstairs get in here," Shiller said to the speaker. She was feeling curiously lightheaded, as if Dandridge's death had spared her.

"Want some company, Shiller?" Briggs asked with an audacity he had learned from Wranswell. "Come outside here."

"I've got company. Dandridge's body's in here. You gonna come in and get it out or do I call the bridge?" It was a bluff: Shiller knew she could never call the bridge and risk the ostracism it would bring, or maybe an end like Dandridge's.

"You don't have to do that," Briggs said quickly. "You said Dandridge's body?"

"Yes. She's dead. Somebody killed her. You better tell Wranswell. He might be anxious about her." Shiller heard Briggs whisper to someone, then he said, "It'll take a couple of minutes. We'll get her out."

It was longer than that when they at last came through the hatch, shapeless in their cold gear, a stretcher slung between them. Shiller saw that the other steward was Mallory, and that he was calm.

"She's at the back under tier number five. You won't be able to lay her flat; she's got stiff."

When they got to the place, Briggs stopped, his eyes widening behind his mask. "Come on, Briggs," Mallory said. "We gotta get'er out of here. Wranswell's waiting."

Briggs pulled himself together, grabbing the out-thrust elbows. "Look at her. She sure got hit," Briggs said. Mallory only grunted.

They wrestled the body onto the stretcher and lashed it down as best they could. Then, without a word to Shiller, they left steerage, carrying their grim trophy between them.

Shiller watched them go, remembering what Wranswell had said. The warning was plain. If she talked, she, too, would be killed. If she did not cooperate with Wranswell's smuggling, she would find herself beaten and frozen at the back of steerage.

"It's too bad that we'd already gone hyper when this happened," Wranswell announced to the stewards. "If we were still in port we could report this to the Babel home office and they could investigate. But since we've gone hyper and we aren't due to touch port for another fifteen days, even preserving the body might be difficult."

Gathering her anger and her courage, Shiller said, "Why not put her in steerage? She'll keep in there."

Wranswell chuckled at the idea. "Well, it's a novel approach," he said as he loomed over her. "But it's not practical. We'll put her in one of the spare capsules and ship her off."

Briggs had got noticeably paler. "Off *where?*" he demanded. "Out there? We don't even know where that is. We won't know where she's gone."

From his side of the room Mallory gave Briggs an impatient sign. "Don't worry about it, Briggs. It's better this way. More'n that, there won't be any hassle at the other end of the line. Nobody'll investigate and we'll all be safe. Captain'll file a report and that'll be the end of it."

"Mallory's right, you know." Wranswell agreed. "Much less trouble for everyone. Believe me, the Babel line doesn't like these occurrences any better than we do. We'll prepare her for burial and send her off tomorrow."

When the others got up to leave, he motioned Shiller to stay behind. "I trust your talk was constructive? I know these one-sided conversations can be trying, but I'm sure she had some information for you." He reached out one hand and tugged at Shiller's hair. "Be reasonable, Shiller. You won't get anywhere if you antagonize me."

"I got the message. Can I go now?" She refused to look at

Wranswell, at his bloated, smiling face and his eyes that raked her body like nails.

"Not quite yet. I want to explain about the next drop out. On Archer Station, the next port, we play the game a little differently."

"I hear you," Shiller said, wishing she could scream.

"There, one capsule more or less makes little difference to my agent's clients. And I find it hard to justify keeping a steward on who is only good for steerage work. Unless I find out you're more versatile, there might be an extra capsule. Archer Station deals with Ranyion slavers. I understand they're most unpleasant."

Shiller felt her teeth grind as she held her mouth shut. There was little she could say now. Archer Station was two weeks away, and they would be her last two weeks of freedom.

In the end they had to break Dandridge's bones to fit her into the capsule. But at last her stiff, distorted body was closed away, sealed for a journey into nothing that would lead nowhere. The stewards gathered at the lock, as Wranswell had ordered.

Briggs arrived last, looking haggard. He watched Mallory through exhausted eyes, fingering a lean statue which he clutched to his chest. Mallory deliberately ignored him, turning away when Briggs started his way.

Wranswell, his big body looking out of place in his first-class uniform, arrived to deliver his eulogy before sending the capsule on its way. He wore a secret smile that grated on Shiller's nerves. Wranswell was obviously satisfied.

"For our comrade who has died in the line of duty," Wranswell began the traditional benediction as the rest of the stewards shifted on their feet and felt awkward, "we praise her now for all she accomplished while she worked among us and did her tasks. . . ."

Before Wranswell could continue, Briggs shouted out, "You killed her!" And he lunged at Mallory, the statue he had been holding at the ready. "I loved her and you killed her!"

Mallory shouted and leaped aside, bringing his arm down on Briggs' back. Briggs staggered under the blow, but turned, his face filled with loathing. "You're Wranswell's errand boy. He gave her to you and when she wouldn't take you, you killed her!" He sloughed around on Wranswell. "You're as bad a slaver as the ones you sell to."

This time it was Wranswell who hit him, sinking his balled-up fists deep into Briggs' gut. Retching, Briggs fell to his knees. Beside him the little black statue lay broken. "You can hit me till I'm dead. It doesn't change anything. You still killed her."

"When you're finished, Briggs, we'll get on with this ceremony." Wranswell turned to Mallory. "You're okay?"

"Sure. Briggs's just upset. He don't know what he's saying. Why, when this is all over, he's gonna forget all about it." Mallory was straightening his uniform as he spoke, adjusting it with strangely finicky gestures.

Briggs looked up. His face was ashen and his voice hoarse, but there was no mistaking his words. "You hear me, Wranswell. So long as Dandridge is out there, we're gonna stay hyper, too."

"Go away, Briggs. If you can't conduct yourself right, go away." Then Wranswell turned from him, ignoring him now. He began the ceremony once more in impressive, sonorous tones. No one but Wranswell spoke.

Above decks the captain played back Wranswell's report, shaking his head, not caring about what went on below decks. He heard the thing out, then connected it to his log, giving his formal acceptance to the report. It was too bad that the steward had died. They would have to lay over a couple extra days at Archer Station while a new one was sent.

It was several hours later when there was the first indication that something was wrong. The *Babel Princess* gave a lurch, like a boat riding over choppy water. But in hyper there were no waves, and there was no reason for the ship to lurch. Alarms began to sound all over the ship.

Shiller tumbled out of the bunk, still half-asleep, knowing that something had wakened her. The shrilling of the alarm broke through and she began to dress automatically. The cold of steerage was still on her and she trembled as she pulled herself into her clothes.

The alarms grew louder. Down the corridor there were other stewards stumbling about, shouting to each other.

Suddenly the ship's master address system came on. "This is

the captain. This is the captain," the system announced. "We have encountered unfamiliar turbulence. For that reason we are going to drop out and see if there is any reason for it. I apologize in advance to our passengers for this inconvenience. I ask your indulgence while we complete this maneuver. The stewards are standing by to take care of you should you experience any discomfort. We will drop out in ten minutes. For that reason, please remain in your quarters. If you need assistance, buzz for a steward. Thank you."

Mallory pounded on Shiller's door. "Get your ass above decks, Shiller. First-class uniform so the tourists can throw up on somebody neat and clean."

"Shut up," she answered.

"The passengers are waiting," he said in a brusk voice.

Sarcastically she asked, "And are you looking after steerage? I thought that regulations required that steerage be manned during every drop out and every pass to hyper. Don't tell me you're going in there, Mallory."

"Not me, but you are," Mallory said, taking cruel delight in this change of orders. "You can take care of the cargo in steerage. You been doing it so long, you're real good at it. Maybe you can snuggle up to 'em and keep 'em warm." He laughed in imitation of Wranswell, then hurried down the hall.

Slowly Shiller changed into her cold gear, a deep worry settling over her with gloom. Unlike the others, she suspected that Briggs was behind the trouble. And when the others discovered it, what would happen to him? Mutiny brought with it an automatic death sentence. Shiller had seen a formal execution once, and it had not been pretty. To watch poor, crazy Briggs die that way . . .

"Hurry up, Shiller," Langly shouted from down the hall. "Time's short! Three minutes!"

"Coming," she answered, and went out into the corridor still pulling on her gloves. When the one-minute warning sounded she began to run.

The drop out did not work. The drive whined, the ship bucked and slid like a frightened horse, the shield room grew unbearably hot, the core reached its danger point, but they failed to drop out.

There was a wait then, while the core cooled down, and then they tried once more. Above decks the tourists in first class watched each other uneasily, not willing to admit that their pleasure jaunt could end this way. The stewards kept to their assigned posts, not daring to show the panic they felt. For if the tourists did not know they were in trouble, the stewards did.

The fear did not touch steerage. Shiller braced the cocoons, strapping the tiers to their stanchions on the walls. She steadied herself between them and stoically rode out the first attempt to drop, and the second. She knew a morose satisfaction: if they were stranded in hyper, she would be free of Wranswell, free of Mallory. She glanced around the familiar bleakness of steerage, thinking of the names stenciled on the cocoons with a certain affection, as she might have thought of plants.

"Don't let this worry you, Ander," she said to the nearest one. "This doesn't matter. If we don't get where you're going, you'll never know about it anyway." Idly she wondered if Ander were male or female. There was nothing on the invoice that mentioned sex. Was Ander a great strapping lad with huge shoulders and hands the size of dinner plates? Was she a strong farm woman who could carry a sheep slung over her shoulders? Was he a small ferocious man with bright eyes and boundless energy? Did she work handily, driving her small frame to greater feats . . . ?

She tightened the cocoon in place and moved on to the next one.

This was Taslit, bound for Dreuten's Spot, an out-of-the-way agricultural planet, the last on their outward run. "Taslit, never mind," she spoke gently, easing the cocoon more firmly into place. "Two to one Wranswell would have sold you to some slaver anyway. You won't have lost anything this way."

Then the alarm sounded once more and another futile attempt to drop out began. As the heat mounted in the core, steerage began to warm up, the temperature rising almost five degrees. Shiller watched with concern as more and more indicators moved into the critical zones. If they kept this up long it would kill her cargo. She couldn't let that happen.

She went like a drunken man across steerage, reaching for the speaker button as she was thrown against the wall. She grabbed for a brace and held on as the *Babel Princess* sunfished about her. At last the attempt was broken off, the core stopped its maddened hum and the ship righted itself in the vastness of hyper.

Again the speaker came to life. "This is the captain speaking. This is the captain speaking." There was silence following that announcement. "We appear to be having some difficulty returning to normal space. As it will take time to effect the necessary repairs, we will continue our journey in hyper until we can drop out without endangering the ship or her passengers . . ."

Shiller stared at the speaker, incredulous. "We're never gonna drop out; you know that," she told it, shaking her head.

"We may be delayed in arriving at Archer's Station . . ."

"We sure will. Forever."

"But the Babel Company will gladly refund part of your fare to compensate for this delay. I trust we will proceed without incident."

When the sound died away, Shiller sank onto the monitor bench. She wondered if the others in the seven percent who never came out of hyper did this, lied to the passengers and to themselves, pretending that everything was all right, promising an end to the voyage they would never live to see.

Shiller started to laugh. In the eerie cold the walls echoed her laughter, making it louder.

Wranswell was left to deal with Briggs; the captain had decided that it was a matter for the chief steward because Briggs was a steward. Wranswell had smiled, accepted the responsibility and sought out Mallory. Together they decided what had to be done.

They attached burners to Briggs' hands and feet and lit them. Then they locked him in steerage, alone with the cocoons. Wranswell and Mallory took turns at the hatch window, watching him as he died. They watched for a long time.

And when at last they dragged the body out, it had burned-off hands and feet, leaving charred, bleeding stumps on a corpse rimed with frost, seered with cold, the skin mottled blue where it was not black.

On Wranswell's orders it was left in the corridor for a day, a silent ghastly reminder of Wranswell's power. Then it was loaded into a capsule and sent out to join Dandridge in the lost places.

There had been trouble above decks. Rations had been short-ened again and a fight had broken out, the stronger taking what little food there was from the weak. Now that most of them knew there would be no escape from hyper they cared less what became of one another. There had been several injuries and medicine was running as short as food.

"Look," said Mallory to a general meeting of the stewards, "we can take the ones that are worst hurt and we can stick 'em in cocoons and hook 'em up like the rest of steerage. We won't have to feed 'em, they won't get any worse, and if we ever get out of this, they'll be alive. They'll be grateful."

"And if we don't get out of this?" Shiller asked, the fear of Mallory all but gone. She had not bothered to change out of her cold gear.

"Then it won't matter, Shiller," Wranswell said from the head of the table. He had lost weight and his flesh hung in folds about him like a garment that no longer fit.

"Then who's supposed to look after 'em?" Shiller went on, seeing with contempt that the other stewards did not challenge him.

"You are."

"What? No more flattering offers?" She barked out a laugh, and found that it no longer hurt to laugh, or to die.

Stung, Wranswell retorted. "I've made other arrangements. You lose, Shiller. Too bad." His greedy eyes fastened on the slender grace of Langly, and the boy pouted in response.

"Lucky you," Shiller said before she walked out.

She woke to the smell of cooking meat. She sat up slowly, for hunger had made her faint. The light over her bunk was off but she did not bother to turn it on; she knew it was dead. More awake, she sniffed again. Yes, it was meat, fresh meat broiling. She felt her way to the door and pulled it open.

"Hey, Shiller, come on down and have some breakfast," Langly called when he caught sight of her. His bony face was wreathed in smiles and grease.

Shiller shook her head as if to clear it. "Where'd that come from?"

"It was Mallory's idea." He turned into the mess to answer a question, then said to her, "You're entitled to two pounds of meat a day so long as you're working."

"What'd you do, kill someone?" she asked without thinking.

Langly's answering giggle told her what she did not know.

"Oh, shit," she cried, ducking back into her room and pulling on her cold gear as fast as she could. It was a slow business in the dark, and she had to pause often to regain her strength. When she was done she stumbled down the corridor, oblivious to the mocking words that Langly sent with her.

When she pulled open the hatch, she knew.

The tiers had been raided, the cocoons pulled apart and the bodies harvested for the stewards. Here and there a few of the cocoons remained intact, awaiting the time when the others would be hungry again. Some held the injured passengers, their new seals not quite dry.

Shiller stood in the door, swaying on her feet. That they had done this to her steerage, that they had damaged her cargo . . . She moved into the cold room, unbelieving. Ander was gone. So was Taslit. And Ettinger. And Swansleigh. Nathan. Cort. Fairchild. Vaudillion. Desperately she searched the tiers for the cocoons and found them empty. Gone, gone, gone . . . She thought of Wranswell, his sagging face full of meat, smiling, gesturing as he ate, his thick hands caressing Langly and his dinner alternately.

Vomit spewed from her before she could stop it, and she sank to her knees until there was nothing left for her to cast up.

"There she is." Mallory's soft words reached across steerage to Shiller as she lay exhausted on the floor.

"Good work," Wranswell said, a contented grin spreading over his shiny face. "I was afraid we'd lost her."

Shiller turned her head slowly, filth and ice clinging to her face. Dully she watched as the two men came nearer.

"Hello, Shiller," Mallory beamed down at her. "We've been looking for you." He was much closer now. He put his boot on the side of her face and pushed.

Shiller gasped and was silent.

"Come now, Shiller. You aren't going to spoil this for us, are you?" Wranswell leaned down next to her. "Let me hear you, Shiller. It's much quicker if you do." He sank his hands in her hair and pulled sharply back. Shiller left blood and skin on Mallory's boot.

Mallory was good at his job. Each time a fist or a boot struck her, Shiller remembered the way Dandridge had looked when she found her. Now she knew how it had happened. She tried to let go, to ride with the punishment and the pain, but she knew that she fought back. In some remote part of her mind she knew that she struck at Mallory, trying desperately to stop him, to give him back hurt for hurt. Once she had the satisfaction of connecting with his eye, and as he beat her into unconsciousness, she could see the slow drip of blood down his face, and she was satisfied.

When she woke it was warm. Her cocoon had thawed around her and the room reeked of putrefaction. Of the few remaining bodies in steerage, only she was alive. Numbly she felt for the feeder lines and found none. They must not have had time to attach them.

Carefully she eased herself off the tier, her hands shaking when she tried to close them around the lip of the tier.

Then she heard the sound. "Wranswell? Wranswell? Where are you?"

The voice was Mallory's, but so changed. Now it was a quavering thread, coming on uneven breaths like an old man's.

"Wranswell?"

Shiller listened for the answer, hardly daring to breathe. She did not want to be discovered, not by Mallory, not by Wranswell. She was not alive for that. Discovering that she was trembling, she willed herself to relax.

"I know you're down here," Mallory went on, his voice reverberating in the still corridors. "I'm hungry, Wranswell."

At the words Shiller felt her own hunger rage in her with fangs as sharp and demanding as some beast's. She knew that her trembling weakness was from hunger, that her bony hands were the face of hunger.

Something stumbled near the shield room. Then lumbering footsteps came down the hall, wallowing, blundering into the walls, no longer careful or cautious, wanting only escape.

Now Shiller understood, and it was what she had feared. It was the hunt. The last hunt. She lay back on the tier, very still, hearing her heart very loud in the stinking room.

There was a scuffle now, flesh meeting flesh, and a mingled

panting of voices, senseless sounds that neither Mallory nor Wranswell knew they made.

Then came the heavy, final sound, as though something large and moist had burst.

"Got you. Got you," Mallory chanted in ragged victory. He was not good to hear. "Got you. Got you. Got you, Wranswell." His high crowing made the hackles on Shiller's neck rise.

Now the sounds were different, a chopping and tearing as Mallory set about his grizzly work.

This was her chance then. Her hunger was gone and her mind had become clear as her terror dissolved. After this, there could be no more terror, no more fear.

Carefully, very carefully Shiller eased herself off the tier. Slowly, so slowly she slid across the room, no longer seeing the slime that oozed underfoot, or seeing the things that rotted on the other tiers, or the wreckage in steerage. That was over and done. That she could not change. There was only one thing now that she wanted, one last act she could perform.

She reached the monitor bench, raising the lid so that it made no sound.

In the hall Mallory began to sing.

Then Shiller had it, the long wedged blade that opened the capsules. Its edge shone purposefully. It had been designed to cut through seventeen inches of steel without slowing down.

Ander was dead, and Taslit. Dandridge, Briggs. Langly, too, she supposed. Wranswell. Cort. Ettinger. Harper. All of them.

The *Babel Princess* was dead, lost in uncharted darkness, derelict, drifting on unknown tides, its last energies draining into emptiness.

She was dead, too.

Shiller fondled the blade with care, testing the edge against her thumb, sucking the blood, tasting the salt. Weak as she was, she would not fail.

In the corridor Mallory was almost finished.

And in steerage, on the other side of the hatch, Shiller was waiting.

SEASCAPE

GREGORY BENFORD

Earlier in this volume Poul Anderson writes that a civilization which has "mastered FTL would explode outward like a dropped watermelon. They'd have bases, colonies, disciple races . . . communicating by tachyons."

Here is a story of just such a disciple race, a sumi-e *painting of technology, religion, and alien culture. While showing us the economics of fairly advanced interstellar FTL travel, Gregory Benford reveals a concern with the ethical and moral problems of technological civilization.*

An FTL culture will exercise power on a grand scale. Benford shows us how this power has reached into the past, present, and future lives of the people of Seascape . . .

Dawn comes redly on a water world.

Shibura sat comfortably in lotus position, watching the thin pink line spread across the horizon. Slowly the Titanic Ocean lost its oily darkness and rippled with the morning wind. Waves hissed on the beach nearby.

The pink line collected into a red ellipse, then into a slowly rising yellow ball. The gathering wetness of the morning fog slowly seeped away. Shibura passed through this transition complete, of a piece, attention wholly focused. Then a small creature, something like a mouse with bat wings and a furry yellow topknot, coasted in through layers of fog and landed on his shoulder. Smiling, he made a finger perch for the animal, noting that its wings were translucent and covered with fine pearly moisture. Shibura and the air squirrel studied each other for a moment. There came the furious beat of wings from above and the faint high cries of pursuit. The squirrel fidgeted; Shibura fished a crumb from his pocket and threw it into the air. The animal leaped, caught it with a snap and coasted away on an updraft. Shibura smiled.

Waterchimes sounded and a small, nut-brown man emerged from his home further down the beach. He began doing excercises on the white beach: hip thrusts, smooth flowing of limbs first one way, then the other, easy leaps into the air. The man's house was a vaulted, delicate structure of curved lattices. The reddish greasewood gave it the appearance of weight and mass, belied by the rakish tilt of the columns and cantilevered beams that would have been impossible in normal Earthgravity. Everywhere there were curves; no angles, no sharpness or sudden contrast to jar the eye.

Shibura enjoyed the man and his house, just as he appreciated the other homes hugging the tide line of the Titanic. But they were people of the world, and given to such things. He was a Priestfellow and lived in a rude hut of rough canewood. His floor was fine ground sand. His food—Shibura reached to the side and found a bowl of red liquid—simple and adequate. His neighbor was a dealer in metals who shipped deposits from the Off Islands for use in the holy factories. The small man had achieved a station in spiritual life adequate to his personality, and now reaped the rewards. So it would come to Shibura. He had but to wait until the Starcrossers made audience on Seascape again. Then—if the audience were successful and reached cusp—he would fulfill his role and pass through the holy lens. The lesson was clear: if the Starcrossers were pleased, if the Paralixlinnes proved functional, then Shibura (indeed, all of Seascape) would have proved holy in the light of the stars, complete again for another generation or more. After that audience would come the material things, if Shibura wished them. Within himself he was sure he would not desire such trappings. He relished the life of austerity and the denial of the body. Not, of course, for its own sake: that was counter to the integrated spirit. But he knew that for himself simplicity was integrity and serenity. Even the coming of the Starcrossers would not deflect him from this.

Down the coast Shibura could see people leaving their homes and walking on the beach, some swimming and others doing morning meditation. Through the thinning fog he could make out the main road, still void of traffic. A lone figure moved down it in the quilted morning shadows: a priestservant, to judge by his robes. Shibura wondered what the man's mission could be. He believed he was the only priestfellow nearby, but he could imagine no task before him which required a summons so early. Perhaps the man was bound out of town, toward the interior farmland.

Well, no matter. He tried to return to his meditation but the focus was not there. The sun had risen slightly and its steam brought him even more into the awakening of the morning. He looked up. The great eye of Brutus hung overhead, a half crescent streaked with brown and yellow bands. As he watched Shibura could see small changes as the great clouds of that turbulent atmosphere swirled and danced. He knew that Brutus was massive and powerful; it sucked the waters away in the second tidetime, stronger than the sun. But now it seemed calm and peaceful, unwracked by storms. So unlike Seascape it was, yet Brutus was the parent of this world. Shibura knew this as a truth passed on from the Starcrossers, but it seemed so unlikely. Seascape was a place of quietness and Brutus usually a drove of storms. There were some in the streets who said Brutus influenced the lives of men, but when asked the Starcrossers said no—men were not born of Seascape and their rhythms were unkeyed to this world, however much it suited man to live here.

Shibura shook his head; this was disturbing, it took him out of his natural place. All hope of further contemplation vanished when there was a loud jangling of his welcome bells. The priestservant was padding quickly down the short wooded path. His sandals scattered pebbles to the side in his haste. Shibura breathed deeply to compose himself and caught the first sharp tang of the morning tide. The man knocked delicately on the thin door and Shibura called to him to enter. He was an old priestservant who, it was said, remembered well the last audience of the Starcrossers. His robe was tattered and retained the old form of pants and vest beneath his flowing purple outer garments. The man smiled, exposing brown teeth, and ceremoniously handed forward a folded yellow parchment. Shibura took it and carefully flattened the message against the sand before him. The calligraphy was hurried and inexact. Here and there the ink was smeared. Shibura noted these facets before reading it; often one could learn more from them than from the literal contents. He prepared himself for an unsettling point.

Slowly, he read. His thumbs bit into the parchment and crinkled it. His breath made a dry rasping sound. After perfunctory salutations and wishes of the day the message was laconic:

They are coming. Prepare.

The great sphere rode through Jumpspace, unseen and unknown.

Its air was stale. The bridge was dark; hooded consoles made pools of light where men sat calculating, measuring, checking. The Captain stood with hands clenched behind him as the calculation proceeded. There were men sealed within the walls and wired forever into the bowels of the computers; the Captain did not think of these. He simply waited in the great drifting silence between stars, beyond real space and the place of men.

Silvery chimes rang down thin, padded corridors, sounding the approach of Jump. The bridge lay in dull red light. Men moved purposefully about it but everyone knew they were powerless to control what was coming.

Justly so. Converting a ship into tachyons in a nanosecond of real space time is an inconceivably complex process. Men devised it, but they could never control the Jump without the impersonal faultless coordination of microelectronics.

A few earnest, careful men moved quietly about the bridge as they prepared to flip over into real space. In the same way that a fundamental symmetry provided that the proton had a twin particle with opposite charge, helicity and spin—the antiproton—there was an opposite state for each real particle, the tachyon.

The speed of light, c, is an upper limit to all velocities in the universe to which man was born; in the tachyon universe c is a lower limit. To men, a particle with zero kinetic energy sits still; it has no velocity. A tachyon with no energy is a mirror image—it moves with infinite velocity. As its energy increases it slows, relative to us, until at infinite energy it travels with velocity c.

As long as man remained in his half of the universe, he could not exceed *c*. Thus he learned to leave it.

By converting a particle into its tachyon state, allowing it to move with a nearly infinite velocity and then shifting it back to real space, one effectively produces faster-than-light travel. In theory the process was obvious. It was Okawa who found the practical answer, some decades after the establishment of Old Nippon's hegemony. The Captain had often wondered why the Jumpdrive did not bear his name. Perhaps Okawa was born of impure strains. Perhaps he was an unfavored one, though passing clever.

Okawa reasoned by analogy, and the analogy he used was the simple laser. In the laser the problem was simply to produce a coherent state—to make all the excited atoms emit a photon at the same time. Okawa reasoned that the same problem appeared in the faster-than-light drive. If all the particles in the ship did not flip into their tachyon states at the same time, they would all have vastly different velocities and the ship in one grinding instant would tear itself apart. Okawa's achievement lay in finding a technique for placing all the ship's atoms in excited tachyon states so that they could all be triggered at the same instant; the particles of the ship Jumped together, coherently.

All this was accomplished by maximizing the cross-section for transition from real particle to tachyon. Complex modulated electromagnetic waves controlled the transition through microelectronic components, which operated on the scale of atomic dimensions. Thus, through a long chain, the ability to cross between the stars depended on controlling the quantum events at an unimaginably small scale.

A slightly audible count came through the padded rooms of the starship. Silvery chimes echoed and the Captain closed his eyes at the last moment. A bright arc flashed beyond his eyelids, so he could see the blood vessels as he heard the dark, whispering sound of the void. A pit opened beneath him, he was falling—

Suddenly they wrenched from tachyon space and back into the real universe. There was really no difference between the two; each mirrored the physical laws of the other. There were stars and planets in tachyon space, surely—but no man had ever stopped to explore them. No one knew if a real spaceship transferred into tachyons could be maintained in the presence of dense tachyon matter. The physicists said it was doubtful, and no one cared to test the point.

The ship trembled slightly—or perhaps it was only his own reaction—and the Captain turned to the large screen of the foredeck. There was the F8 star, burning hot and yellow.

"A minute, Cap'n," the Executive Officer said. "Looks like we blew a few on that last one."

"What?"

"The ferrite banks. A lot of them failed."

"The Paralixlinnes, you mean," the Captain said precisely.

"Right. Some are showing flashover effects, too."

The Captain frowned. "I am afraid this might put us over the margin."

"What?"

The Captain grimaced at this insolence. "We may not have enough ferrite memory to make the transition back into Jump. I want a detailed report, if you please."

"Oh." The Executive Officer nodded and turned slightly away, fumbling at his fly. "You think it's that bad?" As he spoke he began urinating into the porous organiform flooring. "I mean, it could trap us here?"

The Captain stepped away and clasped his hands behind his back. "Well, uh, yes, it might." He knew this public passing of water was acceptable practice on some worlds, the product of crowding and scarcity. He knew it was not supposed to be a sign of contempt. But something in the Executive Officer's manner made him think otherwise. Certainly actions like this were forbidden on his own home world . . .

"What happens if we try it without getting more ferrites?" the Executive Officer said, looking back over his shoulder. His urine spattered on the organiform and quickly disappeared. Many spots in the ship had such floors and walls; in the long run it was the only way to insure cleanliness. Dust, liquid, odd bits of paper—all were absorbed and gradually bled into the fuel reserve, to be chewed apart in incandescent fusion torches and converted into thrust.

"The ship's mass will not trigger coherently."

"So?"

A political appointee, the Captain guessed. "We would

emerge into tachyon space with each particle traveling at a different velocity."

"Ah, I remember." The man finished and zipped his fly. "Tear ourselves apart. Grind us to atoms."

"Uh, correct."

The Executive Officer had made no attempt to hide himself from view while urinating. The Captain wondered whether the man had any convention of privacy at all. Did he defecate in public? It seemed impossible, but—

"Okay, I'll get that report. Might take a while." The man did not bother to salute."

"See that it doesn't," the Captain said sharply and returned his attention to the phosphor screen. He expanded scale a hundredfold and found the banded gas giant planet. It was enormous, he knew, and radiated strongly in the infrared. At the very center of it, according to theory, hydrogen atoms collided and stuck, fusing together and kindling some weak fire. But this vast giant of a world was not their aim. There, not far from the methane-orange limb of the planet, gleamed a blue-white moon: Seascape. He smiled.

Shibura sat, feeling the exquisite rough texture of the floor mat on his ankles and yet at the same time not feeling it at all. There was no sound, and all was sound. He was listening and shimmering in the sweet air of incense, relishing the sticky pull of damp robe on his flesh.

"Thus we proceed to fullness," finished the Firstpriest. "Quit of our tasks. Gathered once more into the lap of sunlight."

Shibura studied the old man's weathered brown face, receptive. The morning had begun with sainted rituals among the crowds of Priestfellows and Priestsisters. As the quiet rhythm of the day wore on each was assigned a task of convergence, expressed gratitude, rose and departed. The damp of the suntide gradually seeped into the high vaulted room. The cold stone walls became clammy at first and then warmed, adding their own moist breath to the layered smoke of incense. From the rear of the great hall the singing reeds brought a clear, cutting edge of sound that aided the mind to become fixed.

"So we come to the end. All roles are suited but one." The Firstpriest paused and looked into Shibura's eyes. "There is left the place of him who stands on the right hand."

Shibura felt a momentary jolt of surprise. Then he extended his hearing and sensing behind and around him. True; he had not noticed the fact, but the other Priestfellows were gone. Only he remained. He felt a swell of elation. That implied—

"It passes to you as it once came to me," the Firstpriest said. From beneath the folds of his robes he produced a copper talisman and handed it to Shibura. It was deceptively heavy. Shibura tucked it into his side pouch and straightened the cloth. He knew no reply was necessary. The ripples of excitement and surprise smoothed and vanished. The Firstpriest began the ritual passes Shibura had heard described but never seen. The old man's hands slipped through the torchlight, now visible, now unseen. Shibura entered into a state of no definition, no thought, no method. To put aside the thousand things and, in stillness, retain yourself. So the motions led and defined him. And inside, the soft tinkling chuckle of joy.

After a time they rose and moved from the great hall. They did not use the usual passage of exit. Instead, they walked slowly through the Organic Portal, as convention required. Shibura had been here only once before, when he was learning the intricate byways of the temple. Their sandals made echoing clicks in the great hall, but when they stepped into the Portal there came a sudden quiet, for they now walked on a firm softness of green. The Portal was a long, perfectly round passage that muffled all sound. It had no noticeable weave or texture, save the uncountable small pores. There were no torches, but the cushioned walls seemed to provide light. It was a hushed and holy place. It was the enduring gift of the Starcrossers.

The two men stopped midway. Near the floor on a small yellow patch was the place of dedication.

Shibura had learned some fragments of the Starcrossers written language, but he could not decipher all the patch contained. No one could. He and the Firstpriest squatted together for a long moment and regarded the yellowed print.

ORGANIFORM. *47396A index 327. Absorbent multilayer.*

They passed out of the Portal and through the temple corridor. The Firstpriest began to unfold his memories of the last Starcrosser visit. There were preparations, always extensive and complex. The citizens of the city had to be prepared and the Priestfellows themselves would have to see to their own personal states of mind as the event approached.

"I received word from the Farseer only this morning. They had been studying the motion of the central band in Brutus, but of course they set aside the usual five time spaces for observation of the Great Bear. That is the ordained place from which the Starcrossers speak."

"But it is not time," Shibura said. "We expected the audience in my third decade."

"I know. I never expected to see another Starcrossing. The last came when I was a boy—almost too young to hold the talisman you now carry. The Firstpriest of that time assured me I would pass through the lens—die—before the Captain came again."

"Why, then?"

"We must remember our place. The Captain is forever Crossing and his path is not so simple that we can understand."

"The men of the Farseer could not be mistaken? They *did* see the lights?"

Shibura knew a few of those patient watchers of the sky. He did not understand the great tube they seemed to worship and saw no true interest in what they did. The stars were but points of light and told nothing. Only the sun and Brutus held any interest for a man of religion, for they alone revealed their structure. The stars were great candles and might possibly say much, but they were too far away. Only through the Crossing did contact with the mightier places come, and then solely in the form of the Captain and his fellows. Nonetheless, only with the Farseer could the dancing of lights be seen and preparations made for the coming of the Captain.

"I have every trust in them. The Farseer was built in the far past, at the command of the Captain. The role of the Farseer is ordained and it is not for a Firstpriest or Priestfellow to question the tenders of the Farseer." The old man's head bobbed in the gesture of instruction. He smiled to show that his words carried no sharp edge and were meant only for reminding. Between the two men there had come a feeling of closeness. The Firstpriest's joy that he would again see a Crossing conveyed itself to Shibura and lightened his step.

After a pause Shibura said, "Was there any message in the dancing light?"

"The tenders of the Farseer said only that it was the ritual message. They come. They are now within the grip of our sun and we must be ready."

Shibura padded ahead and put his weight against the great door of the temple. They passed out into sunlight. Going down the steps, the bare baked stone face of the temple at their backs, the murmur of life swelled up around them. The great square before them was host to hundreds of people. Knots of friends drifted past amid the flicking echoes of hundreds of sandals.

The shops which lined the tiled walkways were small and displayed their wares with abandon, letting robes spill from their holders; beads and books and spices competed for the same spot in a display case. The two men passed through the crowd. Shibura relished the grainy feel of this uncomplicated existence: talking, laughing, some barterers greeting the price of items with a feigned sharp bark of disbelief.

The sun lay on the horizon, burning a hole in heaven. A few men and women clad in religious raiments spoke of their missions in life, advising of the latest revelation. Shibura bore them no malice, for they were simple people who followed their own blind vision.

Five of the women formed a circle and chanted:

> I am
> Not great or small
> But only
> Part of All

Shibura smiled to himself. It was comforting to know that the purpose of their world was writ large in even the minds of the most common. These people were, of course, no less than he. They formed the base of the great pyramid at whose peak were not priests or merchants or the men of government, but a holy article: the Paralixlinnes. Shibura had learned much from those infinitely detailed and faceted cubes. As objects of meditation they were supreme; how fitting that they played the crowning role even in the vast universe of the Starcrosser.

The Firstpriest made a gesture and they turned down a bumpy avenue of black cobblestone. Rice bins towered over them, their great funnels pointing downward to the rude shop where the grains were sold. The tubs carried indecipherable scrawls in red denoting the strains.

Here the air had its own texture, the sweat of work and reek of spices. Where the two men walked the crowds separated and let them through. Word had passed in the early morning, once the Priestfellows had met in the temple. Now surely everyone in the city knew the time of cusp was approaching. Thus and so: in the damp morning the two men journeyed through the city to the foundry that was the focus of the city itself; the birthplace of the Paralixlinnes.

Shibura glanced upward at friend Brutus, thanking the brown and pink giant for this day. His senses quickened.

The Captain listened intently to the whine of the air circulator. So that was breaking down, too. Nothing in this ship seemed to work anymore.

The last transit through Jumpspace had fractured an entire encasement of Paralixlinnes, even though they were rated to stand up for longer than a year. The ship—indeed, the whole Jump network—was well over into the red zone. With that many encasements gone the ship might well fail at the next Jump. Perhaps the Captain could make it through by enforcing absolute discipline on the next Jump, but he doubted it. Many of the backup men were not well trained; it seemed a corollary of life that political appointees never knew their jobs. But if he ran the calculation through a dozen times perhaps the errors would iron themselves out. A slight mistake in the measurement of the metric tensor, some small deviation in the settings, a flashover in the encasements—any of these, and the ship would blossom into a thousand fiery fragments.

The Captain clenched his hands behind his back and paced the organiform deck. The hooded computer modules were lit and the sullen murmur of the bridge would be reassuring to one who did not know the facts. The Captain turned and glanced down the bridge. His Executive Officer was talking earnestly to one of the lieutenants. The Captain could be sure that whatever the conversation, it would not concern ship's business. The Executive Officer was a Constructionist and most of the lieutenants were sharp enough to have fallen directly into line as soon as the ship left its last major port. The Captain knew there were lists aboard of each staff member's political inclination, and he expected the list would soon be used.

Half the mercantile worlds they visited were Constructionist. The others were teetering, watching the drift of events and deciding which way to jump. Against the Constructionists were arrayed a motley crew of T'sei Ddea followers, Old Formists and the bulk of the rest of the apathetic human race. Most people—with a singular wisdom—wished only to be left alone. If the Constructionists had their way, the days of liberality would soon be past.

The Captain shrugged and turned away. Let the Executive Officer do what he would, this voyage was not finished and the ship was in far more peril than most of the officers realized. Politics could wait. If there was some failure at Seascape this ship might very well never leave real space again. He turned his attention back to the large screen. They were following a smooth ellipse in toward the gas giant that loomed ahead. At the terminator the Captain could see flashes of gigantic lightning, even at this distance.

This planet was at least nine Jupiter masses; its compressed core burned with a lukewarm fusion reaction. The physics of the thing would make an interesting study. He had never visited this system before, and while reading the description had wondered why an experimental station did not orbit the gas giant for scientific purposes. But then he realized Seascape had a telescope and would see the station. No one wished to perturb the priests of Seascape with an artificial construct in their skies. Such things had proved unsettling on other worlds. So the great gas planet went unstudied and Seascape, according to the computer log, displayed very little social drift. The society there had lasted over ten thousand years and the Captain was quite aware that he should do nothing to upset it.

He gave an order and the view shifted from the swirling bands to a point of light that orbited the great planet. The view expanded, focused. Seascape shimmered in blue-white. At first it appeared to have nothing but vast oceans, but as the eye accommodated to its light a few details emerged. Lumps of brown were strewn randomly, as though by a careless Creator. At the edge of the horizon lay the only continent. The Captain wondered idly if a drone Ramscoop was by chance making delivery now, but a quick scan of the orbital index indicated nothing around Seascape that would fit the parameters. He made a mental note to complain—for the nth time—about the lack of communication with the drone operation. Worlds like Seascape needed tools, cutting bits, sometimes rare metals and ceramics; if the drone were off schedule or failed in flight there was no way of knowing whether the client world was carrying on manufacture any longer. More than once the Captain had brought his ship out of Jump to find a servant world without necessary materials. Without the few pieces of crucial high technology that the Ramscoop should have brought the manufacturing process broke down. Without a cause to move them the priests had to search for some other aim, and usually they failed. The world began to come apart at the seams. Not only was the Jumpship's mission worthless, but sometimes fatal damage was done to the client society itself.

The Captain ordered a further magnification and the mottled brown continent became a swollen mark on the planet's limb. There was a belt of jungle, a crinkling gray swath of interior mountains, convoluted snake-rivers and—in the island chains to the north—frigid blue wastes.

An orderly passed by; the Captain accepted a warm mug of amber liquid. He sipped at it gingerly, made a face. He paced the deck again till he came to an area of organiform and then poured the cup into the floor. In the light gravity the drink made an odd slapping sound as it hit the organiform and was absorbed.

The Captain glanced back at the screen, where the single continent was spreading over the edge of Seascape. He felt a certain sadness that this would be one more world he visited for only a day or two, pressed by the demands of economy. There were thousands of worlds like this. Each made its own small contribution to the Fleet, each was a mirror of the original Planet. Yet the Captain wished he could see more of this world: hear the hum of insects in the hazy air, witness the eternal lazy rhythm of the Seascape orbit. Seascape was tidelocked so that the single continent always faced the banded giant. It was rare for an Earth-like planet to be a moon and even rarer when the geological mix in its crust was hospitable to man. The Captain wondered what it would be like to live on a world where the Sun was regularly eclipsed by a gas giant planet; what color was the halo? There were so many unique things about any world: winds that deafened, oceans that laughed, tranquility beside violence. Even the routine miracles of the xenobiologists could not wash away the taste and sound and smell of what was new and alien.

"Cap'n!"

The Captain turned. It was totally unnecessary to shout on the bridge. The Executive Officer was taking his time; he stopped and spat expertly into the organiform carpet. The Captain felt his spine go rigid.

"About time we sent them a burst, don't you think?" the other man said casually.

"It's day at their observatory."

"So what?"

"They cannot read laser flashes in broad daylight, obviously."

"Use radio. Hell—"

"Their culture was not designed to need or use radio. They haven't developed it and if we don't introduce it, perhaps they never will."

The Executive Officer regarded him shrewdly. "That's probably right."

"I know it is right," the Captain said.

"Yeah, I guess I could look it up if I had the time. I thought we ought to tell the natives we were coming in faster than usual."

The Captain regarded him with distant assessment. "And why is that?"

"We can't afford to spend much time here. Get the components and leave. There are good political reasons to be ahead of schedule this time."

"I see," the Captain said evenly. He glanced up at the screen where the ocean world was rolling toward them and savored the view one last time. His few moments of introspection had lifted some of his troubles but now the weight of working with such men returned. He breathed deeply of the cycled air and turned back to the Executive Officer.

Men might fly between the stars, threading across the sky, but they were still only men.

The message found them as they entered the Kodakan room. Shibura padded quietly behind the Firstpriest. They had reached the door when he felt a slight tap on his shoulder and turned. A man stood beside him panting heavily in the thick air. The chanting from within drowned out his words. Shibura gestured and the man followed him out into the foyer of the holy foundry.

"We are beginning the game," Shibura said rapidly. "What is it?"

The man still gasped for breath. "From the Farseer." Pause. "Starcrossers."

"What?" Shibura felt a sudden unease.

"The Watcher sent me at the run. The Starcrossers will not circle the sky five times. They come two circles from now."

"That is not congruent with ritual."

"So the Watcher said. Is there a reply for the Watcher?"

Shibura paused. He should speak to the Firstpriest but he could not now interrupt the Kodakan. Yet the Watcher waited.

"Tell him to omit the Cadence of Hand and Star." He juggled things in his mind for a moment. "Tell the Watcher to spread word among the populace. The Firstpriest and I shall go to the small Farseer to watch the next circling of the sky. The Firstpriest will want to see if events are orderly among the Starcrossers."

The man nodded and turned to leave the foundry. Shibura reflected for a moment on his instructions and decided he could do no better without further thought. And he could not miss the Kodakan.

He entered the chamber quietly. He made the canonical hand passes diagonally across his body to induce emotions of wholeness and peace. The low hum of introduction was coming to an end. Shibura took his place in the folded hexagon of men and women and began his exercises, sitting erect. He aligned his spine and arms and found his natural balance. He raised his hands high and brought them down in a slow arc, breathing out, coming *down* into focus, outward-feeling. In his arm carrier he found the gameballs and beads. He began their juggling and watched as they caught the light in their counter cadences. Sprockets of red and blue light flashed as they tumbled in the air. The familiar dance calmed Shibura and he felt the beginnings of congruence in the men around him. Across the hexagon the Firstpriest juggled also and a feeling of quietness settled. The sing-chant rose and then faded slowly in the soft acoustics of the room. The factory workers signaled readiness and Shibura began the game.

The first draw came across the hexagon where a worker of iron fingered his leaves nervously. The man chose a passage from the Tale and unfolded it as overture. The play fell first to the left, then to the right. It was a complex opening with subtle undertones of dread. Play moved on. Gradually, as the players selected their leaves and read them, the problem gained in body and fullness.

For the older man came down from the hills on the day following, and being he of desperate measure, he sought to bargain on the rasping plain. Such was his mission of the flesh that he forgot the custom. There are things of trade and there are things not of trade; the old man forgot the difference. He sought gain. The things he loved he had made himself, but he knew not that to give of himself it was necessary to find himself and others. There came a time . . .

All entries made, the play passed to Shibura. Shibura began the second portion of the Kodakan: proposal of solution. The draw danced among the players and the air thickened.

It came to this: you are one of two players. You can choose red or black. The other player is hidden and you hear only of his decisions. You know no other aspects of his nature.

If you both pick red, you gain a measure. If both choices are black, a measure is lost. But if you choose red and your opponent (fellow, mate, planet-sharer) votes black, he wins *two* measures, and you lose two.

In the end it gains most measure for all if all play together. He who cooperates in spirit, he who senses the Total—it is he who brings full measure to the Kodakan.

Kodakan is infinitely more complex than this simple trading of measures, but within the game there are the same elements.

Today the problem set by the workers carried subtle tension.

> The Starcrossers come in audience yet they
> take from us our most valued.
> If the Paralixlinnes be our consummation—
> —Apostles of first divinity—
> —Why should we give them over to the Starcrossers?
> We shall suffer loss of Phase.
> We shall lose our moorings. Go down into darkness.

But now the play returned to Shibura. He pointed out the automatic ships that came to Seascape. Did these machines without men not bring valued supplies, components for the working of the Paralixlinnes? Bore they not new and subtle devices? Delicate instruments, small lenses to bring insight to the making of the Paralixlinnes?

The gameballs danced and the spirit moved out from Shibura. The workers caught the harmony of the moment. Shibura indicated slight displeasure when divergent moods emerged, rebuked personal gain; and drew closer to the workers. The Firstpriest added tones of his own; praise of the workers; admiration of the delicate iron threads that honeycombed the Paralixlinnes. Love of workmanship.

So, Shibura asked then, as one casts food upon the Titanic and through the mystery of the eternal currents there returned the fishes and the deepbeasts; so the Starcrossers gained the Paralixlinnes and Seascape received the Ramships with their cargo of delights.

The mood caught slowly at first and only with the rhythm of repetition did the air clear, the tension submerge. Conflicting images in the game weakened. The players selected new leaves, each bringing to the texture of events some resonance of personal insight.

Shibura caught the uprush of spirit at its peak, chanting joyfully of the completion as the play came to rest.

> In pursuit
> Of infinity
> Lose the way
> Thus: serenity.

The Firstpriest imposed the dream-like flicker of gameballs and beads. The muted song was clothed in darkness. Then stillness.

Accept them as the flower does the bee. The fire burning, the iron kettle singing on the hearth, an oiltree brushing the leadened roof, water dripping and chiming in the night.

The hexagon broke and they left, moving in concert.

Shibura stood with his arms folded behind him and listened to the clicking of the implements. The Firstpriest was engaged with the small Farseer and attendants moved around the long tubular instrument making adjustments. Shibura looked out the crack of the great dome and down at the sprawling jumble of the town as it settled into dusk. Even at this distance he could see the flicker of ornamental torches and make out the occasional murmur of crowds.

In the main street the canonical pursuit was in progress. Bands of young men in tattered rough garments ran down the avenues, laughing and singing and reenacting the sports of the Fest. There came the muffled braying of domestic animals. The *segretti* were loose; Shibura could see one of the long-limbed animals chasing a group of men under the yellow torchlights.

The *segretti* snapped at a lagging man, but he dodged away at the last moment. The animals were fairly harmless anyway, since most of their teeth had been pulled. Their three legs still carried the sharpened hooves that could inflict wounds, but these were easily avoided by rolling away if the man was quick about it. The *segretti* chase was the most ancient of the Fest ceremonies. It spoke of the earliest days of man on Seascape, when he had not tamed the animals of the inner continent and was prey as often as he was hunter. Shibura had run like that once, taunted the *segretti* and felt the quick darting fear as the animal brushed too close. But that was behind him. He would not know it again.

"It is there," said the Firstpriest. "All seems in order."

Shibura turned away from the view. He murmured a phrase of pleasure and relief but he still felt a gnawing anxiety. Things were askew; the Starcrossers should not perturb the ancient ceremony this way. He felt restive. Perhaps the Game earlier in the day had not truly brought him to completion.

The Firstpriest was conferring with the attendants of the instrument. Shibura knew its function, just as he knew the role of the machines in the foundry and the mines and the optical shops, all of which came together to make the Paralixlinnes. It was only necessary to know their role, not the details themselves. These were the only rightful machines for life on Seascape. Occasionally, through the long scroll of history, men had tried to extend the principles in the Farseer or devise new ways in the foundry. Sometimes they even succeeded, but the radical nature of what they did caused unease and loss of Phase. History showed that when these men died their inventions passed with them.

One of the attendants stepped around the long tube and her flowing robe caught his eye. She had long delicate fingers and moved with grace across the gray stone floor. Her sandals seemed to make a quiet music of their own.

Ah, Shibura thought. *Ah* it was and *ah* it did.

When the audience was over, the Starcrossers gone and he was released from his priestly vows, this was what he would seek. A woman, yes. A woman to have in the yearly fortnight of mating. A woman for companion in the rest of the long year. A warm molecular bed of cellular wisdom, receptive. Shadowed inlets of rest. He would not seek adventure or wealth. No, he would seek a woman.

There came a hollow clanking as the Firstpriest came down from the perch.

"The Starcrossing is as before. Their ship is not changed from the last audience." The Firstpriest smiled at Shibura and took his arm. "Would you like to see?"

Shibura nodded eagerly and mounted the iron stair. He settled into the carved oaken chair and another woman attendant helped him strap in. She turned a massive crank and heavy oiled gears interlocked. It required several moments to bring the tube around and beads of sweat popped out on her brow. Shibura watched her with interest until the eyepiece swung down to meet his face.

He pressed his eye against the worn slot. At first the field of view seemed dark but as his eye adjusted he caught a fleck of light which moved from the left into the center. As his eye adjusted the dot seemed to grow until suddenly it was a silvery ball moving lazily through the great night. Shibura had heard of this but never seen it: The ship that crossed between stars in the wink of a moment. Not like the Ramship which required more than a man's life to make the journey, and carried only instruments or supplies. This ship knew the dark spaces too well for that.

Tomorrow a smaller craft would detach itself from this sphere and dip down into the air of Seascape. Tomorrow was so soon. He and the Firstpriest and all the others would have to labor through the night to make adequate preparations. The people had to be brought to awareness in large meetings; there was no time for the usual small gatherings.

Shibura felt a gathering tightness in him. It was not well to rush things so.

"Come," the Firstpriest called up. "We must go."

The woman labored and the gears meshed again. Shibura wished he had more time to study the ship, to memorize its every line. Then he hurried down the cold stone steps and went to help.

The morning air shimmered over the Canyon of Audience. A swarm of birds entered it from the south and flew its length in W formation. They fluttered higher as they came toward Shibura, probably rising to avoid the murmur of the gigantic crowd. Shibura stood with the others at the head of the valley, the crescent of Brutus at their backs.

The hills were alive with people. They were encamped in the low hills that framed the valley; most had been waiting since yesterday. Delegations were here from the inner continent, an entire fleet from the Off Islands, pilgrims of every description. These were more people than Shibura had ever seen before. The massive weight of their presence bothered him and he had difficulty focusing on the moment. He knew he was tired from the long night of performing blessings and meditations before the Paralixlinnes.

"*Seistonn,*" the Firstpriest murmured, placing a gentle hand upon Shibura's shoulder.

"I am distracted. I hope the Paralixlinnes prove suitable."

"I am sure the workers have done well."

"Would that I were a foundry worker," Shibura said. "They have only to watch now."

"For others there is process. For us there is the comfort of duty." The Firstpriest smiled. To Shibura the crescent of Brutus seemed to form a halo around the Firstpriest's head. The halo rippled and danced in the rising warm air of morning.

Shibura nodded and turned, hands behind back, to regard the incredible view before them. A Prieststeward said there might be a million people here. It was probably no larger than the audiences of antiquity, since the population of Seascape varied little, but the variety astonished Shibura. This was the most important spiritual event of their lives and the most impassioned were demonstrating their prowess to pass the time. There were men who could pop metal bands wrapped around their chests; women who babbled at visions; children who whispered to dice and made them perform; a wrinkled gray man who could stop his heart for five minutes; walkers on water; religious acrobats; a man who had been chanting hollowly for three days. All this added to the murmurs that came from the hills, aswarm with life.

Far down the valley, toward the west, they saw it first. An excited babble of sound came toward them as the word spread and Shibura looked up into the gathering blue sky. A white dot blossomed. He prepared himself. The Priestfellows arrayed themselves in the formal manner and watched the dot blossom into a winged form. It fell smoothly in the sky, whispering softly as the evening wind. Abruptly it grew and a low mutter came from it. There was a distant roll of thunder as the ship glided down the valley, turned end for end and slowed. A jet of orange flame leaped out of the tail with a sudden explosion. Shibura wrinkled his nose at the sulfurous stench. The ship came down with lazy grace in the middle of the prepared field.

The sound of its arrival faded slowly and there was no answering mutter from the crowd. All lay in silence. The Priestfellows paced forward under the direction of the Firstpriest, who carried the banner and welcoming tokens.

A seam opened in the side of the pearl-white ship. A gangplank slid out and after a moment a human figure appeared. He wore a helmet which after a few moments he removed. Other people appeared beside him, all clothed in a ruddy golden cloth.

Shibura watched the ancient ritual and tried to memorize as much as he could of each moment. In a way it was hard to believe these men had spanned the stars. Their aircraft was beautiful and sleek but it was only a small shuttle compared to the spherical ship he had seen the night before. These men were taller and moved differently, to be sure. In the universe at large they were like the Manyleggers of the Off Islands who spun gossamer webs, bridging the gap between distant orange flowers. Yet they seemed only men.

His time came: he stepped forward and was presented to the Captain, a tall man with a lined face full of character. Shibura presented the log of Seascape's history since the last audience. There were records of crop yields and births, accidents and deaths, details of factory and farm. The Captain turned and introduced the Executive Officer in prescribed manner. Shibura looked at this man and saw an unbuttoned pocket in his vest; a snagged bit of cloth near his knee; brown hair parted wrongly near the crown of the head; dirt beneath the finger-nails; one thumb hooked into a wide belt. The Executive Officer stood with one knee bent, hips cantilevered.

Shibura greeted him. The man pursed his lips and looked at the Captain. The Captain whispered the opening two words and the man picked it up, completing about half the ceremonial response before bogging down. The Captain shifted uneasily and prompted him again. The Executive Officer stumbled through the rest of the reply.

The ceremony proceeded on a raised, hardpacked field near the ship. They were visible all the way down the vast canyon but their words could only be heard by those nearby. Nonetheless there was no distant murmur of conversation from the other hundreds of thousands in the canyon. All stared raptly at the Starcrossers. All Starcrossers but the Captain and Executive Officer stood together in a group, smiling but not partaking actively in the formal ceremony. Shibura stood at the right hand of the Firstpriest and noted carefully each movement and word. When the moment came the Captain turned and addressed the people at large. His voice boomed out in the canyon. He knew the words well. Something caught Shibura's eye and he glanced to the side. The Executive Officer was not standing in place. Instead the man paced impatiently and studied the faces on the nearby hillsides. As Shibura watched he produced a shaped instrument from his belt and began fiddling with it. He raised it to his mouth and green smoke billowed up into the soft air. Occasionally, as the Captain continued speaking, the Executive Officer would take the implement from his mouth and begin pacing again. The smoke smelled of something like barley. Shibura knew this was not correct. The Firstpriest seemed oblivious and did not take his vision from the Captain. As the Captain concluded the Executive Officer put away the implement and took out a polished metal cylinder. He tipped it up to his mouth and appeared to drink from it. When Shibura next looked back at him he was wiping his mouth with the back of his hand.

When the Captain finished there was a sudden crescendo of windbells in unison and the formal procession began. Shibura led the Priestfellows up the slight rise and over the lip of the canyon. The Firstpriest and the Captain entered the waiting ornamental carriage. The Captain said something to the Executive Officer and the man turned to look at Shibura. There were masses of people everywhere but aside from the music there was silence. Shibura bowed to the Executive Officer and gestured at the second carriage. The Priestfellows knew what to do; they arrayed themselves in the remaining carriages and with a lurch the procession began back toward the city.

Though their driver was expert the carriage creaked and groaned with the strain. It was probably several thousand years old and had completed this task many times before. It seemed to know the ruts of the worn road.

The Executive Officer appeared uninterested in talk. Shibura studied him in the filtered light as they rocked and jounced their way along. The man had a day's growth of beard and gritted his teeth at the sway of the carriage. Something caught his interest on a hillside and he leaned out the window to look at it. He screwed up his eyes against the sun's glare and then beckoned to Shibura with his finger. Shibura leaned forward.

"What're they doing up there?"

Shibura followed his pointed finger. "They are performing religious exercises." Near the road a man was rippling his stomach, hands locked behind spine, balanced on the balls of his feet.

"What whackers. That's what you skinheads do?"

Shibura did not know what to say. True, he had no hair. Every Priestfellow was required to symbolize his renunciation of the flesh and a shaved head was the most common selection.

"No," he said finally. "We perform other tasks."

That seemed to end the matter. The Executive Officer slumped back in his seat and closed his eyes. There he remained for the rest of the journey.

The noise of arrival wakened him. Shibura climbed down and held the door for the Executive Officer. The two followed the Firstpriest and the Captain through the great doors of the temple. The vaulted hall was cool and refreshing. In the flickering of the torches the crucibles seemed to glow with pearly moisture. The Starcrossers trooped in and began opening the carryslings they had brought. The Firstpriest and the Captain moved to the far end of the great hall and finished the ritual of welcome. Then they began to speak as they watched the examination of the crucibles.

The Executive Officer paced around the great hall with his hands behind his back. Shibura followed him at first but when he realized the man was going nowhere in particular he returned to the center of the hall in case he was needed for some other purpose. Each Starcrosser was accompanied by a Priestfellow. Several Starcrossers set up a bank of machinery near Shibura.

Near him a Starcrosser knelt before a crucible and waited for the Priestfellow to unfasten the latch. Inside was a Paralixlinne cushioned in velvet reedwork. Shibura avoided looking too closely at the work; he did not wish to become fixed on the Paralixlinnes and be unready if he was summoned. At each crucible the Priestfellow turned away as the examination proceeded. The block of orange within was about a meter on a side, with delicate black ferrite stains imbedded along fracture interfaces and slippage lines. Each corner was dimpled with an external connection; a Starcrosser slipped a male interfacer into each and studied the meters he carried with him. The intricate array within the Paralixlinnes seemed to dance in the flickering light with hypnotic regularity.

Shibura tried to allow the slow rhythm in the room to relax him. He felt a welling unease but he could not place the cause. Abruptly he realized that the Executive Officer was nowhere in the great hall. He glanced around but no one else seemed to notice it.

He padded quickly to one of the side antechambers and found nothing. Then he crossed to the side foyer and glanced among the columns there. Against one of them, in near darkness, something stirred. As his eyes adjusted Shibura recognized one of the Priestsisters standing rigidly, back pressed against the stonework. Her eyes were wide, her hands clenched. The Executive Officer had his knee between her legs, his hand caressing her hips. He was speaking to her and she stared straight ahead, rigid. He moved his knee to widen her legs beneath the folds of her robes and Shibura came forward.

The Executive Officer caught the faint slap of sandals on stone. He turned and saw Shibura. Casually he released the woman and stepped back. She stared at him, still frozen. He regarded Shibura for a moment and then turned and walked casually away.

Her eyes showed too much white. She was on the verge of hysteria. Wordlessly he gestured toward the great hall and after a moment she seemed to comprehend what he meant; she nodded and shuffled away. The Executive Officer was gone, but the man had not walked in the direction of the great hall.

Shibura followed him, not quite knowing what to do. Beyond the foyer was a maze of meditation chambers; he spent several moments threading his way through them fruitlessly. He stopped and listened for a telltale sound. Even the talking from the great hall did not penetrate this far into the temple and there was a pensive silence so still that Shibura could hear the sound of his own breath. Normally one could pick out the sound of sandals approaching, but the Starcrossers wore some form of boot with a padded sole which made no noise.

Shibura moved quickly along the torchlit corridors. He found nothing. In a few moments he reached the Organic Portal and decided to go back. Probably the Executive Officer had returned to the great hall.

Turning, he glanced down the bore of the Portal. The Executive Officer stood with his back to Shibura, his knees slightly bent in a familiar stance. Shibura felt a sudden rising premonition. In the dull glow of the Portal walls he saw a thin yellow-amber stream appear between the man's legs. It spattered soundlessly on the floor.

Shibura rushed forward. The soft padding muffled the sound

of his approach. Something welled up from within him. He smacked the man smartly on the back with the flat of his hand.

"No. This is a most holy place!"

The Executive Officer took a half step forward to catch himself. He fumbled at his fly, blinking at Shibura. Then his jaw tightened.

"What in hell—?" He shoved Shibura away. "You just take off."

"No. This is the Portal from the Captain. It—"

"You don't know what this is. We don't run off into the bushes the way you do." He kicked at the floor. "This stuff absorbs it."

Shibura stared at him, uncomprehending. "And you stroked the woman, the Priestsister, in an inappropriate manner."

"Spying, huh?" The Executive Officer had regained his composure. He shook his fist. "You guys want to tell *us* about women? Huh—you're unqualified."

Shibura said slowly, "We have our own—"

"You have *nothing*. Nothing we didn't give you. *We* fixed you so you wouldn't screw too much, wouldn't overpopulate, so you've got a mating season, like animals. *We* did it."

"The mating fortnight is the natural Fest time of all men—"

"No, skinhead. *I'm* a man. You're a test-tube experiment."

"That is an untruth!"

"Yeah? You're trained for obedience. To kneel down to Jumpship men—real men."

The Executive Officer's lip curled back. Casually, open-handed, he cuffed Shibura. The Priest's head snapped to the side. "See? Made to take it."

Shibura felt something terrible and strange boil up in him. His pulse quickened. Sweat beaded on his forehead. He could not find focus in this swirling of intense new feeling.

"We . . . are following the path of certitude . . ." he began, quoting from the ceremony of dedication.

"Right, that's a good boy. You just run along now, I've got some more business to attend to here."

Shibura started to turn away and suddenly stopped. The Executive Officer was unbuckling his pants. With a muffled grunt he started to squat and then looked at Shibura again. "What are you waiting for? Get going."

"No. No!"

The man hitched up his pants and held them together with one hand. He stepped forward, bringing a fist around—

Shibura blocked the arm. He clutched at the man's hands, not knowing what to do and felt a sharp blow in his ribs. The pain startled him and he pushed, nearly losing his balance. Cloth ripped. He grappled at the other man as they fell together. The floor seemed to rush upward into his eyes and he landed with the Executive Officer's weight on top. His face pressed into the softly resistant foam. He caught the stench of urine and gasped. He wrenched upward and got free of the weight. He rolled away. His breath came hot in his nostrils. The Executive Officer was flailing after him and Shibura came up on his heels, ready to spring.

There was some distracting noise but he ignored it to concentrate on his opponent, who was slowly getting to his knees. The noise came again. It was a voice.

"Hold! Shibura, get back—" It was a Priestfellow.

Shibura froze. He allowed arms to encircle him, half listened to their river of words and exclamations. His thoughts ran furiously and the Organic Portal seemed bathed in hot red light. The Executive Officer glared at him and raised a hand to strike, but another hand appeared and blunted the blow. The other man's face moved away, saying something, and was gone.

The sounds came as though from a great distance, hollow and slow. He stumbled away from there on the arms of two Priestfellows.

There was a sharp burning in his nose. He wiped at it and his fingers came away smeared scarlet. He tried to speak and found his mouth clotted, as though stuffed with acrid cotton.

Word of the event had reached the great hall. There was a babble of voices. With carryingholds and slings the Priestfellows were removing the Paralixlinnes.

Shibura stood and watched numbly. The two Priestfellows still held his arms. He saw the Captain looking over at him, lines furrowed on his brow.

After a time he blinked and saw the Firstpriest standing before him. The old man regarded him for a long moment and then said softly, "No word will be repeated of this. I have heard of the event. I think it best you do not follow us to the canyon. The Captain wishes to depart soon."

There was another long silence and then, "I know this is a difficult time for you. Let this moment pass away."

Shibura nodded and said nothing. The two Priestfellows at his side went to help with the loading of the crucibles and after a pause Shibura moved to the doorway of the great hall. The sudden silence of the room reminded him that he was now alone. All else were making preparations and entering the carriages. At the doorway he watched them go, a long line of ceremonial carts. The Paralixlinnes were sealed in their crucibles, which were in turn sheathed in sleeves of polished dark-wood. Each neatly filled a cart.

At a call the procession began to move. The carriages departed first and then the long line of carts rattled away down the cobblestone streets and into the damp heat of the early afternoon. Dust curled in their wake.

Shibura stood with one hand on the massive burnished temple door as the procession slowly wound away. His mind seethed. The Executive Officer's words had battered Shibura more than the fists. The picture endlessly repeated itself in Shibura's mind: the unbuckling, the abrupt squat, the grunt as he settled himself—

It had been the act of an animal. Not a man. A man knows the time to fondle a woman. A man senses what is sacred.

Such animals as that Officer now had the Paralixlinnes and would carry them away. The purity of those forms would be profaned by the touch of the Executive Officer. The work of a generation was delivered into the hands of that—

Out of the confusion in Shibura's mind came a thought. Shibura was a young man. The Firstpriest would pass away and Shibura, he-who-stands-on-the-right-hand, would become Firstpriest. He would supervise the slow, serene craftsmanship that made the Paralixlinnes. He would follow the right path.

But when next the Starcrossers came, the Paralixlinnes would be safely hidden in distant mountain caves. They would be revered as they were meant to be.

Shibura clenched his jaws tight and smiled a terrible smile.

The Canyon of Audience would prove a different host next time.

A landslide starts with the fall of a single pebble. Thus did the Empire begin to erode.

FAST-FRIEND

GEORGE R. R. MARTIN

George R. R. Martin has mixed mythical archetypes, imagination, and speculation to create a future where men clone angels and yearn to become spirits that travel faster than light.

Here is a dream of new chariots, a quest for freedom and love foiled by fear and all the other walls of men.

Brand woke in darkness, trembling, and called out. His angel came to him.

She floated above him, smiling, on wings of soft gauze gold. Her face was all innocence, the face of a lovely girl-child, softness and light and wide amber eyes and honeyed hair that moved sinuously in free-fall. But her body was a woman's, smooth and slim and perfect; a toy woman fashioned on a smaller scale.

"Brand," she said, as she hovered above his sleep-web. "Will you show me the fast-friends today?"

He smiled up at her, his dreams fading. "Yes, angel," he said. "Yes, today, I'm sure of it. Now come to me."

But she moved back when he reached for her, coy, teasing. Her blush was a creeping tide of gold, and her hair danced in silken swirls. "Oh, Brand," she said. Then, as he cursed and reached to unsnap his web, she giggled at him and pouted. "You can't have me," she said, in her child's voice. "I'm too little."

Brand laughed, grabbed a nearby handbar to pull himself free of the web, then whipped himself around it toward the angel. He was good in free-fall, Brand; he'd had ten years of practice. But the angel had wings.

They flowed and rippled as she darted to one side, just

274

beyond his reach. He twisted around in midair, so he hit the wall with his legs. Then, immediately, he kicked off again. The angel giggled and brushed him with her wings as he flew by. Brand hit the ceiling with a thump and groaned.

"Ooo," she said. "Brand, are you hurt?" And she was at his side, her wings beating quickly.

He grinned and put his arms around her. "No," he said, "but I've got you. Since when is my angel a tease, eh?"

"Oh, Brand," she said. "I'm sorry. I was only playing. I was gonna come to you." She was trying to look hurt, but despite her best efforts, a tiny smile escaped the corner of her mouth.

He pulled her to him, hard, and pressed her strange coolness against his own heat. This time there was no reluctance. Her delicate hands went behind him, to hold him tight while he kissed her.

Floating, nude, they joined, and Brand felt the soft caress of wings.

When they were finished, Brand went to his locker to dress. The angel hovered nearby, her wings barely moving, her small breasts still flushed with gold.

"You're so *pretty*," she told him, as he pulled on a dull black coverall. "Why do you hide, Brand? Why can't you stay like me, so I can see you?"

"A human thing, angel," he said, hardly listening to her chatter. He'd heard it all before. His boots made a metallic click as they pulled him to the floor.

"You're beautiful, Brand," the angel murmured, but he only nodded at her. Only angels said that of him. Brand was close to thirty, but he looked older; lines on a wide forehead, thin lips set in a too-characteristic frown, dark eyes under heavy eyebrows, and hair that curled tight against his scalp in sculptured ringlets.

When he was dressed, he paused briefly, then opened a lockbox welded to the locker wall. Inside was his pendant. He took it out and stared. The disc filled his hand, a coolness of polished black crystal with a myriad of tiny silver flakes locked within. The pale silver chain it hung from curled up and away, and floated in the air like a metal snake.

He remembered then how it had been, in the old days, under

gravity. The chain was heavy then, and the crystal stone had a solid heft to it. Yet he'd worn it always, as Melissa had worn its twin. And he wanted to wear it now, but it was such a nuisance in free-fall. Without weight, it refused to hang neatly around his neck; instead it bobbed about constantly.

Finally, sighing, he slipped the chain over his head, pulled the crystal tight against his neck, then twisted the chain and doubled it over again and again. When he was finished the stone was secure, now more a choker than a pendant. It was uncomfortable. But it was the best he could do.

The angel watched him in silence, trembling a little. She'd seen him handle the black crystal before. Sometimes he'd sit in his sleep-web for hours, the stone floating above him. He'd stare into its depths, at the frozen dance of the silver flecks, and his face would grow dark, his manner curt. She avoided him then, lest he scold her.

But now he was wearing it.

"Brand," the angel said as he went toward the door panel. "Brand, can I come with you?"

He hesitated. "Later, angel," he said. "When the fast-friends come, I'll call you, as I promised. Right now you stay down here and rest, all right?" He forced a smile.

She pouted. "All right," she said.

Outside was a short corridor of grey metal, brightly lit; the sealed airlock to the engine compartment capped one end, the bridge door the other. A few other closed panels broke the spartan bleakness: cargo holds, screen generators, Robi's room. Brand ignored them, and proceeded straight to the bridge.

Robi was strapped in before the main console, studying the banks of viewscreens and scanners with a bored expression. She was a short, round woman, with high cheekbones and green eyes and brown hair cut space short. Long hair was just trouble in free-fall. The angel had long hair, of course, but she was just an angel.

Robi favored him with a wary smile as he entered. Brand did not return it. He was a solo by nature; only circumstances had forced him to take on a partner, so he could complete the conversion of his ship. Her funds had paid for the new screens he'd installed.

He moved to the second control chair and strapped himself

down, his expression businesslike. "I'll take over," he said. Then he paused, and blinked. "The course has been altered," he stated. He looked at her.

"A swarm of blinkies," Robi said, trying her smile again. "I changed the program. They're not far out of our way. A half-hour standard, maybe."

Brand sighed. "Look, Robi," he said, "this isn't a trap run." His hands moved over the controls, putting new patterns on most of the scanners. "We're not bounty hunting, remember? We're going to the stars, and coming back. No detours."

Robi looked annoyed. "Brand, I sold my *Unicorn* to invest in this scheme of yours. A bounty or two would be nice, in case the gimmick doesn't work, you know. And we're going out to the Changling Jungle anyway, so we might as well bring a dark or two with us, if we can trap some. That swarm is right on top of us, nearly. A couple darks have got to be nearby. So what's the harm?"

"No," Brand said, as he wiped off the program she'd fed into the ship's computer. "We're too close to fool around." He checked the console, reprograming, compensating for the swerve she'd fed in. The newly christened *Chariot* was two weeks out from the orbital docks on Triton, where she'd been overhauled. A few short hours ahead, out toward the dark, the Changling Jungle swung around the distant sun, a man-made trojan to Pluto.

"You're being stubborn and unreasonable," Robi told him. "What do you have against money, anyway?"

Brand didn't look up. "Nothing. The idea will work. I'll have all the money I need then. So will you. Why don't you just go back to your room, and dream about how rich you're going to be."

She snorted, spun her chair around, unstrapped, and kicked off savagely. If it had been possible to slam a sliding panel door, she would have done that too.

Brand, alone, finished his reprograming. He hardly thought twice about the argument. Robi and he had been arguing since they'd left Triton; about bounties, about the angel, about him. It didn't matter. Nothing mattered, nothing but his idea, the Jungle ahead, and stars.

A few hours, that was all. They'd find fast-friends near the

Jungle. Always there were fast-friends near the Jungle. And somehow, Brand knew he'd find Melissa.

Unconsciously, his hand had gone to his neck. Slowly, slowly, he stroked the cool dark crystal.

Once they'd dreamed of stars together.

It was a common dream. Earth was teeming, civilized, dull; time and technology had homogenized it. What romance there was left was all in space. Thousands lived under the domes of Luna now. On Mars, terraforming projects were in full swing, and new immigrants flooded Lowelltown and Bradbury and Burroughs City every day. There was a lab on Mercury, toehold colonies on Ceres, Ganymede, Titan. And out at the Komarov Wheel, the third starship was a-building. The first was twenty years gone, with a crew who knew they'd die on board so their children could walk another world.

Yes, it was a common dream.

But they were most uncommon dreamers.

And they were lucky. They were born at the right time. They were still children when the Hades Expedition, bound for Pluto, came upon the blinkies. Then the darks came upon the Hades Expedition.

Twelve men had died, but Brand felt only a child's thrill, a delicious shiver.

Three years later, he and Melissa had followed the news avidly when the Second Hades Expedition, the lucky one, the one with the first primitive energy screens, made its astonishing discoveries. And a crewman named Chet Adams became immortal.

He remembered a night. They'd walked hand in hand, up a winding outside staircase atop one of the city's tallest towers. The lights, the glaring ceaseless lights, were mostly below. They could see the stars, sort of. Brand, a younger smooth-faced Brand with long curling hair, wrapped his arm around Melissa and gestured.

Up. At the sky.

"You know what this *means?*" he said. The news had just come back from Hades II; dreamers were everywhere. "We can have the stars now. All of them. We won't have to die on a starship, or settle down on Mars. We're not trapped."

Melissa, whose hair was reddish gold, laughed and kissed him.

"You think they'll find out how it's done? How the darks go ftl?"

Brand just hugged her and kissed her back. "Who cares? I suppose ftl ships would be nice. But *hell*, we can have more now. We can be like *him*, like Adams, and the stars can all be ours."

Melissa nodded. "Why fly an airplane, right? If you could be a bird?"

For five long years they loved, and dreamed of stars. While the Changling Jungle swelled, and the fast-friends sailed the void.

Robi returned to the bridge just as Brand activated the main viewscreen. Surprise flashed across her face. She looked at him and smiled. Above, the picture was alive with a million tiny lights, pinpoints of sparkling green and crimson and blue and yellow and a dozen other colors. Not stars, no; they shifted and danced mindlessly, constantly, blinking on and off like fireflies and making the scanners *ping* whenever they touched the ship.

She floated herself to her chair, strapped down. "You kept my course," she said, pleased. "I'm sorry I got so angry." She put a hand on his arm.

Brand shook it off. "Don't give me any credit. We're dead on. The blinkies came to us."

"Oh," she said. "I might have known."

"They're all around us," he said. "A huge swarm. I'd guess a couple cubic miles, at least."

Robi looked again. The viewscreen was thick with blinkies in constant motion. The stars, those white lights that stood still, could hardly be seen. "We're going right into the swarm," she said.

Brand shrugged. "It's in our way."

Robi leaned forward, spread her hands over the instruments, punched in a few quick orders. Seconds later, a line of flashing red print began to run across the face of her scanner. She looked up at Brand accusingly. "You didn't even check," she said. "Darks, three of them."

"This is not a trap run," Brand said, unemotionally.

"If they come right up to us and ask to be trapped, I suppose you'll tell them to go away? Besides, they could eat right through us."

"Hardly. The safe-screen is up."

Robi shook her head without comment. The darks would avoid a ship with its safe-screen up. So, naturally, you couldn't trap them that way. But Brand wasn't trapping this time.

"Look," Brand said.

The viewscreen, suddenly, was empty again; just a scattering of stars and two or three lost blinkies winking a lonely message in blue and red. The swarm was gone. Then, with equal speed, it came into sight again. Far off, growing smaller; a fast-receding fog of light.

Brand locked the viewer on it; Robi upped the scopes to max magnification. The fog expanded until it filled the screen.

The blinkies were fleeing, running from their enemies, running faster than the *Chariot* or any man-built ship had ever gone or could ever hope to go, unaided. They were moving at something close to light-speed; after all, they were mostly light themselves, just a single cell and a microscopic aura of energy that gave off short, intense bursts of visible radiation.

Despite the lock, despite the scopes, the viewscreen was deserted less than a second after the blinkies began to run. They'd gone too far, too fast.

Robi started to say something, then stopped. Instead she reached out and touched Brand by the elbow, squeezing sharply. Up in the viewscreen, the stars had begun to dim.

You can't see a dark, not really, but Brand knew how they looked, and he'd seen them often enough in his imagination and his dreams. They were bigger than the blinkies, vastly bigger, almost as big as a man; pulsing globes of dark energy, seldom radiating into the visible spectrum, seen only by the drifting flakes of living matter trapped within their spheres.

But they did things to the light passing through them: they made the stars waver and dim.

As they were dimming now, up on the screen. Brand watched closely. Briefly, oh so briefly, he thought he saw a flash of silver as a flake of darkstuff caught the tired sunlight and lost it again. The old fear woke and clutched at his stomach. But the dark was keeping its distance; their safe-screens were up.

Robi looked over at Brand. "It's begging," she said, "it's practically begging. Let's drop screens and trap it. What's the harm?"

Brand's face was cold. Irrational terror swirled within him. "It knows," he said, hardly thinking. "It didn't go after the blinkies. It senses something different about us. I tell you, it knows."

She gave him a curious stare. "What's wrong with you?" she asked. "It's only a dark. Come on. Let me trap it."

Brand mastered himself, though the fear was alive and walking, the Hades fear, the trapper's companion. Creatures of energy, the darks ate matter. Like the blinkies they swept clean the scattered dust and gas on the fringes of solar space. And they moved through blinkie swarms like scythes, carving tunnels of blackness in those living seas of light. And, when they found a lonely chunk of nickle-iron spinning through the void, that too was food. Matter to energy, converted in a blinding silent flash. An incandescent feast.

A hundred times Brand had faced the fear, when he sat before his computer and prepared to drop his screens. When the ship was naked, when the screens were down, then only the mindless whim of the dark said if a trapper lived or died. If the dark came slow, moving in leisurely towards its sluggish steel meal, then the trapper won. Once the dark was in range, the safe-screens would blink on again, covering the ship like a second skin. And, further out, the trapping screens would form a globe. The dark would be a prisoner.

But if the dark moved *quickly* . . .

Well, the blinkies ran at light-speed. The darks fed on the blinkies. The darks ran faster.

If the dark moved quickly, there was no way, no defense, no hope that man or woman or computer could raise the screens in time. A lot of trappers died that way. The First Hades Expedition, screenless, had been holed in a dozen places.

"Let me trap it," Robi said again. Brand just looked at her. Like him, she was a trapper. She'd beaten the fear as often as he had, and she had luck. Still, maybe this time that luck would change.

He unstrapped, pulled himself up, and stood looking down on her. "No," he said. "It's not worth the risk. We're too close. Leave the dark alone. And don't change course, you hear, not five feet. I'm going down to angel."

"Brand!" Robi said. "Damn you. And don't bring that thing up here, you understand? And . . ." But he was gone, silently, ignoring her.

She turned back to the viewscreen and, frustrated, watched the dark.

Asleep, awake, it never mattered. The vision would come to him all the same. Call it dream, color it memory.

There were four of them, inside Changling Station, on the wheel of rebirth. It was a doughnut, the Station; brightly lit, screened. Around it, in all direction, ships—trapper ships with their catch, bait ships hauled by timid trappers, supply ships out from Triton, couriers from Earth and Mars and Luna with commissions for the fast-friends. And derelicts. Hundreds of ill-fit hulks, holed, abandoned, empty, filling up the Jungle like hunks of cold steel garbage.

Between the ships moved the fast-friends.

The airlock where they donned their spacesuits had had a window in it; it was a large, empty chamber, a good place for long looks and last thoughts. Brand and Melissa and a fat blond girl named Canada Cooper had stood there together, looking out on the Jungle and the fast-friends. Canada had laughed. "I thought they'd be different," she said. "They look just like people, silly naked people standing out in space."

And they did. A few stood on the hulls of derelicts, but most of them were just floating in the void, pale against the starlight, small and stern and awesome. Melissa counted fourteen.

"Hurry up," the government man had said. Brand hardly remembered what he looked like, but he remembered the voice, the hard flat voice that whipped them all the way out from Earth. They were the candidates, the chosen. They'd held to their dream, they'd passed all the tests, and they were twenty. That was the optimal age for a successful merger, the experts said. Some experts. Adams, the first-merged, had been nearly thirty.

He remembered Melissa as she put on her suit, slim and clean in a white coverall zipped low, with her crystal pendant hanging between her gold-tan breasts in the imitation gravity of the spinning Station. Her hair was tightly bound. She'd kept it long, her red-blond glory, to wear between the stars.

They kissed just before they put on helmets.

"Love you," she said. "Love you always." And he repeated it back to her.

Then they were outside, them and Canada and the government man, walking on the skin of Changling Station, looking down into the Pit. The arena, the hole in the doughnut, the energy-screened center of the whole thing, the place where dreams came true.

Brand, young Brand, looked down at where he'd have to go, and smiled. There was nothing below but stars. He'd fall forever, but he didn't mind. They'd share the stars together.

"You first," the government man said to Melissa. She radioed a kiss to Brand, and kicked off toward the Pit.

She didn't get far. There were darks in there, three of them, trapped and imprisoned. Once she was beyond the screens, one came for her. The sight was burned deep in Brand's memory. One moment there was only Melissa, suited, floating away from him towards the far side of the Station. Then light.

Sudden, instantaneous, quick-dying. A flash, nothing more. Brand knew that. But his memory had elaborated on the moment. In his dreams, it was more prolonged; first her suit flared and was gone and she threw back her head to scream, then her clothes flamed into brilliance, and lastly, lastly, the chain and its crystal. She was naked, wreathed in fire, adrift among the stars. She no longer breathed.

But she lived.

A symbiote of man and dark, a thing of matter and energy, an alien, a changling, a reborn creature with the mind of a human and the speed of a dark. Melissa no longer.

Fast-friend.

He ached to join her. She was smiling at him, beckoning. There was a dark waiting for him too. He would join it, merge. Then, together, he and Melissa would run, faster than the starships, faster than light, out, out. The galaxy would be theirs. The universe, perhaps.

But the government man held his arm. "Her next," he said. Fat Canada kicked free of the place where they stood, hardly hesitating. She knew the risks, like them, but she was a dreamer too. They'd tested and traveled with her, and Brand knew her boundless optimism.

She floated towards Melissa, chunky in her oversize suit, and reached out her hand. Her radio was on. Brand remembered her voice. "Hey," she said, "mine's slow. A slow dark, imagine!"

She laughed. "Hey, little darkie, where are you? Hey, come to mama. Come and merge, little . . ."

Then, loudly, a short scream, cut off before it started.

And Canada exploded.

The flash was first, of course. But this time, afterwards, no fast-friend. She'd been rejected. Three-quarters of all candidates for merger were rejected. They were eaten instead. Except, this time, the dark hadn't enveloped her cleanly. If it had, then, after the instant of conversion, nothing would have been left.

But this dark had just sheared her off above the waist. Her legs spun wildly after the explosion of violent depressurization. Her blood flash-froze.

It was only there for a second, less than a heartbeat, a pause between breaths. Then another flash, and emptiness. Just Melissa again, her smile suddenly gone, still waiting.

"Too bad," the government man had said. "She did well on the tests. You're next."

Brand was looking across at Melissa, and the stars behind her. But his vision was gone. Instead he saw Canada.

"No," he'd said. For the first time ever, the fear was on him.

Afterwards he went down into the Station and threw up. When he dreamt, he woke up trembling.

Brand left Robi with her dark, and sought the comfort of his angel.

She was waiting for him, as always, smiling and eager for his company, a soft winged woman-child. She was playing in the sleep-web when he entered, singing to herself. She flew to him at once.

He kissed her, hard, and she wrapped her wings around him, and they tumbled laughing through the cabin. In her embrace, his fears all faded. She made him feel strong, confident, conquering. She worshiped him, and she was passionate, more passionate even then Melissa.

And she fit. Like the fast-friends, she was a creature of the void. Under gravity, her wings could never function, and she'd die within a month. Even in free-fall, angels were short-lived. She was his third, bred by the bio-engineers of the Jungle who knew what a trapper would pay for company. It didn't matter.

They were clones, and all alike, more than twins in their delicate sexy inhuman angelic simplicity.

Death was not a threat to their love. Nor fights. Nor desertion. When Brand relaxed within her arms, he knew she'd always be there.

Afterwards, they lay nude and lazy in the sleep-web. The angel nibbled at his ear, and giggled, and stroked him with soft hands and softer wings. "What are you thinking, Brand?" she asked.

"Nothing, angel. Don't worry yourself."

"Oh, *Brand.*" She looked very cross.

He couldn't help smiling. "All right then. I was thinking that we're still alive, which means Robi left the dark alone."

The angel shivered and hugged him. "Ooo. You're scaring me, Brand. Don't talk of dying."

He played with her hair, still smiling. "I told you not to worry. I wouldn't let you die, angel. I promised to show you the fast-friends, remember? And stars too. We're going to the stars today, just like the fast-friends do."

The angel giggled, happy again. She was easy to please. "Tell me about the fast-friends," she said.

"I've told you before."

"I know. I like to hear you talk, Brand. And they sound so *pretty.*"

"They are, in a way. They're cold, and they're not human anymore, but they are pretty sometimes. They move fast. Somehow they can punch through to another kind of space, where the laws of nature are different, a fifth dimension or hyperspace or what-you-will, and . . ."

But the angel's face showed no comprehension. Brand laughed, and paused. "No, you wouldn't understand those terms, of course. Well, call it a fairyland, angel. The fast-friends have a lot of power in them, like the darks do, and they use this power, this magic, for a trick they have, so they can go faster than light. Now, there's no way we can go faster than light without this trick, you see."

"Why?" she asked. She smiled an innocent smile.

"Hmmm. Well, that's a long story. There was a man named Einstein who said we couldn't, angel, and he was a *very* smart man, and . . ."

She hugged him. "I bet *you* could go faster than light, Brand, if you wanted." Her wings beat, and the web rocked gently.

"Well, I want to," he said. "And that's just what we're going to try to do now, angel. You must be smarter than you look."

She hit him. "I'm *awful* smart," she said, pouting.

"Yes," he laughed. "I didn't mean it. I thought you wanted to hear about the fast-friends?"

Suddenly she was apologetic again. "Yes."

"All right. Remember, they have this trick, like I said. Now we know they can move matter—that's, well, solid stuff, angel, like the ship and me and you, but it's also gas and water, you see. Energy is different. The darks are mostly energy, with only little flakes of matter. But the fast-friends are more balanced. A lot of smart men think that if they could examine a dark they could figure out this trick, and then we could build ships that went fast too. But nobody has been able to figure how to examine a dark, since it is nearly all energy and nearly impossible to hold in one place, you see?"

"Yes," the angel lied, looking very solemn.

"Anyway, the fast-friends not only move energy and little flakes of matter, they also move what once were the bodies of the human members of the symbiosis. You don't understand that, do you? Hell, this is . . . ah, well, just listen. The fast-friends can only move themselves, and whatever else they can fit inside their energy sphere, or aura. Think of it as a baggy cloak, angel. If they can't stuff it under their cloak, they can't take it with them."

She giggled, the idea of a baggy cloak evidently appealing to her.

Brand sighed. "So, the fast-friends are sort of our messengers. They fly out to the stars for us, real fast, and they tell us which suns have planets, and where we can find worlds that are good to live on. And they've found ships out there, too, in other systems, from other kinds of beings who aren't men and aren't fast-friends either, and they carry messages so that we can learn from each other. And they keep us in touch with our starships, too, by running back and forth. Our ships are still real slow, angel. We've launched at least twenty by now, but even the first one hasn't gotten where it's going yet."

"The fast-friends caught it, didn't they?" the angel interrupted. "You told me. I remember."

"Yes, angel," he said. "I don't have to tell you how surprised those people were. A lot of them were the sons and daughters of people who'd left Earth, and when their parents left there were no fast-friends, and they hadn't even found out about the blinkies yet, or the darks. But now the fast-friends keep all the ships in touch by running back and forth with messages and even small packages and such. Once we have colonies, they'll link them too."

"But they're crippled," angel prompted.

"For all their speed," Brand continued, smiling, "the fast-friends are strangely crippled. They can't land on any of the planets they sail by; the gravity wells are deadly to them. And they don't even like to go in much further than the orbit of Saturn, or its equivalent, because of the sun. The darks and the blinkies never do, and the fast-friends have to force themselves. So that's one drawback.

"Also, frankly, a lot of men want to travel faster than light themselves. They want to build ships and start colonies. So whoever finds a way to do what the fast-friends do, so that regular men can do it without having to merge and maybe die, well, they'll make a lot of money. And be famous. And have stars."

"You'll do it, Brand," the angel said.

"Yes," he said. His voice was suddenly serious. "That, angel, is why we're here."

"No."

The word had haunted him, its echoes rolling through his dreams. He'd thrown away his stars, and his Melissa.

He couldn't force himself to go back to Earth. Melissa was gone, off to the stars on her first commission, but he loved her still. And the dream still gripped him tightly. Yet he would not get another chance. There were more candidates than darks, and he'd failed his final test.

He worked in Changling Station for a while, then signed on a supply run from Triton to the Jungle and learned to run a ship. In two years, he saved a substantial amount. He borrowed the rest, outfitted a derelict drifting in the Jungle, and became a trapper.

The plan was clear then. The government wouldn't give him another chance, but he could make his own. He'd prowl until he found a dark, then trap it. Then he'd go outside and merge. And he'd join Melissa after all. Brand, fast-friend. Yes, he would have his stars.

A good trapper can support himself in fine style on four catches a year. On six he gets rich. Brand was not yet a good trapper, and there were months of fruitless lonely search. The blackness was brightened only by the far-off lights of distant blinkie swarms, and the firmness of his vision, and Melissa.

She used to come to him, in the early days, when she wasn't out among the stars. He'd be on his tedious prowl when suddenly his scanners would flash red, and she'd be there, floating outside the ship, smiling at him from the main viewscreen. And he'd open the airlock and cycle her in.

But even in the best days after, the very early ones, it wasn't the same. She couldn't drink with him, or eat. She didn't need to; she was a fast-friend now, and she lived on stardust and blinkies and junk, converting them to energy even as a dark did.

She could survive in an atmosphere, and talk and function, but she didn't like it. It was unpleasant. The ship was cramped, and it was a strain to keep her aura in check, to keep from converting the molecules of the air that pressed on her from every side.

The first time, when she'd come to him in Changling Station, Brand had pulled her lithe body hard against him and kissed her. She had not resisted. But her flesh was cold, her tongue a spear of ice when it touched his. Later, stubborn, he'd tried to make love to her. And failed.

Soon they gave up trying. When she came to his ship in those months of hunt, he only held her hard, slick hand, and talked to her.

"It's just as well, Brand," she told him once, in those early days. "I wanted to make love to you, yes, for your sake. I'm *changed*, Brand. You have to understand. Sex is like food, you know. It's a human thing. I'm not really interested in that now. You'll see, after you merge. But don't worry. There are other things out there, things that make it all worthwhile. The stars, love. You should see the stars. I fly between them, and, and . . . oh, Brand, it's glorious! How could I tell you? You have to feel it. When I fly, when I punch through, everything changes. Space isn't black anymore, it's a sea of color, swirling all around me, splashing against me, and I'm streaking right through it. And the *feeling!* It's like . . . like an orgasm, Brand, but it goes on and on and on, and your whole body sings and feels it, not just one little part of you. You're *alive!* And there are things out there, things only the fast-friends know. What we tell the humans, that's only a little bit, the bit they can understand. There's so much more. There's music out there, Brand, only it isn't music. And sometimes you can hear something calling, far away, from the core stars. I think the call gets stronger the more you fly. That's where the first-merged went, you know, Adams or whatever his human name was. That's why the older fast-friends sometimes vanish. They say it's wearying after a while, playing messenger for the humans. Then the fast-friends go away, to the core stars. Oh, Brand, I wish you were with me. It would be the way we dreamed. Hurry, love, catch your dark for me."

And Brand, though strange chills went through him, nodded and said he would.

And finally he did.

For the second time the fear came. Brand watched his scanners as they shrieked of dark proximity. Five times his finger paused over the button that would kill his safe-screens. Five times it moved back. He kept seeing Canada again, her legs a-spin. And he thought of the Hades I.

Finally, his mind on Melissa, he forced the button down. The dark came slowly. No need to hurry, after all. This was no light-fast blinkie swarm; just dead metal creeping through the void.

Brand, relieved, trapped it. But as he put on his spacesuit, the fear hit again.

He fought it. Oh, he fought it. For an hour he stood in the airlock, trembling, trying to put on his helmet and failing. His hands were shaking, and he threw up twice. Finally, slumped and beaten in the fouled lock, he knew the truth. He would never merge.

He took his catch back to the Changling Jungle for a bounty. The Station offered its standard fee, but there was another bidder, a middle-aged man who'd run an old supply ship out here on his own. As dozens did each year. Brand sold the dark to him, to this hopeful unqualified test-failing visionary. And Brand watched him die.

Another derelict, abandoned, joined the Jungle, floating in a crowded orbit with all the other hulks, the debris of other dreams.

Brand sold his dark again, to Changling Station. A month later, when Melissa returned, he told her. He'd expected tears, a storm, a fight. But she just looked at him, strangely unmoved. Then he asked her to come back to him.

"Maybe we can go back to Earth," he said. "We'll stay in orbit, and the scientists can look at you. They might be able to un-merge you, or something. They'll certainly welcome the opportunity. Maybe you can tell them how to build ftl ships. But we'll be together." His words were a child's hopeful gush.

"No," Melissa had said, simply. "You don't understand. I'd die first."

"You said you loved me. Stay with me."

"Oh, Brand. I did love you. But I won't give up the stars. They're my love now, my life, my everything. I'm a fast-friend, Brand, and you're only a human. Things are different now. If you can't merge, go back to Earth. That's the place for men, for you. The stars belong to us now."

"*No!*" He shouted it to keep from weeping. "I'll stay out here then, and trap. I love you, Melissa. I'll stay by you."

Very briefly, she looked sad. "I'll visit you, I guess," she said. "When I have time, if you want me."

And so she did. But as the years went by, the visits came less often. Brand, more and more, hardly knew her. Her gold-tan body turned pale, though it kept the shape of a twenty-year-old while he aged. Her streaming red-blond hair became a silvered white, and her eyes grew distant. Often, when she was with him in orbit near the Jungle, she wasn't there at all. She talked of things he could not understand, of fast-friends he did not know, of actions beyond his comprehension. And he bored her now, with his news of Earth and men.

Finally the talk stopped. There was nothing left but memories then, for Melissa did not come at all.

Robi rang him on the intercom, and Brand dressed quickly. "Now," the angel said eagerly. "Can I come now?"

"Yes," he told her, smiling again his fond indulgent smile. "I'll show you the fast-friends now, angel. And then I'll take you to the stars!"

She flew behind him, through the panel, up the corridor, into the bridge.

Robi looked up as they entered. She did not look happy. "You don't listen, do you? I don't want your pet on the bridge, Brand. Can't you keep your perversions in your cabin?"

The angel quailed at the displeasure in Robi's voice. "She doesn't like me," she said to Brand, scared.

"Don't worry, angel, I'm here," he replied. Then, to Robi, "You're scaring her. Keep quiet. I promised to show her the fast-friends."

Robi glared at him, and hit the viewscreen stud. It flared back to life. "There, then," she said savagely.

The *Chariot* was in the middle of the Jungle. Brand, counting quickly, saw a good dozen derelicts nearby. Changling Station was low in one corner of the screen, surrounded by trapper ships and screens. Near the center was a larger wheel, the spoked and spinning supply station Hades IV, with its bars and pleasure havens.

Floating close to Hades, a group of fast-friends were clustered, six at least, still small and white at this distance. There were others visible, but they were closest. They were talking, even in the hard vacuum of the solar fringe; with a simple act of will, the fast-friends could force their dark aura up in the range of the visible spectrum. Their language was one of lights.

Robi already had the *Chariot* headed toward them. Brand nodded toward the angel, and pointed. "Fast-friends," he said.

The angel squealed and flew to the viewscreen, pressing her nose against it. "They're so *little,*" she said as she hovered there, her wings beating rapidly.

"Increase the magnification," Brand told Robi. When she ignored him, he strapped down beside her and did it himself. The cluster of fast-friends doubled in size, and the angel beamed.

"We'll be right on top of them in five minutes," Brand said.

Robi pretended not to hear. "I don't know about you, Brand," she said in a low serious voice, so the angel would not hear. "Most of the men who buy sex toys like that are sick, or crippled, or impotent. Why you? You seem normal enough. Why do you need an angel, Brand? What's wrong with a woman?"

"Angels are easier to live with," Brand snapped. "And they do what they're told. Stop prying and get on the signal lights. I want to talk to our friends out there."

Robi scowled. "Talk? Why? Let's just scoop them up, there's enough of them there . . ."

"No. I want to find one, a special one. Her name was Melissa."

"Hmpf," Robi said. "Angels and fast-friends. You ought to try having a relationship with a human being once in a while, Brand. Just for a change of pace, you understand." But she readied the signal lights as she talked.

And Brand called, out across the void. One of the fast-friends responded. Then vanished. "She'll come," Brand said firmly, as they waited. "Even now, she'll come."

Meanwhile the angel was flitting excitedly around the bridge, touching everything she could reach. Normally she was not allowed up here.

"Calm down," Brand told her. She flew down to him, happy, and curled up in his lap.

"What are the fast-friends doing?" she asked, with her arms around him. "Are they going to tell us their trick, Brand? Are we going to the stars yet?"

"Soon, angel," he said patiently. "Soon . . ."

Then Melissa was there, caught in the viewscreen. Brand felt a chill go through him.

Her skin was milk-white now, her hair a halo of streaming silver. But otherwise she was the same. She had the firm curves of a twenty-year-old, and the face that Brand remembered.

He shooed the angel from his lap, and turned to the console. He hit some buttons.

Outside, the stars began to flicker. The bright dot of the distant sun dimmed. The hulks of the Jungle, the Hades wheel, Changling Station; all darkened slightly. Only Melissa and the other fast-friends were unchanged.

Caught within the globe.

Robi smiled, and started to speak. Brand silenced her with a look. His signal lights called Melissa. When she acknowledged, he cut the safe-screens to let her through.

He met her in the corridor after the airlock had cycled her, in. Robi stayed up on the bridge.

They stood ten feet apart. They did not touch or smile.

"Brand," Melissa said at last. She studied him with ice-blue eyes, from a cold and steady face, and her voice had a husky quality he had not remembered. "You . . . what are you doing? We are not . . . not darks. To be trapped." Her speech stumbled and halted awkwardly.

"Have you forgotten how to talk, Melissa?" Brand said. As he spoke, the bridge panel slid open behind him. The angel flew out and hovered.

"Oh," she said to Melissa. "You're *pretty.*"

The fast-friend's eyes flicked to her quickly, then dismissed her and went back to Brand. "Some, I've forgotten. Ten years, Brand. With stars, the stars. Not . . . *I'm* not a human now. I'm elder now, an elder fast-friend. My . . . my call comes soon." She paused. "Why have you screened us?"

"A new kind of screen, Melissa," Brand said, smiling. "Didn't you notice? It's *dark.* A refinement, just developed back on Earth. They've been doing a lot of screen research, and I've been following it. I had an idea, love, but the old screens were no good. This kind, well, it's more sophisticated. And I'm the first one to realize the implications."

"Sophisticated. Implications." The words sounded odd, foreign, *alien* on Melissa's tongue. Her face looked lost.

"We're going to the stars together, Melissa."

"Brand," she replied. For a moment her voice had an almost-human tremor. "Give it up, Brand. Give up . . . me. And stars. They . . . they're old dreams, and they've gone sour on you. See? Can't you see?"

The angel was swooping up and down the corridor, coming closer to Melissa each time, clearly fascinated by the fast-friend, but afraid to come too close. They both ignored her.

Brand was looking at Melissa, at the dim far-off reflection of a girl who'd loved him once. He shook it away. She was just a fast-friend, and he'd get his stars from her.

"You can take me to the stars, Melissa, and other men after me. It's time you fast-friends shared your universe with us poor humans."

"A drive?" she asked.

"You might . . ."

But the angel interrupted him. "Oh, let me, Brand. Let me tell her. I know how. You told me. I remember. Let me talk to the fast-friend." She'd stopped her wild circles, and was floating eager between them.

Brand grinned. "All right. Tell her."

The angel spun in the air, smiling. Her wings beat quickly to underscore her words. "It's like horses," she told Melissa. "The darks are like horses, Brand said, and the fast-friends are like horses with riders. But he's got the first chariot, and the fast-friends will pull him." She giggled. "Brand showed me a picture of a chariot. And a horse too."

"A star chariot," Brand said. "I like the image. Oh, it's a cartoon analogy, of course, but the math is sound. You can transport matter. Enough of you, locked into a dark screen, can transport a ship this size."

Melissa floated, staring, shaking her head slowly back and forth. Her silver hair shimmered. "Stars," she said softly. "Brand, the core . . . the songs. Freedom, Brand. Like we used to talk. Brand, they won't . . . no running . . . they won't let us *go* . . . can't *chain* us."

"I have."

And the angel, emboldened by Melissa's sudden stillness, flew up beside her. In a childish tentative way, she reached out to touch, and found the phantom solid. Melissa, her eyes on Brand, put an arm around her. The angel smiled and sighed and moved closer.

Brand shook his head.

And the angel suddenly looked up, childish pique washing across her face. "You fooled me," she said to Brand. "She's not a horse. She's a person." Then, brightly, she smiled again. "And she's so *pretty.*"

There was a long, long silence.

The bridge panel slid shut behind him. Robi was waiting. "Well?" she asked.

Wordlessly Brand kicked himself across the room, strapped down, and looked up at the viewscreen. Out in the darkness, in the screen-dimmed gloom, Melissa had rejoined the other fast-friends. They spoke with staccato bursts of color. Brand watched briefly, then reached up to the console and hit a button.

The stars flared cold and bright, and the flanks of Hades shone.

Before Robi had a chance to speak the fast-friends had vanished, spinning space around them, moving faster than the *Chariot* ever would. Only Melissa lingered, and only for a second. Then emptiness, and the derelicts around them.

"*Brand!*"

He smiled at her, and shrugged. "I couldn't do it. We would never have been able to let them outside the screens. They'd be animals, draft animals, prisoners." He looked sheepish. "I guess they're not. Not people either, though, not anymore. Well, we always wanted to meet an alien race. How could we guess that we'd create one?"

"Brand," Robi said. "Our investment. We *have* to go through with it. Maybe we can use darks?"

He shook his head. "No. We couldn't get them to understand what we wanted. No. Fast-friends or . . . nothing, I guess."

He paused, and looked at her. She was staring up at the viewscreen, with an expression that shrieked disgust and exasperation. "I'll make it up to you," Brand said. He took her hand, gently. "We'll trap. We're well equipped."

Robi looked over. "Where's the angel?" she asked, and her voice sounded a shade less angry.

Brand sighed. "In my cabin," he said. "I gave her a necklace to play with."

HYPERSPACE

DICK ALLEN

I place the coin beneath
the paper, rub it so the Lincoln's face appears
dimly in a circle,
            like a cosmonaut's head
emerged from hyperspace,
passed through the luxon wall.

I think of Gettysburg,
            the crowd assembled there,
and Brady's photographs,
            the long gray line,
the sound of wireless,
            then a picture burst
upon a television screen.
            The cities grow
and vanish in a weather map;
            the moon
is safely walked upon.
            How insignificant
the life of one man seems
            when placed beside
inventions and events and dreams.

Imagine tachyons moving faster than
    the speed of light.

Your body vanished in a haze of blue,
    arisen in the night
beside your weekend lover of Andromeda.

296

Imagine being warped through death
it is
    a going out of self
                and coming in,
like what is done with gospels
                     rightly played
and love surrendered to upon a mighty bed.

OUR MANY ROADS TO THE STARS

POUL ANDERSON

There are countless varieties of science fiction these days, and I would be the last to want any of them restricted in any way. Nevertheless, what first drew me to this literature and, after more years than I like to add up, still holds me, is its dealing with the marvels of the universe. To look aloft at the stars on a clear night and think that someday, somehow we might actually get out among them, rouses the thrill anew, and I become young again. After all, we made it to the Moon, didn't we? Meanwhile, only science fiction of the old and truly kind takes the imagination forth on that journey, Therefore I put up with its frequent flaws, and so does many another dreamer.

But are we mere dreamers, telling ourselves stories of voyages yonder as our ancestors told of voyages to Avalon and Cíbola? Those never existed, and the stars do; but, realistically, does any possibility of reaching them?

The case against interstellar travel traditionally begins with the sheer distance. While Pioneer 10 and 11, the Jupiter flybys, will leave the Solar System, they won't get as far as Alpha Centauri, the nearest neighbor sun, for more than 40,000 years. (They aren't actually bound in that direction.) At five times their speed, or 100 miles per second, which we are nowhere close to reaching today, the trip would take longer than recorded history goes back. And the average separation of stars in this galactic vicinity is twice as great.

If we could go very much faster—

At almost the speed of light, we'd reach Alpha Centauri in about four and a third years. But as most of you know, we who were faring would experience a shorter journey. Both the theory of relativity and experimental physics show that time passes "faster" for a fast-moving object. The closer to the speed of light, the greater the difference, until at that velocity itself, a spaceman would make the trip in no time at all. However, the girl he left behind him would measure his transit as taking the same number of years as a light ray does; and he'd take equally long in coming back to her.

In reality, the velocity of light *in vacuo*, usually symbolized by c, cannot be attained by any material body. From a physical viewpoint, the reason lies in Einstein's famous equation $E = mc^2$. Mass and energy are equivalent. The faster a body moves, the more energy it has, and hence the more mass. This rises steeply as velocity gets close to c, and at that speed would become infinite, an obvious impossibility.

Mass increases by the same factor as time (and length) shrink. An appendix to this essay defines the terms more presisely than here. A table there gives some representative values of the factor for different values of velocity, v, compared to c. At $v = 0.7$ c, that is, at a speed of 70% light's, time aboard ship equals distance covered in light-years. Thus, a journey of 10 light-years at 0.7 c would occupy 10 years of the crew's lives, although to people on Earth or on the target planet, it would take about 14.

There's a catch here. We have quietly been supposing that the whole voyage is made at exactly this rate. In practice, the ship would have to get up to speed first, and brake as it neared the goal. Both these maneuvers take time; and most of this time is spent at low velocities where the relativistic effects aren't noticeable.

Let's imagine that we accelerate at one gravity, increasing our speed by 32 feet per second each second and thus providing ourselves with a comfortable Earth-normal weight inboard. It will take us approximately a year (a shade less) to come near c, during which period we will have covered almost half a light-year, and during most of which period our time rate won't be significantly different from that of the outside cosmos. In fact, not until the eleventh month would the factor get as low as 0.5, though from then on it would start a really steepening nosedive. Similar considerations apply at journey's end, while we slow down, Therefore a trip under these conditions would never take less than two years as far as we are concerned; if the distance covered is 10 light-years, the time required is 11 years as far as the girl (or boy) friend left behind is concerned.

At the "equalizing" v of 0.7 c, these figures become 10.7 years for the crew and 14.4 years for the stay-at-homes. This illustrates the dramatic gains that the former, if not the latter, can make by pushing c quite closely. But let's stay with that value of 0.7 c for the time being, since it happens to be the one chosen by Bernard Oliver for his argument against the feasibility of star travel.

Now Dr. Oliver, vice president for research and development at Hewlett-Packard, is definitely not unimaginative, nor hostile to the idea as such. Rather, he is intensely interested in contacting extraterrestrial intelligence, and was the guiding genius of Project Cyclops, which explored the means of doing so by radio. The design which his group came up with could, if built, detect anybody who's using radio energy like us today within 100 light-years. Or it could receive beacon signals of reasonable strength within 1000 light-years: a sphere which encloses a million suns akin to Sol and half a billion which are different.

Still, he does not fudge the facts. Making the most favorable assumption, a matter-antimatter annihilation system which expels radiation itself, he has calculated the minimum requirement for a round trip with a stopover at the destination star, at a peak speed of 0.7c. Assuming 1000 tons of ship plus payload, which is certainly modest, he found that it must convert some 33,000 tons of fuel into energy—sufficient to supply the United States, at present levels of use, for half a million years. On first starting off from orbit, the ship would spend 10 times the power that the Sun gives to our entire Earth. Shielding requirements alone, against stray gamma rays, make this an absurdity, not to speak of a thousand square miles of radiating surface to cool the vessel if as little as one one-millionth of energy reaches it in the form of waste heat.

Though we can reduce these figures a good deal if we assume it can refuel at the other end for its return home, the scheme looks impractical regardless. Moreover, Dr. Oliver, no doubt deliberately, has not mentioned that space is not empty. Between local stars, it contains about one hydrogen atom per cubic centimeter, plus smaller amounts of other materials. This is a harder vacuum than any we can achieve artificially. But a vessel ramming through it at 0.7 c would release X-radiation at the rate of some 50 million roentgen units per hour. It takes less than 1000 to kill a human being. No material shielding could protect the crew for long, if at all.

Not every scientist is this pessimistic about the rocket to the stars, that is, a craft which carries its own energy source and reaction mass. Some hope for smaller, unmanned probes, perhaps moving at considerably lower speeds. But given the mass required for their life support and equipment, men who went by such a vehicle would have to reckon on voyages lasting generatons or centuries.

This is not impossible, of course. Maybe they could pass the time in suspended animation. Naturally radioactive atoms in the body set an upper limit to that, since they destroy tissue which would then not be replaced. But Carl Sagan, astonomer and exobiologist at Cornell University, estimates that a spore can survive up to a million years. This suggests to me that humans should be good for anyway several thousand.

Or maybe, in a huge ship with a complete ecology, an expedition could beget and raise children to carry their mission on. Calculations by Gerald K. O'Neill, professor of physics at Harvard, strongly indicate that this is quite feasible. His work has actually dealt with the possibility of establishing permanent, self-sustaining colonies in orbit, pleasanter to live in than most of Earth and capable of producing more worldlets like themselves from extraterrestrial resources. He concludes that we can start on it *now*, with existing technology and at startlingly low cost, and have the first operational by the late 1980's. Not long afterward, somebody could put a motor on one of these.

The hardened science fiction reader may think such ideas are old hat. And so they are, in fiction. But to me the fact is infinitely more exciting than any story—that the accomplishment can actually be made, that sober studies by reputable professionals are confirming the dream.

True, I'd prefer to believe that men and women can get out there faster, more easily, so that the people who sent them off will still be alive when word arrives of what they have discovered. Is this wishful thinking? We've written off the rocket as a means of ultra-fast travel, but may there be other ways?

Yes, probably there are. Even within the framework of conventional physics, where you can never surpass c, we already have more than one well-reasoned proposal. If not yet as detailed and mathematical as Oberth's keystone work of 1911. If the time scale is the same for future as for past developments, then the first manned Alpha Centauri expedition should leave about the year 2010. . . .

That's counting from R. W. Bussard's original paper on the interstellar ramjet, which appeared in 1960. Chances are that a flat historical parallel is silly. But the engineering ideas positively are not. They make a great deal of sense.

Since the ramjet has been in a fair number of stories already, I'll describe the principle rather briefly. We've seen that at high speeds, a vessel must somehow protect its crew from the atoms and ions in space. Lead or other material shielding is out of the question. Hopelessly too much would be required, it would give off secondary radiation of its own, and ablation would wear it down, incidentally producing a lot of heat, less readily dissipated in space than in an atmosphere. Since the gas must be controlled anyway, why not put it to work?

Once the ship has reached a speed which turns out to be reasonable for a thermonuclear rocket—and we're on the verge of that technology today—a scoop can collect the interstellar gas and funnel it into a reaction chamber. There, chosen parts can be fusion-burned for energy to throw the rest out backward, thus propelling the vessel forward. Ramjet aircraft use the same principle, except that they must supply fuel to combine with the oxygen they collect. The ramjet starcraft takes everything it needs from its surroundings. Living off the country, it faces none of the mass-ratio problems of a rocket, and might be able to crowd c very closely.

Needless to say, even at the present stage of pure theory, things aren't that simple. For openers, how large an apparatus do we need? For a ship-plus-payload mass of 1,000 tons, accelerating at one gravity and using proton-proton fusion for power, Bussard and Sagan have both calculated a scoop radius of 2,000 kilometers. Now we have no idea as yet how to make that particular reaction go. We are near the point of fusing deuterons, or deuterons and tritons (hydrogen nuclei with one and two neutrons respectively), to get a net energy release. But these isotopes are far less common than ordinary hydrogen, and thus would require correspondingly larger intakes. Obviously, we can't use collectors made of metal.

But then, we need nonmaterial shielding anyway. Electromagnetic fields exert force on charged particles. A steady laser barrage emitted by the ship can ionize all neutral atoms within a safety zone, and so make them controllable, as well as vaporizing rare bits of dust and gravel which would otherwise be a hazard. (I suspect, myself, that this won't be necessary. Neutral atoms have electrical asymmetries which offer a possible grip to the force-fields of a more advanced technology than ours. I also feel sure we will master the proton-proton reaction, and eventually matter-antimatter annihilation. But for now, let's play close to our vests.) A force-field scoop, which being massless can be of enormous size, will catch these ions, funnel them down paths which are well clear of the crew section and into a fusion chamber, cause the chosen nuclei to burn, and expel everything aft to drive the vessel forward, faster and faster.

To generate such fields, A. J. Fennelly of Yeshiva University and G. L. Matloff of the Polytechnic Institute of New York propose a copper cylinder coated with a super-conducting layer of niobium-tin alloy. The size is not excessive, 400 meters in length and 200 in diameter. As for braking, they suggest a drogue made of boron, for its high melting point, ten kilometers across. This would necessarily work rather slowly. But then, these authors are cautious in their assumptions; for instance, they derive a peak velocity of just 0.12 c. The system could reach Alpha Centauri in about 53 years, Tau Ceti in 115.

By adding wings, however, they approximately halve these travel times. The wings are two great superconducting batteries, each a kilometer square. Cutting the lines of the galactic magnetic field, they generate voltages which can be tapped for exhaust acceleration, for magnetic bottle containers for the power reaction, and for inboard electricity. With thrust shut off, they act as auxiliary brakes, much shortening the deceleration period. When power is drawn at different rates on either side, they provide maneuverability—majestically slow, but sufficient —almost as if they were hugh oars.

All in all, it appears that a vessel of this general type can bring explorers to the nearest stars while they are still young enough to carry out the exploration—and the preliminary colonization?—themselves. Civilization at home will start receiving a flood of beamed information, fascinating, no doubt often revolutionary in unforeseeable ways, within a few years of their arrival. Given only a slight lengthening of human life expectancy, they might well spend a generation out yonder and get home alive, still hale. Certainly their children can.

Robert L. Forward, a leading physicist at Hughes Research Laboratories, has also interested himself in the use of the galactic magnetic field. As he points out, the ion density in interstellar space is so low that a probe could easily maintain a substantial voltage across itself. Properly adjusted, the interaction forces produced by this will allow mid-course corrections and terminal maneuvers at small extra energy cost. Thus we could investigate more than one star with a single probe, and eventually bring it home again.

Indeed, the price of research in deep space is rather small. Even the cost of manned vessels is estimated by several careful thinkers as no more than ten billion dollars each—starting with today's technology. That's about fifty dollars per American, much less than we spend every year on cigarettes and booze, enormously less than goes for wars, bureaucrats, subsidies to inefficient businesses, or the servicing of the national debt. For mankind as a whole, a starship would run about $2.50 per head. The benefits it would return in the way of knowledge, and thus of improved capability, are immeasurably great.

But to continue with those manned craft. Mention of using interstellar magnetism for maneuvering raises the thought of using it for propulsion. That is, by employing electromagnetic forces which interact with that field, a ship could ideally accelerate itself without having to expel any mass backward. This would represent a huge saving over what the rocket demands.

The trouble is, the galactic field is very weak, and no doubt very variable from region to region. Though it can be valuable in ways that we have seen, there appears to be no hope of using it for a powerful drive.

Might we invent other devices? For instance, if we could somehow establish a negative gravity force, this might let our ship react against the mass of the universe as a whole, and thus need no jets. Unfortunately, nobody today knows how to do any such thing, and most physicists take for granted it's impossible. Not all agree: because antigravity-type forces do occur in relativity theory, under special conditions.

Physics does offer one way of reaching extremely high speeds free, the Einsteinian catapult. Later I shall have more to say about the weird things that happen when large, ultra-dense masses spin very fast. But among these is their generation of force different from Newtonian gravity, which has a mighty accelerating effect of its own. Two neutron stars, orbiting nearly in contact, could kick almost to light velocity a ship which approached them on the right orbit.

Alas, no such pair seems to exist anywhere near the Solar System. Besides, we'd presumable want something similar in the neighborhood of our destination, with exactly the characteristics necessary to slow us down. The technique looks rather implausible. What is likely, though, is that closer study of phenomena like these may give us clues to the method of constructing a field drive.

Yet do we really need it? Won't the Bussary ramjet serve? Since it picks up everything it requires as it goes, why can't it keep on accelerating indefinitely, until it comes as close to c as the captain desires? The Fennelly-Matloff vehicle is not intended to do this. But why can't a more advanced model?

Quite possibly it can!

Before taking us off on such a voyage, maybe I'd better answer a question or two. If the ship, accelerating at one gravity, is near c in a year, and if c is the ultimate speed which nature allows, how can the ship keep on accelerating just as hard, for just as long as the flight plan says?

The reason lies in the relativistic contraction of space and time, when these are measured by a fast-moving observer. Suppose we, at rest with respect to the stars, track a vessel for 10 light-years at its steady speed of $0.9 c$. To us, the passage takes 11 years. To the crew, it takes 4.4 years: because the distance crossed is proportionately less. They never experience faster-than-light travel either. What they do experience, when they turn their instruments outward, is a cosmos strangely flattened in the direction of their motion, where the stars (and their unseen friends at home) age strangely fast.

The nearer they come to c, the more rapidly these effects increase. Thus, as they speed up, they perceive themselves as accelerating at a steady rate through a constantly shrinking universe. Observers on a planet would perceive them as accelerating at an ever lower rate through an unchanged universe. At last, perhaps, millions of light-years might be traversed and million of years pass by outside while a man inboard draws a breath.

By the way, those authors are wrong who have described the phenomenon in terms of "subjective" versus "objective" time. One set of measurements is as valid as another.

The "twin paradox" does not arise. This old chestnut says, "Look, suppose we're twins, and you stay home while I go traveling at high speed. Now I could equally well claim I'm stationary and you're in motion—therefore that you're the one flattened out and living at a slower rate, not me. So what happens when we get back together again? How can each of us be younger than his twin?"

It overlooks the fact that the traveler does come home. The situation would indeed be symmetrical if the spaceman moved forever at a fixed velocity. But then he and his brother, by definition, never would meet to compare notes. His accelerations (which include slowdowns and changes of course) take the whole problem out of special and into general relativity. Against the background of the stars, the traveler has moved in variable fashion; forces have acted on him.

Long before time and space measurements aboard ship differ bizarrely much from those on Earth, navigational problems will arise. They are the result of two factors, aberration and Doppler effect.

Aberration is the apparent displacement of an object in the visual field of a moving observer. It results from combining his velocity with the velocity of light. (Analogously, if we are out in the rain and, standing still, feel it falling straight down, we will feel it hitting us at a slant when we are walking. The change in angle will be larger if we run.) At the comparatively small orbital speed of Earth, sensitive instruments can detect the aberration of the stars. At speeds close to c, it will by huge. Stars will seem to crawl across the sky as we accelerate, bunching in its forward half and thinning out aft.

Doppler effect, perhaps more widely familiar, is the shift in observed wavelength from an emitting object, when the observer's velocity changes. If we move away from a star, we see its light turned more blue. Again, these changes become extremely marked as we approach c.

Eventually our relativistic astronaut sees most of the stars gathered in a ring ahead of him, though a few sparsely strewn individuals remain visible elsewhere. The ring itself, which Frederik Pohl has dubbed the "starbow," centers on a circle which is mainly dark, because nearly all light from there has been blue-shifted out of the frequencies we can see. The leading or inner edge of the ring is bluish white, its trailing or outer edge reddish; in between is a gradation of colors, akin to what we normally observe. Fred Hollander, a chemist at Brookhaven National Laboratories, has calculated the starbow's exact appearance for different v. It gets nerrower and moves farther forward, the bull's-eye dead ahead gets smaller and blacker, the faster we go—until, for instance, at 0.9999 c we perceive a starbow about ten degrees of arc in width, centered on a totally black circle of about the same diameter, and little or nothing shows anywhere else in the sky.

At that speed, 0.9999 c, we'd cross 100 light-years in 20 months of our personal lifetimes. So it's worth trying for; but we'll have to figure out some means of knowing where we are! Though difficult, the problem does not look unsolvable in principle.

It may become so beyond a certain velocity. If we travel under acceleration the whole way, speeding up continuously to the half-way point, thereafter braking at the same rate until we reach our goal: then over considerable distances we get truly staggering relativity factors. The longer a voyage, the less difference it makes to us precisely how long it is.

Thus, Dr. Sagan points out that explorers faring in this wise at one gravity will reach the nearer stars within a few years, Earth time, and slightly less, crew time. But they will cross the approximately 650 light-years to Deneb in 12 or 13 years of their own lifespans; the 30,000 light-years to the center of our galaxy in 21 ship-years; the two million light-years to the Andromeda galaxy in 29 ship-years; or the ten million light-years to the Virgo cluster of galaxies in 31 ship-years. If they can stand higher accelerations, or have some way to counteract the drag on their bodies, they can cross these gulfs in less of their own time; the mathematical formula governing this is in the appendix.

But will the starbow become too thin and dim for navigation? Or will they encounter some other practical limit? For instance, when matter is accelerated, it radiates energy in the form of gravity waves. The larger the mass, the stronger the radiation; and of course the mass of our spaceship will be increasing by leaps and bounds and pole-vaults. Eventually it may reach a condition where it is radiating away as much energy as it can take in, and thus be unable to go any faster.

However, the real, practical limit is likelier to arise from the fact that we have enough stars near home to keep us interested for millennia to come. Colonies planted on worlds around some of these can, in due course, serve as nuclei for human expansion ever further into the universe.

Because many atoms swept through its force-fields are bound to give off light, a ramjet under weigh must be an awesome spectacle. At a safe distance, probably the hull where the crew lives is too small for the naked eye. Instead, against the constellations one sees a translucent shell of multi-colored glow, broad in front, tapering aft to a fiery point where the nuclear reaction is going on. (Since this must be contained by force-fields anyway, there is no obvious reason for the fusion chamber to be a metal room.) Thence the exhaust streams backward, at first invisible or nearly so, where its particles are closely controlled, but becoming brilliant further off as they begin to collide, until finally a nebula-like chaos fades away into the spatial night.

It's not only premature, it's pointless to worry about limitations. Conventional physics appears to tell us that, although nature has placed an eternal bound on the speed of our traveling; the stars can still be ours . . . if we really want them.

Yet we would like to reach them more swiftly, with less effort. Have we any realistic chance whatsoever of finding a way around the light-velocity barrier?

Until quite recently, every sensible physicist would have replied with a resounding "No." Most continue to do so. They point to a vast mass of experimental data; for instance, if subatomic particles did not precisely obey Einsteinian laws, our big accelerators wouldn't work. The conservatives ask where there is the slightest empirical evidence for phenomena which don't fit into the basic scheme of relativity. And they maintain that, if ever we did send anything faster than light, it would violate causality.

I don't buy that last argument, myself. It seems to me that, mathematically and logically, it presupposes part of what it sets out to prove. But this gets a bit too technical for the present essay, especially since many highly intelligent persons disagree with me. Those whom I mentioned are not conservatives in the sense of having stick-in-the-mud minds. They are among the very people whose genius and imagination make science the supremely exciting, creative endeavor which it is these days.

Nevertheless we do have a minority of equally qualified pioneers who have lately been advancing new suggestions.

I suppose the best known idea comes from Gerald Feinberg, professor of physics at Columbia University. He has noted that the Einsteinian equations do not actually forbid material particles which move faster than light—if these have a mass that can be described by an imaginary number (that is, an ordinary number multiplied by the square root of minus one. Imaginary quantities are common, e.g., in the theory of electromagnetism). Such "tachyons," as he calls them, would travel faster and faster the *less* energy they have; it would take infinite energy to slow them down to c, which is thus a barrier for them too.

Will it forever separate us, who are composed of "tardyons," from the tachyon part of the cosmos? Perhaps—but not totally. It is the meaningless to speak of anything which we cannot, in principle, detect if it exists. If tachyons do, there must be some way by which we can find experimental evidence for them, no matter how indirect. This implies some kind of interaction (via photons?) with tardyons. But interaction, in turn, implies a possibility of modulation. That is, if they can affect us, we can affect them.

And . . . in principle, if you can modulate, you can do anything. Maybe it won't ever be feasible to use tachyons to beam a man across space; but might we, for instance, use them to communicate faster than light?

Needless to say, first we have to catch them, i.e., show that they exist. This has not yet been done, and maybe it never can be done because in fact there aren't any. Still, one dares hope. A very few suggestive data are beginning to come out of certain laboratories—

Besides, we have other places to look. Hyperspace turns out to be more than a hoary science fiction catchphrase. Geometrodynamics now allows a transit from point to point, without crossing the space between, via a warp going "outside" that space—often called a wormhole. Most wormholes are exceedingly small, of subatomic dimensions; and a trip through one is no faster than a trip through normal space. Nevertheless, the idea opens up a whole new field of research, which may yield startling discoveries.

Black holes have been much in the news, and in science fiction, these past several years. The are masses so dense, with gravity fields so strong, that light itself cannot escape. Theory has predicted for more than 40 years that all stars above a particular size must eventually collapse into the black hole state. Today astronomers think they have located some, as in Cygnus X-1. And we see hypotheses about black holes of less than stellar mass, which we might be able to find floating in space and utilize.

For our purposes here, the most interesting trait of a black hole is its apparent violation of a whole series of conservation laws so fundamental to physics that they are well-nigh Holy Writ. Thus many an issue, not long ago considered thoroughly settled, is again up for grabs. The possibility of entering a black hole and coming out "instantly" at the far end of a space warp is being seriously discussed. Granted, astronauts probably couldn't survive a close approach to such an object. But knowledge of these space warp phenomena and their laws, if they do occur in reality, might well enable us to build machines which —because they don't employ velocity—can circumvent the c barrier.

Black holes aren't the sole things which play curious tricks on space and time. An ultra-dense toroid, spinning very rapidly in smoke-ring fashion, should theoretically create what is called a Kerr metric space warp, opening a way to hyperspace.

The most breathtaking recent development of relativity that I know of is by F. J. Tipler, a physicist at the University of Maryland. According to his calculations, not just near-instantaneous crossings of space should be possible, but time travel should be! A cylinder of ultra-dense matter, rotating extremely fast (velocity at the circumference greater than 0.5 c) produces a region of multiple periodic spacetime. A particle entering this can, depending on its exact track, reach any event in the universe, past or future.

The work was accepted for publication in *Physical Review*, which is about as respectable as science can get. Whether it will survive criticism remains to be seen. But if nothing else, it has probably knocked the foundation out from under the causality argument against faster-than-light travel: by forcing us to rethink our whole concept of causality.

The foregoing ideas lie within the realm of accepted physics, or at least on its debatable borders. Dr. Forward has listed several others which are beyond the frontier . . . but only barely, and only to date. Closer study could show, in our near future, that one or more of them refer to something real.

For instance, we don't know what inertia "is." It seems to be a basic property of matter; but why? Could it be an inductive effect of gravitation, as Mach's Principle suggests? If so, could we find ways to modify it, and would we then be held back by the increase of mass with velocity?

Could we discover, or produce, negative mass? This would gravitationally repel the usual positive kind. Two equal masses, positive and negative, linked together, would make each other accelerate in a particular direction without any change in momentum or energy. Could they therefore transcend c?

A solution of Einstein's field equations in five dimensions for charged particles gives an electron velocity of a billion trillion c. What then of a spaceship, if the continuum should turn out to have five rather than four dimensions?

Conventional physics limits the speed of mass-energy. But information is neither; from a physical standpoint, it represents negative entropy. So can information outrun light, perhaps without requiring any medium for its transmission? If you can send information, in principle you can send anything.

Magnificent and invaluable though the structure of relativity is, does it hold the entire truth? There are certain contradictions in its basic assumptions, which have never been resolved and perhaps never can be. Or relativity could be just a special case, applying only to local conditions.

Once we are well and truly out into space, we may find the signs of a structure immensely more ample.

The speculations have taken us quite far beyond known science. But they help to show us how little known that science really is, even the parts which have long felt comfortingly, or confiningly, familiar. We can almost certainly reach the stars. Very possibly, we can reach them easily.

If we have the will.

Appendix

Readers who shudder at sight of an equation can skip this part, though they may like to see the promised table. For different velocities, it gives the values of the factors "tau" and "gamma." These are simply the inverses of each other. A little explanation of them may be in order.

Suppose we have two observers, A and B, who have *constant* velocities. We can consider either one as being stationary, the other as moving at velocity v. A will measure the length of a yardstick B carries, in the direction of motion, and the interval between two readings of a clock B carries, as if these quantities were multiplied by tau. For example, if v is 0.9 c, then B's yardstick is merely 0.44 times as long in A's eyes as if B were motionless; and an hour, registered on B's clock, corresponds to merely 0.44 hour on A's. On the other hand, mass is multiplied by gamma. That is, when B moves at 0.9 c, his mass according to A is 2.26 times what it was when B was motionless.

B, in turn, observes himself as normal, but A and A's environs as having suffered exactly the same changes. Both observers are right.

v	Tau	Gamma
0.1c	0.995	1.005
0.5c	0.87	1.15
0.7c	0.72	1.39
0.9c	0.44	2.26
0.99c	0.14	7.10
0.9999c	0.014	71.5

The formula for tau is $(1 - v^2/c^2)^{1/2}$ where the exponent "½" indicates a square root. Gamma equals one divided by tau, or $(1 - v^2/c^2)^{-1/2}$.

As for relativistic acceleration, if this has a constant value a up to midpoint, then a negative (braking) value $-a$ to destination, the time to cover a distance S equals $(2c/a)$ arc cosh $(1 - aS/2c^2)$. For long distances, this reduces to $(2c/a) \ln (aS/c^2)$ where "$\ln$" means "natural logarithm." The maximum velocity, reached at midpoint, is $c[1 - (1 + aS/2c^2)^{-2}]^{1/2}$.

THE CONTRIBUTORS

THE AUTHORS

DICK ALLEN's books of poetry include *Regions with No Proper Names* and *Anon and Various Time Machine Poems* He has published over 500 poems, essays, and reviews in such periodicals as *Antioch Review, The New York Times, Poetry,* and *Writer's Digest,* and his work is represented in numerous anthologies. He has edited the anthologies *Science Fiction: The Future, Detective Fiction: Crime and Compromise* (with David Chacko) and *Looking Ahead: The Vision of Science Fiction* (with Lori Allen). Mr. Allen is the winner of the Robert Frost Fellowship in Poetry, the Hart Crane Memorial Poetry Fellowship, the Union League Arts and Civic Foundation Prize for poetry, and an Academy of American Poets Prize for Poetry. He lives and teaches at the university level in Bridgeport, Connecticut. His poem "Hyperspace" was written after reading Isaac Asimov's article "The Ultimate Speed Limit."

POUL ANDERSON is the author of over fifty books, including *Brain Wave, The High Crusade, Three Hearts and Three Lions,* and *Tau Zero.* His writing outside science fiction includes science fact, mystery, historical fiction, poetry, criticism, and translations. He has won five Hugo Awards (given annually by the members of the World Science Fiction Conventions), two Nebula Awards (given each year by the members of the Science Fiction Writers of America), a Cock Robin Award for a mystery novel, and other honors. He is also a past president of the Science Fiction Writers of America. His most recent books include *The Day of Their Return, Fire Time,* and *The Winter of the World.* He lives in the San Francisco Bay Area with his wife, poet and writer Karen Anderson.

ISAAC ASIMOV is noted for his many published works, including over 150 books, and his knowledge of many fields. His science fiction books include *The Caves of Steel, The Naked Sun, The Foundation Trilogy, I, Robot,* and others. His nonfiction works include *Asimov's Guide to Science, Asimov's Guide to Shakespeare, The Left Hand of the Electron, Opus 100,* and many others. He has won two Hugo Awards and a Nebula Award. He lives in New York City with his wife, J. O. Jeppson, psychiatrist-author.

GREGORY BENFORD has written over thirty science fiction short stories and two novels, *Deeper Than the Darkness* and *Jupiter Project.* He has also written scientific articles for *New Scientist, Natural History, Smithsonian,* and *Vertex.* He is the co-author of a text, *Astronomy and Life in the Universe,* and the editor of a textbook anthology, *Physics Through Science Fiction.* His work has been nominated for Hugo and Nebula Awards. His novelet *If the Stars Are Gods* (written with Gordon Eklund) received a Nebula Award in 1975. He is Associate Professor of Physics at the University of California at Irvine.

BEN BOVA, editor of *Analog* magazine, has three times won the Hugo Award for best editor of the year. He is the author of more than 30 books, novels, and nonfiction on scientific subjects; his short stories and articles have appeared in all the major science fiction magazines as well as in *Vogue, Astronomy,* and *Smithsonian* magazine. He is a former newspaperman, television consultant, and aerospace executive. Born in Philadelphia, he lives in New York City. One of his latest books is *The Starcrossed,* a science fiction satire.

ARTHUR C. CLARKE is a member of many scientific organizations and a past chairman of the British Interplanetary Society. He is the author of many science fiction novels and story collections, among them *Prelude to Space, Childhood's End, The City and the Stars, The Deep Range,* and others. His nonfiction works include *The Exploration of Space, Profiles of the Future, Voices from the Sky, The Promise of Space* and others. He was co-author, with Stanley Kubrick, of the screenplay for the film *2001: A Space Odyssey;* the script was nominated for an Oscar.

He has won the UNESCO Kalinga Prize for science writing and the Stuart Ballantine Medal of the Franklin Institute for having originated the communications satellite in a technical paper published in 1945. He has also won two Aviation/Space Writers Association Awards. More recently his awards have included two Nebula Awards, a Hugo Award, and a John W. Campbell Award. His newest book is *Imperial Earth*. He lives in Sri Lanka.

HAL CLEMENT sold his first story, "Proof," to John W. Campbell while a junior at Harvard. His novels include *Needle, Iceworld, Mission of Gravity*, and *Star Light*. His work has been nominated for the Hugo Award. He is also a painter of astronomical art under the name George Richard and has sold over forty paintings. He lives in Massachusetts, where he teaches science at the Milton Academy.

HARLAN ELLISON is the author of over 800 stories, articles, and critical essays. His work has appeared in the *New Yorker, New Times, Esquire, Show, Playboy, Cosmopolitan*, and many other publications. He is the editor of *Dangerous Visions, Again, Dangerous Visions*, and *The Last Dangerous Visions*. His short story collections include *Partners in Wonder, Alone Against Tomorrow, The Beast that Shouted Love at the Heart of the World, Approaching Oblivion*, and *Deathbird Stories*. His most outstanding teleplays are "Demon with a Glass Hand" and "Soldier," both written for *The Outer Limits* Anthology Series; and "The City at the Edge of Forever," for *Star Trek*. He has won several Hugo Awards, two Nebula Awards, an Edgar Award (given annually by the Mystery Writers of America), and three Writers Guild of America awards for Most Outstanding Television Script. He is a past Vice President of the Science Fiction Writers of America. He lives in Los Angeles.

A. A. JACKSON IV received his B.A. and M.A. in physics from North Texas State University. He worked for NASA in Houston from 1966 to 1970, training astronauts to use the Abort Guidance System in the Lunar Module. Returning to school, he received his Ph.D. in 1975. He is responsible for proposing the intriguing speculation (with Mike Ryan) that the Tungus event of 1908 in Siberia may have been due to a black hole.

KEITH LAUMER has been a Foreign Service Officer, Vice-Consul, and Third Secretary in the Diplomatic Service. His work has appeared in *If, Analog, Galaxy, Fantasy & Science Fiction, Fantastic, Orbit,* and other magazines and anthologies. His novels include *Dinosaur Beach, The Infinite Cage, The Glory Game, The Worlds of the Imperium, The Shape Changer,* and many others. His work has been nominated for the Nebula and Hugo Awards.

GEORGE R. R. MARTIN's work has appeared in *Analog, Galaxy, If, Universe, New Dimensions, Emphasis, Stellar, Best of Galaxy II,* and other magazines. He has been nominated for the Nebula Award and the John W. Campbell Award for Best New Writer. His novella, "A Song for Lya," won a Hugo Award in 1975. His present occupation is directing chess tournaments. He lives in Chicago.

HOWARD WALDROP's fiction has appeared in *Analog, Galaxy, If, Universe, New Dimensions, Emphasis, Stellar, Best of Galaxy II,* and other magazines; and his articles and reviews have been published in *Crawdaddy* and *Zoo World.* His first novel, written with Jake Saunders, was *The Texas-Israeli War: 1999.*

IAN WATSON was born in Great Britain and educated at Oxford University. He lectured in literature for two years at the University of Tanzania. He then taught for three years at various universities in Tokyo, Japan. His first novel, *The Embedding,* won second place in the John W. Campbell Award for best science fiction novel of the year. His first science fiction stories were published in *New Worlds.* His newest novel is *The Jonah Kit.* He now lives in Great Britain, where he teaches courses in science fiction at Birmingham Polytechnic.

CHELSEA QUINN YARBRO has worked with mentally disturbed children and as a statistical demographic cartographer. She is also a trained musician and composer and teaches voice. She began writing professionally in 1961 for a children's theatre company; four of her plays have been produced. Her stories have appeared in *If, Galaxy, Infinity, Strange Bedfellows, Planet One,* and other magazines and anthologies. She is the co-editor, with Thomas N. Scortia, of the anthology *Two Views of Wonder.* Her work has been nominated for the Edgar Award. She is also a past Secretary of the Science Fiction Writers of America. Her novels include *Ogilvie, Tallant and Moon,* and *A Time of the Fourth Horseman.* She lives in the San Francisco Bay area with her husband, Donald Simpson, an artist and inventor.

THE ARTIST

TIM KIRK is an artist whose work has appeared in a number of books and periodicals, including the *1975 J. R. R. Tolkien Calendar, The Last Dangerous Visions,* and *Vertex.* He is a four-time Hugo winner. He is currently employed by a well-known greeting card company.

THE EDITORS

JACK DANN was born and raised in upstate New York. He studied drama at Hofstra University and received his B. A. in political science from the State University of New York at Binghamton (Harpur College). He studied law at St. John's University and did graduate work in comparative literature at S.U.N.Y. at Binghamton. His short fiction has been published in *Orbit, New Dimensions, The Last Dangerous Visions, New Worlds, If, Fantastic, Gallery,* and other magazines and anthologies. He is the editor of *Wandering Stars, Future Power* (with Gardner R. Dozois), *The Speculative Fiction Yearbook* (with David Harris), and *Immortal.* He is the author of a novel, *Starhiker* (Bobbs-Merrill, Gold Medal Books), and is currently at work on a novel based on his novella *Junction,* which was a Nebula Award finalist. Mr. Dann has taught science fiction at Cornell University and Broome Community College. He was managing editor of the *Bulletin of the Science Fiction Writers of America* from 1970 to 1974. Mr. Dann resides in Johnson City, New York.

GEORGE ZEBROWSKI is a freelance writer and anthologist. His more than thirty stories and articles have appeared in such magazines as *Fantasy and Science Fiction, If, Amazing Stories, Current Science,* and in many original collections, including *New Worlds Quarterly, Future City,* and *Strange Bedfellows.* He was a Nebula Award finalist for his short story "Heathen God," and his first novel, *The Omega Point,* has been translated into six languages. He is the co-editor of *Human-Machines* (with Thomas N. Scortia), from Vintage, as well as the *Planet Series* of original collections from Unity Press. He was editor of the *Bulletin of the Science Fiction Writers of America* from 1970 to 1975. He has lectured and taught science fiction at the college level. He attended the State University of New York at Binghamton, where he studied philosophy. His other novels are *Star Web,* and the forthcoming long work, *Macrolife,* (Harper & Row). He lives and works in upstate New York.

A SELECTED BIBLIOGRAPHY

INTERSTELLAR TRAVEL

NOVELS:

Starship by Brian Aldiss (Avon)
Tau Zero by Poul Anderson (Doubleday)
The Enemy Stars by Poul Anderson (Doubleday)
Cities in Flight (a tetralogy) by James Blish (Doubleday)
Islands of Space by John W. Campbell (Doubleday)
The Listeners by James E. Gunn (Scribner's)
Orphans of the Sky by Robert A. Heinlein (Putnam)
Starman Jones by Robert A. Heinlein (Scribner's)
Time for the Stars by Robert A. Heinlein (Scribner's)
Destination: Void by Frank Herbert (Berkley)
The Skylark of Space by E. E. Smith (Pyramid)
The Star Maker by Olaf Stapledon (Penguin)

STORIES:

"Brake" by Poul Anderson (*Astounding,* Aug. 1957)
"Take A Match" by Isaac Asimov (*Buy Jupiter,* Doubleday, 1975)
"Thirteen to Centaurus" by J. G. Ballard (*Passport to Eternity,* Berkley)
"Common Time" by James Blish (*Mirror of Infinity,* ed. Robert Silverberg, Harper & Row)
"The Shadow of Space" by Philip José Farmer (*Alpha 3,* ed. Robert Silverberg, Ballantine)
"The Lion and the Lamb" by Fritz Leiber (*The Second Book of Fritz Leiber,* DAW, 1975)
"The Living Galaxy" by Lawrence Manning (*Wonder Stories,* Sept. 1934)

320

"First to the Stars" by Chad Oliver (*Astounding,* July 1952)
"The Gold at the Starbow's End" by Frederik Pohl (*Analog,* March 1972)
"No Matter Where You Go" by Joel Townsley Rogers (*Best from Fantasy & Science Fiction, 9th Series,* ed. Robert P. Mills, Doubleday)
"Beyond Space and Time" by Joel Townsley Rogers (*A Treasury of Great Science Fiction,* ed. Anthony Boucher, Doubleday)
"Far Centaurus" by A. E. Van Vogt (*Astounding,* 1943)

NONFICTION:

The Next Ten Thousand Years: A Vision of Man's Future in the Universe by Adrian Berry (Saturday Review Press, E. P. Dutton, 1974)
Bibliography of Interstellar Travel and Communication by Robert L. Forward and Eugene F. Mallove (Hughes Research Laboratories, 1972)
Beyond the Solar System by Willy Ley and Chesley Bonestell (Viking, 1964)
How We Will Reach the Stars by John W. Macvey (Collier, 1969)
Challenge of the Stars by Patrick Moore and David Hardy (Rand McNally, 1972)
Intelligent Life in the Universe by Carl Sagan and I. S. Shklovskii (Holden-Day, 1966)
The Cosmic Connection by Carl Sagan (Doubleday Anchor, 1973)
Flight to the Stars by James G. Strong (Hart, 1965)
We Are Not Alone by Walter Sullivan (McGraw-Hill, 1972)

ARTICLES:

"The Science in Science Fiction" by James Blish, in *Vector 69,* Summer 1975
"Interstellar Space Flight" by Eugen Sänger, *Space Flight* (McGraw Hill, 1965)